I0818237

GILA BEND

Also by Tom Hansen

Seminole Bend

What readers have said about ***Seminole Bend***:

"How Tom wove the web of characters, countries, technology, and sports into this story is genius! You can't put this book down once you start. I can't wait for his next book!"

"I just finished ready Seminole Bend and utterly enjoyed the entire book. The detail and complexity that the author wrote were amazing. I didn't want to miss a single written word as it was all relevant and added interest to the story."

"I literally couldn't put it down! Lots of twists and turns, action, great characters, and edge of your seat excitement! I anxiously await the next novel from this new and talented storyteller!"

"The detailed references to what was happening in the time frame of the book is impressive, and living in South Florida makes it even more interesting by knowing of the places where the action occurs in the book. If you want to read an exciting new novel by a new novelist I would highly recommend this book."

"Hansen's creativity and commitment to detail, along with realistic referrals to places and events make this book a must-read for the conspiracy-minded community."

"I am a BIG fan of this genre (Daniel Silva, Lee Child, Nelson DeMille), and I would rank this novel right up there with them. Characters are very well developed and become surprising right up until the very end. I can't recommend this book strongly enough. A must-read for fans of this genre!"

"Seminole Bend is a fast-paced mystery thriller using a literary style that is innovative, humorous, and simply put, quite fun. Hansen is the most detailed, imaginative writer on this planet. My head is still spinning."

GILA BEND

Tom Hansen

2018

Gila Bend is a work of fiction. All incidents, dialogue, and all characters except some well-known historical figures are products of the author's imagination and are not to be construed as real. Some locations, businesses, and organizations are real but are used only to support the fictitious nature of this novel. In all other respects, any resemblance to actual persons living or dead, events, or locales is entirely coincidental.

Cultural Unity Publishing
4106 N. St. Elias
Mesa, AZ 85215

Cultural Unity Publishing is a division of Educational Video Training Concepts, LLC.

ISBN: 978-1-7328182-0-0

Printed in the United States of America

Open Book Clipart by http://www.clipartbest.com/cliparts/ace/y8q/acey8qMc4.jpeg

Cover Design by Luke Hansen

For my grandson, William,
and my parents and in-laws,
Bud, Jean, Hugh, and Nona:
You are now and always will be my inspiration!

For your reading pleasure and reference,
a cast of characters chart is included in the appendix.

Part I

Arabian Connection

"The punishment of those who wage war against Allah and His messenger and strive to make mischief in the land is only this, that they should be murdered or crucified or their hands and their feet should be cut off on opposite sides or they should be imprisoned; this shall be as a disgrace for them in this world, and in the hereafter they shall have a grievous chastisement"

Quran (5:33)

Chapter 1

Friday, April 20, 2018 (4-Shaban-1439)
Rub' al Khali Desert, Saudi Arabia
2:00 pm (Arabia Standard Time: Post-Midday Prayer Time)

Lying face down in the scorching, gritty sand, the young man opened his eyes, tried to blink, and realized he was suffocating. A thick, guttural cough loosened the crud in his throat, and he raised his neck just enough to spit out the disgusting filth that was blocking his air passages. Crawling out of the repulsive muck-covered saliva was a dung beetle. The scarab had been feasting on a feces dinner dropped from the back end of a camel, and based upon the damp moisture content, not all that long ago. The young man must have fallen face first with his mouth wide open on the camel dropping! As he discharged what remained in his oral cavity, his first thoughts were bewildering. Where was he, or even more important, who was he?

With the back of his hand, he wiped off a tiny blood droplet from his severely chapped lips. Then he reached around to the base of his skull and felt a soft lump the size of a golf ball that was steadily throbbing. The pain was edging down his neck into his torso. He wanted to get up, but the agonizing sting forced him back to the earth. Where was he? Who was he? Why couldn't he remember?

The young man could feel an extreme heat sensation sizzle over his entire body. He was desperate for water! The hot, arid atmosphere coupled with blowing sand was miserable, and he needed to find answers soon. Despite the sharp twinge in his neck, he managed to roll on his back. The wind and sand had dulled the sun's brightness, but the intense rays were piercing through the dusty air with little trouble, scorching whatever living thing that was foolish enough to get in its way. As he bent forward into a sitting position, the man could see what looked to be the tops of several palm trees about 200 yards away behind a sand dune ridge. Only the palm fronds were visible as the trunks hid below the crest. In the distance beyond the trees were more dunes that appeared to be small mountains on the horizon. The wind was blowing very fast, and grains of sand were cutting at his face and eyes. The young man's only chance for survival was to find water and shelter soon.

Steadying himself with both hands pressed against the blistering earth, he pushed himself into a wobbly stance and moved cautiously toward the palm trees. Although unstable, the promise of shade motivated him to move quickly toward his target. Ascending the steep dune proved more complicated than he imagined, and as he neared the peak, he stumbled. To keep from losing ground, he dug his fingers into the sandbank. While maintaining a firm grip in the supple sand, the young man managed to inch his way to the top of the dune. Sweat from his chest bonded with the sand that snaked through his torn denim shirt, creating mud splotches on what he hoped would not soon become a corpse.

As his head emerged above the apex, a wave of optimism surged through his blood. Glancing downward, he caught an image that appeared to be a small lake or pond perfectly surrounded by lush greenery. Perhaps the green was some sort of crop. On the far side of the water was a domed marble building that resembled a small mausoleum. Was this oasis a shrine honoring a great leader from the past? Or, was it a mirage, a horrible hallucination eating away at what little remained of his sanity?

Believing he was alone in this empty wasteland, the young man once again scrambled to his feet and hastened down the dune toward the pond. He wanted to quickly quench his terrible thirst. But as he descended, he caught a glimpse of movement to his left beyond a cluster of palm trees in the distance. He heard the faint sound of a drum. Ducking back down to keep out of sight, he observed black stumps of all sizes that seemed to be alive and marching in a circle to the whistling wind.

The young man slid down the embankment and clambered behind a group of shrubs. Squinting through the brittle branches, his eyelids and mouth opened wide at the sight of what was unfolding beyond the palm trees. The black stumps were human! Through the ringing in his ears from the injury to his head and the wind piping unharmonious tunes over the desolate desert, he could make out a faint chant coming from the circle. Aching with every silent step, he crept slowly around the shrub toward the alien congregation. To keep from being heard, he concealed his awkward movements behind the desert foliage.

He was no more than twenty yards away now, and as he squinted through the relentless sun and commanding wind, he could see several women in black abayas walking in a circle. Each was carrying a rusty, tin bucket of rigid stones the size of baseballs. Their faces were carefully veiled behind a thin black cloth with gold lace trim, and only the dim shadow of their lips, nose, and chin could be seen through the wispy material. As they were walking, the women would glance up at the sun and unload terrifying shrieks and clicking sounds; then, they would look down into the circle and chant in low-toned, sickening voices. Goosebumps appeared on the young man's arms beneath the red, scaly patches of dry skin. Suddenly, the women stopped their circular parade, and together in unison, they each lifted their veils to reveal pairs of dark, uncertain eyes. The young man stared intensely at the fatigued faces of the Arab women through the slight openings in their niqab, and as unlikely as it seemed, he could swear those eyes told a story. A story of sacrifice, servitude, fear, and hopelessness. But why were they carrying buckets of stones, and why were they moving in a spiral direction?

Then he saw it. In the center of the circle was the head of a young Arab girl. She could be no older than fifteen; her black, curly hair was partially covering youthful dimples and tearful eyes of fright. The girl's head was moving frantically back and forth. Sand covered her body to the top of her shoulders, trapping her in this horrifying position. She was unable to move her extremities even the slightest bit.

The chant abruptly ended. Each Arab woman genuflected and offered praise and glory to Allah, and then each took a stone out of their bucket and gripped tightly. A stout gal, whose worn and wrinkled forehead made her appear many years older than her actual age, raised a jagged rock and aimed at the sobbing girl's face. Her throw was weak and missed by two feet. The young girl began to scream in Arabic; it was a panicked call for forgiveness that needed no translation. Within seconds, the next woman launched a solid, grapefruit-sized stone that was so heavy it required an arcing trajectory to reach the target. It landed directly on the girl's upper forehead causing cranial bones to crack. The human circle of black cloaks turned away momentarily, several covering their mouths with their hands, as the girl blasted a curdling scream of terror.

The young man was covered in a cold sweat and frozen in time. His pain was unconsciously stored somewhere outside his body. A sweeping mixture of fear and anger over what he was witnessing replaced the soreness. Could he possibly save this girl, or was the situation hopeless? A brave attempt at heroics might cost him his own life by tortuous means that he could not even begin to imagine. What had a seemingly innocent child done to deserve this type of death?

Before he could gather his thoughts, a third stone hit the girl on her fragile temple, sending a gushing flow of blood down her chin and neck. The next rock was the last one. The impact forced the girl's head backward, and a wicked snap echoed through the desert.

Chapter 2

Two Years Earlier
Wednesday, July 6, 2016 (1-Shawwal-1437)
Siri Fortress, Aden, Yemen
11:00 am (Arabia Standard Time)

The Rub' al Khali, better known as the Empty Quarter, is the largest sand desert in the world. It is over a quarter-million square miles and covers a majority of the southern one-third of the Arabian Peninsula, including parts of Saudi Arabia, Omen, Yemen, and the United Arab Emirates. The terrain is composed of colossal sand dunes mixed with a few gypsum plains. The climate is arid and sweltering. A cool summer day would be 110 degrees Fahrenheit, but most temperatures are in the neighborhood of 120 degrees. The one inch of rainfall that accumulates each year evaporates within minutes of touching the ground. But underneath that ground is an overabundance of wealth. It's called oil, and the Empty Quarter has enough to run the earth's cars, boats, trains, and planes for the next 200 years.

From his office in Omsk, General Leonid Sokolov oversaw aviation operations for all the Russian Air Force east of the Ural Mountains. He desired to become a chief marshal; however, he was passed over for promotion because of his temper and lack of respect for authority, namely towards President Vladimir Putin. Sokolov met Prince Wasim Nassar during the Sira Fortress Tenth Century Celebration in Aden, of which the general was a guest speaker.

The Nassar family ruled the Al Mahrah district of eastern Yemen since the end of the Ottoman Empire. But Wasim's father, King Ra'id Nassar XIV, was demoted to Governor Nassar when new administrative regions began replacing ancient ones. Ra'id was not happy with the title of governor because he believed he was losing his royalty. The new regime could call him governor, chief, or minister for all he cared, but he would always be a king. It was in his blood. His oldest son, Prince Wasim, headed up the military division of Al Mahrah and was an expert fighter pilot. He had been trained by Al-Qaeda's General Ekram Ganim himself at a makeshift airfield in Oman.

Wasim had been reviewing his first assignment for Al- Qaeda, the elimination of the Eiffel Tower, when a US Fairchild A-10 Thunderbolt lit up the training base, killing twenty-seven Al Qaeda pilots, including General Ganim. Wasim watched in horror as a thirty-millimeter bullet ripped through the general's right eye and gray matter spattered around the room, including a large chunk that came to rest on Wasim's left cheek. The next night, Osama Bin Laden was fatally shot by a Navy SEAL team in his Pakistani compound in Abbottabad. Wasim decided to quietly return to the old palace in Al Mahrah and work for his king-turned-governor father as the head of the district's military, even though the position was not officially recognized by the Yemen government in Sana'a. However, ex-President Ali Abdullah Saleh was a longtime friend of King Nassar, so he let the eccentric ruler of Al Mahrah do as he pleased and create any type of unconventional methods of reigning the old man desired. After all, Al Mahrah was just an empty wasteland, and who would really care if it had its own military?

The rededication of the Sira Fortress was the first such ceremony honoring the island military complex that protected Aden's significant harbor. It was called the *Rock of Gibraltar East* for its unique resemblance to Britain's promontory on the southwestern tip of the Iberian Peninsula. The new president, Abdrabbuh Mansur Hadi, decreed that the fortress be rededicated once each century as long as it was standing tall and mighty. The Russians wanted to control the shipping entrance to the Red Sea, and that would only be accomplished by being good friends to the Yemeni's. Thus, Putin sent Leonid Sokolov to represent the Russians at the first ceremony of the Siri Fortress, despite the general's insistence that he had more important things to do in Omsk.

Along with his native Russian, Sokolov was fluent in Arabic, French, and English. After the speech that was delivered in perfect Arabic, Prince Wasim invited Sokolov to his favorite juice bar tucked into the back corner of the Mualla vegetable market. There, the prince emptied an airplane-sized bottle of Beluga Nobel Russian Gold Vodka into the general's glass of orange nectar. Then he winked at the stunned Russian officer. Sokolov glanced nervously around the tiny bar looking for mutawa, the Islamic religious police. The last thing he needed was to spend the rest of his life in a Yemeni prison cell prancing around its ten-by-ten-foot dirt floor all day trying not to step into the earthen commode with his bare feet. Alcohol was illegal in Yemen, so what was Prince Wasim trying to prove?

"Worried that a little man with a big machine gun is going to sweep you off to jail?" asked the prince with a smile on his face. "Here, I have another bottle. Try it. Screwdrivers are my favorite drink of choice!"

"I'll pass, sir. I plan to return to my fine apartment in Omsk with no bullet holes in my butt," replied Sokolov sarcastically.

"No risks, no rewards, my dear General. I'm assuming that you'll pass on the pork rind chips in my pocket too!" The prince laughed aloud after Sokolov glanced at Wasim's pants pouch.

"I'm assuming you're not a man of your faith, Prince Wasim?" asked Sokolov as he stared directly into his new acquaintance's eyes while taking a sip of juice. The prince looked away and smiled but did not respond. Then, out of nowhere, Wasim changed the conversation from Arabic into perfect Russian. The general was impressed!

"I listened closely to your speech, General. Your willingness to support the Yemen nation and protect our shipping lanes is admirable. But most intriguing to me is that you oversee military aviation for a vast part of your home country. And I, sir, am the best fighter pilot in the Middle East." Once again, Prince Wasim cracked a smile.

"You are most humble, Prince," said Sokolov cynically. "May I ask what it is that you want from me?"

"A job. I would like to work for the Russian government. It would be an honor to help protect your skies from the likes of nasty Americans."

"I don't suppose finding Russian vodka on every city block has anything to do with your motives, does it?" Now it was time for Sokolov to laugh at his own rhetoric. Prince Wasim chuckled, raised his glass, and toasted with the general.

"Before you leave for Omsk, there is something I would like for you to see," stated Wasim. "Would you be able to postpone your return for a few days?"

"Why? What could possibly be in this godforsaken country that would interest me enough to spend a few more days in it?"

"How about an opportunity to amass a fortune and rule the world." Prince Wasim's smile was becoming infectious.

"I guess a tour of your fine nation is worthy of a few extra days of my time." Leonid Sokolov's grin matched the beam on Prince Wasim's face. They raised their glasses and toasted one more time.

Chapter 3

Wednesday, July 6, 2016 (1-Shawwal-1437)
Rub' al Khali Desert, Saudi Arabia
5:00 pm (Arabia Standard Time)
Day 1

"What the hell is this? I'm not getting on that damn thing!" stated General Sokolov while shaking his head.

"It's the only way to see what I want to show you. My uncle is a sultan, and he rules over an oasis community in the desert. He is building a private runway on his oasis, but it won't be finished for several months. To make a long story short, my uncle doesn't want outsiders to find him, so we cannot risk someone finding a dune buggy's tire tracks. Besides, these camels know the way to their home. Call it a sixth sense or something. I'm not sure I could find my uncle's oasis with a GPS and a compass. I have only been there twice, and both times I rode camels. The Rub' al Khali is a vast, wide-open land of hot nothingness. If you get lost, it will eat you alive!"

Prince Wasim owned a 1974 Beechcraft Bonanza four-seater airplane that was used merely to commute small distances from his palace in Al Mahrah. It was also a relaxing way to spend an afternoon in a country that offered little in the form of entertainment. He would fly it out over the Rub' al Khali and perform heart-stopping aerobatic maneuvers that even seasoned veteran pilots would never attempt. Wasim especially loved the Trifecta, a series of three aileron rolls in succession. Like a maestro playing a concerto in Carnegie Hall, he would gently tap the rudder pedals and correct the yawing motion while guiding the elevators to directional and pitch perfection. After completing the loop-de-loop, he would perform a 120-degree vertical climb, drop nose down, kill the engine and soar as far as the desert winds would allow him. Wasim enjoyed tipping his wing and lightly dusting the sand dune peaks.

Before the Siri Fortress ceremony, the prince had parked his Beechcraft at Aden International Airport, which was a short drive from the Mualla vegetable market. General Sokolov was wearing the suit and tie he had on while giving his speech, and Wasim knew he would need a change of outfit for the desert. They walked a block up to a clothing store on Saidi Street, and both men bought a pair of khakis, a long-sleeve white shirt, cushioned sandals, and a wide-brimmed Stetson Yukon hat. The store owner gave them each a paper bag for their dress clothes. Sokolov hadn't asked Wasim where he was taking him, mainly because he wasn't sure he wanted to know the answer. After giving the prince a look that could kill, he rolled his eyes and followed him out the door and into a taxi that was waiting on the street. Ten minutes later, Wasim and Sokolov were boarding the Beechcraft that was sitting just a few yards from the general's Gulfstream G650. No Russian military pilot would be waiting for him at the Aden airport because Sokolov always flew solo to government meetings and events.

Prince Wasim and General Sokolov departed Aden International at 1:30 pm. With a cruising speed of 200 mph, the Beechcraft landed at its destination, a private airfield just south of the Saudi Arabian border near Al Kharkhir, around five in the afternoon. Prince Wasim had built the airstrip for his pleasurable aerobatic outings into the Empty Quarter.

Tucked neatly into Wasim's oversized hangar was a Buckshot XR-2 dune buggy with its 1,300 horsepower V8 engine begging to be fired up. Sokolov hesitated for a moment, then shook his head, laughed, and hopped into the passenger seat. With a grin from ear to ear, Wasim jumped into the driver's seat and cranked the ignition. The monster roared with pleasure as the prince pumped the accelerator while in neutral. After slowly pulling out of the hangar and shutting the door, Wasim gunned the dune buggy, and the two dignitaries became kids again, sand-storming without restraint over the border into the Saudi Arabian arid wasteland. An hour later, they stopped at a small oasis that had a tent, gasoline storage tank, and water well. Two camels were lapping up the water, the last they would drink for at least a week. An old man wearing a full-length white thobe and red-checkered scarf appeared from the tent and kissed Wasim on both cheeks. Then he kneeled and kissed Wasim's hand.

"Marhaba," said Wasim as the weather-beaten elderly man stood up.

"Assalamualaikum," responded Khadim. The old man had served the Nassar family since he was five years old and never knew his own last name. Now at the ripe old age of ninety-four, he was in charge of looking after Wasim's secret outpost and making sure that his uncle's camels were fed and watered.

Wasim handed Khadim the keys to the dune buggy. "Gas it up, then hide it well, my friend."

"Yes, sir, as usual, my dear prince," responded Khadim.

6:00 pm (Arabia Standard Time)

Leonid Sokolov tightened his belt to ensure the Makarov semi-automatic pistol was secured firmly to his back. Then, with the help of Khadim, who steadied the camel, he climbed up onto the wooden saddle. The leather pad covering the seat had worn so thin that the cotton stuffing was bulging out of tiny rips in the hide. "Exactly how far am I riding on this confounded contraption aboard this malodorous creature?"

"A mere four or five days, my friend," replied Wasim with a wink. "My uncle's camp is about 120 miles from here." Sokolov shook his head in disgust and looked out into the orangish-brown mountains of sand surrounding him. Meanwhile, Khadim draped two soft-leather, five-gallon water flasks over each camel's neck and tied them firmly to the saddle.

"I'm assuming this water is for us. What are the damn dromedaries going to drink?" asked Sokolov.

"My dear General, these camels can go weeks at a time without water. Whereas, we need to take precautions and sip carefully. If our twenty-gallon supply runs out before we reach our destination, our final moments before eternal heavenly peace will be filled with dizziness, delirium, and hallucinations." Prince Wasim smiled and winked again at Sokolov, who was struggling to find the humor in death by dehydration.

"If I'm to make this journey and most likely die with you, I'd appreciate it if you would call me by my first name. Leonid—just call me Leonid."

"Okay, Leonid, then it's time to get dirty and sweaty! Here, you're going to need this." Wasim reached into a pack that was attached to the camel saddle and pulled out a spare ghutrah that had been rolled up into a ball. "Wrap this scarf around your face. Make sure you are totally covered except for your eyes."

While Sokolov was trying to figure out the best way to wrap the ghutrah, Khadim tied a large burlap sack filled with goat jerky and unshelled green peas to Wasim's saddle. He then handed each man a large ginger root.

"This will cure the terror in your tummies," stated Khadim proudly like any good medicine man would do. He then whipped each camel with a small leather rope, and the hoofed mammals lurched forward. Sokolov grabbed the saddle grip and held on for dear life.

Under his breath, whispering to himself, the general grunted, "What was I thinking?!"

11:30 pm (Arabia Standard Time)

The men had covered roughly twenty miles the first night, which was a relatively unchallenging ride for the novice camel jockey Leonid. They left Khadim's outpost a few hours before dusk, and the temperatures dropped continually throughout the evening. The general was concerned that the camels wouldn't be able to follow their own tracks in the dark.

"How do these overgrown creatures know where to go?" asked Leonid sarcastically.

Wasim raised his right arm towards the sky while holding onto the grip with his left hand. He pointed his finger and waved his hand back and forth. "The stars, my friend, they follow the stars. Their tracks would have been blown away by now, anyway. Camels have a keen sense of smell. Trust them, they know their next meal is waiting for them at my uncle's oasis."

At midnight, the men made camp in a small valley tucked between two dunes. Wasim guided the camels to a resting position on their bellies, then tied the reigns together so they would be unable to leave without breaking each other's neck. He pulled two large beach towels out of his pack and spread them on the soft sand for beds. The temps had dropped down to a balmy ninety-six degrees, but the ground retained the hot daytime solar heat. Sokolov munched on a piece of goat jerky, then stripped away all his clothes and settled in for a restless night's sleep. At 5:40, the most beautiful sunrise he had ever seen awakened him as it crept slowly over the eastern horizon while the fading moon sank below the western skyline. He glanced over to Wasim's beach towel bed, but the prince was nowhere in sight. After turning in all directions to see where his partner had gone, Leonid looked up towards the horizon and shaded his eyes with his hand. Prince Wasim was prostrating at the top of the dune, but strangely, he was facing opposite the gorgeous sunrise. Leonid put his clothes on and sat down on his towel, chomping fiercely on another goat jerky while he waited twenty minutes for Wasim to return.

"What was that all about?" Leonid asked the prince.

"Call to prayer, my friend," replied Wasim bluntly. "You should try it."

"Why weren't you facing the sun? Isn't that what you are supposed to do?"

"I'm not a sun worshipper, Leonid. I was facing west to the holy city of Mecca. I was offering my salat prayer, but I was also praying for a safe journey for us."

"Well, it seems to me you missed a few prayers yesterday. Like, perhaps, after you guzzled down that screwdriver in the juice bar!" Sokolov laughed and playfully slapped Wasim on the back.

"I don't usually pray the required five times, my friend. However, we may need Allah's help today to get us where we're going." Wasim smirked, then looked to the heavens and placed his fingertips together in prayer. Leonid's smile vanished.

"Let's get back on them damn beasts and get the show on the road," ordered Leonid. "And where do I get some coffee around here?"

Thursday, July 7, 2016 (2-Shawwal-1437)
3:00 pm (Arabia Standard Time)
Day 2

By mid-afternoon, on the second day of their journey, the temperature peaked at 130 degrees, and there was no breeze. Leonid decided he did not need to wear the uncomfortably hot ghutrah when there was no blowing sand. A few moments later, he decided he didn't need the long-sleeve shirt or his khakis, so he stopped, climbed down from the saddle, and undressed down to his birthday suit. If Lady Godiva could do it, so could he! Wearing just the sandals on his feet, Leonid remounted the desert beast. The camel grunted and shook his head wildly before lurching forward. You just knew what the dromedary was thinking!

Prince Wasim had stopped his lead camel to watch the spectacle taking place behind him. When Leonid got closer, Wasim stared and waved his forefinger around his ear in a circular motion indicating that what he was witnessing was simply loco! "Have you gone mad, my friend? An hour in this sun and you will roast like a chestnut!"

"Too damn hot, Wasim! There's nothing more to take off to stay cool. This insane trip better be worth it!"

"You will pay for your stupidity, Leonid." Wasim shook his head and continued the journey.

That evening, after traveling thirty miles since sunrise, Leonid spent another restless night itching his badly sunburned skin. When he was certain Wasim was sleeping, he poured water all over his body. Drinking water. Bad idea.

Saturday, July 9, 2016 (4-Shawwal-1437)
10:00 pm (Arabia Standard Time)
Day 4

A five-degree drop in temperature can be a welcome relief for sizzling summer days. The third and fourth day of the journey maxed out at 125 degrees, which was not exactly chilly but was undoubtedly cooler. However, Leonid's demeanor was not. His skin was beginning to blister and form dark, red blotches, but he still refused to wear clothes that served as his only protection from the ultraviolet rays that were shattering what was left of the melanin in his epidermis. To top it off, the northwesterly breeze picked up gradually and became a violent windstorm by the fourth afternoon. Thankfully, the camels were used to shamals and needed no special gear to protect themselves. But Leonid did, and finally, he wrapped the ghutrah over his scorched face and donned his shirt and pants, letting out shrieks of pain with each tug of his trousers.

The camels progressed another fifty miles in the two days, and now Uncle Nassar's oasis was becoming the light at the end of the tunnel. Leonid consumed the last drop of water in both flasks shortly after munching on his final strip of goat jerky. He needed to let Wasim know his situation.

"My dear prince, I have some bad news," said Leonid as he grabbed Wasim's wrist.

"I can just imagine," replied Wasim. "You are hot and itchy, right?"

"Worse. I have no more water in my flasks."

"How can that be, Leonid? You were only supposed to drink when I drank." Wasim jerked his wrist free from Leonid's grip and gave him an evil stare.

"My body was hot. I used some water to cool off."

"You imbecile!" shouted the prince. "We have another thirty miles to travel, and I have less than two liters of water myself! I told you to keep your damn clothes on, but no, you wouldn't listen!"

"Your anger will not solve the problem, Wasim."

"No, but leaving you in the desert to rot certainly would!" Wasim picked up his towel and walked to the other side of the camels. He didn't want to be anywhere near the general.

Leonid laid down on his towel and stared at the abundant stars that lit up the desert sky. He was overly exhausted from four days riding on the hump of a camel and three nights of restless sleep. The general closed his eyes and was in dreamland within seconds. Just before midnight, he awoke with chills and a feeling of nausea. Leonid tilted his head to the side and puked, providing a warm refreshment for a nosy scorpion that stopped in its tracks only inches from Sokolov's lips. Leonid reached out and picked the Leiurus quinquestriatus up by the tail and let it squirm madly in the air. Although he didn't know much about life in the desert, he remembered from his high school biology class that the vomit-covered arachnid writhing above him was a full-fledged yellow scorpion, better known as a deathstalker due to its potent venom. With the fingers of his free hand, Leonid squeezed the scorpion so hard that a stream of liquid oozed out of the insect's body. He raised the scorpion high into the air to get a good, focused look at the dead little rascal. Leonid then placed it into his mouth and chomped away on the crispy critter.

"Yum, tasty," Leonid whispered to himself while patting his belly. "Let's hope I squeezed all of the venom out of your ugly carcass."

The arachnid snack caused Leonid to become very thirsty, and his inflamed skin was feeling like hundreds of pins were being pushed into each pore. He wriggled around on the towel, trying desperately to scratch his itchy back, but the discomfort only grew worse. His sleep-deprived brain was in survival mode, unable to process the long-term consequences of the actions he was contemplating. He needed water for his throat and his back, and he needed it now!

Wasim was sound asleep on his towel when Leonid tiptoed around the camel searching for the last water flask. But the soft, insulated leather container was no longer tied to the camel saddle. "Where did you hide the flask, you little bastard," muttered Leonid to himself, quiet enough so he couldn't be heard.

Then he noticed the vessel cuddled in Wasim's arms. Apparently, the prince wasn't taking any chances with the general's deranged mental state. Leonid gripped the Makarov pistol and aimed it at the sleeping prince with his right hand while he reached for the flask with his left.

The tug on the water flask woke the lightly-sleeping Wasim. He rolled into a fetal position and instinctively clutched the container with his hands, arms, and tucked-up knees. Leonid squatted on his haunches and placed the pistol on Wasim's forehead. "Hand over the water now, my prince, or I will bury you in the dust with the carcasses of all the spiny-tailed lizards that couldn't hack this godforsaken piece of eternal damnation!"

Wasim scurried backward away from the gun, his arms still cradling the flask. "Leonid, come to your senses, man! This is the last of our water. It's a full day's ride tomorrow to our destination in scorching temps with a killer-sized wind blowing right in our faces! We won't survive without water!"

"Either you give me that water now, or I will blow you to Kingdom come!" Leonid disengaged the safety and cocked the trigger. The weapon was aimed directly at the eyes of the prince.

Wasim carefully tossed the flask at Leonid, then raised his hands. "Peace be with you, brother, because once you finish that water, eternal peace will be the only pleasant thing left following your last few torturous hours on earth. Don't do it, my friend!"

The prince's appeal fell on deaf ears. Leonid unscrewed the cap and guzzled until he couldn't breathe, then poured the remaining water over his blistering back. Wasim scrunched his knees up to his chin and buried his face in his hands. The end was near, very near. In normal circumstances, the human body can last three days without water, maybe a week in a cool home with a humidifier running. But in the arid desert with temperatures nearing 130 degrees? One day possibly, but the brain would be on the brink of insanity if full psychosis hadn't already set in.

Minutes later, Leonid was back on his towel, sound asleep, gun in hand, finger still on the trigger.

Sunday, July 10, 2016 (5-Shawwal-1437)
4:00 am (Arabia Standard Time)
Day 5

An hour before dawn, Wasim nudged Leonid on the shoulder with his foot. "Get up, Leonid, we must get started." Awakened from the best dream he had in months, Leonid sprang alive and instinctively aimed his gun at the prince.

"What, what is it? It's still nighttime. Don't bother me!"

"In case you may have forgotten, we have no water and a journey of thirty miles to complete before delirium settles into our heads. We need to make haste early if we have any chance of surviving the day. But should you choose to sleep, then fine. Ma'a as salama, General! I am on my way."

"Hold on, Wasim. I'm coming with you. But I need food. I didn't want to tell you this, but I ate the last of my goat jerky yesterday, and I ran out of vegetables before that." Leonid looked at the prince hoping for some sympathy, but Wasim had none to offer. After a moment of complete silence, Leonid was becoming agitated. "Last night I devoured a scorpion. I'm in need of some protein, and I could use a good cup of coffee, damn it!"

"You ate a scorpion?" asked Wasim with a mix of disgust and concern. "You fool, the only scorpions out here are the deathstalkers. Their venom will paralyze, then kill you!"

"Do you believe me to be a ninny? I squeezed the venom out of that ugly creature before swallowing it. It was quite delicious, I might add!"

"Saddle up, Leonid. Let's move out." Wasim started walking toward his camel, then stopped and turned to the general. "And wear your clothes today. You will not endure the brutal sun and nasty wind with no skin protection."

10:00 am (Arabia Standard Time)

By mid-morning, the sun was more than brutal, and the wind was beyond nasty. Leonid was extraordinarily thirsty but dared not tell Wasim. The temps had risen above the 130 mark, and the winds were gusting smack dab into their faces at eighty miles per hour. The camels stopped in their tracks and refused to move unless encouraged by kicks to their ribs and lashes to their rear ends. In the first eight hours of the day's journey, the dromedaries had only covered slightly more than five miles. The prince and the general were about twenty-five miles away from their destination, but Wasim knew they wouldn't arrive by nightfall. And chances were good they wouldn't make it tomorrow either if this atrocious weather held up. Shortly before noon, Leonid became dizzy and fell off his camel.

Wasim jumped down and slapped Leonid on both cheeks. Sokolov gasped but did not awaken. The prince placed two fingers on the general's neck and felt his pulse. Leonid's heartbeat was irregular, racing out of control one minute and completely stopping the next. Death was near.

Wasim led the camels fifty yards to a small valley nestled between two dunes. It offered a little pocket of protection against the wind, but not much. He ran back to Leonid and lifted him on his shoulders, then carried him quickly back to the camels. With no water, Leonid would be dead within an hour.

When camels finally get the chance to drink, they do so with great haste and can store thirty gallons of water in their stomachs. That water gradually diffuses into the ellipsoid red blood cells, expanding to more than twice their average size to prevent dehydration during long journeys into the desert. The liquid in the stomach is absorbed into the bloodstream at a rate of about two gallons a day. A dromedary is a one hump camel, and any homegrown Arab boy worth his salt understands that there is no water in that hump, only fat tissue. Unless these camels were abnormally osmosing water faster than usual because of the immense heat, there should be at least twenty gallons left in their bellies.

Knowing that the camels had filled their guts at Khadim's oasis before the journey began, Wasim had only one choice. He grabbed Leonid's pistol and placed the barrel on the largest camel's head, directly between the eyes. Wasim's hands began to shake, and he looked away. Momentarily frozen, he thought about the dromedary and the general. The camel was utterly innocent, sent to the earth by God for one simple purpose: to serve his master. On the other hand, Leonid Sokolov tested God's forbearance with his stupidity. He deserved to die.

Wasim pulled the trigger. The camel's brains and blood splattered in all directions, but his eyes remained open, staring sadly back at his executioner. The prince dropped to his knees, cradled the camel's neck into his chest, and looked up to the sky. "Allah yaghfir li," he pleaded.

When his tears subsided, Wasim used a rope that was tied to the surviving camel to roll the half-ton corpse on its side. The extant dromedary was reluctant to move at first. It appeared to Wasim that he was mourning the loss of his brother in a way that only a camel would know how. The prince patted the forlorn beast above his nose and asked for forgiveness.

With his razor-sharp Helle Sylvsteinen knife, Wasim ripped open the carcass and allowed the blood to drain into one of the empty flasks. The nutrients in the plasma might save Leonid's life if he could keep from regurgitating. The camel's stomach sac still had plenty of undigested water, and Wasim filled the other flask up with the warm liquid, complete with gastric juices that included a delicious combination of hydrochloric acid, pepsinogen, and mucus. Perhaps death didn't sound so bad!

After setting the flasks next to Leonid's cataleptic body, Wasim returned to the carcass and cut off chunks of fatty tissue from the hump. With the blubber, he rubbed Leonid's skin to try and soothe his sunburn pain. Wasim then cut large strips of hide from the carcass and wrapped them around Leonid's upper torso for maximum protection from the sun's ultraviolet rays. Finally, he dressed the general in his clothes, stretching the long-sleeve shirt around the camel's hide the best he could.

Leonid's pulse and breathing remained irregular as Wasim propped him into a sitting position that allowed the general to lean his back onto the prince's chest. Wasim tilted Leonid's head and poured a few ounces of camel blood down his throat which immediately caused the general to choke and cough it back out. But this also woke Leonid from his coma, and he leaned forward to spit out the putrid plasma. Weak and dazed, Sokolov turned his head and looked back at the person who was steadying him.

"Good, you're awake," said Wasim. "But you are on the verge of death, my friend. I have slaughtered one camel so you may live. You must drink some blood from its carcass and some water from its stomach. It is your only hope for survival. Should you decide to return to your old irksome self and refuse God's gifts, I will leave you here to rot through eternity with this poor camel that didn't deserve to die! Are you with me?"

"I believe I have no choice," replied Leonid feebly. "But I'm too weak to stand and board that beast."

"You will mount the dromedary by holding on to my shoulders, and you will then hold on to me for dear life. And pray to Allah that you don't let go because if you do and you fall off, your grave will be where you lie!"

With that said, Wasim gave Leonid another sip of blood and water, then drank the same amount himself. Both men became nauseous but held the fluids down. The general climbed onto the prince's back, and with a high degree of difficulty, they awkwardly mounted the camel. The mid-afternoon sun was still scorching the desert, but fortunately, the shamal had whipped up the sand into a thick, brown-hazed filter. Impossible to see through the grit, the dromedary journeyed onward using only his senses. He wanted to be home even more than his rapidly perishing cargo.

7:00 pm (Arabia Standard Time)

Leonid fell back into a coma shortly before dusk, and Wasim clenched the general's limp arm with his left hand while gripping the camel's reigns with his right. To keep Sokolov from falling, Wasim bent forward in the saddle to allow Leonid to lean on him. Knowing he would be unable to get the general back on the dromedary if he fell, Wasim relieved his bladder twice into his pants while the camel drudged on. There was no point in stopping to rest now that the sun had set, and the wind had finally subsided. Getting to the oasis before dawn was Wasim's one and only goal. Leonid's life hung in the balance.

Wasim poured a mixture of camel water and blood over his shoulder, drenching his shirt with the reddish-gray substance that looked and smelled like sewage. Knowing his passenger's face was propped up on his back, he hoped that the unconscious Leonid would somehow be able to absorb the gooey fluids into his digestive system through osmosis from his severely chapped lips.

Chapter 4

Monday, July 11, 2016 (6-Shawwal-1437)
The House of Sultan Tariq ibn-Nassar
Rub' al Khali Desert, Saudi Arabia
5:00 am (Arabia Standard Time)

Sensing he was close to home, the camel moved swiftly through the starlit night. Wasim's back was aching with unyielding pain due to his uncomfortable position on the dromedary as it began to climb an enormous dune. The sun was rising behind him when Wasim noticed the shadows of palm tree fronds appear in the distance. A new day was dawning, and the prince pulled back on the reigns to stop the camel after reaching the dune's peak. Looking down, Wasim could see his uncle's oasis, an old Bedouin community of roughly twenty men and boys and nearly one hundred women and girls. But no longer was the tribe nomadic, thanks to the leadership of Uncle Tariq ibn-Nassar, who decreed himself a sultan. He believed he was an overlord: a master of power, might, strength, reign, and rule, unlike his brother Ra'id who was simply a king. All who lived in Sultan Tariq's oasis were relatives, mostly distant cousins, nieces, and nephews. But Tariq was a devout Muslim, and his oasis sultanate was ruled strictly by the word of the Koran. Each adult male was required to marry at least four females before they reached the age of twenty. As Wasim peered down from the dune, he watched intently as those men completed a mixture of standing, bowing, and prostrating on their prayer rugs while facing west toward the Kaaba in Mecca. Inside eight large tents set a hundred or so yards behind the main camp would be the harem of women also performing their daily salat. Only a flock of thirty-three camels sleeping in a corral were allowed to shun their duties to Almighty God by missing the Fajr prayer.

The main camp consisted of colorful tents encompassing a small pond that was surrounded by papyrus reeds and other green vegetation. Shade and nutritional sustenance were provided by an abundance of tall date palm trees and smaller fig trees. The tent walls were made from intricate Persian tapestry woven from goat hair and stanchioned by wooden poles, while the roofs were a hardened mixture of thatch and camel dung.

Behind the reflective pond, looking like a miniature Taj Mahal, was Sultan Tariq's palace built from marble and covered by a bronze dome. Wasim knew his family was not rich, but you would never know it from the looks of his uncle's mansion. Only Ra'id and Wasim knew his secret to success. Tariq had formed a business alliance with one of the wealthiest people on the planet that resulted in the creation of his sultanate. However, Tariq was the only resident of this oasis allowed to display any sign of opulence. He demanded complete obedience from each of his servants, which was everyone who lived in the hidden community. In return, Tariq promised them eternal life in heaven alongside the great prophets of Islam. No one dared question how he could do that!

Next to Tariq's palace was a deep underground well that supplied the entire community with clean and fresh water. Wasim stared at the well and the pond in wonderment. What miraculous geological factors underneath this desolate desert shaped how Tariq's oasis was blessed with water? There had to be a fault line below the surface that trapped and channeled natural spring water in pockets to a nearby aquifer. Intense heat from the earth's substrata pressured the water upward to form the pond, but Wasim couldn't even imagine how long it took human servants to dig the well with the type of tools and equipment available in the 1800s.

Suddenly, a brilliant beam originating somewhere behind the palace streaked through the dawn sky like a lightning bolt. A split second later, an explosion could be seen and heard beyond the crest of the nearest dune. General Sokolov opened his eyes and watched a small plane disintegrate into ashes.

"What … the … hell?" he muttered with all the energy he had left in him after five excruciating days on the camel.

"This is why I brought you here, my friend." Wasim shifted in the saddle. It was time to get the general off his back—literally and figuratively.

Chapter 5

Monday, July 18, 2016 (13-Shawwal-1437)
The House of Sultan Tariq ibn-Nassar
Rub' al Khali Desert, Saudi Arabia
8:00 am (Arabia Standard Time)

Sultan Tariq's personal doctor, Sachit Laghari, tended to General Sokolov for a week in the private clinic inside the sultan's palace. Dr. Laghari induced Sokolov into a comatose state, then treated the general for severe dehydration and ultraviolet radiation poisoning—better known to ordinary people as brutal sunburn. Wasim was at his side when he regained consciousness.

"Thought I lost you there for a moment," said Wasim grinning. "Thought maybe that might be a good thing, you stubborn old fool! You owe me a camel!"

"I believe I owe you more than that," replied Sokolov in a faint voice. "I'm trying to forget the camel ride, but please tell me about that light beam and explosion I saw."

"The beam of light was a laser weapon. Uncle Tariq's engineers created it to protect his oasis from enemies."

"Enemies?! Why would anyone be his enemy? Who was in that plane that was blown up?"

"Research geologists and petroleum engineers who survey the land periodically fly near here. Unfortunately, they never return home to their families. My uncle doesn't want to be discovered!"

"So, he uses a—what do you call it—ray gun to protect himself from harmless oil men?" asked Sokolov curiously. "Why on earth would you need such a potent weapon out here in this wasteland?!"

"Perhaps you should know a little of the history of my family, dear General."

"Perhaps I should!" replied Sokolov.

"We, the Nassar family, had ruled this tiny area of the Rub' al Khali since soundly defeating the Saud family raiders with swords a century ago. Back then, nomadic tribes fought for the right to claim the Arabian Peninsula as their own. After our victory, the Nassar clan moved south into what is now Yemen and settled there where the land wasn't as harsh as the Rub' al Khali."

"After your family left, didn't the Saud family try to reclaim the region?"

"They didn't have to," replied Wasim. Then his voice turned to anger. "The House of Saud no longer needed religious warriors to conquer Bedouin tribes and behead nonbelievers in the name of the Prophet Muhammad!"

"What do you mean?"

"In 1938, petroleum engineers from the United States struck oil near Dammam on the Arabian Gulf. After tapping into the black gold, the Saud family went from rags to riches virtually overnight. The onetime massive sandbox of nothingness was suddenly coveted by every nation on earth. Every president, emperor, prime minister, king, queen, and dictator wanted a piece of the action!"

"Did your family try to stake a claim to the oil around this oasis?"

"We didn't even bother trying! The Saudis had America to protect them! We had swords—they had atomic bombs! So we stayed in eastern Yemen and declared our tiny region a kingdom, which was a joke! No one cared because no one wanted to live there anyway! When the Yemen Arab Republic was formed in 1978, the government allowed us to oversee the sparsely populated area merely for historical and cultural reasons. If someday they allowed tourists in their country, our clan would be the main attraction! I can picture the blurb printed in those colorful travel pamphlets: *Come see how the Yemeni nation tamed the vicious Nassar warriors!* But they also wanted our family to be isolated from modern politics and not become an embarrassment to their new country. Uncle Tariq and my father, Ra'id, were appointed co-governors of Al Mahrah, our mundane region of nothingness!"

"How did that work out?" asked Sokolov.

"Ra'id at once denounced the title of governor and proclaimed he and his brother as kings. But Tariq knew the title of king would never be recognized in Yemen. So, he had a better idea. His hobby was falconry, and he was a master, well known throughout the elite hunting circles as the world's finest birds of prey trainer and huntsman. Wealthy people from all corners of the globe hired Tariq for his falconry skills, primarily to watch with morbid pleasure as the Saker falcons searched and killed the cute little fennec foxes that roamed the desert. What more could rich corporate executives want than to have a stuffed omnivorous mammal with big ears standing on their oak desks watching them work?!

"Tariq's best client was John Shaffer, a member of the British House of Lords and the Old Hawking Club of London. Seems the young chap had more wealth than the owners of Harrod's and the House of Windsor put together, and falconry was his beloved diversion from the London rat race. Lord Shaffer offered to pay Tariq handsomely to be his private falconer, ready to hunt at his beck and call.

"So, banking on a financial twist of fate from the billfold of his new parliamentarian friend, Tariq decided to move permanently across the Saudi-Yemeni border and reclaim this abandoned oasis that rightly belonged to the Nassar family anyway. There wasn't much here at the time except for the pond and an old well dug a century before. But thanks to his new business alliance with Lord Shaffer, Tariq gave up his governate in Yemen and formed a new sultanate in the Rub' al Khali with all the essentials befitting a sultan. Mainly, a palace and a harem!"

"You're telling me that a British politician funded this estate so he would have his own personal hunting lodge in the middle of nowhere?! Incredulous!"

"Yes, General, my uncle is indebted to that man."

"What about that laser weapon?" asked Sokolov. "You know, the reason I'm assuming you dragged me out here on the back of a camel!"

"What do you want to know?"

"Who designed it?"

"An MI6 double agent," replied Wasim bluntly. He smiled again as he watched the general try and assess what he just heard. "Yes, you heard me right. A renegade member of the British Secret Service. A friend of the rich and powerful Lord Shaffer!"

Chapter 6

Wednesday, July 20, 2016 (15-Shawwal-1437)
The House of Sultan Tariq ibn-Nassar
Rub' al Khali Desert, Saudi Arabia
8:00 am (Arabia Standard Time)

Tariq's conference room inside his palace resembled a miniature Westminster Abbey. Perhaps that was because four oil paintings that once graced the walls of England's mother church now hung in the sultan's meeting room along with bookshelves direct from the Abbey's library. Lord Shaffer never hesitated to use his connections within the royal family to please someone! But one painting was unexpected; it was a 15th Century canvas by Florentine artist Bicci di Lorenzo that showed the Madonna enthroned and holding a rose with the Christ child and angels kneeling at her feet. Not something you would expect to see in the palace of a devout Muslim! Tariq didn't care. If hanging the gift from Lord Shaffer would solidify their friendship, then he would gladly do so and ask Allah for forgiveness later!

From a large picture window, Tariq could see the entire oasis, which was oddly beautiful considering its isolated location in the Rub' al Khali. Windswept dunes provided a stunning backdrop to the pond and palm trees in the foreground. And from this same room, stonings and executions could be clearly observed—a feature Tariq thought his guests would enjoy. None did.

Tariq sat in an oversized, high-back chair that resembled a miniature throne at the head of a long ebony conference table. There were plenty of leather chesterfields placed around the table that were comfortable but not easy to move. The sultan believed in showing off wealth ahead of practicality.

Tariq introduced himself to General Sokolov, then sat quietly in his chair, sipping tea. Next to him was a tall man whose physique resembled that of the Incredible Hulk. A pistol bulged from the back of his elastic waistband. Sokolov assumed he was Tariq's bodyguard. Prince Wasim whispered to the general that his uncle was waiting for someone to arrive before the meeting would begin. Wasim assured Sokolov that everything would be explained shortly. But when the helicopter that was landing could be seen through the window, Sokolov glared angrily at the prince.

"You told me that your uncle only allowed visitors to arrive by camel! What is this all about?!"

Sultan Tariq cut in. "My nephew is correct, General Sokolov. Only one person is allowed on my oasis without arriving on a dromedary. That would be Lord Shaffer."

Sokolov was about to respond but decided to hold his tongue. Wasim was glad he did!

A few minutes later, Lord Shaffer entered the conference room wearing khaki shorts and a Burberry short-sleeve shirt. He was ready to hunt with Tariq after the meeting ended. Alongside Shaffer was an elderly man who was incredibly fit for his age wearing a perfectly tailored Giorgio Armani wool suit. General Sokolov's mouth opened wide in surprise, not because someone would wear wool in this extreme heat, but because he recognized the elderly man.

"Yegor. What the hell are you doing here?"

*****

Yegor Bovnik was immortal. At least he thought he was. In November of 1956, at the age of twenty-two, he crushed all hopes the revolutionist Hungarians had for a life of democracy. Yegor was the commander-in-charge for Russia's mission to squash the uprising in Budapest, and he did so with expediency and vigor. He sat in the gun turret of the lead T-55 armored tank and personally killed more than a thousand young men, women, and teenage protesters who were armed with empty beer bottles. After killing the defenseless "hooligans," he rammed his tank into the Yugoslav embassy and arrested Chairman Imre Nagy and hauled him to a secret location where he was convicted of treason and hung. Nagy's lawyer was not invited to the trial.

Immediately following the Hungarian revolution, Yegor was reassigned to the KGB because of his leadership skills. The young soldier was intelligent, fierce, and cunning, but most importantly, he despised failure—in himself and in his followers. Yegor was destined for greatness—a premier in the making, but he preferred to work in the shadows where no one would take notice. Yegor was a loner and only needed his own corrupted soul to be happy. The fewer people on the earth, the better off he would be. And like all his fellow communists, he hated Americans.

In October of 1959, Yegor was appointed the Directorate Chief of the KGB, and his boss, First Secretary Nikita Khrushchev, gave him only one directive: create and carry out a plan that would end the Cold War with the USSR being victorious! Shatter the American dream and that confounded democracy along with it! Yegor wasn't sure where to start. The United States was a tough egg to crack.

Then, acting on clandestine intelligence from KGB spies in America, Yegor procured the services of a disgraced, court-marshaled US Marine named Lee Harvey Oswald. Four years later, Oswald was asked to perform one simple act of treason against his former country: put a stop to President Kennedy who was doing everything in his power to dismantle the Communist regime. The young commander-in-chief had ordered the Bay of Pigs invasion, stockpiled nuclear weapons, and supported the Truman Doctrine by creating a military presence in Vietnam.

Oswald did his part, but when the assassination of America's beloved president failed to end the Cold War, the Central Committee of the Communist Party of the Soviet Union reorganized. They fired Khrushchev and appointed Alexei Kosygin as premier and Leonid Brezhnev his first secretary. Then, the Committee gave Kosygin and Brezhnev a mandate: win the space race or face disgrace! The new leaders delegated that mission to Directorate Chief Yegor Bovnik.

In the early morning hours of July 21, 1969, Brezhnev and Kosygin sat defeated in front of the television that displayed black and white video feed coming from the moon. The words would haunt them until the day they died: "That's one small step for man, one giant leap for mankind." Neil Armstrong and Buzz Aldrin were now steadfast enemies of the Soviet Union, and that damn CBS anchor, Walter Cronkite, needed to stick a sock in his mouth!

Yegor was ordered to meet with Brezhnev and Kosygin in Brezhnev's Kremlin office. The space race was over, and the Americans had won. The mood was grim, and Yegor wished his bosses would have drunk their morning coffee before the meeting.

"We lost, Directorate Chief Bovnik," said Brezhnev sternly. "Where in Siberia would you like to spend your remaining years?!"

"Please, sir," replied the morose Yegor. "I will create a new plan. One that will collapse America from inside its own beating heart!"

"It better be good," retorted Kosygin. "There is no room for any more failures!"

"What is your grand scheme, Yegor?" asked Brezhnev.

"We will bring down America by clogging the arteries and veins of Washington, DC!" Yegor pounded his fist on the table in anger. "From inside the capitol legislative chambers to the bench of the Supreme Court and all the way to the damn White House, they'll never know what hit them! The United States of America will crumble from within!"

Deep in thought, Brezhnev stood up and paced the room. He assumed the specifics of Yegor's plan would unfold in due time. Although he blew it on the space race, the directorate chief was a man of his word. Whatever this proposal would entail, it had the total enthusiasm of Yegor, which was good enough for the General Secretary. Brezhnev then headed for the door, stopped at the entryway, and turned to look at Yegor.

"Well then," said Brezhnev cracking a smile and giving a nod to Kosygin. "You better get to work."

8:30 am (Arabia Standard Time)

"I'm eighty-two years old," said Yegor directly to General Sokolov. "It's high time I completed my life's mission."

The conference room was silent. Yegor shook Sokolov's hand, bowed to Tariq, nodded at Wasim, then looked at the well-built man sitting next to the sultan and smiled. "Nice to see you again, Bond." Bond glanced at Yegor but remained expressionless.

"What's this all about, Yegor?" asked Sokolov.

"In 1969, I promised my superiors that I would devise a plan to end American democracy. I tried, but luck wasn't on my side. In the 1980s, I hired a team of five scientists who had come close to developing a laser weapon in a secret laboratory underneath the Chernobyl Nuclear Power Plant. The station was generating electricity for much of Ukraine, but more importantly, the facility was producing energy packs to be used in the new death ray gun that the scientists were creating. But the entire project ended suddenly after the power plant's reactor failed and caused a nuclear meltdown. The catastrophe killed thirty-one workers, including all five scientists.

"Then, five years later, the Iron Curtain collapsed, as did the Union of Soviet Socialist Republics. The country I loved was tearing apart from the inside. Poverty was spreading, and the Russian leaders had no answers. Oh, how I wished for another Bolshevik Revolution! I even contemplated suicide, but I'm not a quitter! I refuse to die until my mission is complete!" Yegor pushed his chair back, stood up, and pounded the table with his fist. His face had turned bright red. General Sokolov thought his Russian comrade was going to have a heart attack!

Yegor regained his composure and walked over to where Lord Shaffer was sitting. He patted the parliamentarian on the shoulders—sort of a love tap that a father gives his son when he is proud of him.

"In 2005, I met this man. He wanted to buy property in Moscow, but he couldn't get approval from the Russian authorities. A British Secret Intelligence Service agent accompanied Lord Shaffer, which was odd because the parliamentarian wasn't on official government business." Yegor then gestured at Bond.

"Have you met Bond?" he asked Sokolov.

"Not really," replied the general. "He doesn't seem to have much to say." Bond finally cracked a smile and winked at Sokolov.

Lord Shaffer cut in. "He's the best MI6 operative that the SIS has! Not one of the best—THE best! And I'm privileged to call him my friend and business partner. I nicknamed him Bond because he reminds me of actor Sean Connery. He could be mistaken for 007, don't you think?!" Everyone grinned except for Sokolov, who still wasn't sure what this meeting was all about.

Lord Shaffer could tell that Sokolov was frustrated and wanted some answers, so he looked at the general and got straight to the point. "Bond and twenty other MI6 operatives work directly for me without the British government's knowledge. I pay them double their current salaries and provide them with shares of ownership in the Manchester United soccer club. Bond has a Doctorate of Quantum and Theoretical Physics from Imperial College London. The British Secret Service found that useful—and so do I!"

Bond finally decided to speak. "I knew Yegor from meetings the British SIS had with the KGB. When Lord Shaffer hit a dead end trying to buy the Moscow property, I contacted the Directorate Chief to see if he could arrange the deal." Bond glanced at Yegor, guessing he would like to continue his story.

"Lord Shaffer slipped me a check for fifty million Russian rubles," said Yegor, then paused momentarily and chuckled. He walked back to his seat and pointed at Shaffer. "Then, that rich Englishman offered to take Bond and me on a falconry hunting expedition to Arabia! That was the clincher, you might say! An hour later, the Moscow property was signed, sealed, and delivered!

"And our hunt was extraordinarily successful! We celebrated right here in this room with fine Russian caviar and vodka mixed with Siberian ginseng. The cape hares, sand cats, and striped hyenas are all mounted and scattered around my office at the Kremlin!

"It was during the hunt that I found out Bond had a physics degree. I had given up hope for developing a death ray after the Chernobyl disaster killed my team of scientists. But I thought there might be a chance that Bond would have the knowhow to develop a new weapon, perhaps a more potent one! And what better place to set up shop but in this desolate hidden oasis in the middle of nowhere?! So, I took a risk and told my three hunting partners about my plan to create a laser weapon to be used against the United States. Then, I asked them to join me. Do you know what they said?"

"Bloody hell!" blurted Lord Shaffer and then roared with laughter. "That's what I said! I had no idea how a laser gun could be used against America, but I didn't really care! I told Yegor to count me in! This should be fun!"

Tariq nodded. "And if Lord Shaffer was all in, well, so was I!"

Yegor walked around the table and stood next to Sokolov. The expression on his face turned serious. "General, I would like for you to take part in my mission to end American democracy. I was the one who asked Prince Wasim to bring you here. I need a comrade from Russia to join me, and I believe you might be interested."

Sokolov got up from his chesterfield and paced around the conference room. Everyone stared at him, waiting for an answer. A minute later, he placed his hands on the table, leaned in, and stared directly into Yegor's eyes. In a firm tone of voice, Sokolov uttered, "On one condition."

"What's that?" asked the directorate chief.

"I decide how the laser weapon will be used," replied the general.

Everyone glanced at Lord Shaffer. After all, it was his money that would finance the entire project.

Shaffer looked reluctantly at Sokolov. He didn't want to relinquish his power, but there appeared to be no other choice. So, he shrugged his shoulders, and his apprehensive face transformed into a childish grin.

"If that's what it takes, General, then welcome aboard!" said Shaffer. He reached out his arm to shake Sokolov's hand. "But one other thing—if the energy packs that fuel the laser gun are going to be used against the United States, then we should build them in the United States. From what Bond told me, the energizers must be stored in a cool and dark location. Once they are exposed to room temperature or above, they must be used within one month. Transporting them out of the Rub' al Khali is slow and difficult."

Sokolov chortled and asked sarcastically, "You think you can find somewhere in America to build a death ray weapon that will be used against them?!" Then he shook his head and snorted.

"As a matter of fact, I think I can, General," replied Lord Shaffer confidently. "We will meet again in three months to create a strategic plan. As for right now, I believe Sultan Tariq and I have a hunting date with some falcons!"

What Lord Shaffer didn't know was that he was about to discover something that would rocket his corporate profit margins off the chart. And it would fit in nicely with Yegor's plan to take down America!

Chapter 7

Saturday, July 23, 2016 (18-Shawwal-1437)
Sadeh, Yemen
1:00 pm (Arabia Standard Time)

Taste Of Arabia was just a middling coffee company, an "average joe" you might say, located in Sadah, a small community nestled in the Sarawat Mountains of northwestern Yemen. When roasted properly, the Arabica beans smelled and tasted perfumey with notes of fruit and sugar tones. Lord Shaffer first sampled a cup of java brewed from the rare beans during the falconry outing with Tariq. They were driving from the Sana'a airport to Khamis Mushait in Saudi Arabia and stopped for a rest in Sadah. One road sign a few miles back claimed that Abadi's Pita Bakery was *To Die For*, the next billboard said *Don't Miss The Freshness.*

Lord Shaffer smiled at Tariq and declared, "I do believe it's time for a pit stop, my dear huntsman!" They found the bakery in an alley a few blocks off the main drag. Parking was a nightmare, but the road signs were certainly truthful. The hot pita bread right out of the earthen oven was simply delectable. But the coffee that Mr. Abadi served with the pita was even better!

"What brand coffee is this heavenly java?!" Lord Shaffer asked the owner. He smelled the fragrance and sipped another taste.

"Ah sir, you are a gentleman who appreciates freshness. This coffee is made from beans that I handpicked a few miles from here in the Sarawats. I roast them in my ovens, as well. You like, no?"

Well, Lord Shaffer loved the coffee so much that he purchased the store from Mr. Abadi right there on the spot. He scribbled two identical contracts onto a couple of napkins, had Mr. Abadi sign each one, then opened the leather satchel that he brought everywhere and handed the bakery owner 100 crisp fifty-pound British banknotes. 5,000 pounds converted into Yemeni rials would equate to a very fine retirement someday! But Lord Shaffer had a strange request to go along with the deal.

"Okay, Mr. Abadi, now that I own this place, I have a few exigencies that require immediate attention. First, I would like you to stay on as my general manager. What do you say?"

"Yes, Lord Shaffer, I would be honored to work for you. Thank you, sir!" Mr. Abadi believed he had died and gone to heaven.

"Second," said Lord Shaffer, "I want you to close down the pita bakery and use the ovens only for roasting those delicious coffee beans."

Now Mr. Abadi was in shock. Yes, the java was excellent, but the pitas were incredible, and the reason that locals and travelers alike came to his place of business. "Are you sure, Lord Shaffer, that you would want to put all your apples into one basket, so to speak?"

"I'm a very successful entrepreneur, Mr. Abadi. I've been around the block once or twice. The pita bread is amazing, yes, but the coffee will make us a fortune. Pitas need to be sold in a day or two after baking, whereas roasted coffee beans could be vacuum-packed to seal in freshness and shipped around the world. There are very wealthy coffee connoisseurs in every country, my friend. My first presentation and major sale will be to Starbuck's CEO, Howard Schultz." Lord Shaffer paused for a few moments and studied Mr. Abadi's face. "Do you see my point, sir?"

"Yes, my gracious lord, I most certainly do!" Mr. Abadi had decided that working for this man would be very rewarding, and it was time to show him all the respect that royalty deserved, even if he was British royalty. Lord Shaffer laughed aloud, stood up, and gave his new general manager a handshake.

"My gracious lord? Please, sir, the Middle Ages ended centuries ago and along with it any resemblance of nobility amongst British politicians. In fact, you may call me John if you wish."

Mr. Abadi walked his unforgettable customers out to their rented Jeep Wrangler, then bowed several times as they headed off on their hunting expedition. As he turned to go back into the bakery, he came to a full stop, slapped himself lightly on both cheeks, and gazed up at the sky.

"What just happened?" he muttered to himself.

Even Allah himself wasn't sure.

Chapter 8

Saturday, August 13, 2016 (10-Dhu al-Qidah-1437)
Sadeh, Yemen
12:05 pm (Arabia Standard Time)

Bassam Bashir was fourteen-years-old and a grade school dropout like ninety percent of his friends who lived in Sadah. Education was required until a child reached puberty, which in the eyes of the local authorities was synonymous with adulthood. There was a need for only one school in Sadah, and the faculty consisted of five primary teachers for prepubescent students and only two for all the rest. Graduation occurred after completing ten grades, and zero percent went on to college. Instead, local businesses set up apprenticeships, and every employee learned on the job. Bassam was one of two teenagers that Mr. Abadi hired to run the new *Taste Of Arabia* factory, but you could hardly ever find him working. He was a lazy apprentice who had mastered the art of daydreaming.

Tungis was a rare, leafy plant found only in the southern Sarawat Mountains of the Arabian Peninsula. It resembled the umbrella leaf of eastern Tennessee, but when dried, it looked and smelled like tobacco. A few Sadah dropouts realized that smoking rolled up leaves from the tungis plant could make all their troubles disappear. It had a powerful chemical effect, which was precisely what the doctor ordered for Bassam, that is, of course, if he had a doctor. So, after another boring day watching green coffee beans pop and crackle into deep brown ones, Bassam rolled and lit up a tungis reefer and dreamt of exotic goddesses awaiting his beck and call. Ten minutes later, the religious police were making their daily rounds checking each business for violations of Sharia law. It was a few minutes past noon, and every worker should now be performing their Dhuhr prayers. Bassam saw them coming just in time and tossed the leaves into the oven with the green beans. Smoking tungis was worse than smoking marijuana in the eyes of the local mutawa and would result in spending the rest of your life in prison.

"Son of Bashir, you should be in prayer now," said one of the mutawa while pointing his AK-47 Kalashnikov at the boy.

"Yes sir, yes sir," replied Bassam with a great deal of anxiety. "I was working so hard that I forgot. I will never let that happen again, sir. Please forgive me! Allahu akbar!"

Bassam retrieved his prayer rug from a closet inside the small factory and began his required ritual. The mutawa waited and watched for a few moments, then nodded and moved on.

Meanwhile, the chemical reaction of tungis leaves and Arabica coffee beans was about to unknowingly create new profitability of monumental proportions for the *Taste Of Arabia* coffee company.

1:10 pm (Arabia Standard Time)

By the time he had completed his midday prayer, the beans in the oven had roasted too long and could not be sold with the consistency that Bassam's boss demanded. But the teenage apprentice believed he would lose his job if he had nothing to show for the time he was getting paid. His colleague and sometimes friend, Dawud Tadros, had roasted ten sacks earlier in the morning that were sitting in a dark corner away from the hot oven. Bassam had a quick decision to make, and when it came to thinking fast on his feet to avoid being caught in unscrupulous acts, well, he was a gold medal winner in that arena! Next to the oven was a flat converted snow shovel used to scoop out the roasted coffee beans, just like it was used for extracting piping hot pita bread back in the old bakery days.

Bassam looked around the room to ensure he wasn't being watched, then scooped the blend of dark beans and tungis ash from the oven and dumped the mixture into a burlap sack. He tied the bag tightly with twine and carried it over to Dawud's pile, then grabbed one of his friend's sacks and placed it in his own collection. After roasting and bagging two more bundles of raw coffee beans, it was time to leave for the day. Bassam wiped the sweat from his forehead as he walked a mile to his home. He had never worked this hard in his life!

When Bassam arrived for work the next morning, Dawud was playing solitaire with a deck of beat up cards while waiting for a batch of beans to finish roasting. Dawud heard the door open but didn't bother looking up from the ace of clubs he had just moved to the top of the pile. "Your late, Bassam, as usual. And now that I think about it have you ever been on time for work?"

"Back off, Dawud, I worked a long and tedious afternoon yesterday. Sweated on the way home, in fact!" Bassam stared at his colleague, but Dawud just ignored him. That's when Bassam noticed it. Just behind where Dawud was sitting was the sack of coffee and tungis he had bagged and exchanged yesterday. Underneath, a black, oily residue was seeping out onto the wooden floor. Curious if tasting the blend of beans and tungis could produce a better high than smoking the dried leaves by themselves, Bassam walked around Dawud, picked up the sack, and caught a whiff. "Wow, heavenly stuff," he muttered to himself.

"What was that?" asked Dawud.

"What was what?"

"What did you say? You just said something."

"Nope, I was just thinking aloud."

"Well, what were you thinking about?"

"Nothing. Hey, I hear your beans crackling. You need to get them out of the oven."

Dawud got up quickly and placed an empty sack on the bag holder, then picked up the shovel and began scooping the beans. Meanwhile, Bassam took the mixture of coffee and tungis and walked out the front door, then placed the sack around the corner of the building so Dawud would not see that he had taken it. He stuck his head back into the factory and yelled over to Dawud, who was busy bagging the newly roasted beans. "Hey, I'll be back soon.

Boss wanted me to pick up some bottled water on the way into work this morning, and I forgot."

"Yeah, right!" replied Dawud. "Chances are slim that I'll see you again today!"

Bassam picked up the sack and hurried down to the alley. Just as he turned the corner and was about to hide behind a garbage bin to taste the divine substance, a shiny black stretch limousine slammed on its brakes to avoid running him over. Bassam was stunned, then turned pale, thinking how close he had come to serious injury or death. But his dark skin transformed into a delicate shade of pastel when the back doors of the limo opened and out stepped Anwar Abadi, Bassam's boss, with some rich-looking dude in fancy clothes. The two men rushed over to Bassam.

"Are you okay, Bassam?!" asked Mr. Abadi with some anxiety in his voice. "What are you doing out here?"

Bassam had to think quickly again. White lies were becoming his mantra. He lifted the coffee and tungis sack and handed it to his boss. "I was trying to find you, sir! I didn't want to tell Dawud, but I roasted this special variety of coffee yesterday that I think you will like. You know me, I'm always trying to make this company better by finding ways to make the coffee better! Anyway, I thought you were at Rashim's restaurant having breakfast, and I couldn't wait to tell you the good news!"

Mr. Abadi took the ten-pound sack and smelled it. The perfume fragrance was very noticeable, as was the sticky residue on the bottom. Mr. Abadi pulled out a hanky and wiped the substance off his hands. "You roasted this too long, Bassam. The oils have bled out of the beans."

"But I brewed a pot this morning to taste it, and it was perfect," lied Bassam—again. "Simply incredible, sir! Please, you need to try it!" Bassam hoped beyond hope that Mr. Abadi was buying his story.

Before his boss could respond, the gentleman who was riding in the limousine with him stepped up and patted him on the back. "Please, Anwar, let's try a cup. This boy, you said his name was

Bassam, right? Perhaps he's on to something good. I like it when my employees are innovative!"

Bassam looked at the dapper man who was now smiling at him. "Ah, who are you, sir?"

"My name is Lord John Shaffer, and I own the company you work for."

1:40 pm (Arabia Standard Time)

Dawud had finished bagging his last roast of beans when Lord Shaffer, Mr. Abadi, and Bassam walked into the factory. Dawud stopped what he was doing and bowed to his boss, then glared over Mr. Abadi's shoulder directly into Bassam's eyes. He noticed Bassam was not carrying any bottled water, which meant his colleague had lied to him again.

"Lord Shaffer, this is Dawud Tadros, who is an apprentice bean roaster along with Bassam." Dawud bowed to the well-dressed gentleman. Only adults were allowed to offer a handshake. "Dawud, this is Lord Shaffer, a member of the British Parliament and owner of *Taste Of Arabia.*"

Lord Shaffer walked over to Dawud and extended his hand. "Nice to meet you, son. And thank you for roasting up some of the finest coffee beans in the world."

While Lord Shaffer was chit-chatting with the boys, Mr. Abadi took the sack of coffee and tungis ash to the countertop, scooped out enough beans for two double shots of espresso, and turned on the burr grinder. He dumped the mixture into the Cecilware Venezia dual espresso machine and placed a small cup under each spout, then pressed the *Turkish Coffee* button. As the espresso was brewing, Mr. Abadi removed several sugar cubes from the cupboard and a stirring spoon from the drawer. He then reached into the fridge and took out two bottles of water, one for Lord Shaffer and one for himself, to cleanse their pallets. Dawud happened to notice that the refrigerator was stocked full of water, more proof of Bassam's lying!

Just then, Lord Shaffer's cell phone rang. It was a call from his parliament secretary asking that he return to London at once. An emergency session of the House of Lords would be commencing the next morning at eight o'clock, and they required his attendance for a vote. He apologized to Mr. Abadi and the boys, then excused himself and hustled back to his limo.

Mr. Abadi asked the boys if they wanted a taste of the new coffee blend seeing that Lord Shaffer didn't get the chance. Dawud was confused. Exactly what new blend of coffee was his boss talking about? He had been roasting the same Arabica beans picked exclusively from the Sarawat Mountains every day since he started working at *Taste Of Arabia.* There was never any mixture of beans.

Bassam glanced at Dawud and motioned for him to take one of the cups. Maybe this act of kindness would help Dawud to forget about his friend's lies, and they could get back on good terms. But Bassam also wanted to observe if the tungis ash had any hallucinatory effects on his boss and colleague. If so, perhaps Bassam could take full advantage of Mr. Abadi's dreamlike state of mind and secure a raise in pay!

Mr. Abadi and Dawud tapped each other's cups in a toast and sipped the neoteric blend of coffee and tungis, neither one knowing what this mélange contained. When Mr. Adabi finished his cup, he smacked his lips and grinned, then nodded approvingly at Bassam. "Son, this java is incredible! You must tell me what you mixed in with the Arabica beans to bring out this flavor!"

Dawud gave his coworker an evil stare, then placed his cup down, snatched his backpack off the floor, and rushed for the door. As he was exiting the factory, he turned to Mr. Adabi and shook his head. "I quit! You and that deceitful bastard are meant for each other!"

Having no clue as to what just happened, Mr. Adabi gave Bassam an inquisitive look.

Bassam beamed back at his boss. "Jealous young man, isn't he, sir?"

Chapter 9

Sunday, August 28, 2016 (25-Dhu al-Qidah-1437)
Sadeh, Yemen
7:30 am (Arabia Standard Time)

"Anwar, I assure you, my friend, that your coffee factory is still standing. I drove past it only one hour ago." Rashim Sarraf was patting his best customer on the back as Mr. Abadi sat on a chair with his hands covering his eyes. Tears and sweat were dripping onto the floor of Rashim's restaurant.

"Where is my factory, Karim? I've looked all over town this morning and can't find it!" Mr. Abadi's face was red, and his body was convulsing.

"Anwar, you know my name is Rashim and not Karim. Are you okay? You are sweating and shaking."

Mr. Abadi left his house for work each morning at daybreak following Fajr prayer, then Bassam would arrive around eight, and Anwar would head to Rashim's restaurant for a breakfast break. But today, he forgot which way Mecca was and performed his prayers facing north rather than west. When he left his house, he couldn't remember how to get to his Taste Of Arabia coffee factory. Because his home was only three blocks from work, he walked each day. Rashim saw him wandering around the streets like a drifter, so he led his friend into the restaurant and sat him down at the first table, which was Anwar's usual spot.

"Please help me find my factory, Hadid. I beg of you!" Anwar's eyes were dilated, and he was squinting at Rashim.

"I believe you need to see a doctor, Anwar. I will take you to the hospital."

"No, please, I need to get to work. Please!"

Rashim walked Anwar to his car that was parked in the back alley, and they drove quickly to Sadah's Prophet Muhammad Hospital. Anwar passed out two blocks from the entrance.

8:15 am (Arabia Standard Time)

Bassam arrived for work a few minutes late, which was the norm for him. As he entered the front door, he shouted the same thing that he did every day, "Sorry I'm a tad tardy, Mr. Abadi! But I'm ready for another momentous day of work!"

There was no response. Usually, Mr. Abadi would reply with an uninterested sigh and mutter, "Uh, huh. Perhaps you will be on time tomorrow, son." But today there was no counter. Mr. Abadi was nowhere to be found.

Bassam was confused. Today was going to be the first shipment of the new coffee blend he had discovered a few weeks ago, the day Dawud quit and left work in a huff. Mr. Abadi asked him to roast and bag fifty pounds to be shipped to Lord Shaffer in London. From there, Lord Shaffer had contracted with Harrod's for the coffee to be sold exclusively in England's famous department store for six months. After six months, Starbucks would retain the rights to sell the world's most expensive java. Because of its rarity and taste, the coffee beans would be priced significantly higher than their current premium product, *Jamaican Blue Mountain Supreme.*

Bassam never revealed to Mr. Abadi that he was roasting the beans with tungis. Instead, he told his boss that the secret ingredient was a vegetable his mother grew in their garden. Mr. Abadi wanted to see the garden, but Bassam lied again and said his mother's garden was within the private quarters of their house, and his father would not allow a male to enter. Bassam figured this was a clever way to ensure his continued employment at Taste Of Arabia. Mr. Abadi would never dare fire him and lose the secret ingredient. So, after dark each night, Bassam grabbed his flashlight and headed into the

Sarawat Mountains to find tungis plants, then would hide them in his backpack as he came into work each day.

Today, Bassam was to use Mr. Abadi's pickup truck to transport five sacks of the new beans to the Sana'a airport, where Lord Shaffer had a Learjet waiting for fast transit to London. If the coffee sold as expected at Harrod's, Shaffer would begin shipping mass quantities from Aden up the Red Sea and through the Suez Canal to England. Bassam twiddled his thumbs with his feet propped up on a table waiting for his boss to arrive. This was a first: Bassam actually coming to work BEFORE Mr. Abadi!

Just then, Dawud walked into the factory and headed over to the workstation he used before he quit. He didn't even look at Bassam, and Bassam's mouth dropped open. He stared at his old colleague with an incredulous look. "What are you doing here, Dawud?"

Dawud glanced over at Bassam, then put on his old fireproof apron. "I work here, Masbali, remember?"

"My name's Bassam, and no, you quit working here last month."

"I've never quit a job in my life, Masham, nor have I ever missed even a minute's work!"

"Masham? What's wrong with you, Dawud? You know my name is Bassam, and you know very well that you walked out on Mr. Abadi two weeks ago because you were jealous that he liked my new coffee bean recipe."

"Who is this Mr. Abadi that you speak of?" asked Dawud.

Bassam was very confused. Was he losing his mind? First, Mr. Abadi didn't arrive for work, then Dawud returned as if he has never left! Bassam grabbed his backpack stuffed with last night's gathering of tungis plants and stormed out of the building. He needed to find a phone to call Lord Shaffer and let him know he would be late to the Sana'a airport. He walked over to Rashim's Restaurant knowing that Rashim would let him make a long-distance call to London—as long as he called collect. Rashim wasn't there when he arrived, but Rashim's brother, who was waiting tables, said it would be okay if he didn't talk long. Bassam didn't have a phone number for Lord

Shaffer, but the British parliament office should know where to find him. Just as he picked up the receiver, Rashim walked into the restaurant and caught a glimpse of Bassam by the phone, then strolled over to him. Bassam placed the handset down on the phone when he saw Rashim heading his way.

"Marhaba, Bassam, kaifa haloka?"

"Ana bekhair, shukran!"

"Are you calling the hospital about Mr. Abadi's health?" inquired Rashim. "I doubt if they have any results yet."

"Hospital? Mr. Abadi? What are you talking about?" Bassam began to panic.

"Ah, you haven't heard, have you? Mr. Abadi was sweating and convulsing in my restaurant this morning and not making much sense when he was speaking, so I took him to the hospital."

"Mr. Abadi's in the hospital?" Bassam asked. "I must go see him!"

"If he's conscious, I doubt if he'll even recognize you. He called me Hadid this morning."

Bassam thought about this and rubbed his forehead. He was thinking about what Dawud had said to him earlier. After a long pause, he said, "My friend Dawud didn't recognize me either. He called me a couple of wrong names."

"That is a strange coincidence," replied Rashim. "Perhaps you should find your friend and make sure he's okay."

Bassam nodded and walked out onto the street. He paused momentarily, not knowing if he should return to Taste Of Arabia to check on Dawud or head for the hospital to see Mr. Abadi. He chose the hospital and began to jog. The staff said Mr. Abadi would be hospitalized for at least a week until they could identify and treat his condition.

Bassam returned to Rashim's Restaurant and called Lord Shaffer. The parliamentarian's assistant reluctantly put the boy's call through to Lord Shaffer's phone after Bassam lied and told the assistant he was the Lord's long-lost Arabian son.

"Who is this?" asked Lord Shaffer sternly. "I am swamped, and you have one minute."

"This is Bassam, you know, the boy who works at your Taste Of Arabia factory in Yemen. I met you a few weeks ago when you arrived in a limousine."

"Oh yes, Bassam, how are you, young man? I do remember you. You found the new roasting ingredients that hopefully will make me very rich. By the way, how did that new coffee taste? I had to leave and didn't get a chance to try it out, but Mr. Abadi phoned me and said it was exemplary! Based on his advice and his advice alone, I've decided to see how it sells at Harrods."

"I haven't tried the coffee either, Lord Shaffer. Actually, I don't drink coffee. I lied to you that morning I met you. I just thought the smell of the roasted beans was amazing, and they would taste just as good. However, Mr. Abadi thought the taste was incredible, best he ever drank. And so did Dawud."

"So why the call, Bassam? I suspect you want to let me know that the first shipment of beans is on the way on my Learjet. Did the pilot say how long before he would arrive in London?"

"Well, sir, that's why I'm calling. Mr. Abadi has taken ill and is in the hospital. I've been unable to transport the beans to Sana'a because he has the keys for the pickup truck."

"Mr. Abadi is in the hospital, you say? What is his condition?"

"I'm not sure, sir, but the people in the hospital say he will need to stay there for at least a week."

"Hmmm. In that case, I think I should give Mr. Abadi a visit and wish him well. I can wrap some things up here and be in Yemen by late next week. Please let me know if his condition changes for the worse, and thank you again, Bassam. You are a good employee!"

Chapter 10

Wednesday, September 7, 2016 (5-Dhu al-Hijjah-1437)
Sadeh, Yemen
8:30 am (Arabia Standard Time)

Charlie, Riley, and Mackenzie O'Connell were molecular geneticists on a voluntary mission to Yemen. The siblings had all graduated in the top five percent of their graduating class at the University of Wisconsin, and fortunately for their parents, each one paid for college via an athletic scholarship. Charlie played baseball and was drafted in the first round by the Milwaukee Brewers, Riley was an All-American volleyball setter destined for the Olympics, and Mackenzie broke all soccer scoring records for the Badgers. But the three of them wanted to give back to the world, so they gave up fame and fortune to live an obscure life in a remote country helping the poor and needy. The Yemen government provided food, housing, and a Jeep for the siblings. In return, Charlie, Riley, and Mackenzie identified several causes of congenital diseases that plagued the Yemeni people and determined the roles that the environmental conditions of the desert played in their development. Working with an undertrained staff of doctors and nurses, the O'Connells found cures for several diseases and saved the lives of many folks. Although not medical doctors by degree, the locals called each one "Doc," and it appeared that the siblings knew more about medicine than the physicians on the hospital's payroll.

But Anwar Abadi's mental condition stumped each one of the local medical heroes. After performing a brain biopsy, the geneticists could not agree on what caused Mr. Abadi's memory loss. The CAT scan revealed no tumor or any apparent abnormality. They had relieved his anxiety with a high dose of Xanax and stabilized his heart palpitations with Digoxin; the combination had effectively dismissed Anwar's sweating and convulsions. However, Anwar was losing both long and short-term memory daily.

"It could be the start of Alzheimer's," said Mackenzie.

"Could be," replied Riley. "But Anwar is only thirty-nine years old and has no family history of Alzheimer's. Also, he hasn't had a previous head injury, hypertension, or case of depression."

While Mackenzie and Riley were studying the medical charts, Charlie was examining Anwar's CAT scan. He noticed something on the computer and zoomed in.

"What is this?" asked Charlie while pointing at the scan.

"What is what?" asked Riley as she moved over to the screen.

"This. Right here. It looks like a bubble." Riley and Mackenzie leaned in to get a closer look.

"I think it's just dust," answered Mackenzie. But she wasn't all that sure herself.

"No, it's not dust," retorted Charlie. "It is something growing, or something has attached itself to the basal ganglia. And if it is a bubble, we are looking at a possible stroke in the very near future!"

Riley looked closer and shook her head. "The bubble isn't near the artery. I doubt if it has the potential for ischemic stroke. And we cannot remove it anyway. No one could survive brain surgery to that location."

"It could be nothing," countered Mackenzie. "We need to search and see if a bubble such as this has ever been previously identified and see if the patient suffered memory loss. If there is no such data, we may be onto a new disease. Unfortunately, and not to sound morbid here, but the only way to identify the causes and effects of this thing is most likely through an autopsy. I don't wish that medical discovery on a nice man like Mr. Abadi!"

"Excuse me," The head nurse opened the door to the genetics lab and interrupted the O'Connells. "Thought you might like to know. A young man has just been admitted with similar symptoms as Mr. Abadi: sweating and cannot remember his own name. But we know him. He lives a few houses down from me. His name is Dawud."

Chapter 11

Friday, September 9, 2016 (7-Dhu al-Hijjah-1437)
Sadeh, Yemen
10:00 am (Arabia Standard Time)

"Normally we are prohibited from sharing a patient's analysis with anyone but family members," stated Doc Charlie. "But Dawud's parents want to find a cure for his memory loss, and we're willing to release any information to anyone if it might help. Mrs. Abadi, Anwar's wife, said you've been like family since you signed the business deal for the coffee factory, so we are happy to share what we know with you. And yes, to find a cure will most likely be very expensive, and we will need some financial assistance."

Lord Shaffer didn't even flinch. He was worth more than the gross national product of Yemen.

Dawud's CAT scan showed a small bubble on his basal ganglia in the exact location of Mr. Abadi's bubble. The O'Connell siblings were explaining their theory to Lord Shaffer and Mr. Abadi's eldest wife, who was very happy to have the wealthy parliamentarian at the hospital to support her. The other three Abadi wives didn't understand English and would not be able to comprehend the geneticists' diagnosis, so they remained at home.

"So where do you go from here, Doc?" asked Lord Shaffer.

"First, we will need to extract brain tissue from each patient," replied Charlie. "It is too dangerous to remove the bubble based on the location deep inside the core. Perhaps we can find commonality within the cell structure of each man's tissue. If so, we can replicate those cells in laboratory rats and try to find a drug that could dissolve the bubble."

"That sounds very time consuming," said Lord Shaffer. "Could they die before you find a fix?"

"That is unknown," inserted Doc Riley. "We know that something is causing their memory loss, but we can't say for sure it will kill them."

Doc Mackenzie cut in. "Does anyone know if Dawud and Mr. Abadi digested something in common? It might give us a better starting point."

"I'm not aware of anything," replied Lord Shaffer. "But Bassam, who works at the factory, is in the lobby waiting for an update. I shall summon him."

A few moments later, Lord Shaffer reappeared with Bassam. The young man bowed to Mrs. Abadi and the geneticists. Lord Shaffer had explained to Bassam why he was invited into the lab. Bassam was fluent in both English and Arabic, as were most students in Sadah. It was the only way to enjoy American-made movies!

"Good morning, Bassam. My name is Charlie O'Connell, but you can call me Doc if you want. Most people around here do even though I'm really just a geneticist and not a doctor. Anyway, we were wondering if you knew of something that Dawud and Mr. Abadi both ate, perhaps a sandwich for lunch or a candy bar for a snack or something. Can you think of anything?"

Bassam thought for a moment, trying to remember. Dawud hadn't been to work for several weeks, and he never watched either his friend or his boss very closely. Dawud always brought a cold shawarma and potato chips for lunch, while Mr. Abadi ate out each day. Every now and then Dawud would chomp down a Snickers as a snack, but Mr. Abadi detested sugar. Except, of course, the sugar he used to dilute his expresso. Wait a minute! The last time Bassam saw Dawud and Mr. Abadi together was when Dawud quit work, and shortly before leaving, Dawud and Mr. Abadi both drank Bassam's new coffee blend of roasted beans and tungis. That day, Lord Shaffer was called back to London and never did try any of the coffee, and Bassam doesn't drink the stuff. Could that be it? Bassam was afraid to tell anyone about the tungis. If he told the geneticists, they would report him to the mutawa!

"No, sorry, I can't think of anything they both ate," lied Bassam. He was a master of fibbing, but this secret could soon become his nemesis. He wanted to tell someone the truth about the tungis and coffee.

"Well, I need to get back to London," said Lord Shaffer. "However, I will return in a week for a falconry trip with my friend Tariq. I will stop in and check on Mr. Abadi's progress then." He turned to Bassam. "You were unable to send that first shipment of your new coffee bean blend because of what happened to Mr. Abadi and not being able to find the keys to his truck. I understand that, so please don't worry. I will pick the bags of coffee up when I return with Tariq. Harrod's will just have to wait."

Bassam nodded but did not smile. He was troubled. Could there be something in that coffee blend that causes memory loss? If Mr. Abadi and Dawud were to die, would he be a murderer? He excused himself and left the hospital quickly, then hid behind a tree next to the entrance. Bassam was waiting for Lord Shaffer to wrap things up with the O'Connells. He was nervous and wished he could smoke a tungis leaf to get his head on straight. Lord Shaffer walked out alone and headed towards the parking lot and his rented Jeep. Bassam jumped out from behind the tree, and Shaffer froze.

"Whoa! Bassam, you startled me!" exclaimed Shaffer.

"There's something else I need to tell you," muttered Bassam frantically. He was shaking. "Tungis."

"Tungis?" asked Shaffer. "What's tungis?"

"It's a secret ingredient in the coffee," said Bassam timidly.

"Mr. Abadi never mentioned tungis to me. What exactly is it, Bassam?"

"I smoke it, and it makes me happy. Very happy if you know what I mean!"

"Are you talking about a hallucinogen? Like marijuana?"

"Yes, sir." Bassam dropped his head in shame. "Please don't tell anyone that I told you! It's illegal, and I could spend the rest of my life in jail! Please!"

"Calm down, Bassam. Your secret is safe with me. But you say you've mixed tungis into the coffee, and you think that might be causing the memory loss, is that right? Why did you do that?"

"Because the mutawa were coming and I had to ditch the stuff, so I threw it into the coffee beans I was roasting."

"Well, that can't be the cause of memory loss. You and I drank the stuff, and we're fine."

"No, sir. You left in a hurry and didn't drink any coffee that day. And I don't drink coffee; I can't stand the flavor! I only smoke tungis. But Mr. Abadi and Dawud both drank the coffee."

"I see," responded Shaffer, thinking hard. "There might be a chemical in the coffee that when mixed with tungis causes memory loss. I think you're on to something, son."

"I guess we should tell the O'Connells, right?" whispered Bassam dejectedly. He thought he would need to leave Yemen quickly or risk life imprisonment. And if Mr. Abadi or Dawud were to die, he would be executed in the town square by a sharp sword crashing down on his narrow neck. Tears were forming in his eyes, and Lord Shaffer embraced him.

"I don't think they need to know," said Shaffer while patting Bassam on the back. "Now, where can I get ahold of this tungis?"

Chapter 12

Wednesday, October 12, 2016 (11-Muharram-1438)
The House of Sultan Tariq ibn-Nassar
Rub' al Khali Desert, Saudi Arabia
8:00 am (Arabia Standard Time)

Following recovery from his comatose state, Sokolov had returned to his post in Omsk and continued to supervise military operations east of the Ural Mountains. Thanks to the soothing oils of the date palm roots, he slowly recuperated from his near-death camel ride through the desert with Wasim. But his skin was covered with red patches from his forehead to his toes. The general really didn't want to travel back to Tariq's palace, but it was time to create the strategic plan that would finally put an end to America!

Sokolov didn't have many friends in Moscow, and he especially despised President Putin. But in recent weeks, he had become good friends with KGB Directorate Chief Yegor Bovnik. During a casual game of chess at a tavern in Omsk, Yegor had mentioned to Sokolov that Lord Shaffer and Sultan Tariq had discovered a phenomenon that could be even more potent than the death ray laser. It was called Taste Of Arabia, a coffee drink that contained a chemical that could destroy brains.

Yegor still expressed shame for the Russians' failure to win the space race in 1969. But his enduring mission to destroy the United States was now on the brink of happening. Yegor was looking forward to drawing up a masterplan that would successfully complete his purpose in life. If this Taste Of Arabia could wipe out the minds of all coffee-drinking Americans, then that combined with the laser death ray would create terror and panic deep down in their souls!

The first meeting of the Power Four (Lord Shaffer, Directorate Chief Bovnik, Sultan Tariq, and Prince Wasim) took place in Tariq's conference room inside his palace. During that gathering, it was agreed that the foursome should never be seen together unless it was an emergency. *Power Four* would be the code phrase used for that emergency should the need exist.

The strategic plan was developed over the course of two weeks and hundreds of miles away from any form of modern civilization. Tariq was a proper host, offering a gala feast each evening consisting of mutton or camel on top of a rice mixture of vegetables, olives, wheat, and strong spices. After dinner, each of the guests was given a sheep's eye served on a shiny brass plate as a token of friendship. And each night, the sultan was generous enough to offer up a young lady from his harem.

Lord Shaffer knew the host was a strict follower of the Koran, and no alcohol would be served. So, he searched the depths of his wine and champagne cellar and brought liquid gifts to share with his new business associates. The first was a bottle of Dom Perignon Charles and Diana 1961 from the house of Moet and Chandon. The second was a very rare bottle of Goût de Diamants that he had stored in a locked safe within his collection. The Dom Perignon warranted a price tag of 4,000 British pounds because it was the official champagne at the royal wedding of Princess Diana and Prince Charles. The Goût de Diamants was valued at 1,750,000 pounds, not only for the delightful bubbly contained inside but for the bottle's design. The skillfully cut Swarovski crystal lain in pewter was created by luxury designer Alexander Amosu. The cost of the rare and valuable champagne was just a drop in the bucket for Lord Shaffer.

Yegor brought nothing to the party; he was there strictly for business. Sokolov asked him politely to lighten up and enjoy the surroundings. By that, he meant the harem.

After the pleasantries ended, Lord Shaffer got down to the nitty-gritty. He described how a young man working in a java roasting facility discovered that the tungis plant could wipe out memories if digested with coffee. Depending on the roast of the bean and the molecular makeup of the person drinking the mixture, memory loss would begin to occur within twenty-four hours but could take up to a month to thoroughly wipe a brain clean.

Yegor had an idea, but first he wanted to know if Lord Shaffer had enough money to pay off an American politician. The directorate chief had someone in mind. Lord Shaffer just laughed. No one had ever asked him if he had enough money for anything.

"I could buy you the White House, my dear new friend, if only it were for sale!" gloated Shaffer.

"I might find someone to sell it to you, my dear Lord," responded Yegor, then winked and smiled.

After the plan was sketched out, assigning players to the game was difficult. There were a lot of them, and all would need to abscond from patriotism to their own countries for the sake of wealth. Hiring a personnel director was the first task—preferably someone with a keen knowledge of the world and the ability to find intelligent, ruthless people who could invoke fear, yet be loyal to the cause. That person would first need to have global connections, then be responsible for screening and ensuring that all the participants had the same evil qualities. General Sokolov volunteered his services. He would start making phone calls at once.

Before breakfast the next morning, Sokolov sent Wasim to Germany to round up his first two employees: Gene Schultz and Loren Schoenholtz, two tough East Berliners who cried in 1989 when the wall was torn down. They were bored with their low-paying jobs as artillery and ammunition designers for ThyssenKrupp and were looking for a change. Schultz and Schoenholtz hated Vladimir Putin and Barack Obama equally! But they loved Russian rubles and American dollars alike, so they shook hands with Wasim and eagerly awaited their first assignment.

After sending Wasim off to Germany, Sokolov phoned his friend Pavel Orlov and tried to lure the ex-KGB officer out of retirement. For 200 million rubles, Sokolov would give Orlov the authority to head up air and ground operations in America. He could hire and train his own troops, and he would answer only to Sokolov. That was the key selling point. Orlov knew Yegor Bovnik was also involved in the masterplan, and there was no love lost between those two. As a field marshal, Orlov gave the KGB everything they asked for, but Yegor prevented him from becoming a directorate, and Orlov never knew why. Orlov spent most of his life working undercover in the USA and spoke perfect English without any hint of a Russian accent. But he would only agree to Sokolov's terms if he didn't have to answer to Yegor.

Sokolov consented to Orlov's request, assuring him that he would have no communication with the directorate chief. He also reluctantly agreed to Orlov's demand to place Bogdan Smirnov second-in-charge. Smirnov was a colonel who had repeatedly disobeyed orders from the Kremlin. In 2014, Smirnov refused to lead his troops into Crimea as part of the Russian incursion into Ukraine. Instead, he hijacked a Sukhoi Su-30 fighter jet that was parked at the Lutsk airfield and flew it to Turkey, where he landed it in the desert near Mardin. From there, Smirnov became an exporter of weapons to the terrorist group ISIS in nearby Syria, a very lucrative occupation. Sokolov respected Smirnov's ballsy attitude toward Putin, but he didn't appreciate the theft of a fighter jet that was under his watch. Regardless, if Orlov wanted Smirnov, then that was fine by him. Orlov was sure that Smirnov would happily agree to be part of the implosion of America. To get into the USA, an expert team of passport counterfeiters would turn Pavel Orlov into Bill Clemons, a name as American as apple pie and Chevrolet.

Realizing the importance of concealment, Lord Shaffer decided to move the entire coffee and tungis operation from Sadah to Sultan Tariq's palace in the Rub' al Khali desert. There, in a newly built factory beneath the mansion, the beans would be roasted and combined with tungis extract, then stored in a refrigerated room awaiting exportation. Digging out sand, constructing support fixtures, and pouring concrete under the palace was laborious. Two workers died from heat exhaustion, and another was killed when railroad ties used as temporary supports collapsed in the shifting sand and crushed him.

Tungis shipments began arriving at the desert palace once a week from the Sarawat Mountains of Yemen via camel caravans. Sultan Tariq could have used large Jeeps or even cargo planes now that his private runway was finished, but he opted for camels to keep outsiders from becoming suspicious. Plus, he had no ambition to become anything other than the simple, powerful ruler he was today. His alliance with Lord Shaffer had made him as rich as all his oil-producing counterparts. If the tungis plant and the coffee beans were delivered on schedule, he could provide enough Taste Of Arabia to wipe out everyone's memories throughout the entire planet if he so desired.

After turning fifteen a few weeks ago, Bassam Bashir was hired to oversee operations. Actually, he was kidnapped and forced into his new position. Bassam had discovered the effects of mixing tungis with coffee while playing hooky from work, and no one knew how to roast the beans and mix in the psychoactive plant better than he did. After he was abducted by Lord Shaffer's hitmen, his parents thought he had run away from home in search of a better life.

But the target of the Power Four's plan was the United States of America. Lord Shaffer knew that if they could set up shop somewhere inside the boundaries of the world's superpower, the ambitious scheme would unfold much easier. Then two words flickered inside his brain: *Breaking Bad.*

Lord Shaffer's favorite television show of all time was the story of Walter White, a financially strapped high school chemistry teacher diagnosed with lung cancer. To pay for treatments, White secretly turned to a life of crime by making and selling crystal meth out of an old RV in the rural New Mexico desert near Albuquerque. Ah, the Wild West, America's first frontier!

Shaffer mentioned the Breaking Bad location to his highly-paid researchers who traveled to New Mexico to see for themselves. They found a better area a few hundred miles southwest of Albuquerque that geographically replicated the arid environment of the Sarawat Mountains: the Sonoran Desert of Arizona. Its climate and soil conditions were also similar to the Sarawat region of Yemen. But before he could begin growing tungis in America, he needed more information about the long-term effects of his new coffee concoction.

Mr. Abadi, the owner of the coffee factory in Sadah where it all began, and Dawud, the young man who had worked there, were now vegetables. The O'Connell family of molecular geneticists were the ones who discovered that something the two Yemenis had digested caused memory loss. Lord Shaffer decided the O'Connells would head up his American research division and study the effects of tungis more deeply. And he found a perfect place to do that—a nondescript convalescent home in Gila Bend, a small, sleepy town in southern Arizona. The entrepreneurial lord of the British Parliament paid cash for a dilapidated center for invalids and seniors who already had one foot in heaven.

A British crew of sixty workers reconstructed the deteriorating nursing home into a fabulous-looking facility, perhaps the most beautiful structure in Gila Bend. It was on the edge of town near the tiny municipal airport, and many weary drivers on I-8 pulled in thinking it was the Motel 6 of their dreams. Unfortunately, Lord Shaffer ordered six elderly seniors to an early departure for the pearly gates to make room for research. The poison was painless. Well, at least it was painless for Lord Shaffer.

For a measly five million dollars each, the O'Connell clan gave up their voluntary mission to help the poor in Yemen so they could staff the facility in Gila Bend. The money was secondary to their decision to return the United States; Lord Shaffer had lied and told them that their research would help cure thousands, maybe millions, from memory loss, including the dreaded Alzheimer's disease. With that incentive, the O'Connells moved into a new home in the countryside just north of Gila Bend. Lord Shaffer built the geneticists a 6,000 square-foot, five-bedroom, five-bath home in the Maricopa Mountains Wilderness area, twenty miles northeast of Gila Bend, with a 40,000-gallon heated swimming pool, an iron security gate, and a mile-long asphalt driveway. Their nearest neighbor lived ten miles away. Lord Shaffer didn't want the O'Connells talking to anyone about their research. He opened a Swiss bank account for five million dollars for each one of them. To access the money, they would email one of Lord Shaffer's personal finance managers requesting a minimum of $1,000 in cash. That money would go from the bank in Zurich to a bank in Zaire to an offshore bank in the Cayman Islands before finally winding up at the Cattleman's National Bank of Gila Bend, where the O'Connells were told to open a local account. The O'Connells had no idea where their money came from, but they made good use of their ATM cards.

Little did they know that Lord Shaffer had hired two private investigators to keep tabs on them day and night. If the O'Connells figured out that their research was used for killing and not saving people, they would become victims of a head-on semi-truck accident while heading home one evening.

Sultan Tariq's nephew Wasim oversaw the worldwide supply chain. His first responsibility was to ensure the tungis and coffee beans arrived weekly to the palace, and he would make sure the final product was shipped out when the blueprint finally became a reality. But until the plan was given the green light, Wasim's primary duty was to ensure that Tariq added a new wife to his harem each month. Most of the young women came from Russia with help from General Sokolov.

As the masterplan unfolded over the next year and a half, young overseer Bassam Bashir was under a lot of pressure to deliver. Oh how he longed for the simple life daydreaming in the Sarawat Mountains.

Part II

Arizona Connection

Chapter 13

Tuesday, April 17, 2018
Maricopa County Sheriff's Office, Phoenix, Arizona
9:00 am (Pacific Daylight Time)

Another unwelcome sales call about put Deputy Ken Smith over the edge. The governor gave Maricopa County Sheriff's Department a written order to improve public relations within the community, so Sheriff Elliot Urdano reluctantly agreed to a few minor changes suggested by Arizona's top official; one was to "dialogue respectfully" to any vendor that came calling.

"What if," explained the governor directly to Urdano, "the salesperson tells his next customer how he was treated rudely at the sheriff's office? It could be a PR nightmare!"

Smith had other things on his mind while the Taste Of Arabia coffee salesman watched from a worn down, uncomfortable chair in the deputy's office. The salesman was an athletic-looking, dark-skinned man with a slight foreign accent that Smith could not quite place.

The deputy pushed the intercom button on his phone. "Rebecca, would you please come here for a minute?"

Smith smiled at the salesman but did not say a word while he waited for receptionist Rebecca Grimm to arrive. He had his head buried in the paperwork on his desk. The salesman smiled back and nervously began to twiddle his thumbs.

"What is it, Ken?" asked Rebecca as she stood in the doorway.

"Come on in and sit down," replied Smith as he pointed to the other uncomfortable chair next to the coffee salesman. Rebecca sat down with a notepad in hand, and the deputy continued. "This is—I'm sorry, sir, I forgot your name."

"My name is James LeBron, and I'm a sales rep for Taste Of Arabia," replied the coffee salesman, offering no disclaimer for the flip-flopped name of the NBA's greatest player! Deputy Smith laughed out loud. Salesman LeBron sat with no emotion, waiting for the guffaws to stop.

"To cut to the chase," continued LeBron, "we simply offer the very best coffee ever made! And to prove my point, I'm offering you a month's supply free and a Keurig machine that you can set up right over there on the shelf. No contracts to worry about. I promise you will enjoy our coffee!"

"Why us?" asked Rebecca. "I've never seen your products down at Albertson's or even Walmart. Maybe you should start with them."

"We only deal with businesses directly. And we have free delivery. Now you can't beat that! Please, let me set up this Keurig and have you taste it. No obligation!"

Deputy Smith nodded at Rebecca while trying to bite back laughter again. He was a diehard sports fan, and the name reversal of a basketball icon was resonating in the frontal lobe of his brain that regulated humor and sarcastic thoughts. Smith was picturing James dunking the ball over Bryant Kobe at the Center Staples in Angeles Los, and then high-fiving Nicholson Jack as he strutted back into defensive position.

James set up the coffee maker, filled it with water, put in the Taste Of Arabia pod, and pushed the start button. He offered the first cup to Deputy Smith, then he made another one for Rebecca. Before they took a sip, James opened two artificial sweetener packets and began to pour the powder into both cups. Smith covered the cup with his hand and shook his head no. "Thanks, but I like my coffee black."

"Please, sir, try this just once. The taste of our coffee with this sweetener is heavenly! I guarantee it!" James opened his arms wide and smiled at the sky in reverence to God who created the epicurean liquid delight. That did it! Deputy Smith bit his lip so hard to keep from roaring with laughter that it started to bleed.

"Well, okay, if you say so." Smith and Rebecca clanged their cups together in a mock toast and took a sip of the hot coffee. They turned and nodded again at each other.

"Excellent!" exclaimed the deputy. "You're right. This is fine coffee!"

"Yes, it certainly is!" copied the sheriff's receptionist. "You said we get a month's supply free, right?"

"Yes, ma'am, that's correct," replied James. "I will return in a couple of weeks to see how your whole department enjoys it." James placed a large box of 500 coffee pods on Deputy Smith's desk. Then, he thanked his new customers and excused himself from the office.

After James was gone, Rebecca mumbled, "Strange."

"What's strange?" asked Ken.

"He didn't make us sign any agreement. Who does that in today's world where no one trusts no one?"

"Well, maybe, just maybe, the world is changing for the better," answered Ken. Then he smiled one more time and shook his head. "James LeBron—are you kidding me?!"

Chapter 14

Tuesday, April 17, 2018
Gila Bend Charter School (K-12), Gila Bend, Arizona
11:30 am (Pacific Daylight Time)
Lunch Recess

Isaac Martinez loved sports. Most fourteen-year-old boys dreamed of a career in the NBA or NFL, and Isaac wasn't picky. If professional table tennis became popular in the United States, he could picture himself on the cover of *Sports Illustrated* as the top-ranked ping ponger in the world. It didn't matter what sport got him to the promised land; it was Isaac's lifelong goal to be featured on *ESPN*. Unfortunately, Isaac was chosen last or close to it for every game ever played in the schoolyard, and today he couldn't face the rejection that awaited him during lunch recess. Instead, he propped himself up on the corner of the brick schoolhouse away from his screaming classmates and sat dejectedly with his head lowered as he started to cry.

"Hey, what's up, Ike?! How's my main man?!" asked Assistant Principal Ted Sanderson, who was doing his daily supervision of lunch recess. He had noticed Isaac sitting alone and wanted to cheer him up. "Are you a little under the weather? A boy with skills like yours should be out dominating the basketball court, son!"

Sanderson could see Isaac crack a smile through the fingers that were covering his face. But he also knew that Isaac didn't want him to notice. The assistant principal had a fantastic ability to connect positively with every student—not just the good kids but every student. To him, discipline was a form of love, and the students referred to his office for misbehavior knew they were loved. Sanderson was a middle-aged ball of energy on campus. Whatever game the students were engaged in, he would loosen his tie during each recess and play. The days when the Arizona heat dialed up north of 110 degrees, Sanderson would come back to the office with a red face and drenched in sweat. His secretary would just shake her head and lock him in his office alone with the odor until he dried up! Two years ago, Sanderson received the prestigious *Administrator Of The Year* award from the Arizona School Boards Association. He was the first assistant principal to be honored in the history of the organization.

"Let me guess—Sam Johnson is controlling the basketball courts again today." Sanderson sat down next to Isaac, leaned back on the brick wall, and put his arm around Isaac's shoulders.

"Yes, sir," replied Isaac weakly. "As usual."

Sanderson paused for a moment. Then he lightly turned Isaac's chin so he could look him in the eye. "Ike, you are destined to become anything you want to be. Why? Simple—because you are smart, athletic, personable, hard-working, and talented! Oh yeah, I forgot—brilliant, too!" Just then, Sanderson's beeper sounded, and his office summoned him. He stood and reached out his arm to help Isaac up. "Now, get over to the court. Be confident, son. You're the best! Do you understand me?"

Isaac smiled and nodded. Then he got up and jogged over to the other boys. After Mr. Sanderson's pep talk, he was fired up and decided it was time to assert himself if he was someday going to be a high draft pick on any pro team. Unfortunately, his new-found self-confidence was short-lived.

"Sam, any chance that I could pick sides for basketball today?" asked Isaac politely. His friends Lucas Hernandez and Diego Garcia walked up beside Isaac and stood there looking at each other, wondering how Isaac dared to ask such a question!

Most of the boys laughed. No, not just chuckled, but let out a loud roar of guffaws. They were all looking at Sam Johnson for approval of their massive chortling. If Sam liked you, you were well on your way as a BMOC apprentice. Big Man On Campus. Yes, sir, a big shot. The girls would smile at you in the hallways, and the wimps would move aside.

Sam grinned while glancing around at all his sidekicks, then he took a step towards Isaac and stuck his forefinger into his classmate's chest. "Haven't you heard, Mexican Midget, you're being deported soon. So that means you won't even be around to play basketball anymore. Now, take your padres and hightail it off our court. This court is sacred ground, you know. Americanos only, dude!"

The crowd howled in laughter and one-by-one took turns high-fiving their beloved leader. Sam and his best friend, Mel Dawkins, began choosing sides as they did every day at lunch recess, be it touch football in the fall, kickball in the spring, or basketball anytime during the year. Isaac, Lucas, and Diego dropped their heads and walked away. They avoided eye contact with the rest of the kids on the playground. They weren't exactly sure who their friends were these days.

America was not their country of birth, but it was the only place they remembered and the place they called home. They would love this land until the day they died. Jim Morgan desperately needed cheap workers willing to pick jalapeno peppers on his 500-acre ranch in Arizona for his salsa company. Reluctantly, because he knew it was illegal, Jim crossed the border in his Chevy cargo van loaded with crates of *Morgan's Southwestern Salsa and Chili* and drove to Rocky Point in search of low-cost labor. Jim sold his popular products to Mexican grocers and became good friends with both the Mexican and American security patrols at the border. When reentering the United States with sacks of pinto, kidney, and black beans grown in the Sonora province, Jim always dropped off jars of salsa for the guards. They waved him through the gate as if he were family, never checking his cargo. The parents of Isaac, Lucas, and Diego all arrived at the Morgan ranch outside of Gila Bend in burlap bags with their children snuggled to their breasts. The boys were two-years-old, barely breathing from the suffocating environ of the van, and scared to death.

Maria Martinez insisted her son learn English, which was not easy since neither she nor Isaac's father spoke anything but Spanish. After removing pepper stems for ten hours each day in blistering temperatures above 110 degrees in the summertime, it was all Mateo Martinez could do to stay awake during the family English lessons on cassette tapes each evening. Jim Morgan needed to be able to communicate with his workers; thus, he gladly purchased the recordings for his Mexican laborers. Enrolling in a community college to take the *English As A Second Language* course was impossible for undocumented residents of the United States.

Because he wanted the Hispanic children to receive a quality education like his own kids, Mr. Morgan sat on the school board and was the chief donor for the Gila Bend Charter School's breakfast program and Parent-Teacher Association. Principal Sebastian Perez knew full well that many of his students were illegally in the United States, but he wasn't about to blow the whistle. As a lifelong educator, his love for children came first. The color of their skin or their birthplace or their religion made no difference to him. Kids were kids, plain and simple, and they deserved a wholesome education. Mr. Perez was well-respected for his passion and unending dedication to students and staff. He was the first and only principal the charter school had since it opened in 1995 in the small desert town. Gila Bend was best known as a gas stop for vacationers traveling on I-8 heading for the beaches of San Diego. It was an hour drive south of the state capital where legislators fought over the interpretation of the Fourteenth Amendment to the Constitution: should children of undocumented workers become United States citizens?

When Isaac enrolled in kindergarten at Gila Bend Charter School, he was not only bilingual, he was reading and speaking at a fourth-grade fluency level. By the time he reached junior high, Isaac was a straight "A" student, a bright and creative kid who enjoyed learning. His teachers loved his imagination, polite manners, and thoughtfulness towards other students and adults. If someone needed lunch money, he would give his last quarter to his classmate. If someone needed help with homework, Isaac would explain the assignment several different ways until his comrade understood the lesson. Most importantly, he considered all his classmates friends—even Sam Johnson. Even after what took place on the basketball court today, if Sam needed help with algebra, Isaac would be there for him.

12:10 pm (Pacific Daylight Time)
Fifth Hour

Rick Frye was an amazing teacher and Isaac's favorite. Just three years removed from college, he taught World History and could bring the past to life simply by telling stories. Last year, when Isaac had Mr. Frye for American History, his instructor's depth of knowledge mesmerized him. Isaac enjoyed all his classes, but for some reason, he longed for Frye's fifth-hour class to start and wished it would never end.

A safe haven existed inside the walls of the school that ran contrary to the intimidation that took place on the playground. Every teacher knew kids whose parents were illegal sprinkled their classrooms, but that didn't stop them from caring for their students. Principal Perez had hired a staff who truly believed in their commitment to the most general law of education: "en loco parentis." During the seven hours on campus, teachers understood and accepted that they were each student's warmth and comfort, and the first line of defense, if need be. A child was a child regardless of skin color or national origin. The consequences of bullying were severe, and Sam Johnson had missed several recesses because he was spending quality time in the detention room for testing his teachers' resolve.

Mr. Frye was the best of the best. He greeted students at the door with hugs and smiles and sent them on their way after the bell with high fives. The forty-eight minutes inside his classroom were spellbinding. When he wasn't telling a story, his students were acting out scenes from history with the chance to change the past. Those scenes were the students' ideas, not his, which gave them the autonomy to become critical thinkers and feel like someday they could transform this country for the better. Yes, even the Mexican kids felt like loyalists when they reenacted the American forefathers' creation of the constitution in Philadelphia. In Mr. Frye's class, every student felt like a patriot!

Athletic Director Cyrus McCool was born and raised in Gila Bend. He had been a 315-pound All-American tackle at Southern Cal before being selected third pick in the 2013 NFL draft by the Washington Redskins. On the first play from scrimmage during the home opener at FedEx Field, Eagles defensive end Fletcher Cox crushed running back Jawan Jamison at the line for a loss of a yard. Both players landed on top of Cyrus, whose legs had splayed out behind him. Cox showed off his muscles to the crowd while the rookie tackle groaned in pain, his helmet buried in the turf. Ten minutes later, Cyrus was carted off the field to the applause of a stunned sellout crowd. He never played another minute in the NFL. Both knees had hyperextended on the play, and Cyrus needed reconstructive surgery to repair torn and detached ligaments on each leg.

Even though he had no teaching or coaching experience, Assistant Principal Sanderson thought Cyrus, being a Gila Bend native and star football player, would make an excellent athletic director. The big fella had majored in Liberal Arts, beer-drinking, and girls at USC—and not necessarily in that order. Principal Perez was skeptical but gave Sanderson his blessing to hire Cyrus.

Cyrus popped his head into Frye's classroom.

"Well, if it ain't the teacher of the year! Coach Ricardo S. Frye! The *s* meaning *superstar*, of course!" Frye had been waiting by the door for his kids to come in from lunch recess. Cyrus gave him a high-five.

"No, sir, you can lay all the compliments you want on me, but I'm not coaching golf again! Sorry, Cy!"

"But you're my hero—the greatest of the great! Olympian master of the past 5,000 years! Besides, we need a golf coach, and you're the only one with experience." Cyrus winked at Frye.

"My, my, you certainly have a way with words! But I can't. First, I need more time to prepare for my classes. Our golf matches take place all over Arizona, and we don't get back from some road trips until midnight. Then, to top it off, you make me drive the dang school van to the meets. But the main reason I'm not coaching golf again is that my handicap is twenty-five! Talk about the blind leading the blind! Sorry, Cy, I'm not going to do it!"

"Ah, my good friend and awesome person, I'll let you think about it for a few days!" Cyrus smiled and waddled down the hallway to check in with other teachers. His knees never completely healed the way he hoped, so he walked with a permanent limp. Cyrus was also the football coach and supervised in-school suspensions. He apparently had a lot of free time because he would cruise the elementary and high school hallways every day just to chat. The high school was a block from the K-8 building. Cyrus would leave during lunch break and ride a golf cart to the elementary school to have lunch in Sanderson's office. Then he would walk a brisk lap through the hallways before heading back to the high school. Besides joking with teachers, he was always buttering up the athletic-looking kids. It was never too early to build the championship teams of the future. His nickname was Friendly Bear. He happened to be at the elementary school on that fateful day.

The afternoon the Immigration and Custom's Enforcement team raided the Gila Bend school was synonymous with the end of the world. Mr. Frye knew something was up. He had strolled to the window while his class was in the middle of a mock presidential debate between Stephen Douglas and Abraham Lincoln. Just as the team of Republicans applauded a solid point against slavery, Mr. Frye shouted out, "To the art room, now, all of you! Leave your backpacks. Move quickly! Go!"

The students were all stunned but weren't about to question the authority of their beloved teacher. Most days, they left classrooms in a single file, a result of Principal Perez's rules for proper behavior. But today was a mess—pure chaos. Zaira Tahan, a Muslim immigrant who happened to be the tiniest kid in the class, was pushed to the floor. Isaac stopped to help her up and dust off her ragged dress, but she was crying, shaking, and afraid to move. Holding Zaira's hand and trying to get her to run, Isaac pulled her to the door. He was hoping to catch up with the rest of the class that was kicking up sparks in the hallway as they followed Mr. Frye to the art room at the end of the corridor.

"Why the art room?" Isaac wondered. It was a converted storage room with a variety of spilled paint covering the cement floors. Then again, Isaac wasn't sure why they were leaving the classroom. He looked around and saw no other class emptying out. It couldn't be a fire drill because the alarm didn't go off.

As Isaac and Zaira started down the hallway, they saw strange people in the distance and froze. Ten or fifteen men in black windbreaker uniforms with assault rifles were aiming their weapons inside the art room. Assistant Principal Sanderson came running from the office and looked like he was pleading with the men to back off. Cyrus McCool stood at Sanderson's door trying to evaluate the situation. Isaac grabbed Zaira by the collar and yanked her back into Mr. Frye's classroom. Without speaking a word, they bolted for the window, but it was locked solidly in place. Isaac grabbed the closest desk and smashed it into the glass, breaking it into tiny shards. After pushing the sharp edges that remained in the window to the ground outside, he lifted Zaira up and threw her out of the building. Then Isaac dove headfirst through the opening and belly-flopped onto the hard dirt. They both jumped up and ran towards the parked busses next to the mechanic's garage. Their faces, arms, and legs were cut and bleeding, and the middle of Isaac's t-shirt was turning red.

Two helicopters were circling the school, and several black Suburban vans with flashing blue lights were surrounding the building. What was going on? Why would men with guns be attacking a school? Zaira began to cry, so Isaac hugged her and then motioned for them to get inside the nearest yellow bus. They pushed the double door open, climbed aboard, ducked down below a passenger window, and gazed back at the school.

Soon curious midday drivers in dusty old pickup trucks and dented gas hogs from the nineties pulled over to see what was happening. They had been working in the fields since sun up and were returning home for a lunch break. After several minutes, the men in windbreakers escorted Principal Perez and Assistant Principal Sanderson out the main entrance with their hands cuffed behind their back. Teachers followed with their arms raised high above their heads as the men in uniforms pointed nasty-looking rifles at them. As soon as they were about fifty yards from the building, the educators were forced to lie down on the ground face first and place their hands behind their backs. Mr. Sanderson laid down, but Principal Perez refused and fearlessly stood his ground. Then a uniformed man struck Perez on the side of his head with the butt of a rifle. Mr. Perez fell to his knees and collapsed forward—his nose smashing into the dirt.

From inside the bus, Isaac scrutinized the school and asked, "Where are the kids? Where are our friends?"

"They must still be in the school," replied Zaira. "Wait! Look over there, Isaac!"

Zaira pointed to the north door that opened onto the playground. The students were being led to the baseball diamond by uniformed men who were aiming guns at them.

"What . . . the . . . heck," mumbled Isaac as he gaped through the bus window at his classmates. "I think we need to get out of here."

"Get out?!" asked Zaira. "How?! Where to?!"

Isaac glanced over at the driver's seat and dashboard. The keys were in the ignition, but Isaac had never driven a motor vehicle of any kind. A long metal rod with a black ball on top extended up from the floor. There were three pedals under the dash; Isaac was baffled!

"Zaira, we need to drive this bus away from here, but I don't know how! I know if I turn the key the bus will start, but I don't know anything about that stick and the pedals!"

"I can help. I heard dad yelling out instructions to my older brother when he was trying to teach him how to drive our pickup truck. The pedal on the left is to shift the gears. When you push it in, you can move that stick. Start with it in the upper left-hand position like it shows on the ball, and then let the pedal out slowly. *Very slowly* is what my dad told my brother. He didn't, and we jerked several times. Then the engine killed. Dad wasn't too patient and yelled at my brother again to go slow with the pedal. I think he called it a clutch. And, oh yeah, push the pedal on the right down as you let out the clutch pedal. That's the accelerator and makes it go. The pedal in the middle is a brake."

"That's a whole bunch of confusing stuff just to make the bus go! Why don't you drive, Zaira?!"

"Me? I don't think I could reach the pedals and see out the windshield. You have to do it, Isaac!"

"Maybe we should just make a run for it. It's only a hundred yards or so to Winston's house. We could hide in the backyard."

"All those guys in uniforms have rifles, Isaac. We might get shot. Let's just stay here, on the bus."

"I don't think that's a good idea," replied Isaac. Then, after glimpsing back out the window, he had second thoughts. "Okay, I'll drive, you stay down!"

Isaac slid into the driver's seat and thought about what to do first. Fear had caused him to forget Zaira's instructions. He reached down and turned the key. The engine fired, and then the bus lurched forward and killed. Isaac tried again, and once more, the bus started, jerked a few feet, and then stopped dead in its tracks.

"What's going on!" shouted Isaac as he shot a panicked glance out the window. The guard who was standing over Mr. Frye noticed something move in the distance out the corner of his eye. He aimed his rifle at the bus that was a couple of football fields away.

"Isaac, you have to push down on the left pedal, the clutch, and hold it in when you start up the bus! Didn't I tell you that?!"

Isaac gave Zaira a perplexed frown but did as she said. The engine started. Isaac held the clutch down and asked, "Now what?!"

"Give it some gas and let the clutch out slowly. After we get going, push the clutch back down and shift it into the next gear, which is the number two on the nob." Zaira said it calmly, but her chest was tightening up with anxiety.

Isaac pushed the accelerator down and slowly let out the clutch, but he had given it too much gas, and the bus jolted forward. The bus began to move faster, and the gears were grinding. He shifted into second and bolted toward the parking lot exit. The uniformed man pulled the trigger, and his Kalashnikov assault rifle unloaded an entire cartridge of 123-grain boat-tail bullets through the emergency exit door and into the padded seats of the school bus. Zaira covered her ears and cried, resting her head on the floorboard in the aisle.

"Just stay down, okay!" ordered Isaac as he began to understand the theory behind a clutch and a transmission. The bus picked up speed in the third gear, and Isaac steered the yellow monster out onto Chavez Avenue. He guided the bus south towards Main Street reaching forty miles-per-hour.

Donnor Colten had been watching the school seizure from his Ford F-150 pickup. He had pulled over when the black Suburban vans were racing into the school's student drop off area. He saw the letters emblazoned on the doors in white letters:

US Immigration & Customs Enforcement

"Why would ICE be emptying out a school?" muttered Donnor to himself. "And why would they need assault rifles to do it?"

When Donnor saw the guard firing rounds into the back of the bus, he believed it was time to stop the nonsense. Whoever was on the bus couldn't be that dangerous, and even if he was, risking the lives of neighbors or school children with stray bullets was unacceptable. Donnor reached around to the gun rack attached to his back window and lifted out the Beanfield Sniper Remington Sendero SFII, and then aimed the hunting rifle at the guard who was firing shots into the bus. Donnor was thrilled with Arizona's lax gun laws, and he was a card-carrying member of the National Rifle Association. He also brought home a Coconino National Forest elk for Thanksgiving every fall because his wife never wanted to spend time basting a turkey. His Beanfield never missed its target.

A split second later, the ICE agent was lying face down on the ground with a seven-millimeter hole in the back of his head.

The gunshot surprised everyone, and the agents all turned their gaze to the pickup truck. Bill Clemons, the ICE sergeant and officer in charge of the operation, barked out an order. "Get the man in that pickup truck! Now! Go!"

The agents ducked down and slowly approached the ominous pickup. The top of Donnor Colten's head was barely visible below the passenger window, but his rifle was aimed at the group of agents that, for some reason, decided to advance together. They were sitting ducks! All Donnor had to do was fire away, and he was bound to hit someone. He thought about sliding over and trying for a quick getaway, but there seemed to be too much firepower to escape without being blasted into eternity. If he could open the driver's door that was on the opposite side of the agents, he could make a run for it. Chances were slim for the success of that plan, too.

Meanwhile, the bewildered and shocked teachers sat up and glanced at one another. Principal Perez and Assistant Principal Sanderson were the only faculty members who had cuffs on, and Mr. Frye realized that his bosses would need help if the staff decided to make a run for it. When the agents who had been watching the kids on the baseball diamond joined in with their counterparts, Officer Clemons gave the next command.

"Stop and take aim, gentlemen," he directed in a low, confident tone.

Ten ICE agents took to one knee and pointed their assault weapons at Colten's truck.

The dazed staff of Gila Bend Charter School stood, covered their mouths, and ambled backward away from the agents. Principal Perez silently motioned for them to head to the baseball diamond. The teachers could read his lips and just barely hear his loud whisper. "Find your students and make sure they're safe!"

Lucas Hernandez's father was parked behind Donnor's pickup, but unlike Donnor, who worked with him out on Jim Morgan's ranch, Pablo Hernandez didn't hunt. He didn't own a gun because he never had any ambition to kill a living creature. In fact, he would flick a mosquito off his neck rather than kill it with a slap. In shock, Pablo had witnessed the atrocity unfold with the teachers and principals led at gunpoint to the school parking lot and the students to the baseball diamond. Were the ICE agents planning to apprehend every person in the school?! Could it be that his son Lucas, who had never hurt a soul in his life, was now under arrest?!

Pablo watched in horror as an agent fired random bullets into the school bus. It was incomprehensible what was happening! Then he watched Donnor Colten shoot the agent with a rifle. Pablo didn't approve of Donnor killing the man, but he understood why his coworker took the shot. As the agents turned and aimed their assault weapons at the F-150, Pablo knew that Donnor wouldn't have a chance if they began firing at his pickup. He had to make a quick decision.

Pablo had left his rebuilt 1971 AMC Gremlin running while he watched the incident. Now, after a smooth shift into drive with the automatic transmission, he gassed the accelerator to the floor and steered directly at the cluster of black windbreakers. Muddled by the turmoil of the moment, the stunned agents started shooting at the Gremlin.

Donnor saw what was happening and slid back into the driver's seat of his truck. He shifted quickly into first gear and darted for the group of stupefied teachers. Then he parked his pickup sideways to partially block the agents' egress and shouted out the window, "Run! Get the kids then spread out and run, damn it!"

The teachers ran as fast as they could to the baseball diamond, passing the other agents who had been watching the students. Those agents were sprinting to help their colleagues who were now stuck between the Gremlin and the Ford F-150.

Pablo had slammed on the brakes just inches before piling into the men, then ducked down in the front seat to avoid the rain of bullets that had shattered his windshield and blew holes in the steaming radiator. He had accomplished his short mission, which was to distract the agents who were focused on eliminating Donnor. In the end, he couldn't kill another human being. One agent's bullet ricocheted off the gravel underneath the car causing a spark to ignite the gas tank. Seconds later, the Gremlin was a charred skeleton of steel, while the pacifist occupant of the vehicle slowly rolled out the passenger door onto the parking lot, his hair and clothes in flames. No one bothered to help. The ICE agents watched in awe as Pablo's face dissolved like a wax candle.

While all eyes were pasted on the Gremlin, Donnor followed the terrified teachers as they scrambled to get their kids. Assistant Principal Sanderson was running back toward the school to help get his support staff out of harm's way. Somehow his cuffs must have loosened because he had freedom of movement in both arms. Donnor saw that Principal Perez was laboring and running awkwardly due to the handcuffs that were clenching his arms behind him. Donnor slowed the vehicle, reached over and opened the passenger door, and then yelled at the principal to hop in. Mr. Perez wiggled his way into the front seat. He had to kneel facing the rear window because he couldn't sit with his hands behind his back. Donnor didn't wait for the door to close before flooring the accelerator. Mr. Perez almost fell out but was able to balance himself.

Mr. Frye had paused momentarily to see how his principal was doing, and he watched him struggle into the F-150. Seconds later, Donnor pulled up next to Frye and told him to jump into the bed of the pickup. Shots rang out as the history teacher climbed over the side panel and dove to the floor. Bullets pierced the back window missing Donnor and Perez by inches. Donnor rammed the gas pedal down, and the truck burst forward with the passenger door flapping in the wind until it finally slammed shut. Perez wobbled around on his knees and watched Frye roll uncontrollably backward into the tailgate. Mr. Perez desperately needed to get the handcuffs off.

As the agents began running towards the baseball diamond, the teachers were yelling at their students to scram. The kids didn't need any encouragement. They all tore out of the diamond, sprinting in every direction possible away from the men with guns who were chasing them. Fifteen teachers jumped into the bed of Donnor's pickup with Frye, and the rest scrambled away with the kids.

At that point, Bill Clemons raised his hand high and screamed at his men to stop. They did as ordered and looked at their boss, waiting for his next command. "Back to the vans! Don't let that truck get away!" yelled the sergeant.

Without hesitation, the agents sprinted for their Suburbans, then gave chase with the guidance of two helicopter patrols flying overhead.

Not one of them noticed or remembered their fallen comrade lying face down in a pool of blood.

Chapter 15

Tuesday, April 17, 2018
City of Gila Bend, Arizona
12:35 pm (Pacific Daylight Time)

Isaac hurtled down Logan Avenue running stop signs and forcing traffic to slam on their brakes to avoid colliding with the bus. But maneuvering around Community Center Park proved a bit tricky when Isaac turned right going forty onto Hunt Street and nearly rolled the big yellow box with wheels. Zaira let out a gasp and grabbed the legs of the seats in front of her. She was lying on her stomach straddling the rubber grip mat that ran down the aisle of the bus. After forcing a pair of elderly tourists to lose control of their Cadillac and ram into the side of Don Jose's Mexican Grill, Isaac picked up speed and looped underneath Interstate 8 and onto Highway 85. He gunned the accelerator, and the bus hit ninety as it headed south towards Ajo and the Mexican border.

Donnor Colten saw the bus in the distance and followed it across the railroad tracks outside of town. The teachers in the Ford F-150's bed were rolling back and forth like liter Coke bottles in a shopping cart. Principal Perez had fallen backward when Donnor pounced on the brakes to avoid a collision, and he was now on the passenger floor jammed in between the dashboard and the seat, unable to move.

The ICE agents were starting to catch up, their Suburbans' blue lights flashing and sirens blaring. The two helicopters were flying directly above the bus and Donnor's truck as it headed southward. Back in Gila Bend, the frightened school children were beginning to arrive at their homes, many with friends and classmates who didn't live in town. On the usually quiet village streets, kids could be heard yelling at their startled moms as they burst through the screen doors. Panic overwhelmed the mothers who were picking up the house or making dinner or taking care of baby brothers and sisters. Why were the kids coming home early? What was happening? Phone calls to the school were unanswered, and the voice messaging system was full.

Myra Adams had been peeking out from behind her living room curtains after hearing a gunshot coming from across the street at the school. She watched astonishingly as an unidentified person in an AMC Gremlin drove directly at a group of uniformed ICE agents and then slammed on the brakes, and a few seconds later saw the car blown to pieces. But in the distance, Myra also saw Donnor Colten load up the bed of his pickup truck with teachers and tear out of the school parking lot as the agents began chasing him. She knew it was Donnor's pickup because she was good friends with Donnor's wife, Ellen. Both Myra and Ellen waitressed the night shift down at the Space Age Restaurant.

Myra could not afford a cell phone, so she hustled over to the AT & T cord phone on the countertop by the toaster and called her friend.

"Hey, Myra, is that you?" asked Ellen after being unable to understand Myra's anxious greeting.

"Yeah, it's me . . . Ellen, just wondering if you knew Donnor was down at the school this afternoon."

"Naw. He came home for lunch and was heading back to Morgan's for work. He wouldn't stop at the school. Why you askin', Myra?"

"Ellen, something's going on down at the school, I tell ya! A bunch of soldiers or people with ICE written on their windbreakers and guns in their hands raided the school. The teachers were lying on the ground when an old Gremlin car blew up, then I saw Donnor race over and pick up the teachers. They all jumped in the back of his pickup, and he drove off like a bat out of hell with the ICE people firing at them!"

"What! Those ICE people are immigration police. I know we got some illegal kids in the school, but why would they need guns? Why would they be shootin', Myra?"

"I don't know, Ellen, but I'm looking out my window right now, and a whole bunch of people are running to the school! They must be parents lookin' for their kids, but I can tell ya for sure they ain't gonna find no one. I saw all them kids running to beat hell after those ICE people got back in their big black vans. Ellen, I'm telling ya again, I think they're after Donnor and those teachers, I do!"

"Oh my God, Myra, what should we do?!"

"This is too big for our own police to handle. We need to call the sheriff's office up in Phoenix and see if they know what's happening. I'll do it, girl! You just sit tight. I'll call you right back." Myra hung up the phone on Ellen, then dialed 1-4-1-1 for directory assistance to get the Maricopa County Sheriff's Office number. She wrote it down on a Post-It, and then punched the phone's keypad. A receptionist answered on the third ring.

"Maricopa County Sheriff's Office, this is Rebecca Grimm. Is this an emergency?"

"Well, I think damn tootin' it sure could be. Don't know, you tell me."

"What's the problem?" asked Rebecca calmly. She heard panicked and frightened callers several times a day, and to be composed and focused was the primary responsibility of her job.

"Men with guns just stormed our charter school down here in Gila Bend and started shooting. They also blew up an old car with someone in it. Then they got back in their big black Suburbans and started chasing a truckload of teachers. And thems good teachers, nice ones who wouldn't hurt nobody!"

"Can I get your name, ma'am?" asked the composed receptionist. "And can you give me any identification for the men who were driving the vans?"

"My name's Myra Adams, and the only thing I noticed besides them guns was everyone was wearing black windbreaker jackets with ICE on it. Like those immigration policemen wear, you know."

"ICE? Are you sure the jackets had ICE on them?"

"Yes, no doubt about it!"

"Hold on, Myra, I'll be right back." Rebecca punched down the red hold button on the phone and ran to Deputy Sheriff Gordy Owen's office. The door was closed, but Rebecca thought that this emergency was more critical than Gordy's daily pro football analysis with Deputy Ken Smith. Gordy was criticizing Carson Palmer's inability to avoid a sack during the Arizona Cardinal's loss to Seattle last season. Ken was trying to tell Gordy that if Palmer could get better offensive line protection, he wouldn't take so many sacks. Then Rebecca barged in.

"Gordy, I've got a gal on the line who claims ICE agents just infiltrated Gila Bend Charter School, blew up a car, and shot at teachers."

"Ain't no way, Becca," replied the sheriff's deputy as he was shaking his head. "ICE wouldn't even carry weapons into a school."

"That's what I thought, too. Can you call the Homeland Security office over on North Central and find out what's going on?"

"I'll get right on it, but are you sure this is a legit call? Someone might be playing a disgusting joke or something."

"I'm pretty certain the gal witnessed the events, Gordy. I have a knack for being able to tell if someone is lying to me."

"Yes, you do, Becca. Please tell the lady to hold on while I call Homeland Security."

Rebecca went back to her desk and asked Myra to be patient for a few more minutes. Myra had been glancing out her window while on hold and noticed the dead agent lying face down in a pool of blood. "I'm gettin' a bit nervous here," stated Myra. "I can see a dead man in one of them ICE windbreakers lying in the school parking lot!"

"Are you sure he's dead?"

"Well, he ain't wigglin' none, so I assume he's gone to heaven or hell, one of the two!"

"Okay, thanks! Hold tight, Myra, I'll be back with you soon."

The Phoenix Homeland Security Investigations Division served as the principal field office for the southwestern United States. They oversaw the Immigration and Customs Enforcement operations from El Paso to Yuma. And they were also skeptical of what Myra witnessed in Gila Bend. After placing Deputy Owens on hold for five minutes, Special Agent in Charge, Earl Kelly, picked up the transferred call. "Your message is alarming to me, Owens. Any ICE operation taking place in Gila Bend would have come directly from this office, and there have been absolutely no orders given. So, first things first—if there is a dead body, call the local police. Then, the sheriff and I need to get down there right away."

"Sheriff Urdano is out of town," replied Owens. "You'll have to take me."

"Then let's do it. I'll pick you up in five to ten." Special Agent Kelly didn't wait for confirmation; he just hung up the phone.

12:45 pm (Pacific Daylight Time)
Maricopa County Sheriff's Office, Phoenix, Arizona

Earl Kelly pulled up in front of the sheriff's office in a red Corvette convertible and parked in a spot with a sign that read *Official Government Vehicles Only*. He dialed Owens' office using his cell phone and heard the ring on his hands-free Bluetooth system built into the dash. The deputy did a double-take when he stepped outside and saw the glistening Vette.

"Homeland Security must have gotten a funding boost," commented Owens sarcastically as he lightly brushed the dust off the paint on the passenger door. "Are the taxpayers okay with this?" He smiled and winked at Kelly. They had never met, but when Kelly smiled back, it appeared a new friendship had begun.

"Just get in. We need to get moving. There's an accident on the Ten slowing traffic to Buckeye, so we'll cut through Dead Cow Road from Maricopa."

Interstate 10 was notorious for bumper to bumper traffic, especially during rush hours. But when an accident occurred at any time during the day, backups were inevitable, and they usually started after the tunnel that ran underneath Margaret T. Hance Park all the way to the accident site. Dead Cow Road was a popular name for Highway 238 and a viable option when traveling to Gila Bend. The turnoff was just north of the town of Maricopa, and drivers could avoid the slow traffic through the bedroom community. The drawback was the cows. Dairy and beef cattle saturated the area, and the underneath-the-road animal guard crossings were minimal. Unfortunately, the livestock would cross the two-lane road in the abundant places that the ranchers strangely didn't feel the need for barbwire fences. The result was a forty-two mile stretch of road littered with dead cows that were stiffened by rigor mortis, swamped with horseflies, and becoming a delectable meal for hungry vultures. Cars traveling on Highway 238 did so at their own risk, and that risk was especially high for fiberglass-framed sports cars weaving around the nasty curves at an Indy pace.

Deputy Owens opened the Corvette's door and climbed in, then reached across and shook Special Agent Kelly's hand. "Hello, Agent Kelly. I'm Deputy Owens, but my friends call me Gordy. Nice to meet you."

"And you can call me Earl. Now, hold on tight!"

Chapter 16

Tuesday, April 17, 2018
Ajo, Arizona
1:20 pm (Pacific Daylight Time)

Donnor and the truckload of teachers caught up with Isaac and Zaira thirty miles south of Gila Bend. It wasn't an easy task by any means because Isaac had the bus in fifth gear, and the pedal pushed to the floorboard. Now and then he would lift his foot from the throttle to slow down, especially when driving over a pothole. The suspension was giving out, and at times Isaac couldn't keep the coach from swerving due to a strong crosswind that was blowing dust and dirt across the road. Zaira had her eyes closed tightly and was praying.

The bus and Donnor's pickup were now traveling ninety miles per hour. The ICE Suburbans could be seen a mile or two back in the rearview mirror, but they were making progress. Overhead, both helicopters were hovering. Knowing the Border Patrol was set up just outside of Ajo, Donnor decided that it was now or never. He hammered the F-150's accelerator down and began to pass the bus. Isaac watched the truck as it overtook him but had no idea who was driving, nor did he know who all those people were in the bed. However, he saw the International Workstar milk truck approaching a quarter-mile down the road in the northbound lane, and he knew the pickup wouldn't make it. Reluctantly, Isaac let up on the accelerator, and the F-150 passed and sliced back into the southbound lane a split second before the shiny semi-truck would have hit them head-on. The driver of the mid-range diesel wasn't about to slow down or move onto the shoulder for a tiny Ford! This was Arizona after all, and on the roads, it was survival of the fittest!

As soon as Donnor regained control in the southbound lane, he lightly touched his brake and gradually slowed down, forcing Isaac to do the same. Isaac leaned forward toward the dashboard and peered into the bed of the pickup. "Oh my God, Zaira, it's our teachers in the pickup in front of us! They're trying to get us to slow down."

Zaira gradually got to her knees and stared out the windshield, then carefully moved into the seat behind Isaac. "What are they doing, Isaac?"

Isaac looked in the rearview mirror and replied, "I'm not sure, but those uniformed men are coming up fast behind us. They're a mile or two back. I think the teachers are trying to escape, too!"

"I think they want us to follow them."

"Okay, but I'm not sure where they are going. But okay, I'll follow them."

A mile down the road, Donnor turned on his left blinker and slowed to twenty. He was planning on cutting down Mead Road toward the small town of Childs, and he knew the bus would roll if it went any faster. Isaac didn't think to shift gears as he slowed to make the turn, and the bus sputtered while trying to maintain the reduced speed until the engine finally killed, and it rolled gradually to a stop. Donnor could see what had happened and pulled over on Mead Road to help. He jumped out of the pickup and ran back to the stalled bus while the terrified teachers watched. Isaac was turning the ignition while pumping the accelerator with the clutch down, but the school bus had flooded, and the spark plugs refused to ignite. Donnor pushed the bus doors open, waved, and shouted, "Come on! Get out now and hop in my pickup. Move it!"

Isaac and Zaira jumped out of the bus, ran to the truck, and dove headfirst into the bed. The teachers had lowered the tailgate in anticipation of what was happening. Mr. Frye was able to grab both of his students by the shirt collars and drag them forward as Donnor quickly got back in the cab and sped off. The helicopters were hovering overhead, and the five Suburbans were only a mile from the Mead Road turn.

"Where are you planning to go?" asked Principal Perez frantically. "We can't possibly lose them, you know!" His kneeling position with hands cuffed behind him was an uncomfortable state of being, but he held no self-pity after seeing the teachers and two kids squished into the bed of the truck.

"The fifth hole. There's a boulder behind the out-of-bounds line near the bunker. That's where I'm heading!"

"What are you talking about? Fifth hole, boulder, bunker. What do you mean?"

Donnor didn't have time to explain as his mind was focused on somehow hauling a truckload of people down Mead Road at speed faster than the approaching black Suburbans. He also didn't have time to think about the helicopters that were tracking his every movement. But the principal deserved an answer, so he made it short. "The Ajo Country Club. I'm going to get off the road up ahead and cut across the fourth-hole fairway to the woods that line the fifth. There's a boulder near the bunker that marks the entrance to a trap door and underground tunnel. The tunnel leads to the airport."

"A tunnel? How do you know about this? And there's no airport in Ajo!" The principal was perplexed.

"Yes, sir, there's an airport. It's called the Eric Marcus Muni, but it's just an airstrip. If we're lucky, I can get us out of this mess from there." Suddenly, he yanked the steering wheel and made a sharp turn off Mead Road and dropped down into a ditch. The pickup emerged onto the fourth fairway, and the passengers bounced uncontrollably, most letting out screams. Perez's head jolted forward then back, hitting his skull hard on the dashboard. He wanted to rub it, but that was impossible with the cuffs.

"If we're lucky, is that what you said?" muttered Perez sarcastically. "How do you plan to get us all out of here and into a tunnel without being seen by the choppers?"

The ICE agents in the five Suburbans turned onto Mead, then slammed their brakes behind the school bus that was parked in the middle of the road. From a distance, they had seen someone from the pickup truck get into the bus but could not see what happened afterward. Not knowing if someone was still inside, the agents cautiously approached the folding door. After the incident at the school, they weren't going to take any chances. The men opened their car doors, ducked down, and slowly emerged, using the doors as a shield. They pulled out their weapons and aimed them at the bus windows.

When shouting commands with a bullhorn for people to come out with their hands up resulted in nothing, Bill Clemons decided to approach the bus. He ordered his men to cover him. Two minutes later, he ran back to the cars yelling, "Get back in your vehicles! The damn thing is empty!"

The stalled coach had given Donnor and his refugees valuable time to make their getaway. The chopper pilots were also confused as to whether they should stay with the bus or follow the pickup. After hovering over the bus, Clemons radioed for them to find the F-150.

No golfers were playing on the fourth fairway, nor the fifth. As a matter of fact, no golfers could be found on any of the nine holes this late on a warm April afternoon. The snowbirds just left for the summer in their diesel bus RVs or fifth-wheel trailers. Until Easter Sunday, the camping park that ran adjacent to the golf course was at capacity with Canadians who could afford the terrible exchange rate with the US dollar, or with American retirees from the north who would gladly accept the Canadian loonies at the poker tables inside the clubhouse.

The boulder was a twelve-foot-wide by ten-foot-tall igneous, light brown volcanic rock called rhyolite. The golf course builders didn't bring it here as part of a landscape package. Instead, they built the fifth hole around the gigantic felsic mineral that landed in the desert about seventy million years ago when a volcano exploded on the Basin and Range fault line. Surrounding the rock were massive mesquite trees, their roots pushing up from underground and tangling with one another. On the out-of-bounds side of the boulder was a six-by-six-foot steel trap door that had a mixture of mesquite branches and desert sand two inches thick glued onto it. One of the sticks was a metal handle painted to look like it had fallen from a tree. It took two muscular human bodies to pull the trap door open that led into a long tunnel. But the disguised landscape was not visible from the fairway, nor from the air due to the compact umbrella of mesquite trees next to it. And there was no worry about duffers finding the trap door while searching for an errant shot. The folks who built the tunnel and trap door took care of that by posting three identical signs near the boulder. The signs read *Rattlesnake breeding grounds – Do not look for lost golf balls!*

Donnor drove the pickup swiftly across the fairway and then cut across the green into the woods where the mesquite canopy would prevent the choppers from seeing them. He slammed on the brakes a few feet short of a tree trunk, then hurdled out of the truck and ran to the tailgate. "Get out! Fast! Wait over there behind the boulder!"

As the sixteen teachers and two students unloaded quickly, Donnor reached out and grabbed Mr. Frye by the shoulder. "I need your help," he pleaded.

Frye nodded, "What do you want me to do?"

"We need to lift a trap door that leads into a tunnel." Donnor motioned for Frye to follow him. Together, with adrenaline pumping through their bloodstream like never before, they pulled back on the steel cover until it was perpendicular to the ground. Then Donnor said to Frye, "Okay, I'll hold it steady. Get in and find the electrical wire attached to the roof of the tunnel. Follow it a few feet until you find the switch. Hurry!"

The tunnel dropped straight down three feet, then turned west in the direction of the airstrip. Frye jumped in and found the wire hanging loosely from the roof. The sunlight from the open trapdoor made it easy to find the switch. Frye rotated it until it clicked, and a series of forty-watt light bulbs placed twenty feet apart were illuminated.

As Donnor waved frantically for the teachers to jump into the tunnel, Frye waited to help them down and shoo them away from the entrance. When everyone was in, Donnor shouted, "Okay, now keep moving to the other end. I'm going to get back into the truck and decoy the ICE agents away from the airport." He started to lower the trap door when Frye stopped him.

"Mr. Perez is still in the truck!" barked Frye. "I'm going with you to help out!"

"You may not get out of this alive!" replied Donnor. "Go with your friends!"

"There's no time to argue! I'm coming with you!"

Donnor shook his head in disbelief but held the door open until the young history teacher emerged. They slammed the gate back down and ran to the pickup. Principal Perez was still jarred between the front seat and the dashboard on his knees with his hands cuffed behind him. Frye climbed into the passenger seat and sat cross-legged to keep from kicking Perez in the face. Donnor shifted into gear and jammed the accelerator to the floor. He bolted through the wooded area, turned south, and came out on the sixth fairway, right where a dogleg ended many a golfer's good day. The helicopters saw him and radioed to the Suburbans that were just starting to cross the fifth fairway. The men in the black SUVs cut through the woods and came out about a hundred yards behind the F-150. But without a loaded bed, Donnor's truck picked up speed and exited the golf course into the desert, and then turned east. He was trying to lure his followers as far from the airport as possible.

Traveling close to ninety miles per hour, veering around saguaro cacti and big rocks, the truck dropped down into a wide ditch and became airborne as it flew over two-thirds of Airport Golf Course Road. The F-150 then landed hard as the front wheels plunged into the ditch on the opposite side, but the truck maintained its speed and raced across the desert until Donnor guided it onto Well Road. Once on the cracked asphalt of the town road, he floored the pickup, and the V8 engine kicked into high gear. The lumps on Principal Perez's head were getting larger.

Chapter 17

Tuesday, April 17, 2018
Gila Bend Charter School, Gila Bend, Arizona
1:30 pm (Pacific Daylight Time)

At one-thirty, Special Agent Kelly and Deputy Owens breezed into Gila Bend. They had dodged only one dead cow. The bovine was lying on its back with all four legs sticking straight up. How it maintained that balanced position upside-down on the asphalt road was very curious. Now it was mid-afternoon, and on ordinary days the students at Gila Bend Charter would be frolicking to the bus pick up area, playfully pushing each other and screaming at the tops of their lungs just to be heard over the typical noise that occurs when school gets out. But today was not a normal day.

Gila Bend's police department consisted of a captain, three officers, and two receptionists, one who worked days and the other who worked nights. Captain Ned Segura and Sergeant Pete Ruben operated the day shift, so both police officers were at the school when Kelly and Owens arrived. A blanket covered the dead ICE agent, but blood and brain matter were noticeable on the ground. The Maricopa County coroner had been summoned and was on his way down from Phoenix.

Myra Adams and Ellen Colten were embracing one another a few yards back. Ellen was both nervous and scared. She had placed a call out to Jim Morgan's ranch and was told that Donnor never showed up for work this afternoon.

Special Agent Kelly and Deputy Owens flashed their badges at Captain Segura and Sergeant Ruben. Kelly spoke first. "The sheriff's office received a call from a lady here in Gila Bend, and they, in turn, called us. What's happening down here, Captain?"

Captain Segura responded with an edge to his voice, "Seems that your ICE agents raided our school, Agent Kelly. Perhaps you could tell me what's happening." Deputy Owens and Sergeant Ruben both looked at the special agent thinking the same thing.

Kelly slipped on rubber gloves from a plastic bag in his pocket, and then carefully pulled back the blanket that covered the dead agent, exposing just the back of his cranium. Kelly then gently turned the man's head to the side so he could see his face. The bullet had entered the base of the skull and exited directly in the middle of his forehead. Kelly's mouth dropped open in shock. Not from the distress of seeing a man with a hole through his entire head, but from something else. He pulled the blanket all the way back and examined the man's jacket.

"He's not one of ours," muttered Kelly, then glanced up and looked at the three other officers who could barely understand him. "I said he's not one of our men."

"What do you mean he's not one of your men?" asked Deputy Owens. "I thought your division covered Arizona. Where were these agents deployed from?"

"I'm not sure. But look at this man's jacket. All ICE agents are now required to wear lettering on the back of their jackets that say *Police ICE*, or if they work for Homeland Security, *Police HSI.* This man's jacket says *ICE* on top and *Immigration and Customs Enforcement* printed below it in small letters. Quite frankly, we've never had jackets that spell out the entire acronym."

"Is it possible they were sent directly from Homeland Security in Washington?" asked Captain Segura.

"Well, I guess it's possible," answered Kelly skeptically. "But even so, they would have given us a heads-up before raiding the school." He paused momentarily. "Unless, of course, it was a top-secret mission involving international terrorists. In that case, there is no protocol for notification. The vice president can approve the mission for the Homeland Security director."

The dead agent had no billfold on him, nor was he carrying a badge or other means of identification. He was wearing an Apple watch and an oversized solid gold ring worth many thousands of dollars. For a man who worked for the government and didn't carry a wallet, he appeared to be very wealthy. But the weapon lying in the blood next to him was strange.

Pointing at the gun but being very careful not to touch it, Special Agent Kelly was deep in thought. "Hmmm. Look at this. I believe the man was carrying an old TT-30 pistol. Odd, really odd."

Deputy Owens crouched down next to Kelly and stared at the weapon. "What's odd, Earl? And what's a TT-30 pistol?"

"It's a Soviet semi-automatic that was built back in the thirties. Russian officers used it during World War Two. I learned about it during training workshops at the Pentagon because the Pakistani's are still making bullets for them in their Khyber Pass factories."

"Let me guess. ICE wouldn't be carrying outdated weaponry, would they?"

"We need to get the FBI involved and have them run prints on this dude. They can search the national database and maybe find out who he is. And we need to get to his buddies before they harm anyone. Any idea where they were headed, Captain Segura?"

"That lady standing over there said the Suburbans chased the pickup truck south out of the parking lot. We sent officers Balboa and Renkins to try and find them, but they worked the night shift yesterday and just got going a few minutes ago. The state highway patrol refused to search when we mentioned they were possibly ICE agents. Wonderful, eh?"

"Where would those teachers most likely go from here?" asked Kelly.

"Your guess is as good as mine. Balboa is heading east on I-8 towards Tucson, and Renkins went west towards Yuma. Those would be the fastest routes. That would leave Highway 85 toward Ajo the only other main road out of here. But, if they chose to get off the beaten path, then who knows!"

"Gordy, get into the Vette. We'll go to Ajo. The Pima sheriff's office is there, and they should be able to assist us. Can you radio them and let them know we're coming, Captain Segura?"

"Sure will. I'll call the FBI first and then the sheriff's office. And, oh yeah, we need to call the coroner. Anything else?"

"Before the FBI gets here, take pictures from every angle, and get a close-up of the TT-30. Make sure the coroner doesn't tag him until the FBI is done with him." Special Agent Kelly then nodded at Captain Segura. "But as soon as they're done get this bloody mess cleaned up. This is a school. No need for the kids to freak out." Segura nodded back.

Seconds later, Kelly and Owens were hightailing through Gila Bend heading for Highway 85. The Vette's wide tires threw gravel in all directions. Standing in the parking lot, Captain Segura and Sergeant Ruben turned their heads to keep rocks from penetrating their eye sockets.

"Did you get all that we need to do, Pete?"

"Yes, I think so."

In their haste, they forgot to call the Pima County sheriff's office.

Chapter 18

Tuesday, April 17, 2018
Sonoran Desert, Arizona
1:45 pm (Pacific Daylight Time)

Colonel Cliff Bullard never wanted to leave the Air Force. Twenty years ago, he graduated first in his class from the Academy in Colorado Springs. His father had been a naval commander during the Vietnam War, and his grandfather was an Army major who was killed by a German sniper while leading his regiment up the banks of Omaha Beach on D-Day. Military leadership was in Cliff's blood. He wanted nothing more.

Cliff had spent the first four years of his career moving from one air force base to another, each time with an increase in rank. On September 11, 2001, he was ordered to provide protective air cover for New York City and Long Island following the terrorist demolition of the World Trade Center. Had any civilian jet, knowingly or unknowingly, violated the newly defined restrictive airspace surrounding our nation's largest city, Cliff had full authority to seek and destroy and blow it to kingdom come over the Atlantic Ocean so it could do no harm to any more skyscrapers. Not knowing how many more madmen hell-bent on suicide lurked aboard the hundreds of airborne jets heading to JFK and LaGuardia, he met the challenge head-on with courage and valor. Cliff was rewarded for his pluckiness by being promoted to captain of Air Force One and given the opportunity to personally transport President Bush to destinations around the world. Five years later, he was one of

America's Ambassadors in Blue, a fearless and distinguished member of the daring Thunderbirds flying team.

On February 4th, he led the Thunderbirds flyover of US Bank Stadium in Minneapolis as the official commencement to Super Bowl LII. Before substitute quarterback Nick Foles could complete the unlikely win for his Eagles over the Patriots, Colonel Bullard was halfway over the Atlantic Ocean heading to Egypt for a secret mission to eradicate terror cells in the Sinai Peninsula. On February 9th, he led a coalition of international airstrikes near Bir el-'Abd that resulted in the killing of eighteen civilians, mostly women and children. Because someone needed to take the fall, Cliff was given a dishonorable discharge in exchange for keeping his name out of the newspapers. He wasn't given a choice.

Two weeks later, while riding his Harley down Route 66, he stopped in Winslow, Arizona, for a cold beer and picked the *Arizona Republic* out of a trash bin to have something to read while quenching his thirst. That's where he saw the want ad posted by Zefron Enterprises for an Aerovictor test pilot. Zefron was a new helicopter company located adjacent to the Boeing Corporation in northeast Mesa. Zefron built the Aerovictor Defender and was well known throughout the military world for quality and excellent workmanship. Miles Zefron, CEO of Zefron Enterprises, thought he could make a better product, so he boldly purchased land and erected an assembly plant next to his chief competitor, a move similar to Sam Walton when he built Walmart shopping centers a stone's throw from K-Marts all around America. The US Army had just signed a multi-billion-dollar contract with Zefron Enterprises for 268 Aerovictors, and Zefron needed a pilot now, so they ignored the fact that Cliff was dishonorably discharged and instead focused on his military successes. Cliff guaranteed that he would need only a small learning curve to pick up on techniques for operating an attack helicopter. And he was right. One training mission was all that was necessary to teach Cliff how to fly the chopper.

Cliff's inaugural test flight came on the Tuesday after Easter. He assumed he would be testing the Aerovictor's cruise speed, climb rate, and payload capability, and he also thought his boss would be flying with him on his first flight. But Barney Kinkel had the ultimate faith in his new employee to handle it solo. After all, the ex-colonel had performed masterfully as a member of the Thunderbirds, and a test mission over the desolate Sonoran Desert would be minor in comparison to the daredevil aviation maneuvers that Cliff had previously performed. However, Barney had overstepped his authority on this one, which was nothing new for Zefron's maverick vice president in charge of foreign sales and service. He was being pressured by Turkish President Recep Tayyip Erdoğan to send twenty-four choppers to Reyhanli quickly to shore up defenses on the Syrian border, and he needed to ensure the four Oracle missile launchers were working correctly. According to Pentagon policy, the Oracles were only to be tested in the Mohave Desert's contained facility near Edwards Air Force Base, but Barney needed to close this sale within ten days, or Erdoğan was going to turn to the Russians for help.

Other than the Oracle trials, most of the Aerovictor's tests took place along the Salt River on the outskirts of Mesa, so Cliff was plotting a flight course that would take him to the base of Red Mountain and back. Moments before the pilot boarded the helicopter, Barney called and informed Cliff that along with performing flight maneuvers, he also wanted him to take some target practice at giant saguaro cacti to test the weapons system. Because of that, Barney provided Cliff with coordinates for a new destination near the Mexican border to conduct the tests. Cliff knew nothing about the Pentagon policy, and he didn't care for the idea of ripping Arizona's arborescent symbols to smithereens, but he couldn't afford to lose a second job in two short months. Five minutes later, Cliff was airborne and flying south-southwest, careful to avoid interfering with the flight paths for both Mesa Falcon Field and Phoenix Sky Harbor airports.

Cliff's first test was to assess the airspeed, and he checked that off his list after topping out at 182 mph over Harrah's Ak Chin Casino south of Maricopa. He then put the four-blade, twin-turboshaft engine to the ultimate test as he attempted a seventeen-degree steep approach near the Table Top Mountain hiking trail. Cliff was careful to maintain a descent rate below 300 feet per minute to avoid settling into his own downwash and creating a vortex ring state condition. After testing slope landings, takeoffs, and basic hovering maneuvers, Cliff set a heading for the Organ Pipe Cactus National Monument, where he would reluctantly destroy Saguaro cacti with Oracle missiles in the UNESCO biosphere reserve. Organ Pipe cacti were protected but not Saguaros, an oversight that Barney Kinkel was happy to exploit in exchange for millions of Turkish liras.

Cliff picked up the radio mic to let Zefron know that the initial tests were satisfactory. He pushed the side button, and a crackling, static sound could be heard over the speakers. He assumed that it was normal white noise. "Zefron HQ thirty-two, this is Aerovictor three. Do you copy?" More static, but no reply.

"Zefron HQ thirty-two, this is Aerovictor three. Do you copy?" Cliff repeated his hailing. Again, no reply. Then the static vanished and so did the digital channel readout. Cliff flicked the switch on and off and turned the channel knobs, but to no avail. The radio was dead. The first failed test for the Aerovictor copter. No problem, Cliff didn't really need communications to complete his test mission. He throttled down.

As he rose above the small mountain range on the southern edge of the Sonoran Desert National Monument, Cliff noticed in the distance two choppers hovering over a school bus that appeared to be broken down in the middle of the road near the small town of Ajo. Then, he curiously watched as five Chevy Suburbans dashed around the bus and followed the helicopters into what looked like a golf course. Cliff slowed down to observe from a distance. He lifted the Sunagor Mega Zoom binoculars from the passenger seat and placed them to his eyes. The powerful field glasses with 160x magnification zoomed to the writing on the lead SUV: *Immigration & Customs Enforcement.*

Cliff assumed the ICE men were merely earning their day wages by arresting hardened Mexican criminals before they could escape over the border at Lukeville. But when he focused the binoculars onto the tail of the trailing helicopter, his heart skipped an extra beat, and he let out a gasp. The logo was a hammer and sickle clearly painted in red on the camouflaged surface of the aircraft. After spending time in Afghanistan, Cliff readily identified the helicopter as a Mil Mi-17. It was a Russian medium-lift transport chopper that was outfitted as a gunship but hadn't been used much by the Soviets since the end of the Cold War. Instead, the Russian military has been producing the helicopters for use by its allies despite NATO warnings to cease and desist. Cliff turned the glasses to the cockpit area and noticed four 7.62mm machine guns by the doors and one located at the nose. Directly below the cockpit were eight Shturm-V missiles that were locked, ready, and loaded for bear. Cliff wasn't sure what he was seeing. Could ICE possibly be chasing Russian helicopters with SUVs? He was doubtful that the Suburbans were carrying surface to air rocket launchers on their roofs! Cliff flicked the radio switch up and down, but no luck. It was still dead.

Moments later, the Russian choppers began following a Ford pickup truck that was kicking up dust in the desert. The Suburbans cut through the fairways of the golf course and followed the Mi-17s. Cliff estimated that the pickup and Suburbans were doing close to a hundred miles per hour. Seconds later, the truck scrambled onto a rural road and was headed for Ajo. ICE was less than a mile behind.

1:50 pm (Pacific Daylight Time)
Ajo, Arizona

"Can you slow down some, Donnor? You're going to get us all killed!" shouted Principal Perez as the back of his head continued beating on the dashboard.

"If I slow down, sir, we're going to get killed anyway. Those choppers are right above us, and I can see the vans in the rearview mirror." Donnor checked the sky, the mirror, and the road in perpetual succession. Fear was beginning to drive his thoughts and emotions.

"What's your plan?" asked Mr. Frye. "Where are you taking us?"

"My cousin is an illustrator for children's books. He lives out at the old Curley School, which is now an apartment building for artists of all types. The author he works with also lives there. Anyway, he owns an old Cessna 172 that's stored in a hangar out at the airport. It's a four-seater."

"So, you think we have enough time to find him and get out to the airport?" asked Perez sarcastically. "Are you crazy?"

"He doesn't exactly use the airplane for artistic work if you catch my drift."

"What the hell is that supposed to mean?" barked the principal.

"I'll explain later. There's an underground parking garage at the apartment for residents. We need to get down there, find my cousin, and have him take us to the airport."

"Well, that sounds simple," mocked Perez as he looked at Frye and rolled his eyes. "I can't imagine anything going wrong!"

"The entry to the underground parking is only wide enough for one car. The exit is on the other side."

Frye and Perez didn't say a word. They were both beginning to understand Donnor's plan.

The F-150 shot down Well Road like a bullet, fast and straight. After flying past the high school, Donnor tapped the brakes slightly, and then merged right onto Taladro Avenue, tilting on two wheels. Skilled driving mixed with an overdose of adrenaline was the only thing that kept the pickup from rolling. Then he noticed that cars approaching the main drag had slowed for the railroad crossing lights that were flashing ominously.

Mr. Frye saw it first.

"Train! Stop, Donnor, a damn train!" Frye reached for the dashboard to brace for impact.

"Nope! I can beat it!"

Donnor gunned the accelerator and soared across the tracks a split second ahead of the diesel engine and its ear-shattering horn blast. Luckily, the train had slowed down for its passage through town. But the road curved slightly to the right after crossing the tracks, and Donnor couldn't avoid sideswiping an old Cadillac that was parallel parked on the opposite side of the road. People walking down Taladro Avenues took notice and covered their mouths.

Meanwhile, the ICE agents all slammed on their brakes to keep from colliding with the train, but the last vehicle rear-ended the SUV in front of him. In the lead car, Sergeant Bill Clemons opened the door, slid out, and pounded the roof of his Suburban with both fists. From the passenger seat, Agent Bogdan Smirnov pulled out the radio mic and hailed the helicopters.

"Stay with them. We're stuck behind the train."

"Da, we have them in our sights."

Donnor regained control after the sideswiping and zipped past the Estrella Restaurant and the National Bank. He turned left onto Lomita Avenue and then right onto Esperanza. Seconds later, he turned into the driveway for the Curley School Apartments and raced to the underground parking garage. There, he slammed on the brakes, then set the pickup sideways to block the entrance. As both helicopters hovered above, Donnor glanced upward while Mr. Frye helped Principal Perez out of the truck.

"Go! Run down to the stairwell that enters the apartments and wait! I'll be just a minute." Donnor then grabbed a five-gallon gas can from the bed of the truck and splashed the fuel into the cab. As he reached into the pocket of his Levi's to pull out a lighter, a blast of machine-gun bullets peppered the truck from the choppers that were now encircling the apartments. Donnor dove to the ground and scampered on all fours to the garage. Meanwhile, a spark from the ammunition ignited the gasoline, and the Ford F-150 was smothered in flames. Donnor got up and sprinted to the stairwell.

As the Aerovictor flew over the freight train and he got a better look, Cliff Bullard was puzzled. Why were two Russian helicopters pelting a pickup truck with ammo on American soil? This didn't seem right. No, this wasn't right! The United States would not be operating joint missions with Russia to keep illegal immigrants in check. Cliff reached for the Hughes M230 Chain Gun control stick and fired a round of thirty-millimeter warning shots over and under the Mil Mi-17's cockpit. The Russian choppers rotated to confront the hovering Aerovictor. From only fifty yards, Cliff picked up the binoculars and could clearly see the faces of the pilots. Both had one hand on the flight controls and the other on the weapon controls.

Cliff throttled down and dove beneath the two Russian choppers and through the thick, black smoke of the burning pickup truck. He then climbed steeply over the apartment complex and neighboring Sonoran Desert Inn and Conference Center, trying desperately to get out of the Ajo area to avoid any collateral damage should the Russian helicopters decide to initiate combat. He turned south and headed for the Mexican border. The Mil Mi-17s gave chase.

Chapter 19

Tuesday, April 17, 2018
Curley School Apartments, Ajo, Arizona
2:16 pm (Pacific Daylight Time)

The Ajo volunteer fire department took only sixteen minutes to round up four men from their day jobs, board the fire truck, and arrive at the charred remains of Donnor's F-150. By then, the black smoke had turned gray, and what little was left of the paint on the chassis was sizzling like bacon in a skillet. Two police officers waited patiently with handheld fire extinguishers until the firemen arrived. It didn't take a super sleuth to determine the pickup was intentionally set on fire. The gas can and cigarette lighter lying next to the open passenger door was evidence enough to declare it arson.

As soon as the truck had cooled down, Officer Bruce Gledich of the Ajo police department removed the license plate that still clung to the rear fender. Although black with soot, the tag number was quickly traced to a Donnor Colten, who lived in Gila Bend. While Gledich was phoning the Department of Motor Vehicles, Officer Tom Sloan donned asbestos gloves and was placing his forefinger through a hole in the side panel. When Gledich noticed that his partner had apparently found something irregular, he asked, "What is it, Tom?"

"These holes. There are several of them on the chassis. I believe they are bullet holes, Bruce. Big ones, too. They came from something bigger than a hunting rifle, that much I know."

"Bullet holes? You think someone shot up this guy's truck? You think he was being chased?"

"Maybe," replied Officer Sloan. "And maybe that cigarette lighter didn't start the fire, if you know what I mean."

The firemen were cleaning up the mess and filling out reports when Captain Kevin Myers overheard the policemen's conversation. He wandered over to Officer Sloan and looked carefully at the holes in the chassis. "Yep, those are bullet holes, all right. I think you ought to call in the sheriff's department while I get ahold of the state fire marshal up in Phoenix. Don't move this vehicle until we get the all-clear."

"The DMV said the truck is registered to a Donnor Colten up in Gila Bend," stated Officer Gledich. "I wonder what he was doing down here at the apartments."

"Did you say Donnor Colten?" asked Captain Myers.

"Yep, that's what I was told. Why?"

"Donnor's cousin is a kid's book illustrator. He lives in the Curley Apartments. Bet that's why he came here."

"Let's check it out, Tom," said Gledich. They started walking to the front entrance as curious onlookers were watching from their apartment windows. One artist was sketching the scene from his balcony on the third floor. All the residents had heard the hovering helicopters and machine-gun fire an hour earlier. None wanted any involvement. An investigation into the Curley School Apartments could reveal a secret too dangerous to disclose.

2:20 pm (Pacific Daylight Time)

After seeing the F-150 pickup truck in flames, ICE sergeant Bill Clemons radioed for the other agents who were driving the black Suburbans to follow him to an overflow parking area behind the Sonoran Desert Inn. They got out of their SUVs and watched the black smoke rising high into the pure blue afternoon sky. The intercom in Clemon's vehicle crackled, and Sergeant Clemons reached through the open window and picked it up.

"Whirlybird One to Ground Lead, come in!" The pilot's voice on the intercom seemed filled with anxiety.

"Ground Lead here, this is Clemons. What's up?"

"We are in pursuit of an unidentified Aerovictor Defender. He fired warning shots at us while we were lighting up the pickup truck."

"What's your twenty?"

"Thirty-two degrees north and one-hundred-thirteen degrees west. Over Organ Pipe, about five miles from the border. Out."

"Where is the Aerovictor?"

"About three miles ahead. We can't catch him. Our airspeed max is 158. We're gradually falling behind. Out."

"Are you locked and loaded?"

"The Shturm-V missiles won't be effective at this distance. Their range is about 6000 meters."

"In that case play defense," replied Sergeant Clemons as he strategized the situation in his head. "Head back towards Ajo and set up a small semi-perimeter until we can ditch the SUVs."

"Yes, sir, we are turning back now," responded the pilot. The Mi-17s quickly about-faced and returned to the F-150 they had just destroyed.

Clemons gathered his agents in a small circle and issued his orders. "We've got a problem, gentlemen. An Aerovictor Defender has engaged our choppers, and we have no idea who the pilot is or where he came from. By now, he would have called his superiors and most likely recognized that our choppers were Russian. It's time to destroy the evidence and clear out. Get your hiking gear on. We're heading for the desert, boys!"

As soon as the Mi-17s were circling overhead, Clemons got back on his mic to the pilots. "Give us ten minutes, then destroy the SUVs. Missile them up good, you hear me? Don't ask questions now, I'll fill you in shortly. Rendezvous at the Alamo Canyon trailhead. Agent Smirnov will give you the GPS coordinates in a minute. Understand?"

"Yes, sir, no problem. Ten minutes and counting."

Special Agent Earl Kelly and Deputy Sheriff Gordy Owens had just arrived at the Pima County Sheriff's Department and were getting out of the red Corvette when the blasts echoed throughout the usually quiet community. They looked up and gazed in disbelief at the two helicopters as they fired one missile after another at some target on the ground.

"Let's go!" shouted Kelly as he and Owens hustled back into the Vette. Tires squealed, and rubber smeared on the asphalt as the sports car fishtailed back onto North Well Road.

From the front seat of the unmarked Ford Crown Victoria, Maricopa County Sheriff Urdano and Pima County Sheriff Mike Morton scrutinized the Corvette's driver and his passenger. Urdano glanced at Morton with a look of concern. "That's Homeland Security Special Agent Earl Kelly driving, and unfortunately, my deputy Gordy Owens in the passenger seat."

"Why are they down here, Elliot?" asked Sheriff Morton.

"I'm not sure I want to know," replied Sheriff Urdano.

2:25 pm (Pacific Daylight Time)

Mack Colten was the same age as his cousin. Their fathers were identical twin brothers, and the dads had been best friends since birth. Mack and Donnor were the same height and weight, and their voice tones both sounded similar. A picture of them together waving on a boat in Saguaro Lake was on the kitchen countertop in Mack's apartment. Good luck guessing which one was which. The only difference between the two boys was that Mack loved to draw and paint, while Donnor failed his high school art class for ditching too many times.

Donnor didn't bother knocking. Mack had a trustworthy attitude towards his fellow human beings and never locked the door. Donnor burst into the apartment with Mr. Frye and Principal Perez a few steps behind. Mack was on his balcony, leaning forward trying to get a glimpse of the helicopters in the distance when he heard his visitors arrive.

"Donny, what the hell are you doing here, Cuz?" asked his alarmed cousin.

"Long story, Mack. I need your help! These here are two teachers from the charter school in Gila Bend." Donnor turned and pointed at Perez. "Well, actually, he's the principal."

"Why does the principal have handcuffs on?" asked Mack. Donnor lowered his eyes and shook his head. That was a long story!

Then Mack pointed toward the smoke. "Don't tell me that was your pickup truck on fire out there. And don't tell me that those helicopters have anything to do with you being here!"

"They do, Mack, and I will explain later. Do you have anything that can cut through those handcuffs?"

"Don't need cutters, just a pin." Mack's latest illustration was fastened to an easel waiting for the watercolors to dry. He grabbed the pin from the bottom right corner of the tray and asked Perez to turn around so he could reach the handcuffs that were behind his back. Mack inserted the pin into a small hole on the cuffs and wiggled it. A few seconds later, the manacles sprung open. Perez rubbed both of his wrists and stretched out his arms.

"How did you do that?" asked Mr. Frye.

"Let's just say I have some experience with locks and leave it at that. Okay, dude?" Frye glanced at Perez, and both men nodded at Mack.

"Mack, can you get us to the airport?" Donnor waited for a reply, but all his cousin could do was stare. "There are fifteen teachers and a couple of students in the tunnel waiting for us."

"Maybe I can, Donnor. But only if you tell me what's going on first."

Donnor knew this wasn't an option. If he wanted Mack's help, he would have to reveal what had taken place. "When I was returning to work after lunch, I noticed five Chevy Suburbans racing like bats out of hell to the charter school in Gila Bend. They were ICE agents. I pulled over to the side of the road to watch and noticed two helicopters also circling the school. The agents went into the school with weapons drawn and a few minutes later were escorting the teachers out the door. At the same time, a couple of the agents were pushing kids out onto the baseball diamond. Two kids escaped and got into a school bus and tried to drive away. That's when an agent started shooting at the bus. Hell, Mack, there's no sane reason anyone would fire at a school kid! I mean, how far could they get in that bus anyway? So, to make a long story short, I pulled out my hunting rifle and killed the agent who was shooting. A guy I work with, Pablo Hernandez, was parked behind me watching everything, and after I shot down the one agent, he tried to run over the rest with his car. They blew up his car with him in it, which gave me time to load up the teachers and hightail it out of there! Pablo saved my life! We followed the bus with the two kids down to the golf course road, but it stalled, so we picked up the kids and headed to the rock. After loading everyone into the tunnel, we needed to decoy the Suburbans that were coming up fast behind us, so we drove the pickup out onto Well Road and here we are. The helicopters blew up my truck, but then a third chopper showed up and started shooting at them.

"So that's it, Mack, we need to get to the airport and help out those teachers!"

"By help out, you're talking about my Cessna, aren't you?" grunted Mack.

"Yes, Cuz, that's right. There's something fishy about these agents. I don't think they're ICE. I mean, ICE can be ruthless, but random shooting at a truckload of innocent teachers don't make no sense."

"Okay, but my Cessna 172 was built in 1951, and I can only take four passengers at a time. Maybe seven if I put three in the cargo spaces. There are twenty of you, which means three trips. We'll head west to Cabreza Prieta, then south across the border and land on our strip in Los Vidrios. I got to tell you, Cuz, all those trips without the Border Patrol seeing us is awfully risky. But getting us to the airport without the Suburbans seeing us could be near impossible."

Chapter 20

Tuesday, April 17, 2018
Sonoran Desert, Arizona
2:35 pm (Pacific Daylight Time)

As he flew near the Mexican border, ex-Colonel Cliff Bullard noticed that the two choppers that were chasing him had made an about-face and were now returning to Ajo. He realized that his Aerovictor Defender could outrun his chasers if need be, so he turned and headed back north. Cliff tried his radio once again, but with no luck.

Something wasn't right. Cliff hovered on the outskirts of town and pulled out the binoculars. The two Mi-17s were near the burning pickup truck, but not directly over it. Seconds later, both helicopters began firing missiles at another target on the ground. The explosions were intense, and the flames rose hundreds of feet into the clear blue sky. It was decision time, and Cliff had never been one to delay the inevitable. He took aim with the M230 Chain Gun at the first chopper. The highly destructive weapon could fire 625 rounds per minute, but the Aerovictor could only hold 1,200 rounds, and Cliff had used up 300 warning shots during the previous encounter. He couldn't afford to miss.

Cliff had the Mi-17 fuel tank in his crosshairs, and the hydraulic actuator on the centerline elevated the gun into position. Cliff pushed and held the trigger button. The closest Russian chopper burst into flames and rotated uncontrollably. It spiraled into a nosedive and landed directly on top of the burning SUVs on the ground. The second Mi-17 turned to face the Aerovictor, but Cliff was too quick. He fired another round into the enemy's cockpit, completely shattering the pilot's face. The throttle lurched back with the dead aviator's grip, and the helicopter rose and rolled before crashing to the ground upside-down.

Cliff moved and hovered over the scene of obliteration below him. He could make out the charred remains of the five Chevy Suburbans that had been chasing the pickup truck. They were lying conspicuously underneath the rubble of the two Russian helicopters. It was a burning junkyard of expensive metal. Cliff knew he had to return to Zefron, but he was dreading the investigation that would take place with Homeland Security, the US Air Force, the FBI, and most likely, the CIA. Cliff Bullard had thoughts about flying up to Winslow, hiding the Aerovictor somewhere in the Painted Desert, and getting back to seeing the great USA on Route 66 with his new Harley Hog.

*****

Trying desperately to follow the black smoke rising from the blasts, Earl Kelly left a long patch of wide rubber on Highway 85 as the Vette squealed and merged recklessly onto the main avenue from Well Road. The Homeland Security special agent didn't know the layout of the local Ajo roads and mistakenly turned left on South Elota, then right on West Elota, which was an unmarked dead-end street. Kelly and Deputy Owens could see that they were only a few blocks from whatever the helicopters were tearing up on the ground, so they decided to ditch the sports car and run across the desert shrubbery to the scene. Seconds later, they stopped abruptly in their tracks and witnessed an Aerovictor Defender gun down the other two choppers.

"What the hell!" exclaimed Kelly as he shaded his eyes with his hand.

"That's an Aerovictor, Earl! You're Homeland Security, what's going on down here?!"

"I honestly don't know, Gordy. But I sure as hell am going to find out! Let's move!"

Kelly and Owens began to run in the direction of the smoke. Jogging at a rapid pace down Orilla Avenue, they watched as the Aerovictor momentarily hovered over the scene, then turned and headed north towards Phoenix at a high rate of speed. Moments later, Kelly and Owens arrived on foot and witnessed chaos in the making. Fire Captain Myers was frantically trying to direct half of his volunteer crew to extinguish the flames with the water that was left in the truck's 1,000-gallon holding tank, while the other half was knocking down Elmer Hatch's chain-link fence. Most of the truck's water had been used up putting out Donnor Colten's smoldering F-150 pickup. The Ajo fire department had two trucks, but the other one was being serviced today at the Pima County vehicle repair facility in Tucson. The nearest fire hydrant was in front of the main entrance to the Sonoran Desert Inn and Conference Center, too long for the 200-foot crosslay hose to reach. Thus, Elmer's small swimming pool would have to suffice.

Elmer had recently purchased the two-bedroom house on the corner of Lomita and Orilla Avenues and was doing some minor renovations to the property. Yesterday, he finished refilling the pool with 10,000 gallons of water after completing an acid wash of the surface. The strong, physically fit, and severely wrinkled elderly gentleman had moved in only two weeks earlier, following the death of his wife in Minnesota. The ninety-year-old chap had shoveled enough snow out of his driveway in Minneapolis to last a lifetime, and now that he was all alone, he just wanted peace and seclusion for his remaining days on earth. That wasn't about to happen!

Elmer had been working in his detached garage when the five Suburbans slammed on their brakes, kicking up enough dust to dirty his newly refilled pool. Then he witnessed a bunch of men in windbreakers run into the desert while two helicopters fired missiles at the SUVs. And if that wasn't enough to ruin his tuna sandwich lunch, a few minutes later, another chopper blew up the first two helicopters in midair! Now the fire department was tearing down his fence and dragging a crosslay hose into his pool while Elmer just stared at them in disbelief. His first water bill would be enormous! Cha-ching!

Special Agent Kelly and Deputy Owens jogged up to Bruce Gledich and Tom Sloan, the Ajo police department officers who were now haphazardly running yellow crime scene tape around the perimeter of the disaster. Kelly and Owens flashed their badges, but Gledich and Sloan were too busy to talk. "Give us a few minutes," Gledich requested without stopping his work.

"Just one thing," stated Kelly adamantly. "Who's in charge here?"

"Haven't figured that out yet," responded a muddled Gledich.

The streets behind the Sonoran Desert Inn were becoming crowded with bewildered residents of the normally sleepy town. Rumors were rampant. One gray-haired lady was scoping the scene in search of Tom Cruise. She was sure he was filming the next *Mission Impossible* movie right before her eyes!

Minutes later, a Pima County sheriff's car with red lights flashing and siren wailing screeched on its brakes. Out stepped two imposing figures in khaki uniforms and shiny badges. Neither seemed to be in a big hurry, though. As they strolled towards the Ajo police officers, the heavy-set man stopped in his tracks after he saw Kelly and Owens, who were suspiciously staring back at him.

"Deputy Owens, what on God's green earth are you doing down here?" asked the sheriff.

"Funny thing, Sheriff Urdano, I was wondering the same about you," responded Deputy Owens.

*****

Mack Colten's golf cart was parked in the garage underneath the Curley School Apartments where he lived. It was a four-seater with one forward-facing bench seat up front and one rear-facing seat on the back. Mack unplugged the electric cord that ran from the motor to a charging receptacle on the wall. Donnor sat in the front with his cousin, while Principal Perez and Mr. Frye sat behind them. The cart had a top speed of fourteen miles per hour and was licensed for the road.

Upon exiting the garage, Mack slammed on the brakes, and all his passengers held on for dear life. He looked skyward and spotted an Aerovictor Defender destroying the two helicopters he had seen earlier. Both doomed choppers fell to earth a few hundred yards away, and the explosion rocked the small community like an earthquake. "Holy crap! Will you look at that!" exclaimed Mack. All eyes were staring at the flames and black smoke. "Let's get the hell out of here!"

Not wanting to dodge traffic on Highway 85, Mack drove the cart to the airport via Wells Road and the empty golf course. It took forty minutes to travel the seven miles, but fortunately, it was an inconspicuous journey as all town folks had pulled over in their cars to watch the fireworks in the sky. They headed directly for the opposite end of the tunnel where the teachers had walked and were now waiting patiently for their rescuers.

The tunnel ran from the boulder on the golf course to Hangar Seven at the airport. The airport only had three hangars, but Mack named his Cessna storage place after his lucky Vegas number. What he was involved in was basically a crapshoot anyway, and a roll of seven could mean good things or the end of a profitable run. Such was his life. Mack had enlarged and redesigned the hangar with two other artist friends that lived in the Curley School Apartments. Archie McCormick was a professional photographer by trade, and Paul Killian sculpted statues of Native Americans. Unlike his carefree personal lifestyle where he didn't even bother to lock his apartment doors, the hangar housing his antique airplane was a different story. Together with a crew from Browning Corporation in Morgan, Utah, they constructed the secure hangar using steel-reinforced concrete walls and a vault door with twenty-two locking bolts. The door opened by lowering it underneath the ground using a hydraulic lift. The lift would only operate if a ten-digit code was entered into an electronic panel, followed by Mack Colten's thumbprint. If Mack died, he gave permission for Archie and Paul to cut off his thumb to reprogram the security codes. Mack only asked that when they were done, his thumb would be stuffed with cotton and placed on the spire atop the domed roof at the Immaculate Conception Catholic Church. He believed his only way to heaven may be to hitchhike, and hopefully, some sweet soul would give him a ride on his or her way up.

After the crew from Browning finished, the three artists dug a tunnel inside the hangar's subterranean compartment that housed the lowered vault door. They had secured the services of twenty Mexican immigrants and a few homeless gentlemen to help them with the massive project. The workers were very well paid and lived in the Curley apartments while the project was being completed. And with the artist's assistance, after they were done, the homeless helpers all found jobs locally while the Mexicans migrated to their next work location.

No one questioned the expensive-looking hangar sitting next to a couple of dilapidated structures that would collapse if a haboob decided to rear its ugly head. Each of the other rundown hangars housed two private planes that didn't get much use. Including Mack's 1951 Cessna, the five flying machines based in Ajo wouldn't make for an eye-popping display of aviation at an air show. The identities of the five owners were not known either, and actually, no one in Ajo really cared to know.

Mack parked the cart in front of the hangar by the electronic security box and jumped out. He punched in the ten-digit code, then placed his thumb on the reader, and the massive door began to lower into the ground. Donnor had helped one weekend digging the tunnel, so he knew the layout.

Questions were spinning in Principal Perez's mind. Why had Mack built the overly secure hangar to house an old airplane, and why had he dug the tunnel from the golf course? When he asked Mack what he was doing, Mack replied, "You don't want to know, sir, so please don't ask again." That's not the type of answer one gives a principal!

Directly under the Cessna were two hinged iron doors that were locked together by a one-inch thick iron bolt. The location of the entries made it look like there was a mechanical pit underneath that was used to repair or maintain the aircraft. Actually, it was the point of egress for the tunnel that ran from the golf course to the airport. Mack climbed aboard the Cessna and fired up the Lycoming O-360 motor. It purred quietly. It should—Mack had performed a field overhaul every 1,000 hours instead of the recommended 2,000, and he had twice replaced the engine. The expense of building the hangar and tunnel combined with the cost of maintenance to the Cessna was prohibitive for a smalltime artist living in Ajo. Principal Perez noticed that idiosyncrasy immediately.

"Where do you suppose Mack gets his money for all of this?" he whispered to Mr. Frye, making sure no one else heard him.

"You got me, sir!" responded Frye under his breath while shaking his head. "And I have a funny feeling his cousin Donnor doesn't even know."

Mack taxied the Cessna out of the hangar and let it sit with the engine running, then he hopped down and ran to the iron doors. After unlocking the bolt, he asked Donnor to give him a hand. The two men lifted and swung the left gate and placed it gently on the floor, then did the same to the right portal. Thirty-four eyes looked up from the tunnel, and all were squinting as the late afternoon sun was blazing in through the hangar door. The fifteen teachers and two students appeared apprehensive and restless. They had been frightened when the steel door was lowered into the compartment where they were waiting to be rescued. Until that time, they had no idea what the hydraulic lift was used for, and they had discussed going back to the boulder on the golf course. But the scared teachers had no leader, so they stayed put and waited.

A small ladder was bolted to the side of the underground wall next to the swinging doors. Mack, Donnor, Frye, and Principal Perez helped the group out of the hole. They were happy to be free of the dark tunnel but befuddled as to what would happen next. The incident at their school was still first and foremost in their minds, and it was difficult to focus on the future.

"I need seven of you to get into my airplane," said Mack. "The two kids should be in the first group. Three of you can get into a cockpit seat, and the rest should crawl into the storage areas in the back. When we're airborne, grab on to the netting and hold tight." Mack paused for a moment, then continued. "I'll return as soon as possible. In the meantime, the rest of you will wait in the hangar with Donnor, Mr. Frye, and your principal. Any questions?"

Isaac Martinez and Zaira Tahan didn't hesitate and sprinted to the plane. Five of their teachers followed them and climbed aboard. The two students and two smallest teachers crammed into the storage area, while the rest buckled up into their seats. A few moments later, the tiny plane lifted off into the clear blue sky. At once, the passengers were startled by what they saw out the window. There was black smoke rising into the atmosphere from somewhere in Ajo.

"What's that?!" asked math teacher Kurt Kellner nervously while pointing at the helicopter and SUV graveyard.

"That, sir, is the reason we're headed to Mexico," replied Mack with a slight smile. Everyone on board dropped their jaws and imparted a puzzled gape at their pilot. Mack pulled back on the yoke and rotated the control wheel to the right. The plane rose and headed in a southwesterly direction towards the border. "I know a great place for cheap shots of tequila. Y'all look like you could use a few."

Chapter 21

Tuesday, April 17, 2018
Ajo, Arizona
2:45 pm (Pacific Daylight Time)

"These SUVs and choppers were at the Gila Bend Charter School just a couple hours ago," said Special Agent Earl Kelly. "Do you have any idea where they came from?"

"Well, Earl, I'm assuming they're your playthings," replied Sheriff Urdano sarcastically. "We don't have that kind of budget at the Sheriff's department."

"There is a dead man posing as a Homeland Security agent lying in the parking lot at the school. The keyword here is posing."

"If he's dead, then I doubt very much he is still posing." Sheriff Urdano's sarcasm was getting under Kelly's skin.

"The man was wearing a fake ICE jacket and carrying a TT-30 pistol. Not knowing how adept you are at weaponry, a TT-30 pistol is a Soviet semi-automatic that was built back before World War Two. The SUVs are most likely not ours, either. As soon as the vehicles cool down, we will search for a transaxle. Homeland Security stamps an identification number on the transaxle to find the vehicle's origin in case of an accident." Kelly was gazing at Urdano to see if the sheriff would flinch. He wasn't sure why, but he had a gut feeling that Urdano wasn't exactly a lawful lawman. It was doubtful that anyone outside of Homeland Security would know about the transaxle identification system.

Sheriff Urdano remained poised; however, Pima County sheriff, Mike Morton, took off his hat and wiped sweat from his forehead.

"So, what's your theory about all of this?" asked Morton. "I mean, you sound as if you have an idea in your head."

Kelly looked away from Urdano and over to Morton. "A theory is what you're asking me?! Are you kidding?! So, let's summarize what we know. Men posing as ICE agents carrying Russian weapons drove five Chevy Suburbans and flew two unidentified helicopters to raid the Gila Bend Charter School. Why they would make that costly effort to scare little children is beyond me. After that, they chased a pickup truck full of teachers down here to Ajo for reasons that I couldn't begin to comprehend. And then to top it off, the unidentified choppers blasted their own SUVs to smithereens just moments before an unidentified Aerovictor helicopter blew both apart!" Kelly stared at Morton with an incredulous look, then firmly placed his hands on his hips. "You think I can make a theory out of this mess, Sheriff Morton? Who did you buy your criminal justice degree from?" Kelly walked away, shaking his head.

"Where are you going, Earl?" asked Sheriff Urdano with a hint of trepidation in his voice.

"To call the Army, Elliot. I want to find out where that Aerovictor helicopter came from."

3:00 pm (Pacific Daylight Time)

"You could have ridden back with your boss," said Special Agent Kelly while biting his lip. Deputy Gordy Owens didn't find the humor in that. Kelly's red Vette was pushing 160 on Highway 85, and at that speed, they would be in Gila Bend in ten minutes or so. Police Captain Ned Segura had texted Kelly saying he needed to show him something before the coroner hauled the dead man away from the charter school parking lot. "Between you and me, Gordy, I don't trust Urdano."

"No comment," replied Owens. "All I can tell you is he doesn't spend a whole lot of time at the office, and most of the time our receptionist, Rebecca Grimm, covers for him."

"Can you trust her?"

"I think so. I hope so."

Fifteen minutes later, Kelly pulled into the Gila Bend Charter School parking lot and stopped a few yards from the dead ICE impersonator. Captain Segura and Sergeant Pete Ruben were trying to get fingerprint impressions off the man's stiff hands, which wasn't all that difficult now that rigor mortis had begun to set in. Coroner Vic Marson was standing over the body, taking notes.

"It's about time," said Marson coldly. "If I don't get this body back to Phoenix in the next hour, I may not know exactly what killed him."

"Well, I may not be a medical expert nor a cadaver connoisseur, but if I was to guess, this man died from a bullet hole to the back of his brain!" After putting up with Sheriff Urdano's contempt and lack of respect, and now Coroner Marson's simplistic knack for stating the obvious, Kelly was wondering how these men were ever elected. Marson looked away, shaking his head.

Segura motioned for Kelly to come closer. He pointed to the dead man's wristwatch. "That's a top of the line Apple watch he's wearing. It has all the capabilities of a Smartphone."

"Okay, I'll buy that. So, what has that to do with this investigation?"

"It has a GPS and phone inside. Not only can we see who the man has called, but we can find out where he has been. A small built-in hard drive stores that data for thirty days."

"Good! That's great! Set up an inventory sheet on this guy, and I'll take the watch with me. I can sign off right here before I go."

"Sure, okay," responded Captain Segura. "But there's one other thing we noticed. Take a close look at the gold ring on his finger. The skin color is constantly changing where the ring meets his finger. It's barely visible, and we almost missed it."

"Take it off and let's look at it."

"Can't. The rigor mortis is preventing us from straightening out the metacarpals and phalanges."

Special Agent Kelly looked up at Coroner Marson. "Why are his hands stiff, Doc? I thought rigor mortis doesn't happen for eight to twelve hours after death. It's only been three or four hours."

"Gee, I thought you were the expert on death and dying," replied Marson sarcastically. "Why don't you tell me."

Marson was wearing a white short-sleeve shirt, paisley tie, and a cowboy hat; business attire in the Wild West. Kelly stood up, grabbed the tie, and yanked Marson so close to his face he could smell onions on the coroner's breath. No doubt, he had stopped for a Big Mac on the way to Gila Bend. "None of us have time for your condescending attitude. Now answer the question." He pushed Marson, and the coroner stumbled backward.

"Okay, okay, calm down," said Marson. "As soon as this guy died, the muscles of his body probably contracted faster than they did when he was alive. His muscle cells built up electricity in the membranes by pumping out calcium ions. Somewhere along the way, his muscle cells got a neuron signal that opened the calcium channels in the membranes, and the calcium ions rushed in due to the voltage difference between the inside and outside of his cells. There you have it in a nutshell, Agent Kelly, unless, of course, you want to know how the ions interacted with actin and myosin filaments to cause muscle contraction. Would you like me to explain that to you, as well?"

"Give it to me in English, Doc, and cut the sarcasm!"

"Bottom line, I'm guessing there is an electrical source in his left hand that is causing rapid rigor mortis to that area. The rest of his body is becoming stiff, but there is still some pliability. If I were a betting man, I'd say the Apple watch could be the source of electricity."

"Or, it could be this damn ring. I want to see it. Cut off his finger at the knuckle, and it will come off."

"I will do no such thing out here in a school parking lot!" declared Marson. "I have proper tools in my laboratory."

Kelly shook his head in disgust and took out a Swiss Army knife from his front pocket. Two minutes later, the ICE impersonator's ring slid easily off his jaggedly amputated finger. Kelly tossed the finger to a startled Coroner Marson, who quickly placed it in a plastic bag. It was now clear what was making the color variations on his skin. On the inside of the ring was a tiny green light that was blinking. Obviously, the ring contained some sort of electrical device beneath its gold exterior.

Kelly wiped the blood from the dead man's finger off his hand and the ring. He then placed the ring into a small evidence box with the watch. Captain Segura ripped off an inventory form from a pad and filled out the necessary details. Kelly signed the form, thanked Segura and Sergeant Ruben, and then he and Gordy Owens dashed for the Corvette. Coroner Marson simply watched with his mouth wide open.

When they got in the car, Kelly glanced out the window at Marson, then turned to Owens. "What an asshole!"

"Be careful, Earl. The coroner and Sheriff Urdano are close friends."

"Doesn't surprise me."

The wide Goodyear tires screeched as the Vette fishtailed out of the charter school parking lot. If the livestock on Dead Cow Road were taking their afternoon siesta, Kelly and Owens would be back in Phoenix in forty-five minutes.

Chapter 22

Tuesday, April 17, 2018
Desert South of Ajo, Arizona
3:30 pm (Pacific Daylight Time)

"Hold on, Sergeant Clemons, something's wrong!" Bogdan Smirnov had stopped in his tracks and was peering down at the iPad in his hand. The other nine ICE agents were happy for a brief rest. They had been jogging several miles with heavy gear since abandoning their Suburbans in Ajo. They were all hot and sweaty as they bent forward and placed their hands on their knees. Their leader, Sergeant Bill Clemons, wanted to quickly get as far away from the SUV inferno before the authorities realized there were no bodies in the vehicles.

"What is it, Smirnov?" asked Clemons.

"Garth's ring and watch are on the move. And quite rapidly, I might add!"

"They must be taking his body to the morgue. Activate the ring so you can wipe out the watch data."

"Well, that's the problem, boss. It appears the ring and the watch have been removed from the body. Without the body as a conduit, the circuitry won't function. The only way it will work now is if the ring touches the watch."

"Why the hell didn't you activate it before we left Gila Bend, you idiot?!" Bill Clemons was turning red in the face, and spit was blasting from his mouth.

"Garth was obviously dead," replied Smirnov defensively. "I didn't need to use the electronic shock function embedded into the ring to kill him and keep him from talking! But I forgot to activate the data wipe function. I'm human; give me a break!"

"Human? That's a stretch! Contact LeBron and have him get the ring and watch before the FBI dissects the hard drive and traces where we came from. Send him an instant message!"

Agent Smirnov typed in the message and hit the "send" button. At that moment, everyone looked upward into the clear blue sky. A small airplane that had been heading southwest was now turning toward them.

3:30 pm (Pacific Daylight Time)

Kurt Kellner moved to Arizona as a last-ditch effort to avoid buying another sweater. His closet cubbies were overflowing with the wool monsters of the north, and he wanted nothing more to do with those itchy beasts. Kurt graduated and received a teaching degree from a Wisconsin state college in Superior, where he was recruited to play baseball. In the four years he played for the Yellowjackets, he started every game. That should have been 140 total contests. However, the seasons ran from mid-March to mid-May, and forty-four games were canceled due to blizzard conditions. One day, Kurt played in a quin header, five games against cross-lake rival Minnesota-Duluth to make up for four games that had been canceled during the season due to icy field conditions. In April, the college's baseball diamond doubled as a skating rink for off-season youth hockey practice.

As a math major, Kurt could virtually pick any location in the United States to teach because the country was desperate for them. Why he chose New Richmond, Wisconsin, was a puzzle even he couldn't solve—and he was an expert at solving puzzles, especially the math variety. The weather was a wee bit warmer in the winter than living next to Lake Superior, meaning that by May 1st, you could turn off your heat. But just when you were beginning to enjoy the fruits of summer, you were sharing those fruits with noisy mosquitoes. After one year teaching math at Warren P. Knowles

Middle School, Kurt decided to search for a state to live in that rejected both snow and mosquitoes. Arizona!

"Mack, what's that?" asked Kurt, pointing east towards a dirt road. "That looks like men out for a jog, but they are all dressed in long pants and windbreakers. Who exercises in Arizona with those clothes?!"

Mack turned the plane eastward to get a better view. "Well, I believe those are the same fellas that raided your school and chased you to the tunnel at the golf course. Obviously, they didn't die in that fire back there in Ajo."

"You mean all that smoke we just saw was their SUVs burning? How do you know that?"

"Long story. I'll tell you later, but all of you need to know that the people down there are not ICE or Homeland Security agents. Those folks don't work that way."

"If they're not ICE, who are they?"

"Not sure. If I said they were bad guys, would that satisfy you?" Mack glanced quickly at Kurt and grinned. Kurt didn't smile back. He grabbed a pair of binoculars that were fastened to the cockpit wall and peered down toward the men, then let out a small gasp.

"They're all looking up at us! We need to head the other way!"

Mack agreed. He pulled the control yoke, pressed down the rudder, and the Cessna banked southward. It was then that the first bullet pierced the port side fuel tanks, and the second penetrated the engine compartment. Sergeant Bill Clemons rarely missed his target.

Dark black smoke was filling the cockpit. The Cessna would not last much longer. Mack held the controls steady as he searched for a flat location to land the plane, but that possibility was fading fast. They were surrounded by rocky hills and huge saguaros. The dirt road, the same one where the ICE agents were standing, was the only hope for a safe landing. Death by cactus or death by guns. Pick your poison.

"We have three parachutes in the storage bins," shouted Mack. "Does anyone know how to use them?"

"I do," replied Kurt. "I've parachuted with a club in Wisconsin."

"Okay. You take one of the chutes and get the kids geared up in the other two. Show them the ripcord and make sure they know not to pull too soon!"

Kurt unbuckled his seatbelt, crouched down, and moved to the back where a teacher and the two students, Isaac Martinez and Zaira Tahan, were clutching each other in fright. The kids heard Mack's orders and were very hesitant to follow them. First, stealing a school bus and being chased by thugs with guns, then jumping out of a smoking airplane into a rugged desert wasn't exactly "just another day" in middle school. Talk at the dinner table most nights was quite blasé, but tonight would be entirely different.

The Cessna 172 was not large enough for anyone to stand, and the only exits were the two cockpit doors. The smoke was becoming thicker. Kurt helped the terrified students move forward and fastened them into the parachutes with no regard for safety assurances. There simply wasn't time to check the straps. Fortunately, each pack had a reserve parachute with an automatic activation device that would deploy at 1,500 feet during a free fall.

"This is the ripcord," said Kurt anxiously. "Do not, I repeat, do not pull it until you are clear from the plane. Got that?!" Isaac and Zaira nodded yes. Both were diligent students!

Kurt then strapped his pack onto his own back while the other distressed teachers panted and prayed. The plane was losing speed and altitude, but Mack was doing his best to keep it steady. Kurt sat back down in the front passenger seat and slammed the emergency discharge button. Two quick CO2 cartridge blasts and the hinges gave way allowing the cockpit door to fall off into the wild blue yonder. Kurt grabbed Zaira's arm and pulled her forward. Her hand was gripping the ripcord, and she was in tears. The plane was at 4,000 feet and dropping rapidly. "Close your eyes, count to five, and pull!" With that, Kurt pushed Zaira out the door. Seconds later, her canopy opened, and Kurt repeated his order to Isaac. He then pushed him out and waited. As soon as Isaac's canopy opened, Kurt looked back at Mack. "Good luck to all of us!" He jumped and went into a dive to position himself above and in between Zaira and Isaac before deploying his chute. It just dawned on him that the kids would have no idea how to maneuver towards a landing target. He hadn't had the time to explain that part.

The Cessna's control wheel began to shake violently, and Mack gripped it even harder. "You folks in the back get into the front passenger seat—NOW! Double up on each other's lap and buckle up! Lean forward and cover the tops of your heads with your hands. Hurry!"

The plane's speed dropped to forty-eight knots and the engines stalled. There was not enough velocity left to bank it in either direction; however, a strong wind had emerged from the south that allowed the aircraft to glide slowly. Any minute now, the old Cessna could burst into flames. Mack knew he wouldn't be able to reach the road. He was hoping to make it over the peak of a large hill packed with giant boulders a hundred yards in front of him. The ground shadows rose to meet the massive stones that loomed like King Kong ready to swat the small plane out of the air just as he did from atop the Empire State Building. Mack wasn't sure what would be waiting on the other side even if he was able to avoid the rocks. The teachers had become eerily silent, their lives now firmly placed in God's hands.

3:50 pm (Pacific Daylight Time)

Isaac and Zaira landed simultaneously but were a quarter-mile from each other in the middle of the desert. Kurt followed Zaira's canopy to the ground and touched down fifty yards from her. Both students hit the earth hard, stumbled, and were dragged for several feet by the surface winds. They had a variety of scrapes on their arms and legs. Kurt unstrapped himself and ran to help Zaira. By the time they reached Isaac, he had already unhooked himself and was brushing off sand from his torn blue jeans.

"Are you both alright?" asked Kurt hurriedly. Both students looked at each other, then nodded. "Then let's get– "

Kurt was interrupted by an enormous blast, and they all turned to see flames and black smoke rising on the other side of a small hill about a mile away. The three clutched one another and huddled together for a group hug. The explosion could only mean one thing: four teachers had perished along with Mack in the Cessna.

"Come on, we need to get moving," urged Kurt, although it was difficult for him to do so. Those teachers had been colleagues and friends. Kurt looked in all directions, then noticed the dirt road they had seen from the air was only two hundred yards away. He pointed, then they all began jogging towards it.

One minute later, they stopped dead in their tracks. Ten guns held by ten men in ICE windbreakers were aimed at their faces.

"Nice of you folks to drop in," Sergeant Bill Clemons said smugly, cracking an ominous smile.

Chapter 23

Tuesday, April 17, 2018
Zefron Enterprises, Mesa, Arizona
4:00 pm (Pacific Daylight Time)

"Why can't a modern hi-tech flying machine have a damn radio that works?!" muttered Cliff Bullard to himself. He pounded the radio with his fist and threw the microphone to the floor. Cliff was approaching the Zefron plant with caution. No doubt the air traffic controller across the street at Falcon Field was frantically trying to hail him so he wouldn't interfere with the small planes trying to land. Cliff glanced down at his radar screen and saw several large passenger jets were making their descent into Phoenix Sky Harbor airport, but his Aerovictor was not going to be a problem for them. However, the small Learjet approaching Falcon Field from Four Peaks Mountain could be trouble. He noticed on the radar several helicopters hovering over a section of the desert a mile or so northeast of Zefron. Must be more Aerovictors or Boeing's Apache Longbows being tested. "I hope they've got radios that work!" said Cliff to himself with more than a hint of sarcasm.

Cliff decided to avert from his landing as a safety precaution for the incoming Learjet. He headed north away from Zefron following Greenfield Road until he came to the South Canal of the Salt River. Off to the east, he could see flames and smoke and fire trucks. The helicopters on the radar weren't Aerovictors or Longbows; they were news and police choppers. Not wanting to interfere with the emergency taking place, Cliff tracked along the canal, planning to circle back after he reached Bush Highway, but a flash of light caught his eye. A split-second later, an explosion blasted the roof off an unknown structure next to Senso-McNamara Corporation. Curiously, that blast was only a hundred yards from Senso-Mac's company headquarters building that was already in flames and being tended to by a whole host of rescue personnel.

Located a mile from the Nammo Talley ammunition and energy plant, Senso-McNamara Corporation manufactured laser surgical devices, sensors, rangefinders, and mapping devices. The nice folks living in the neighboring Mesa subsection of Red Mountain Ranch thought Senso-Mac also made traffic speed guns for police use, which they did. What they didn't know was the plant produced a variety of shoulder-held laser weapons (a modern-day death ray, you might say) for the Department of Defense. Homeland Security constructed a wide-area perimeter fence to keep the curious at bay, but resident desert hikers found ways to get a closer look thanks to wire cutters purchased at Home Depot. Cliff diverted from his original plan to fly wide and avoid interference; instead, he moved towards the latest blast.

Two Hours Earlier

Joe Freeman was an avid hiker and photographer who lived on Ranier Street. His house was adjacent to Senso-Mac's property, which was no big deal for Joe. He built his home three years before Senso-Mac moved next door, primarily because his backyard provided a spectacular vista of the saguaro-laced desert and an uncompromised view of the Phoenix skyline, Camelback Mountain, and the McDowell Mountains. The Valley of the Sun, my oh my, and it was all Joe's when the sunset lit up the western sky like a bonfire. Joe sold Arizona landscape photographs worldwide. Most were so extraordinarily beautiful straight from the camera that they didn't even need retouching.

Joe had blazed several trails through the desert that started right from the gate in his backyard to a variety of scenic locations, including one that went four miles to the base of Red Mountain. He hiked twice a day—once at sunrise and the other at sunset. His trusty Canon dangled at his side, and the camera was given quite a workout. That was, however, until Homeland Security constructed their barbed wire fence with an electric current running through it.

Joe met with the mayor and complained during a city council meeting, all to no avail. Homeland Security was a federal agency that, quite bluntly, could do anything they damn well pleased. But Joe was also used to doing anything he damn well pleased, and a wire fence with sharp points and a little buzz wasn't going to stop him. He bought a pair of wire cutters and a pair of electrician's protective rubber gloves and continued his daily hikes.

One April afternoon, Joe wanted to complete a ten-mile hike that, if his timing were right, would end at sunset. He had just recovered from the flu that kept him from exercising the previous week, and he was trying to compensate for all the missed activity in one day. Joe was tying his shoe on a trail when the ground shook. Could it be an earthquake? He had never experienced one, so he wasn't sure. Arizona tremors were rare, yet the California fault lines weren't all that far away. Joe shrugged it off and started walking down the trail but stopped suddenly when he saw a herd of thirty howling javelinas charging towards him. Classified as herbivores, hungry javelinas have been known to slurp down roadkill. If Joe didn't get off the trail quickly, that's what he would become! He ran and hid behind the trunk of a mesquite tree as the javelinas hustled by without even giving Joe a second thought. Something had spooked them—perhaps the tremor. Joe watched them gallop away in the direction of the homes on Ranier.

Then he felt another tremor, much more violent than the first. But this one was accompanied by four bursts of bright light flashing out of the ground. Joe never did well in earth science during his school days, but he was pretty sure that an earthquake didn't produce subterranean flares. Perhaps it was a volcano. He hoped not.

Joe walked cautiously ahead until he came to the source of the lights. Four lead pipes, six inches in diameter, were sticking up from the ground about two feet. They appeared to be air vents leading into an underground chamber. Joe knew that Senso-Mac made traffic speed guns and tested them often, but if the speed gun that was being tested here shook the ground and produced a massive amount of blinding light rays, then he hoped he was never riding in the car that was traveling over the posted limit!

Just then, a four-foot square iron door opened from the earth, and two men in asbestos spacesuits and helmets emerged. Both were holding a three-foot laser gun on their shoulders. Joe ducked behind a huge saguaro cactus, pulled out his camera, and started shooting. As the men walked away, Joe quickly attached a 1,300-millimeter zoom lens onto the Canon and switched the shutter button to continuous mode. About two hundred yards away, the men took off their spacesuits, got on board a military Humvee, then drove off. Joe was a Pulitzer prize winner, an accomplished veteran photographer who never missed the perfect shot. He now had in his possession a flawless closeup of the men's faces.

After the Humvee left, Joe exchanged the telephoto lens with a macro lens. He wanted to get a closeup of the four pipes that were sticking out of the ground. To his surprise, he noticed that the iron door the men had appeared from was not only unlocked, but it was also left wide open. Curiosity was supposed to kill cats but not humans. Joe decided to see what the heck was under there.

A long ladder was secured to the steel-reinforced concrete wall next to the opening, and Joe carefully stepped down into the underground vault. He looked up to the entrance door and estimated that he was about twenty feet underground. He then looked all around and decided that the place could use an interior decorator. The walls, ceiling, and floors were made of steel—and painted white. Very white. Almost like an insane asylum, or at least that's what he pictured from the movies. There were two rooms: the ten-by-ten-foot entrance area that he was now standing in, and something behind a massive round door that resembled the one you would find in a bank vault. Joe tried to turn the handle, but the door was locked and there was no combination dial. Instead, he noticed a digital timer that read *00:53:16* and was counting backward. Joe guessed that meant the door would open in a little over fifty-three minutes. He assumed someone was controlling the lock from a central location. The bad news was that the spacemen would probably be back in less than an hour.

Joe's nosiness got the best of him. He decided to wait out the time and see what was in the second room. Whenever he hiked, Joe carried a Ruger LCP .380 caliber pistol in his camera bag. He had no desire to be poisoned by a rattlesnake or eaten by a coyote. If the men in spacesuits returned, Joe would just threaten them. He could never kill a human being.

Joe climbed back up the ladder and looked around for a hiding place. He found a robust netleaf hackberry tree that had grown out of control and had reached stately proportions—a perfect place for concealment in the desert. He pulled his wide-brimmed, floppy safari hiking hat down over his eyes and waited. Joe gripped the gun tightly in his right hand while he nervously checked his watch every few seconds. If he had synchronized his timepiece correctly, there should be thirty-five minutes before the underground vault door opened. Drops of sweat beaded on his forehead.

Five minutes before the timer approached zero, Joe heard an engine noise. It didn't sound like the Humvee, rather more like a motorcycle. Joe peeked around the tree trunk and saw a four-wheel ATV with an attached cargo basket heading his way. It stopped a few feet from the entrance to the vault. A very large man with a bushy beard got off and removed the same type of laser weapon from the basket that Joe had seen earlier. The man inspected the barrel and electronic trigger mechanism, then placed it back into the cargo hold. The big fella was wearing blue jeans and an oil-stained t-shirt with some gobbledygook written on it:

Будем здоровы!

In contrast to the two men Joe saw just an hour ago who were wearing spacesuit type uniforms, this guy had no protective gear. It appeared his t-shirt was no match for his muscles either. The bulk of his biceps had ripped the short sleeves open. Joe looked at his Ruger and back at his intended target. He wasn't sure a .380 caliber bullet would do much damage to this man. So, instead of jumping out and scaring the dude, he hesitated and watched from behind the tree as Mr. Mass descended the steps.

Joe guessed that the electronic vault door would open and stay that way until a human being closed it. Then, the automatic timer would be reset at the central operations building. Joe wasn't sure which structure that was because he had noticed on previous hikes that two buildings existed.

Two minutes later, the man emerged from the tunnel with a long and slender cylinder container that looked like a perfectly-shaped, oversized cucumber. It had a green light on it that was blinking. Mr. Mass walked over to the ATV and slid the cylinder into the handle of the laser weapon. That's when an alarm rang from inside the vault, but another bell could be heard somewhere in the distance.

Joe was confused. What was happening? The alarm in the vault and the one in the distance started at the same time. They both must have been triggered when the gigantic man exited the chamber. Joe placed the Ruger at his feet and quickly pulled out his camera, then exchanged the macro lens with the telephoto. Mr. Mass took out goggles from the glove compartment of the ATV, put them on, and then tramped several yards into the desert. He was heading towards the sound coming from the remote alarm. When he was a football field length away, the man kneeled, placed the laser gun on his shoulder, and aimed it towards the area of the alarm. Joe panned the direction of Mr. Mass's aim with the telephoto lens, and he realized the man's target. Joe zoomed all the way to the max and saw a sign on the building that read:

Senso-McNamara Headquarters.

The sign was underneath a flashing red light, which Joe assumed was part of the alarm system that had been triggered. He set the camera back to continuous shooting mode, focused in on Mr. Mass, and pushed down the button. Seconds later, a narrow beam of light blew the headquarters to smithereens. Although it was from a back angle, Joe got a clear picture of the man firing the weapon, and a clear picture of Senso-Mac engulfed in flames. When Mr. Mass turned around and hustled back to the ATV, Joe had a mug shot for the ages. The network television stations would make him rich and famous!

But Joe wanted more. After the man took off in the ATV, Joe changed his camera back to a regular lens, then ran to the vault's entrance and climbed down. The alarm was driving him batty, as were the flashing red lights coming from behind the open vault door. Thank God the man left the door open! When he reached the bottom of the steps, Joe debated going any further. The alarm was deafening, and the red lights were causing him headaches! But just when he was about to get back onto the steps and leave, mysteriously, the alarm and lights stopped.

Joe quickly surveyed the plain entryway where he was standing and saw that the circular door with the timer was wide open. He noticed that it led to another nondescript chamber. Joe ducked and entered. In this room, the floor slanted downward at a small incline and continued for a hundred yards until it reached the far wall. There was no paint on the walls, floor, or ceiling—just a dark, bronze-colored metal trapdoor. Joe looked up and saw the four air vents in the roof, then he glanced down at the six-by-three-foot trapdoor that had no handle. "So, how does someone open this contraption?" thought Joe.

The entire vault was very well lit with LED lights running the length of the ceiling. Joe found two buttons on the wall next to the door that he assumed were light switches. He pushed the first one to test it out, and the trapdoor began to rattle. Joe had one foot on the door at the time and jumped back. The trapdoor lowered itself electronically beneath the steel base, then automatically slid parallel to the floor and tucked itself neatly out of the opening. Joe gazed into the chamber and gasped. Everyone who thought Senso-Mac was testing police radars was dead wrong. Underneath the vault was another subchamber filled with cylindrical containers labeled with a minatory warning:

EXTREME DANGER!!
CONTAINS A MIXTURE OF
NEUTRON, ULTRAVIOLET, & INFRARED
RADIOACTIVE MATERIALS!!

Joe lifted out his camera and snapped away, getting explicit close-ups of serial numbers embedded on the oversized laser bullets of mass destruction. After filling a full gigabyte of digital pictures onto his SanDisk flash memory card, he stood back up and decided to push the other button on the wall. Surely it must be the light switch! Wrong. Moments later, the room dimmed, the far wall opened, and a hologram of a Boeing 777 airplane appeared. The plane rose and fell, moved across the backdrop, disappeared off to the right, and reappeared on the left. On the fuselage was painted a red circle, no doubt the laser gun's target.

Joe was confused as he stared at the hologram. He understood the concept of target practice, but he couldn't grasp how shooting a weapon filled with a highly radioactive laser beam at a wall one hundred yards away would be considered safe operating procedures outlined in the company's employee handbook! He knew that ultraviolet rays could blind you, and infrared radiation could burn you, which wasn't what concerned him at the moment. Neutron radiation was associated with nuclear fission, and flying neutrons could penetrate lead, iron, and steel! What kept the laser beam from crumbling this entire chamber?

Joe walked through the hologram and saw that a nine-foot square wooden frame an inch deep was attached to the back wall directly behind the target. There was some kind of hard material inside the box. Joe touched it gently with his fingertips. Concrete? He looked down and noticed cement residue on the floor by his feet, and he was puzzled. A laser beam powerful enough to shake the ground like an earthquake is rendered harmless by a piece of driveway?!

Then he remembered the question he missed on his high school physics test. Neutrons can penetrate virtually everything—except hydrogen-rich materials such as water. And concrete.

Joe felt the steel wall behind the frame, looked down at the corners of the chamber, then looked up at the ceiling. Behind a small, yet thick, rectangular plexiglass plate was a series of tiny lenses that produced the hologram. Joe craned his neck and peered up to see what was flashing below the lenses. It was a digital readout with a warning:

Laser Photon Activated!

"Laser photon? What laser photon?" Joe was talking to himself. He aimed his camera and took pictures of everything he could see. Six hundred to be exact! When he was sure he had photographed every square inch of the vault, Joe decided to get out of there fast, and he ran back to the entrance. As soon as the chaos at Senso-Mac ended, no doubt there would be investigations taking place right where he was standing.

Joe pushed the button to close the trapdoor, then he noticed it. There was a dial switch on the side wall that he hadn't seen. The letters *VR* were imprinted on the center of the dial. Perhaps this was the on-off-dimmer switch for the LED lights. Joe was about to test the dimmer, then hesitated.

"VR. What does VR stand for?" Joe whispered the question to himself. "Well, what the hell. I ain't got much to lose at this point." He pushed the button and waited for the lights to go off. They didn't. Instead, the hologram flickered, and a new one appeared. On this image, though, only the nose and cockpit of the 777 could be seen off to the left. It was just frozen there like a nebulous specter waiting to explode.

Not knowing what to do, Joe thought about turning the dial. Would that make the hologram brighter? Yes, that's it! It must be a dimmer switch for the hologram. Joe turned the dial to the right. Instead of the jet becoming brighter, it started to move slowly across the far wall. Joe stopped, and the 777 stopped too. He twisted the button to the left, and the image shifted back to where it started. Now it dawned on Joe. *VR* must be *Video Replay.* He pushed the button several times, and each time a different type of aircraft appeared in a hologram on the left side of the far wall. Joe glanced at his watch. He had already been in the vault too long, but he needed to see what happened to the airplane images. The hologram now on display was a Boeing 747.

Joe turned the dial slowly to his right, and the plane moved into full view. It banked and rose, then circled and dropped. Joe was controlling the speed of the previously recorded image. Once, he rotated the dial back to the left and watched the plane fly in reverse just to see if he was missing something. Then he stopped and peered at the letters marked clearly on the plane's fuselage: *United States of America.* On the tail of the jet was the presidential seal. The hologram was an image of Air Force One.

Joe again turned the dial to the right very gently, and the 747 moved across the screen in slow motion, gaining altitude and banking left and right. When the hologram was centered, a red target appeared on the jet's emergency door. Almost instantaneously, an explosion could be seen. Joe turned the dial back to the left for a replay. Then he deliberately moved the image forward, frequently stopping to inspect the entire hologram. As he inched the 747 forward frame-by-frame, Joe noticed a laser beam coming into view. When it hit the target, Air Force One disintegrated in midair, and concrete chips could be seen flying in the background. The hologram suddenly ended its feed. Joe turned the dial and replayed the video several times. He needed to find out where the hard drive for the video recorder was hiding. CNN would make him a millionaire!

Joe went back to the far wall to get a picture of the hologram lenses and digital laser photon warning that was still flashing. He wasn't tall enough to snap a close-up shot of what was behind the plexiglass, but his telephoto certainly could. Joe fastened the lens to the Canon and zoomed in. He could distinctly see the optical components that created the holograms, but he couldn't find the video recorder or the hard drive. Then it occurred to him that the video lens must be on the other end of the vault near the entrance because the images showed the hologram and chipped concrete, not the hologram and the shooter.

As he turned to go back and examine the opposite wall, the floor began to shake, and Joe froze. The section he was standing on was collapsing slowly downward like an elevator. He was standing on another trapdoor as it descended eight feet and stopped abruptly. Joe turned 360 degrees, but he was afraid to move forward. He was now in another vast underground chamber that extended in all directions. Directly in front of him was a plastic recycling container. Joe moved cautiously and lifted the lid. It was filled with empty cylinders, the same type Joe found loaded in the other subchamber.

"Hmmm, recycling the laser energy packs," whispered Joe to himself. "Those that seek to kill the president seem to want to save the environment. Penance for breaking the sixth commandment, I guess."

A few feet from the recycling bin was a long, wide, and thick wooden bench. Stacked on it were bags of cement, cartons of water, and crates of aggregate—sand, gravel, and pebbles. Apparently, the back wall of the shooting gallery needed to be frequently repaired with new concrete. Joe took a step forward, then stopped dead in his tracks. He dropped the camera, shattering the telephoto lens.

Behind one of the crates was a man lying in a pool of blood with a knife wound in his back. He was gasping for air. Joe regained his composure and dashed for the man. He turned him on his side to keep the man from choking on his own blood, then grabbed a box of lens cleaners from his camera bag and placed all fifty of them onto the laceration. Joe pressed hard on the tissues with his right hand while lifting the man's head off the ground with his left. He wasn't a medic, nor did he much care for the sight of blood, but he could see that the one-inch gash was just below the neck. It was too high for the heart or a lung, but the blade might have caught an artery or vein. Regardless, the man was in shock and had lost a lot of blood. Joe kept pressure on the cut and put several nearby towels on him for warmth.

Visions and thoughts were scrambling around in Joe's mind, and he was having a difficult time processing what had taken place since seeing the light flash from the pipes during his hike. Trying to make sense of it all, he assumed the two men in spacesuits had been testing the lasers by firing them at a hologram image of a jet aircraft. To prevent the vault from disintegrating, Joe guessed the radioactive beam was absorbed into the concrete frame, but some particles in the aggregate were not hydrogen-rich. One foreign particle could cause the concrete to chip and vibrations to occur; many foreign particles would ultimately cause the earth to shake. If a beam happened to miss the concrete frame altogether, the chamber would dissolve, leaving an enormous sinkhole in the ground. His own home and the whole neighborhood would then be at risk!

The man now bleeding in his lap must be the lab's maintenance guy who cleaned up residue after tests and reinstalled new concrete in the frame for the next experiment. Whoever the gigantic man was that he saw from behind the tree most likely entered the vault to steal the laser energy packs. He must have arrived while the man was cleaning up, stabbed him in the back, and left him to die while he blew up the Senso-Mac headquarters building.

Joe muttered again to himself, "That mammoth man is obviously the enemy, right? But if that's true, why were the men in the spacesuits shooting at a hologram of Air Force One?" He lifted the red-stained tissues just enough to check out the man's wound, and it appeared the blood had stopped flowing. The man coughed and blinked, then closed his eyes and took a deep breath. Joe kept holding the tissues while he gently shook the man. "Wake up! Are you awake? Can you hear me?"

The man nodded slightly and blinked again. He was straining to keep his eyes open. Joe decided that it was time to get them both to safety. He knew he couldn't carry both the camera bag and the injured man at the same time, so he ejected the SanDisk from the Canon and slipped it into his pocket. The camera was unfunctional after he dropped it and would have to be replaced anyway. But the flash memory had a valuable record of the day's events.

The man was over six-feet tall and weighed around 220 pounds. "Can you hold on if I carry you on my back?" asked Joe. The man nodded. Although Joe had a slightly herniated disk that caused sciatic pain, it was his only option if he was to get the man out of the vault.

Joe had a roll of masking tape in his camera bag that he used to label items during a shoot. He pulled off several strips and fastened the semi-dried bloody tissues to the man's back, then rolled the remainder of the tape around the man's torso. Hopefully, it would hold until he got the man to a hospital. Joe bent over. The man was able to stand and slide into position onto Joe's back and wrap his arms around his neck. Joe grunted and struggled to lift the man; the sciatic nerve was causing overwhelming pain. He labored a hundred yards to the ladder, held tight onto the rail, and grappled with each agonizing step. Sirens could be heard in the distance, a sign that fire trucks were racing to Senso-Mac headquarters. After finally reaching the vault's door and exiting, Joe collapsed onto the desert rocks. The man unlocked his grip from Joe's neck, slowly slid off his back, and was lying face-to-face with him in the dirt. He was now very much conscious, probably from all the bouncing.

"By the way, my name is Roger. Roger Bennett. Thanks, man." Joe and Roger needed a short rest, and they both closed their eyes. The sirens were getting louder.

When they heard the rattle, both men opened their eyes but did not flinch. Roger murmured, "Don't move. Not one muscle. Stay still." Seconds later, a seven-foot Western Diamondback rattlesnake slithered between their noses—and stopped! Its black-forked tongue was waving back-and-forth just inches from their terrified faces. Any sudden movement and the pit viper would strike either Roger's or Joe's neck. If its fangs sunk into the carotid artery, the venom would kill within minutes. Joe needed to sneeze.

A KPNX news helicopter that had been flying along the Salt River Canal moved in for a closeup view of the Senso-Mac fire. The roaring of the whirlybird's propellers distracted the rattlesnake, and the reptile continued down the path, wiggling back and forth between Joe and Roger's legs. After holding their breaths for almost a minute, both men exhaled at the same time. Joe stood up and prepared himself to transport Roger on his back, but Roger shook his head no.

"I'm okay, thanks to you. I think I can do this on my own." Roger struggled a bit but was able to stand. The masking tape had torn but was still effectively holding the bloodstained lens tissues firmly on his wound. "You mind telling me your name?"

"Joe. Joe Freeman. Glad you're alive, but we need to get to a hospital to make sure you're okay."

"No, I'm good. What's burning over there?" Roger pointed. More and more sirens could be heard in the distance.

"It's the Senso-Mac headquarters," replied Joe.

"What?! That's where I work! How can that be?!"

Joe shot a perplexing look into Roger's eyes. How much does this guy know? Did he not hear the explosion after Mr. Mass blew the Senso-Mac building to kingdom come with his laser weapon?

"Who was the man that stabbed you?" asked Joe.

"I don't know. He surprised me. Bud and Jack had come down for a laser weapon test-firing experiment, as they do twice a week. I was cleaning up the debris and mixing concrete when a huge bulk of a man jumped down into the pit with a knife. I started to run, but he caught me and stabbed me. The next thing I remember was you pressing on my neck."

Joe looked all around to make sure Mr. Mass was nowhere in sight. He was in a hurry but needed to know what Roger did for Senso-Mac. "What do you mean by test-firing a laser weapon? I thought Senso-Mac made sensors and things like that."

Roger looked down at the ground and paused. "I can't tell you, Joe. It's classified, and I've been sworn to secrecy."

"I just saved your life, damn it! And after what I just witnessed out here, chances are it may need saving again! Along with my own!" Spittle was ejecting from Joe's mouth. "That Goliath of a man that stabbed you also fired a laser beam that destroyed your company!"

"Did he shoot at the Homeland Security building, too?" Roger took a few steps forward into a clearing to try and get a good look.

"Homeland Security has a building here? Why? I knew they built a fence around the Senso-Mac property, which ticked off all my neighbors and me, but I didn't know they also had a building. What's the purpose of that?"

"I don't know, they just do. No one at our company knows about it except Bud and Jack. I heard them talking about it one day. It's over there, and it appears to be okay." Roger pointed in the direction of the structure. "We should go there; it would be safe. I'm sure they have agents who could protect us if that giant returns."

Joe hesitated but decided that Roger might be right. The building was closer than his home, and it was in the opposite direction of the seven-foot rattlesnake and that herd of javelinas! Could all this really be happening? He just wanted some lovely photographs of a springtime sunset. What on God's green earth had he stumbled upon?

They moved only as fast as Roger could go, which fortunately was a faster pace than Joe would have expected for a man who just recovered from a near-death episode. Amazing what a little adrenaline will do for the human motor! But even though Joe was behind Roger, he saw it first.

"Stop!" Joe shouted, and Roger froze in his tracks. Roger was sure another rattlesnake was approaching.

"Where's the dang snake? I don't see it!"

"Not a snake, Roger. Worse. We need to turn around and get out of the desert fast!"

"Worse than a rattlesnake?! What is it?"

"Look ahead about fifty yards," said Joe as he pointed down the path they were heading.

"I only see the Homeland Security building, Joe. That's where we are going."

"There's a rather large man guarding the front door."

"Probably because of the explosion at Senso-Mac. What's the problem?"

"The problem is that guard. I recognize him and the ATV that's parked next to the building."

"Are you thinking that could be the SOB that knifed me?!"

"I have no doubt. Not only did he try to kill you, but he was also the one who blew up your employer!"

"Who is he? Why me?!"

"An even bigger question—why is there a Homeland Security division hidden out here in the desert next to a police speed radar plant?"

"Because Senso-Mac also makes deadly laser weapons. I think you know that now."

"No one else seems to know that except for the workers like you who have been sworn to secrecy. Everyone else in Mesa thinks it's just a harmless sensor and rangefinder factory."

"Sorry, Joe," said Roger. "I do not understand you."

"Okay, follow me. Senso-Mac has a secret underground vault that stores highly destructive laser energy packs. Those energy packs are tested with laser weapons and hologram targets. One of the hologram targets is of Air Force One, the others are of passenger jets. Obviously, there is some plan being devised by Senso-Mac to take down Air Force One and other jets. If not, why would they use them as targets? So that brings me to this: how could Homeland Security not know that their next-door neighbor is producing laser technology that could kill the president? And why did they build a fence around both Senso-Mac and the Homeland Security property? They are working together, Roger! And working to do something that could change history if my guess is right."

Roger stared at Joe, pondering everything he just heard. He was dumbfounded and didn't know how to respond. Roger thought that if Joe was correct, then he was in big trouble. After all, he worked for Senso-Mac! Roger didn't know much about Senso-Mac's operations. He just cashed his weekly paycheck and asked no questions.

"The holograms—I know this sounds awfully flimsy, but I never thought twice about the targets being Air Force One or civilian jets," said Roger remorsefully. With a pleading look for pity, he continued, "Honestly, Joe, I'm telling the truth. I should have wondered, but I didn't."

"Back to my house," ordered Joe. He believed that Roger was oblivious to covert actions taking place inside his company. "As fast as we can go! Are you able to make it, Roger?"

"Have to," replied Roger. "I'm beginning to think the other option would be even more hazardous to my health!"

Joe felt into his pocket to make sure he still had the SanDisk memory card. He needed to get a backup copy onto his computer's hard drive quickly, and then upload the files to the cloud. Roger and Joe hastened back to Red Mountain Ranch as smoke from the Senso-Mac fire drifted overhead.

*****

Until the screened flashed and went dead on his security monitor, Homeland Security Agent Gene Schultz had watched Agent Loren Schoenholtz enter the vault, slash a Senso-Mac worker in the back with a knife, then leave with an activated laser energy pack in his gigantic hand. As Senso-Mac employee Roger Bennett was writhing in agony in his own blood and approaching death, his long arms were able to reach out and press the emergency button embedded into the floorboard. When the alarms sounded in the vault, it caused a power surge, which in turn blew a fuse that knocked out power to Schultz's tiny spy cameras that had been placed strategically throughout the chamber and couldn't be seen with the naked eye.

"We need to get back to the vault and extract those laser energy packs. While we're there, we need to replace that fuse," stated Schultz as he walked past Schoenholtz to the ATV. "Let's go!"

"Replace the fuse. Why? The plan was to grab the energy packs, blow this Homeland Security building sky-high just like I did Senso-Mac, and get the hell out of here! There's to be nothing left of either Senso-Mac or this building for the firemen or FBI or whoever to find! What purpose does replacing a blown fuse down in the vault serve?"

"We may need those cameras again sometime, Schoenholtz! Don't argue with me! Once the fuse is replaced, we can secure the vault. Every Senso-Mac employee who knows about the vault just perished from your death ray or was knifed to death inside the vault."

"How do you know they all died?"

"Well, take a look, genius!" Schultz pointed at the flaming wreckage that was now being surrounded by fire trucks, ambulances, and police cars. "Do you really think anyone could survive that?"

"What about employees that may have been absent today, or on vacation, or playing hooky on the golf course?" Schultz was his boss, but Schoenholtz wasn't about to be intimidated. After all, he was six-foot-eight and weighed in at 300 pounds, all muscle. Both he and Schultz had been German artillery and ammunition designers for a company contracted by the US government, and they were the best of friends. You couldn't tell that by listening to them.

"I verified that all the Senso-Mac employees who knew of the vault were at work. Only those with a security clearance of nine or above were in the loop about that operation. Their human resource and payroll files are online, which I've hacked. So, yes, I know they were at work today."

Schultz went behind the building and came back riding an ATV while Schoenholtz mounted his own four-wheeler. The ATV's were identical twins, designed and built by Schultz and Schoenholtz after the men were hired by Homeland Security as border patrol agents and assigned to a remodeled apartment complex in Sells, Arizona. They became friends with Miguel Santos, who owned a garage next to the Tohono O'odham Justice Center. Miguel knew how to change oil, but anything more problematic than that and your car was at risk.

But Miguel had a bunch of space, and at night he would host poker games for the border patrol agents who were being paid to secure the border while his brother Angel smuggled family and friends into Sells from Mexico. Schultz and Schoenholtz didn't much care about gambling, so they spent the time building ATVs and other fun stuff out of metal scraps from cars that Miguel ruined. When the two German friends were reassigned to monitor the Homeland Security building next to Senso-Mac, they brought all their toys with them.

After kicking up a dust storm with their ATVs, Schultz and Schoenholtz arrived at the vault three minutes later. Schultz glanced at the entryway, then he looked at Schoenholtz and shook his head in disgust.

"What?!" demanded Schoenholtz when he noted Schultz's aversion.

"The damn door," announced Schultz. "You left it open!"

"I was in a hurry! I just killed a man and was about to kill many more. Pardon my lack of attention to detail! Besides, if I would have shut the inside door, the timer would have reset."

"We can override the damn timer, you idiot! Just get the energy packs and load them on the ATVs! I'll change the fuse."

"You think you can handle it? I mean, a fuse must weigh in at an ounce or two." Sarcasm was another weapon in Schoenholtz's armory.

Schultz descended the ladder first and stopped when he reached the floor. Schoenholtz was right behind him and wondered why he wasn't moving. Schultz pulled a pistol out of a small holster on his belt, then motioned to Schoenholtz to take his knife out of its sheath. Loren didn't like guns, except for the laser variety!

"What is it?" asked Schoenholtz in a low voice. "You see something?"

"Look at the floor—and here on the steps. Blood!"

"Blood!" repeated Schoenholtz. "Where did it come from?"

"Were you bleeding when you took the cylinders out?"

"No, I don't think so."

"Where is the body of the guy you sliced?"

"Down at the end in the compartment under the floor. You're not thinking a dead man could walk out of here, are you?

"No, not a dead man, you nincompoop! But if he was still alive, that means you failed!

"No way he could survive. I slashed him good."

Schultz and Schoenholtz moved slowly through the circular door into the shooting chamber, then towards the far wall where the trapdoor had dropped. They climbed down, Schultz with his gun drawn and Schoenholtz resting his hand on the knife. They saw a small pool of dried blood where Schoenholtz had attacked the man, but no body.

"Well, I'll be damned," said Schoenholtz while pondering what could have happened to the man.

"Yeah, you'll be damned, alright!" stated Schultz. "You let him get away. Now you need to find him before he spills his guts!"

"I'm afraid it may be too late," mused Schoenholtz.

"What's that supposed to mean?!"

"Look over there," he pointed to the broken camera lying on the floor. "That camera wasn't here when I knifed that guy. I'm guessing whoever it belongs to found our man and tried to save him. The man I sliced must be dead, right?"

"You better hope so," said Schultz. He squatted down, picked up the camera, and then checked the memory slot. "But we better find out who owns this camera. The flash memory is missing. I'm assuming it's filled with all sorts of goodies that we don't want people to know about."

"And how do we do that?"

"The Canon camera body is professional-grade, but it can probably be found in most camera stores. However, this telephoto lens is very powerful and unique. I'm assuming it's not sold in many places around the Valley. Too expensive for a hobbyist, which means whoever owned the camera is most likely a professional photographer."

"What are you thinking, Gene?"

"First, we need to demolish the Homeland Security building as planned. Then, we need to blow up the vault to destroy any evidence of a crime. And then—"

Schoenholtz interrupted, "How do you expect to do that?! This vault is very solid."

"The workbench," said Schultz. "That's how."

"The damn workbench is made of wood!" responded Schoenholtz. "Wood ain't gonna make a dent in this solid steel chamber!"

Schultz smiled at Schoenholtz, grabbed a screwdriver from a nearby toolbox, and then crawled underneath the bench. Lying on his back, he reached up and unfastened a long, oddly-shaped metal cylinder and laid it gently on the ground. It resembled an oversized baseball bat, like the plastic kind that small children use to hit whiffle balls.

"What the heck is that contraption?!" asked Schoenholtz.

"That there contraption is our only option. The boss had plans to use it in the future, and he asked me to hide it in a safe spot. This subchamber under the vault was the safest place I could find."

"That's not what I asked!" retorted Schoenholtz. "What is it?!"

"I'll tell you later. We need to get it out of the vault, and we need to remove the rest of the energy packs from the storage area near the entrance. Grab the camera and put it in that garbage bag over there. We'll take it with us."

Schoenholtz put the camera into the plastic sack and tossed it over his shoulder. The bat-shaped cylinder weighed fifty pounds, and Schultz struggled as he carried it to the entryway. After moving it the length of a football field, Schultz placed it on the ground next to the ladder so he could take a rest. His back was killing him.

"You take it up the ladder, and I'll take the camera," ordered Schultz. "You could use the exercise. All that German beer has gone straight to your belly!"

"Smartass," replied Schoenholtz. "But, I ain't gonna do nothing unless you tell me what this damn thing is!"

"Just get it up the ladder, and I'll show you!"

With minimal effort, Schoenholtz placed the cylinder on his shoulder and climbed out of the vault. He laid it on the ground and reached down to help his partner exit. While Schultz was brushing himself off, Schoenholtz said sarcastically, "Perhaps you're too old and feeble for this line of work. I hear they're hiring Walmart greeters these days!"

Schultz ignored the comment and kneeled next to the bat-shaped container. He unscrewed a cap from the smaller end, peered inside the cylinder, then placed the lid back on and turned it just once.

"Wait here. I'll be right back." Schultz hustled to Schoenholtz's ATV, placed the camera into the cargo basket, grabbed the laser weapon, and hurried back to his partner. Without saying a word, Schultz once again uncapped the end of the container, then inserted the barrel of the laser weapon inside to see if it fit as designed. When he was satisfied that it fit perfectly, he pulled the gun out and handed it to Schoenholtz.

Schoenholtz took the weapon and stared at Schultz, more confused than ever!

"Okay, big fella, do your thing," said Schultz as he pointed at the Homeland Security building in the distance.

Scratching his head, Schoenholtz asked, "Will you please tell me what's inside the bat? Sometime before your grandchildren have grandchildren!"

"Uranium-235," responded Schultz calmly.

Schoenholtz's eyes widened, and he let out a gasp. "Nuclear fission?" he asked rhetorically. "You've created an atomic bomb!"

"Just a small one, Loren. It will easily take care of this vault and a few desert critters that live nearby. The coyote population is getting out of hand, anyway!"

"So, now you're an expert on nuclear reactions?! How can you be so sure it will be just a small one?! If you're wrong, there won't be much left of Mesa. And worse yet, how are we going to get far enough away before this whole thing blows?!"

"First, we need to place the container back into the vault and remove the rest of the energy packs. After you're done lighting up Homeland Security, we'll attach the gun to the container and pull the trigger. The laser neutrons will react with the uranium, which will cause fission. If my estimates are right, we'll have about twenty minutes to get away before the bomb explodes."

"Sure thing, Einstein! I can't imagine a renowned scientist such as yourself would be off on any of your calculations! Well, I guess that means we don't need to change the stupid fuse!"

Schoenholtz carried the uranium-235 container back down the ladder and placed it next to the subchamber storage trapdoor. Both men hurried to get the energy packs out of the vault and into their ATV cargo hold. At the same time, at least thirty fire trucks and emergency vehicles had descended on Senso-Mac headquarters. Red lights were flashing, and hosed water was spraying from all directions. Television news helicopters were competing for airspace even though the police choppers had warned them to stay back.

With the ATVs running and ready for a fast getaway, Schoenholtz loaded an energy pack into the laser gun and walked quickly into a clearing that would give an unobstructed view of the Homeland Security building. He was an avid hunter who never missed his target. He hunted red deer stags each fall in the Bavarian forest of his German homeland, providing delicious food for the table and deer head mounts for the wall of his cabin. He built the cabin away from roads and any form of civilization near the Czech border. No electricity, just water from a well he dug out back. Someday, Loren would retire to that cabin to live out his days, but for now, he needed to make sure he didn't miss his target. He was still upset about failing to kill the man in the vault.

The missile found its mark, and the Homeland Security building was no more. The explosion startled every firefighter and police officer who were tending to the Senso-Mac headquarters. The fire chief called the Scottsdale, Glendale, and even Tucson fire departments asking for backup, while the police chief called the Department of Public Safety, pleading for as many officers as they could spare. That call was intercepted by the Phoenix Homeland Security Office, who monitored all police activity throughout major cities in the southwest.

Needless to say, the receptionist who was minding the radio was disconcerted. She immediately pulled up a satellite image of the area. Sure enough, it was their top-secret remote center near Senso-McNamara that was now in flames! No firefighters or policemen at the site would have any idea it was a Homeland Security building; they would most likely think it belonged to Senso-Mac. The receptionist wasn't sure of protocol now. Their special agent in charge, Earl Kelly, was busy working a disaster that occurred earlier in Gila Bend and Ajo. Should she notify Washington, or get ahold of Kelly and let him sort things out? She opted to call Kelly's cell phone.

"What?!" exclaimed Kelly as he was about to pull into the Maricopa County Sheriff's Office parking lot in Phoenix. He and Gordy Owens had just dropped off the dead ICE agent's Apple watch and gold ring at the FBI lab, and Owens needed to check in with his partner, Ken Smith. From the front passenger seat of the Corvette, Owens gave Kelly a puzzled look.

Kelly shouted into the mouthpiece, "You've got to be kidding me! Blown up! Are you sure?" Kelly and Owens sat in neutral with the motor running as his receptionist filled him in on the details.

He glanced over at Owens. "I hope you don't have a late afternoon tee time planned! After all that has happened today, I think you should come with me."

"Come with you where? What's going on?"

"Someone or something has destroyed a covert Homeland Security building next to the Senso-Mac building in Mesa. And to top it off, the Senso-Mac building had been destroyed moments earlier." Kelly shifted into drive, and the wide Vette tires squealed out onto Third Avenue. The rubber treads had taken quite a beating today.

"I assume you're treating me to dinner?" asked Owens sarcastically.

Chapter 24

Tuesday, April 17, 2018
Skies Over Senso-McNamara Corporation, Mesa, Arizona
4:05 pm (Pacific Daylight Time)

"What . . . the . . . hell?!" said Cliff Bullard aloud, although no one could hear him in the Aerovictor cockpit except himself. "Not this again!"

Cliff had noticed a rather large man in blue jeans and a t-shirt scrambling towards a four-wheel ATV carrying what appeared to be a shoulder-held weapon of some sort. Then he noticed another man waiting near a second ATV. Is it possible they were the culprits who had obliterated Senso-Mac? Cliff was beginning to wonder what the actual job description of his new career as a test pilot really entailed! First, he had destroyed a Russian Mil Mi-17 on what was supposed to be an unmemorable mission over the desert wasteland south of Gila Bend, and now this!

Cliff dropped altitude and flew only a few feet above the saguaros as he cruised towards the men. Neither had noticed Cliff approaching, most likely because the noise from the news choppers had drowned out the sound from his Aerovictor's propeller blades. But as Cliff was closing in, both men glanced up at him.

"It's an Aerovictor!" yelled Schoenholtz. "How did they get the Army out here that fast?! We need to leave! Now!"

"We ain't gonna outrun an Aerovictor! Are you kidding me?! If the chain gun is loaded, we're history! I'm taking him out!" Schoenholtz picked up the laser gun and was ready to reload when the Aerovictor buzzed his ATV only a few feet overhead.

Schoenholtz dropped his weapon and dove to the ground. Schultz did the same. Cliff banked quickly and circled back. He had used up most of the thirty-millimeter rounds in Ajo and really didn't want to engage in any more combat. He was just a damn test pilot, for God's sake!

While Cliff was banking, Schoenholtz slammed the camouflaged door shut. He and Schultz then hustled to their ATVs and gunned the throttles. Blowing up the underground chamber was no longer an option. If they survived this getaway, perhaps they would return and finish the job. Better yet, if they survived this getaway, perhaps they would escape to Schoenholtz's cabin in Bavaria and live happily ever after! Joe Freeman's broken camera bounced around in the basket of Schoenholtz's ATV next to the laser gun and a load of energy packs taken from the vault. As the two perpetrators escaped into a dry wash, the Aerovictor was close behind.

Cliff lifted the Sunagor Mega Zoom binoculars to his eyes to get a better look at the men, and then struggled to catch his breath. "Huh?" he muttered when he saw it. The license plates on both ATVs read ***US Department of Homeland Security***. It was imprinted inside a circular coat of arms along with an eagle wearing a shield. Cliff pulled back on the cyclic and raised the collective. The Aerovictor rose and turned towards the Salt River. He wasn't about to mess with Homeland Security.

Schultz and Schoenholtz stopped in the wash, and both squinted towards the sky when they noticed the Aerovictor had given up the chase. They looked at each other and shrugged. Puzzling indeed!

"What the heck?" said Schultz. Both men were perplexed.

"He could have wasted us with the chain gun. Why didn't he?" asked Schoenholtz.

"We probably don't want to know. Let's move. We need to find out who owns that camera!"

*****

Cliff circled back and hovered over the desert a mile away from all the action taking place on the ground. He was careful not to interfere with the police helicopters and news choppers, although he assumed the police wished the reporters would keep their distance. There were now two fires a short span from the Red Mountain Ranch subsection of Mesa: one had turned into dark black smoke, while the second was blazing away with red and orange fury. Emergency vehicles were haphazardly scattering about trying to deal with both fires simultaneously.

Cliff kept pressing the call button on his radio, but still no response. That would be the only failure on this test mission. The maneuverability and weaponry had worked just fine. He was about to circle around and return to Zefron when a thought occurred. What if the events in Ajo today were somehow related to the events going on below him? Cliff was certain those were Russian helicopters he destroyed earlier. If the men he had chased down below were Russian and not working for Homeland Security, well that would be more than just a coincidence. Could it be possible that Arizona was under attack by Russia? For the sake of his country's welfare, Cliff needed to find out. But once he was done, he would park the Aerovictor back at Zefron, fire up his Harley, and ride off to greener pastures. His test pilot days would end on the day they started. Cliff turned back around in search of the two Homeland Security ATVs and those big dudes driving them.

4:30 pm (Pacific Daylight Time)

Special Agent Kelly and Deputy Sheriff Owens exited the Red Mountain Freeway at Higley Road and sped north towards Senso-McNamara headquarters. A quarter-mile from Senso-Mac was a one-lane gravel road with a locked steel gate and a sign that read: ***No Trespassing - Keep Out!*** That was the entrance to the private driveway for the Homeland Security building. Senso-Mac employees drove past it every day and never once questioned what was beyond the gate. They assumed it was a testing ground for their company's speed guns.

Kelly carried the gate codes for all the Homeland Security properties located in the southwest. They were written in a small manual that he stored in the Corvette's glove compartment. He kept them there for convenience's sake, although he knew it was against regulations. Kelly pulled the car up to the digital security device that stuck up from the ground near the gate and punched in the code. The gate opened, and Kelly gunned the Vette through. Two fire trucks and three police vehicles had driven across the desert from Senso-Mac and were just starting to set up shop, while the remainder of the emergency team stayed with the first blast.

Owens noticed something peculiar. "Both buildings are almost burnt out," he stated.

"What do you mean?" asked Kelly as he surveyed the Homeland Security building, then glanced over at Senso-Mac a few hundred yards away.

"The firefighters couldn't put out a normal structure fire that fast. Which means that whatever walloped the buildings turned them to rubble almost immediately."

"I don't know about Senso-Mac, but the Homeland Security building was built of a one-foot solid steel core," said Kelly. "Only a mighty explosion could make even a dent. Whatever hit it is beyond my comprehension!"

"Any ideas?"

"We have two agents assigned to that building. Both are ex-German munitions experts who immigrated and were hired as border patrol agents. I know what you're thinking—immigrants protecting our border from immigrants, right? Anyway, they were reassigned to staff this facility. Don't ask me why; I had no say in the matter. It was a direct order from the vice president. So, if they were in that building a few minutes ago, most likely their fingers would now be in Apache Junction and their toes in Buckeye! But, my bigger concern is their work history. Senso-Mac secretly designs laser weaponry for our military, and coincidently, the two Homeland

Security agents are munitions experts. I think you can guess where I'm going here. Simply put, I didn't get a chance to do a background check on our German employees."

"The one coincidence I can plainly see is Ajo and Mesa. I've seen nasty things happen during my time at the sheriff's department, but never anything like I've seen today. This is bigger than both of us, Earl. We need to find some help."

"Yes, we do, but which direction we turn to find that help is our biggest problem."

"How so?"

"From what we saw in Ajo, I doubt we can ask Sheriff Urdano for help. And I'm not sure who we can trust in Washington."

Chapter 25

Tuesday, April 17, 2018
Salt River Canal, Mesa, Arizona
6:00 pm (Pacific Daylight Time)

When they heard the rumble of whirlybird blades, Schultz and Schoenholtz drove their ATVs out of the dry wash and parked next to the bank of the Salt River Canal, tucked neatly under cover by desert shrubs.

"He's back," stated Schultz ominously as he crouched next to his ATV and peered up into the sky.

"So why are we running, Gene?" asked Schoenholtz.

"What the hell do you mean, 'why are we running,' you idiot?! Perhaps it's because we just torched a private company, say nothing of a Homeland Security outpost!"

"I've been thinking that the helicopter chasing us can't be Army. Yes, it's an Aerovictor, but that probably means it was on a test mission for Zefron and not Army deployed. The pilot most likely is some peon dude who gets paid to fly around and have fun."

"Probably? Most likely? Those words aren't too assuring when you're in the business of terrorism! Regardless, whoever he works for is a moot point. He's a damn witness!"

"Think about it, Gene. It's doubtful he could have gotten a good description of us from that distance. And there are a ton of ATVs in the desert these days."

"What are you saying, Loren? That we should just mosey on like nothing ever happened?"

"I'm saying we hide here until he flies away, then we return to the Homeland Security building. I mean the ex-Homeland Security building."

"Are you completely nuts?! Are you suggesting we return to the scene of the crime and turn ourselves in?"

"Not turn ourselves in but offer some assistance. We work for Homeland Security, and some unknown entity just ruined our workplace. We can show our badges and offer to help out with the investigation."

"So, when they ask where we were when the building got blown up, what do we tell them?"

"We were securing some fences that hikers have torn down," replied Schoenholtz. "Them damn desert trekkers do it all the time. And that brings me to another idea."

"I hesitate to ask," said Schultz sarcastically.

"The underground vault is still intact. That Senso-Mac employee's blood is all over the place. And whoever owns the camera would have his fingerprints and DNA all around the chamber, too. I believe we can set up the hiker to take the fall for attempted murder—and blowing up the buildings. We just need to plant the camera back in the vault."

"What motive would a hiking photographer have to kill the Senso-Mac dude?! And we don't even know for sure if the dude died! How do we plant the camera without getting caught, genius?"

"We can come up with a motive later. Right now, the investigators will be circling the perimeter of the Senso-Mac building and Homeland Security building. On our way there, we stop at the vault and plant the camera. No one will see us."

"There's a damn container of uranium-35 lying on the vault floor! Won't that be suspicious when the feds start investigating?!"

"Not if we feed them what we want them to think. We say that we suspect the hiker was a terrorist that made atomic bombs in his garage or something. He was going to torch the place to cover up what happened but got scared. We can control the whole investigation of the vault. We work for Homeland Security, remember? I'm sure I can get the vice president to sign off on that if need be!"

"Okay, you may be right, Loren. But what about the Senso-Mac guy? If he survived your botched killing, he would corroborate the hiker's story."

"Yes, that could be a problem. If the Senso-Mac employee survived, he's most likely on the way to a hospital or urgent care center. We just need to make sure he doesn't survive, that's all. After we plant the camera and check in with whoever's investigating this mess, we'll find him. There are two urgent cares nearby. You go to the one next to Falcon Field over by the Walmart, and I'll check out the Regal Health Hospital that used to be a pizza place on Power Road. Flash your badge, but don't let them see your name. Ask if the dude was referred to a hospital or patched up and sent home. Get addresses! If he is still there, end him!"

"A pizza place turned hospital? What's this world coming to?!"

The chop-chop of the Aerovictor's blades was getting louder.

*****

Cliff circled back towards the canal and moved slowly at a low altitude, searching for the ATVs. The two riders couldn't have left the area that quickly, so they must be hiding. He rose forty feet and hovered to get a better view, then swept the desert with his binoculars.

"The son-of-a-bitch is going to find us and waste us!" exclaimed Schoenholtz. "I ain't gonna let that happen!" He yanked the laser gun from the ATV and loaded an energy pack.

"Calm down, Loren, and stick to our plan. If we blow up an Aerovictor, well, then there will be three investigations going on, and we'll be swarmed with feds."

"The Aerovictor is hovering low enough and hidden by those mountain hills, or whatever you call them. Everyone's attention is focused on Senso-Mac and the Homeland Security building right now. The noise of sirens will drown out this explosion. They won't even notice."

"Not now, but sooner or later, someone will discover it. We can't take the chance!"

"Well, I'm not about to get chain-gunned to death!" Schoenholtz stepped around the shrub and aimed at the Aerovictor that was hovering a hundred yards in the distance. Schultz shook his head in disgust—his big ox partner was a stubborn fool!

Cliff saw the gigantic man holding a weapon on his shoulder that was pointed directly at him. He had no time to aim his guns and fire, so instead, he shoved the cyclic stick down and nose-dived toward the canal. Schoenholtz pulled the trigger, and the laser sliced through both rear rotors of the Aerovictor, ripping off the tail boom. The cockpit slammed into the canal and was forced to the bottom quickly due to the swiftly moving flowage. The White Mountains had record snowfall this past winter causing water runoff that filled Lake Saguaro and maximized the dam's capacity. Thus, the Salt River canals were high and flowing fast. Cliff never stood a chance.

Pieces of the entire Aerovictor helicopter had fallen into the canal and were sinking rapidly to the bottom.

"There!" bellowed Schoenholtz. "Perfect! No scraps of metal for anyone to find unless the canal dries up completely. By the time anyone finds the Aerovictor, our mission will have been finished!"

"You don't suppose Zefron might miss one of their expensive toys, do you? You dumb ass!" replied Schultz. "They'll be searching all over for the chopper and the pilot come tomorrow!"

"Well, if they happen to find it, I'm sure they will claim it was pilot error. They certainly wouldn't want prospective clients to think they had a dysfunctional product, now would they?" Schoenholtz paused for a moment, then added, "Dumb ass!"

Schoenholtz and Schultz both gazed down the river to make sure Cliff Bullard's body wasn't floating to the top.

"Don't worry," laughed Schoenholtz. "Whoever that dude was flying that thing is in multiple pieces. Catfish need to eat, too!"

After digging a three-foot hole next to the shrub, Schultz and Schoenholtz buried the laser gun and remaining energy packs in the sand, then covered the hole with rocks. Ten minutes later, they arrived at the underground vault. Schoenholtz planted the camera near the uranium-35 container, then he and Schultz headed for the demolished Homeland Security building. They pulled up next to Earl Kelly and an officer of the Maricopa County Sheriff's Department that they didn't know.

"What's happened here?" asked Schultz to Kelly, pretending to be stunned at the damage caused by the fires. Kelly did a double-take, glanced over to Schoenholtz on the other ATV, then back to Schultz.

"Well, thank goodness you two are safe," said Kelly sarcastically, looking back and forth at both men with a culpable stare. "I was worried you may have been inside the building when it was demolished." He didn't ask where they had been; he just wanted to see how they would respond. Deputy Owens could detect the cynicism in Kelly's voice, and Kelly was sure the two German immigrants could as well. He really didn't care.

"We were about a mile away when we heard the blasts," lied Schoenholtz. "We were fixing the perimeter fence that some hikers had torn down."

"Which blasts did you hear?" asked Kelly with the look a prosecutor gives a defendant in court.

"What do you mean? The blasts that we assume flattened these buildings." Schoenholtz gave a puzzled glance at Kelly.

"Well, the first blast 'flattened' the Senso-McNamara headquarters, and I doubt there were any survivors. There was a gap in time before our Homeland Security building was blown up. So, why didn't you come back after the first blast?"

Schultz decided to take over. He was sure Schoenholtz would find a way to destroy their alibi. "We heard the first blast, Agent Kelly, and thought an air-conditioning compressor had exploded. It's that time of year, you know, when factories switch over from the heat pumps used in winter to the refrigerants used in summer. The pressurization in those big AC units can be a problem, you know."

Schultz paused a moment for the BS to sink in! "We didn't see the fire because we were busy working on the fence. When we heard the second explosion, we knew something was wrong. We thought it was at Senso-Mac, not the Homeland Security building. When we got closer, we realized the fire was our building, not theirs."

"And you're just arriving now?" asked Kelly in disbelief. "You weren't in much of a hurry to return to your workplace, a federal outpost in charge of protecting our nation! We all know that Senso-Mac makes more than just surgical lasers and traffic speed guns; it makes a death ray that's sold to our armed forces. That didn't make you want to hustle back to the office?!"

"As I said, sir, we thought it was an AC compressor accident. Also, we had secured the Homeland Security building. No one could get in. Now, if you don't mind, we would like to help investigate these events."

Kelly was building up steam. He couldn't hold it back. He stuck his face two inches from Schultz and shouted, "Events?! What makes you think that the total destruction of a government laser weapon plant and a Homeland Security building would be an event?! You said it was just an AC—" Deputy Owens grabbed Kelly's arm and pulled him back.

"Earl, relax. We need to approach this calmly." Owens nodded at Schultz and Schoenholtz as he led Kelly away from them. When the German men were out of earshot, Owens whispered, "A shouting match isn't going to solve anything."

"They did it, Gordy!" uttered Kelly in a muffled voice. "By God, they blew up both buildings! I just know it, damn it! I can feel it! Who knows how many innocent victims were in the Senso-Mac headquarters!"

"I think you're right," replied Owens. "But let's not lose it. Think about it. We don't have any proof they did it, so we can't detain them. If you scare them, they'll run, and we may never know why they did it. So, I have an idea. How bout we let them investigate and see what they come up with. That might give us a clue as to what they are trying to accomplish."

Kelly took a deep breath and nodded. "Your right. I'm tired and just uptight from everything that's happened today. First, Gila Bend, then Ajo, and now this. I need some downtime to wrap my head around it."

Kelly and Owens walked back to Schultz and Schoenholtz.

"Sorry about that," Kelly said half-heartedly. "It's been a long day. Yes, I think you two should be part of the investigation."

"No problem. We'll get started right away, Agent Kelly. We will take a helmet-cam to record where we are going and what we find."

"That's a good idea. But the fires are still smoldering. You won't be able to do much until the ashes cool down. Could be a couple of days."

"We thought we could comb the perimeter and see if we can find something. And, Senso-Mac has an underground vault that they use to test laser weapons. We'll check that out, too."

Kelly nodded, then Schultz and Schoenholtz got back on their ATVs and rode off. Kelly then looked at Deputy Owens and smiled.

"You were right, Gordy. If they find something in that vault, it could be our first clue to see what they are up to. As for us, it will be getting dark soon, and things are too hot to start searching. We'll need to return tomorrow. The Senso-Mac holding company is in London, and if they can track down how many employees were in the building, then they should be able to provide us with an estimated death toll by midday. I'll check in with the fire chief, then let's get something to eat."

"You're buying!" Owens slapped Kelly on the back playfully.

"Yep, I'm buying."

Chapter 26

Tuesday, April 17, 2018
Senso-McNamara Headquarters
Underground Vault Testing Area, Mesa, Arizona
7:00 pm (Pacific Daylight Time)

Schultz and Schoenholtz spent ten minutes rehearsing what they were going to say. Neither were actors, but both were accomplished liars. Schultz placed the helmet-cam on his head and turned on the video recorder. The digital storage in the camera could not be deleted or edited, a technology that frustrated the two Germans. The first take had to be excellent.

As they descended the stairs into the entry chamber, the first lie came out of Schoenholtz's mouth. "Wow! There is an intense smell of gasoline in here!"

"There must be a fuel leak somewhere," stated Schultz. He was having a hard time keeping a straight face, but the helmet-cam was on his head, and nobody would notice.

"Yes," replied Schoenholtz. "It has a powerful and penetrating odor. But I don't see a fuel line, do you?"

"No, definitely no fuel line. But look here." Schultz knelt, then pretended to wipe the floor with his right forefinger and thumb as he zoomed the camera in for a close-up. "This is gasoline residue, I'm sure of it." Schultz had stuck his hand in the ATV's fuel tank moments before descending the ladder.

"Where do you think that came from?" asked Schoenholtz as seriously as his acting limitations could be stretched.

"It appears to be splashed all around the vault. Obviously, someone was trying to start this place on fire. I wonder why?"

"A better question would be why the person didn't light the fire after going through all this work?"

"Good question, Loren. Let's keep moving."

Schultz and Schoenholtz moved into the second chamber through the electronically-timed circular door that was open. Schultz turned his head to show the trap door and compartment that stored the energy packs.

"Look!" exclaimed Schoenholtz. "The storage door is open!" Schultz knelt and zoomed in with his camera. "There are only two energy packs in here! Someone seems to have stolen the others! Must have been in a hurry. Probably wanted to destroy the vault with the packs but couldn't find a laser gun to use. That must be why he splashed gasoline all over—you know, to ignite the place! But something must have spooked him, and he ran before lighting the match!" Schoenholtz thought he could qualify for an Emmy or an Oscar with that performance.

Schultz then moved his head, and the helmet-cam was focused on a bat-shaped container lying on the floor. "What could this be?"

"Well, I'm no expert, but this appears to be a homemade atomic bomb."

Schultz cringed! That wasn't in the script! Schoenholtz was supposed to just say he didn't know what the object was and leave it at that. Let the feds find it and open it up. Time to cover for the dumb ass again!

"Nah, I doubt it," said Schultz as he was scrambling for the right words. "It's probably just a new police speed radar gun that Senso-Mac was testing. I'm sure they forgot that they left it here, that's all!" Schultz glared at Schoenholtz with an evil stare. The dumb ass better not say another word! Schultz wasn't going to give him a chance. Before Schoenholtz could speak, Schultz said, "Hey, look at the far wall! It appears the trap door on the other side is open. Let's check it out."

Schultz and Schoenholtz hurried through the shooting chamber to the end of the room, then climbed down into the subterranean space below the vault. Schoenholtz quickly pointed to the blood on the floor, which upset Schultz again. The plan was to wait a few minutes before discovering the splotches.

"Look! Blood!" shouted Schoenholtz in his most fearfully-fake voice. If he had covered his mouth in despair to show off his dramatic skills, Schultz would have whacked him silly!

"Don't touch it! We might need to get some DNA evidence. Hey, what's that laying over there." Schultz turned his head so the video could focus on the Canon camera and telephoto lens. "It's a camera. Probably the killer's!"

As soon as Schultz said it, he knew he made a mistake. He had jumped the gun, so to speak. First, he forgot that Schoenholtz's DNA may be somewhere in the room. But he could explain that away by saying it happened during their investigation. Second, they had not made a case for murder yet. Any investigator, prosecutor, or judge would catch that slip of the tongue. The blood could have come from an accident. With his arms, Schultz shrugged his shoulders and motioned for Schoenholtz to say something that could get them back on track. Schoenholtz got the hint, but he wasn't much for improvisations. He wasn't much good with a script, either!

"Ah, why did you say killer, Gene? Do you think that a murder may have taken place down here?" Schultz rolled his eyes so Schoenholtz could understand his contempt! Thank goodness the eyeballs were tucked under the helmet-cam!

"Well, I may be a bit ahead of myself," responded Schultz, "but with the energy packs missing and gasoline spread all around, the blood could indicate a murder, yes!"

"And why do you think the murderer was the owner of the camera?" asked Schoenholtz. Schultz's face turned several shades of red. If looks could kill, Schoenholtz was a dead man.

"I don't know for sure, but the camera is shattered. Whoever owned it must have dropped it. Let's bag it for evidence. Most likely, there will be fingerprints on it. Also, there is a serial number on both the camera body and telephoto lens that can be traced back to the store where it was purchased." Schultz knew fingerprints were out of the question. After Schoenholtz had picked it up earlier, his prints were all over it. He had scrubbed every inch of the camera before placing it back in the vault. But the serial number would undoubtedly lead to the camera's owner.

After Schultz and Schoenholtz finished their rehearsed investigation, Schultz switched off the helmet-cam.

"Is that everything?" asked Schoenholtz. "Seems like we're forgetting something."

"Well, our security cameras are still here, but the hard drive that stores the footage was in the Homeland Security building that you destroyed. Investigators might wonder what the cameras were used for, but there is no way to trace what was recorded on them, including you knifing that guy."

"Then, turn on the helmet-cam one more time. All good movies have a wonderful ending. I'll take care of that." Schoenholtz waited for his partner to wipe off the skeptical stare on his face. After a moment, Schultz shook his head, then switched on the helmet cam and pointed it at Schoenholtz.

"We need to secure the vault and get this evidence back to our investigation team! Pronto, Mr. Schultz!"

Schultz turned off the camera and flashed his middle finger at Schoenholtz. Neither would be receiving an award at the next International Thespian Festival! They placed the bagged camera, telephoto lens, and helmet-cam into Schultz's ATV basket and headed back to the Salt River Canal, which was in the opposite direction of Senso-Mac and the demolished Homeland Security building. They didn't want Agent Kelly to see them until they had finished the task at hand. When they arrived at the canal, they split up; Schultz headed for the urgent care center by Walmart, and Schoenholtz sped towards the Regal Hospital. They decided to rendezvous at two o'clock the next morning back where they had buried the laser gun and energy packs. If either one found the Senso-

Mac dude who had a knife wound in his back, they were to extract the information about the photographer from him, then drop the dude off at the morgue. Fortunately for Roger Bennett, he never showed up at any healthcare facility.

Joe Freeman helped Roger back to his house in Red Mountain Ranch, returning on the same route he had hiked when he left. Roger had lost some more blood, but for the most part, the lens tissues and masking tape had done the trick. They had heard the blast when the Homeland Security building was blown up, but they didn't know exactly what was happening. They thought it was more of the Senso-Mac headquarters exploding.

"Can I lie down for just a few moments?" asked Roger. "I'm feeling a bit dizzy."

"We should go to urgent care and get you checked out!"

"Just let me rest for an hour or so, then if I'm still feeling faint, I promise we will go."

Joe rolled his eyes and helped Roger to the couch in the living room. "Just sit up for a minute so I can put on a new dressing." He unwrapped the masking tape and gently tugged the bloody tissue from the wound. Then he walked to the bathroom and returned with a three-inch square gauze, which he placed firmly on Roger's laceration. Roger laid down on his side and fell asleep in seconds.

Joe went into the kitchen and made himself a peanut butter and jelly sandwich, then brewed a whole pot of coffee with a few extra scoops of roasted beans. This was going to be a long night.

8:00 pm Pacific Daylight Time (Tuesday evening)
4:00 am British Summer Time Zone (Wednesday morning)
London, England

Lord Shaffer awoke at dawn most days for a five-mile run before heading off to Parliament. He loved money, power, and macho-man fun, but not necessarily in that order. Although he had several girlfriends in the past who would make lovely wives, he broke off every relationship after six months. Not six months and one day—six months on the nose! The good lord even circled the "day of departure" from a relationship on his private calendar shortly after the conclusion of a first date. He believed it wasn't fair to lead a girl on a wild marriage goose chase when he had no plans to share his money, power, and macho-man fun with anyone!

So when the cell phone woke him up at four o'clock, he was wearily confused. The cell phone doubled as his alarm clock, and he couldn't figure out why it was going off before the sun began to rise. Most days, the London fog didn't allow the sun to intrude on sleeping Englanders, but Lord Shaffer's internal clock always knew it was time to get up. Today his internal clock didn't go off and neither did his cell's alarm clock. It was the phone ringing very persistently.

"It's four o'clock," muttered Lord Shaffer as he answered his iPhone. "This better be good."

"Senso-McNamara is no more," said the voice on the other line.

"Were all employees at work?" asked Shaffer.

"Yes," replied the voice.

"So, all are dead? You are sure of that?"

"Yes. I think so."

"You think so! What the hell does that mean?!" Lord Shaffer asked, with his voice rising.

"One man, I believe his name is Roger Bennett, works maintenance in the vault. He was stabbed and presumed dead."

"Presumed dead? Why is he not confirmed dead?"

"Body is missing, sir. He may have been aided by a hiker who was passing by. But it is doubtful he could survive the attack. He most likely is lying somewhere in the desert, bled to death."

"Even so, this hiker is now a witness. Find both of them! Now, do you understand me?!"

"Yes sir, there is no chance they will be a problem. Guaranteed!"

"Anything else?" asked Lord Shaffer.

"Yes. Federal investigators will be contacting the holding company as soon as you open for business. London is eight hours ahead of Arizona, so they will be making the call around midnight here. They will want an exact number of employees who were working for Senso-Mac."

"Yes, that makes sense. But why are you letting me know?"

"Because that number needs to be two less than the actual count. Do you follow me?"

"Of course. I'm not stupid. I will email Trisha, our receptionist, as soon as I hang up. Now find that hiker, do you hear me?!" Lord Shaffer didn't wait for an answer.

Chapter 27

Tuesday, April 17, 2018
Ajo Airport, Ajo, Arizona
11:00 pm (Pacific Daylight Time)

"How long would you say it takes an old Cessna to fly to Mexico and back?" asked Principal Sebastian Perez. The administrator and his ten remaining teachers who escaped in Donnor Colten's pickup truck were sitting on the floor and leaning against the interior walls of the hangar. It had been an incredibly long day, but none were even a bit sleepy.

Donnor didn't want to talk truth to a frantic lot of anxious educators, but it was time they faced a very possible reality. "Mack should have returned by now. I'm afraid something's gone wrong."

"Gone wrong?!" shouted Margo Litweiler, the Gila Bend girl's physical education teacher. "There are two sweet kids on board that plane, say nothing of five teachers who are close friends!"

Principal Perez stood up and motioned the teachers with his hand to stay calm. Margo bit her lip and shook her head, but nothing could turn the bright red of her face a lighter shade. How was anyone supposed to relax at a time like this?

Perez walked over to Donnor and whispered, "Do we have a backup plan?"

"I need a cell phone. Mine was in my truck. Can I borrow one of yours?"

"We all left our cell phones locked in our desks at school. School board policy. No phones allowed, including staff. We're trying to be role models for the kids."

Donnor opened the roll-up hangar door just enough to scoot outside. Perez followed him. Both stood up and brushed themselves off, then looked up at the starry night sky. It was eerily peaceful outdoors. A few crickets could be heard chirping, but that was it. The ladle of the Big Dipper looked like it was smiling down at them.

"That tunnel. This hangar with all the expensive equipment. The airplane. How can a small-town artist afford all this?" Perez looked directly into Donnor's eyes. "Any idea what your cousin is doing on the side?"

"Mack has never told me much," replied Donnor meekly. "I know he moonlights in another business. He keeps things pretty much to himself." Principal Perez thought Donnor might be hiding something.

"He's running drugs," stated Perez in a matter-of-fact tone. "It's pretty obvious. I didn't need my doctorate to figure that out."

Donnor looked down to the ground, where he was nervously kicking gravel off to the side. "Yeah, it does seem obvious, I agree. But, I want you to know Mack is a good person. I've known him all my life."

"We need a new plan. Those were bad men who raided my school. Yes, we have kids whose parents came here illegally, but they are good kids. Never cause any trouble. And their parents are wonderful supporters of the school. They work in the fields all day long, then they come to family functions at night. Anyway, those men can't be ICE agents. No way would ICE bring guns into a school. We need to get out of here before they come looking."

"What do you need me to do?" The voice startled Perez and Colten. They turned to see teacher Rick Frye brushing himself off after rolling under the hangar door. "The staff is getting restless, Mr. Perez. We need a Plan B. How can I help?"

"I think we need to contact the sheriff in Ajo," replied Principal Perez. Donnor and Rick rolled their eyes, then nodded their reluctant approval.

"The sheriff's office is on Well Road," said Donnor. "Best bet to avoid suspicion would be to take the tunnel back to the golf course and hike on down from there. Shouldn't be much traffic on Well Road this time of night. If we see lights approaching, we can scramble quickly into the desert."

"We've been gone from Gila Bend all day. There must be people coming to look for us," said Rick. "If we hide, how will they find us?"

"Good point," replied Perez. "But how will we know who are the good guys and who are the bad guys? Better safe than sorry. The sheriff will be able to protect us."

"Well then, let's get back in the tunnel," said Donnor. He and Perez moved towards the hangar, but Rick Frye just stood in place. He was focused on something in the distance.

"Are you coming, Rick?" asked Perez.

Rick pointed to the large object lying in the shadows on the far side of the runway. "That's a crop duster over there."

Perez and Donnor turned and looked.

"So what?" asked Perez irritably. He was in a hurry to get his staff to the sheriff's office.

"I think I can fly it, Mr. Perez. My father had a private pilot's license and would take us up for joy rides when we were young. I remember how he operated the controls."

"That is a biplane, for God's sake! Even if you could fly it, which I have my doubts, where are you planning on going?"

"I could get to the Gila Bend airport out on the Phoenix Bypass."

"This time of night? I don't think they have landing lights on the runway."

"Then I'll land it in the dark! We need to let someone know where we are. You take the teachers and go on to the sheriff's office, I'll fly that damn thing!"

"It's too risky, Rick. You'll kill yourself!"

"If I can remember how to get it airborne, then I will remember how to land it. Let's see if we can get it started. We may need to pull off the cobwebs."

Frye, Perez, and Donnor jogged across the runway to the Stearman C3B biplane. Initially owned by Delta Airlines back in the 1930s, the one-time mail-carrying plane turned crop-duster appeared to be sound asleep. It evidently hadn't been flown for quite some time. Starting the aircraft was simple—the pilot gave it some gas while someone else spun the propeller. Rick climbed onto the wing brace and checked out the two open cockpits. The pilot's seat was in the rear, and two side-by-side passenger seats were in the front. There were three leather head coverings and three pairs of goggles, but that was about it. A radio clamped between two brackets was caked in rust. Chances were slim that it had much range if it worked at all. There was no radar system built into the dashboard, just the basic flight controls for a pre-World War Two airplane: altimeter, speedometer, gas gauge, and an anemometer to measure wind speed. Wind direction would have to be figured out by watching it blow something on the ground.

Rick scrambled into the cockpit. The yoke, rudder, and elevator seemed to move smoothly. He could only hope that the bracing, flying, incidence, and landing wires were strong enough for a short flight. He pushed the throttle and asked Donnor to spin the propeller. On the third spin, the Wright J-5 Whirlwind engine's spark plugs ignited, and all nine cylinders began to roar. Principal Perez and Donnor took several steps back and covered their ears.

As Rick was about to taxi out onto the runway, Donnor waved his arms and approached the wing.

Rick leaned over the fuselage and yelled down to him. "What are you doing?! Get back!"

"I'm coming with you," shouted Donnor as he grabbed a wing brace and clambered into a passenger seat. "You need some night eyes! I can help!"

Rick didn't have time to argue. Principal Perez nodded and gave him the international okay symbol by making an "o" with his thumb and forefinger. Then he ran back to the hangar, but by the time he got there, every teacher was standing outside the door watching in disbelief.

The plane labored down the runway with gears grinding, but moments later, Rick and Donnor were airborne. The gas tank was full, at least if the gauge was accurate. The altimeter appeared to be working, but that was it. The speedometer and anemometer were stuck on zero, and the radio would only crackle. The compass on the dashboard was spinning out of control. Their only source of direction was the array of constellations glimmering in the night sky. Astronomy wasn't exactly Rick's best subject in college. Donnor never went to college.

11:15 pm (Pacific Daylight Time)

The black Hummer H3 limousine bounced over the desert rocks with ease, taking down a few saguaro cacti on the way. It slammed on its brakes a few feet short of the ICE agents who were admiring the amazing vehicle as it approached.

"It's about damn time!" exclaimed ICE Sergeant Bill Clemons. "What took you so long?"

"We had to make sure Senso-Mac and the Homeland Security building were taken care of first," replied the man. "We knew you would be well hidden in the night desert, so back off Clemons. Plus, I had to notify Lord Shaffer. Besides, if you hadn't screwed up, we wouldn't need to be here rescuing you!"

"I didn't screw up! What was that Aerovictor helicopter doing out here? You were supposed to be monitoring Border Patrol ops, so why didn't you know they were using Aerovictors these days?"

"They aren't using Aerovictors, you fool. I don't know what it was doing out here, but it sure wasn't part of Border Patrol operations."

"You will address me as sir! I am your commander!" Bill Clemons' blood was beginning to boil.

"You ain't crap, sir!" replied the man with a mocking emphasis on sir. "Without me, you would be bottling vodka somewhere in Moscow. I opened up Arizona for you all, and I can close it down just as fast!" The man strode towards Clemons with both fists clenched. Agent Bogdan Smirnov stepped in between Clemons and the man.

"Gentlemen," said Smirnov. "We are on the same side now, so perhaps we should work together and get moving."

The man unclenched his fists and stepped back, trying to regain his composure. "Okay, you mentioned hostages on the phone. What do you got?"

Clemons motioned for another agent to bring Kurt Kellner, Isaac Martinez, and Zaira Tahan to him. With cloth wrapped over their eyes and hands tied behind their backs, they stumbled forward. Then they were pushed to their knees in front of the man.

"These two here are just kids," said the man pointing at Isaac and Zaira. "Why are they here?"

"Well, you should know. These troublemakers were the ones who stole the bus from the charter school to get away from the raid."

The man looked around. "I don't see the school bus. Where is it?"

"They ditched the bus north of Ajo and got into a pickup truck with a bunch of teachers who also escaped. We followed them, but when we caught up, most of the teachers weren't around. I think they were dropped off somewhere on the golf course and snuck over to the airport where they stole a small Cessna."

"If they stole a small Cessna, how is it that you now have them firmly on the ground?"

"We shot the plane down, but these three parachuted before it crashed. We caught them right away."

"You could have told me about this on the phone when you said you had hostages!" said the man angrily.

"There was no need to bother you. We just needed transportation out of here. What difference does it make?"

"Children! Missing children can be a problem. A few teachers missing and people will think they just walked away from their jobs. But kids missing will cause an endless search, and I will have my hands full!"

"I have plans for that one already," said Clemons while pointing at Zaira. "Tariq will pay a nice bonus for her to be part of his harem." He smiled at the other agents, and everyone began to chuckle. Furiously, Kurt Kellner wrestled with the rope that was secured to his wrist. The man stared at Clemons angrily.

"As for the other two," continued Clemons, "they will be our ticket to safe passage out of the country, seeing we no longer have vehicles or helicopters. We'll use them as hostages if need be."

"No!" shouted Kellner. "Let the kids go! My family has more money than whoever this Tariq person is. I can make sure you are very wealthy if you will just let them go!"

"Take his blindfold off, Bogdan. I want to look him in the eyes and see if he's telling the truth." Smirnov untied the knot and removed the cloth. Clemons stooped down and placed his face a foot away from Kellner's. "So, just how wealthy is this family of yours?"

Kurt was about to lie and embellish, but something stopped him dead in his tracks. He glanced over Clemons' shoulder to the man standing a few feet away. The hair on his arms stood straight up, and goosebumps spread like wildfire over his skin. He raised his head and peered at the man, then mumbled fearfully, "What the hell?!"

Chapter 28

Wednesday, April 18, 2018
Salt River Canal, Mesa, Arizona
2:00 am (Pacific Daylight Time)

"Any luck?" asked Gene Schultz.

"No, how about you?" replied Loren Schoenholtz. They had met at the agreed-upon rendezvous location where they buried the laser gun and energy packs by the Salt River Canal.

"Nope. He is either with the camera dude somewhere or died trying to go with him." Schultz pulled his iPhone out of his pants pocket, unlocked it, and tapped on the Safari app.

"What are you doing?" asked Schoenholtz.

"Read me the serial number on the telephoto lens. I'm going to Google it."

"You think Google can tell you what that number means?"

"You'd be surprised what Google can do. Just read me the number, okay?!"

Schoenholtz took out a flashlight and shined it on the serial number. He had to squint to see it clearly.

"Eight-six-six-nine-four-four-three-eight-seven-six-six, then the letter b, one-one-five."

Google responded: *Your search - 86694438766B115 - did not match any documents. Suggestions: Make sure all words are spelled correctly; Try different keywords; Try more general keywords.*

Schultz inserted the words *Serial Number* before the numbers and hit the return key. Google listed a variety of web pages, most being advertisements. Schultz then clicked on the hyperlink to *www.findmyserialnumber.com*. A red, white, and blue webpage opened with fireworks exploding in the background. Schultz chuckled. Patriotism had found its way into covert activities for German immigrants.

In the search box, Schultz retyped the serial number. After five seconds of thinking, the iPhone's processor displayed a new page: *We have located serial number 86694438766B115. You can display the results for $9.95. FMSN also has monthly and yearly plans available.*

"Ten bucks!" shouted Schultz, yelling directly at his iPhone's screen. "This is a rip-off! No wonder they have the red, white, and blue background with fireworks. Only in America would you pay too much for too little!"

"Just pay the damn thing," stated Schoenholtz. "You'll be reimbursed!"

Schultz touched the *Purchase* button, which generated a response from the iPhone: *Please enter your Apple ID*. Schultz tapped in his personal code. Seconds later, a webpage opened with all the details he was looking for, plus a hearty *THANK YOU!* from Find My Serial Number.

"Hmmm. The lens was purchased online two years ago from Pro Camera Limited in Dallas. It was shipped to the buyer's address: 4166 Ranier Street, Mesa, AZ 85215. Guy's name is Joe Freeman. Bingo!"

Schultz searched the address on Google Maps.

"He lives about a mile away from here. It's time we go and plant some evidence and find that damn SD card."

2:30 am (Pacific Daylight Time)
Red Mountain Ranch, Mesa, Arizona

The pot of coffee mixed with the anxiety over what he witnessed in the desert kept Joe Freeman wide awake in his La-Z-Boy recliner. He was watching the original *Star Wars* movie on TNT, one he had seen six times. He thought it might put him to sleep but not a chance. Meanwhile, Roger Bennett was snoring up a storm on the couch.

"How can a man snore so loud on his side?!" muttered Joe to Han Solo, aka Harrison Ford, in a low voice. Suddenly, the scene changed to R2D2 and 3CPO.

"I suggest a new strategy, Artoo: let the Wookie win," said 3CPO.

"Well, that Wookie snoring on my couch seems to be winning, you confounded robots!" Joe said to the TV screen. He was tired and obviously losing it!

The volume on the TV was low, but that mixed with Roger's grunts was loud enough to keep Joe from hearing the random sounds coming from his garage. Meanwhile, Gene Schultz watched Joe place the SD card on the coffee table in front of the couch. Schultz was keeping his eye on the photographer from behind a bush that brushed up against the house next to the living room window. The blind was open a crack, just enough for him to see Joe sitting in the recliner and the other man lying on the sofa. He assumed the sleeping man was the same man his partner failed to kill earlier. Schultz hoped all the racket Schoenholtz was making didn't wake either of them.

Schoenholtz had pried open the side-door entrance into the garage with a screwdriver. Inside was a pair of steel shelves filled with things you normally would find on them. He hid the laser gun and four energy packs under a folded canvas boat cover that was lying on the bottom shelf. Schoenholtz then exited through the side door and made his way to Schultz. There was no time to fix the deadbolt lock he had jimmied to get in.

"What about him?" asked Schoenholtz as he pointed through the blind to the snoring Roger Bennett. "We can't let him live. And how the hell are we going to find that SD memory card? It's like finding a needle in a haystack. Freeman could have hidden it anywhere!"

"Relax. The SD card is on that coffee table. And I've been thinking. I have an idea that would keep that dude you knifed from talking and make this Joe Freeman fella look even more guilty."

"What kind of plan do you have that doesn't include killing him? You must have lost your mind!"

"Coffee. Taste Of Arabia coffee, to be exact. Come on, let's get out of here. I'll explain on the way home."

Chapter 29

Wednesday, April 18, 2018
Red Mountain Ranch, Mesa, Arizona
8:00 am (Pacific Daylight Time)

Gene Schultz knocked on Joe Freeman's door. He was dressed in khaki shorts, a peach t-shirt with the words *Coffee Man* stenciled on the front, and a pair of Nike tennis shoes. Schultz shaved the gray stubble from his face before leaving and now looked like an energetic fifty-year-old coffee salesman instead of a seventy-year-old terrorist. He was holding a can of Taste Of Arabia coffee and a box of Dunkin Donuts. Loren Schoenholtz was hiding with a pistol in the backyard behind the same bush he and Schultz were hiding behind a few hours ago. If Schultz's plan failed, he would storm the house and kill both Roger Bennett and Freeman.

"Yeah, what is it?" asked Joe wearily. He had little sleep last night.

"Only the best coffee you will ever drink, my friend!" replied Schultz with a wink and a deep grin. He offered his right hand out to Joe. "My name is Don Johnson, and I'm here to serve you breakfast. I have donuts and coffee. No pressure to buy. If you like the coffee, I will set you up on my route. If not, que sera sera."

Joe thought it might not be a bad idea. He was too tired to make breakfast anyway. Why not?

"Okay, come on in. My name is Joe." Joe led Schultz to the kitchen. "What do you need to brew the coffee?"

"That Mr. Coffee machine over on the countertop will work just fine, Joe. So, how many cups would you like me to make? Is your wife awake or anyone else who might like the finest coffee in the land?!" Schultz hadn't seen the dude with the knife wound, but he figured the man would still be in the house.

"I'm not married, Don, but I have a friend in the other room that could probably use a caffeine wakeup call. I'll be right back."

Gene measured out the coffee and started brewing a full pot. One eight-ounce cup would work just fine, but two or three cups might speed up the memory-loss process. Meanwhile, Joe went to the living room where a groggy Roger Bennett was sitting up on the couch, rubbing his injured neck.

"How you doing this morning, Roger?" asked Joe.

"I'm fine. Just really tired."

"How about some coffee and a couple of donuts to get you started. Then, I'll take you to my doctor and get you checked out. That sound okay?"

"The coffee and donuts sound fantastic! But, I think I'll pass on the doctor. The bleeding has stopped, and I'm feeling better. We need to call the police as soon as possible."

"There's some guy who sells coffee brewing up a pot in the kitchen. He brought donuts, too."

"A door-to-door coffee salesman," said Bennett while shaking his head in disbelief. "In this day and age. That's unheard of! You can buy coffee most anywhere—grocery stores, drug stores, and office supply stores. He must have some kind of gimmick."

"No, I don't think so. He just says he sells the best coffee in the world. I've never seen it in stores."

"Well then, let's get crackin'! I love coffee, but I love donuts even more!" Joe was helping Roger stand up when Schultz entered the living room with a tray he found in the kitchen. On it were three mugs of coffee, the carafe, and a plate of donuts.

"No, no! Sit down, please!" said Schultz. "I'm here to serve you the finest coffee in the world!" He placed the tray on the coffee table and nonchalantly picked up the SD card. His back was to Joe and Roger; they had no way of noticing that he had stolen the camera's flash memory. While Joe and Roger were feasting, Schultz slipped the SD card into his pocket.

Joe and Roger each downed three cups of java and two donuts. They were having a good time joking with Schultz, trying to put the memories of yesterday behind them for a moment.

"Don Johnson is it?" asked Bennett. Schultz nodded his head yes. "Weren't you the star of *Miami Vice*?"

All three laughed and clanged their coffee mugs in a toast. Joe and Roger took another swig. Schultz, aka Don Johnson, simply faked it.

9:00 am (Pacific Daylight Time)

After Joe and Roger had downed three Taste Of Arabia mugs of java and shared fond memories of old TV shows, Schultz thanked them and left. Joe asked him to reserve a spot on his route, preferably once a month. Schultz pretended to jot it down on a fake order form. On his way out, he placed an unopened box of premeasured filter pods on the kitchen counter that each made twelve cups of coffee.

"Man, that was terrific coffee!" exclaimed Joe. "I'm wide awake!"

"May have to drink another pot," retorted Roger. "It never hurts to be alerts!" Both men laughed at the play on words.

"Why not? Might as well drink it while it's fresh." Joe walked into the kitchen, opened the box, and brewed another carafe full of coffee. While he was wiping off donut crumbs from the tray, he said, "Hey, call the sheriff's office while this is brewing. We need to file a report as soon as possible."

"Then what? I'm never going back to work at Senso-Mac."

"No one will be going back to work at Senso-Mac for a long time, Roger. If Senso-Mac is conspiring to kill the president and we can tell someone what we saw, show them pictures of the hologram and all, your bosses won't have to think about rebuilding. They'll be busy staring at the ceiling of their ten-by-ten-foot cell block at Leavenworth! But don't worry about that now—just make the call."

"Do I dial 9-1-1 or the office number?"

"Call the Maricopa County Sheriff's Office. If you dial 9-1-1, it will be deemed an emergency, and the Mesa Police will be sent. Considering what has happened, I think we need to elevate this to a higher level of authority."

Roger used Joe's landline phone that was attached to the wall. Emergency numbers for fire, ambulance, Mesa PD, and the sheriff's office were on a sticker that was on the receiver. He dialed the number, and a receptionist picked up the phone.

"County cop's office, I mean sheriff's office," said Rebecca Grimm. "Is there a reason you are calling?"

Roger was puzzled. Who answers a phone like that? And in a sheriff's office, no less!

"Yes, I'd like to report that I was an eyewitness to the blast at Senso-Mac last night. I have information to tell you, and I'm afraid that my life is in danger."

"There was a blast at Senso-Mark last night? Really?"

"No, not Senso-Mark, Senso-Mac! You haven't heard?"

"Yes, yes, now that you mention it, I did hear something. Hold on, let me find a notepad." There was a long pause, then Rebecca said, "Just a minute, sir. I'm still looking. Hmm, I know I have one around here somewhere. What did I do with it?"

Roger was rolling his eyes and tapping his fingers on the countertop. Joe looked over at him and saw the frustration in his face.

"Okay, there, I found it! Go ahead, what were you saying?"

Roger took a deep breath and tried to stay calm. "I said that I have information about the Senso-Mac blast, and I think my life is in danger."

"Have you called the police?" asked Rebecca matter-of-factly.

"You are the police!" yelled Roger into the receiver. So much for being calm.

"Okay, sir. There's no need to shout. What's your name?"

"Roger Bennett. I work at Senso-Mac."

"Okay, great! We'll send someone over to you right away."

"Over where?! You don't have my address!"

"Well, then I'll send someone over to Senso-Mark."

"Senso-MAC, not Mark! And I'm not there because it doesn't exist anymore! Who are you?! What's your name?!"

"My name is Becky, and you need to relax. So, what is the address where you are now?"

Roger took another deep breath and slowly gave her Joe's street and phone number.

"Okay, thank you, Mr. Bennett. I'll send someone out there soon." Rebecca hung up while Roger stood there with the receiver resting on his shoulder. He couldn't believe the conversation he just had.

"What's up?" asked Joe. "What's the matter?"

"You wouldn't believe it if I told you! Just keep your fingers crossed that an officer comes out. I'm not going to hold my breath!"

Rebecca was about to call a duty officer on the two-way radio when she heard a knock on the door. She thought that was odd because the entrance was never locked during business hours. She put the notepad down and hustled to open the door. In walked a uniformed man she didn't recognize at first.

"Hi Mary," said Deputy Ken Smith to Rebecca. "I think you parked in my spot today. No worries. I just parked in Sheriff Ur—Urla--Urman. Damn, I'm having a mind warp! What's the sheriff's name? It's on the tip of my tongue."

"Urdano," replied Rebecca Grimm. "And who you calling Mary? You're kidding me, right?"

"Did I just call you Mary?!" laughed Smith. "Why did I do that?" The deputy scratched his forehead and rubbed his temples until they were red. "What is your name? For some reason, I can't think today!"

"Becky. My name is Becky." Rebecca stared at Ken for a moment, then wiped a tear from her eye. "But mom's the only person who ever called me that. For some reason, I can't remember my real first name."

"What's going on here?" asked Ken. "This is sure strange."

"Maybe we just need some coffee to wake us up!" Rebecca went to the counter where the boxes of Taste Of Arabia pods had been left since yesterday's meeting with James LeBron. She brewed two mugs of coffee and handed one to Ken. "What was the name of that java salesman yesterday? I remember he had a bizarre name."

"Oh yeah. It was Curry Stephen, I think. Pretty funny, I remember."

Ken and Rebecca sat down at their desks and sipped the coffee. Both looked puzzled, and neither had any idea what they were supposed to be doing. Then the phone rang, and Rebecca picked it up.

"Sheriff's office. How may I help you?"

"It's me," replied the voice of Deputy Gordy Owens. "Hey, Rebecca, I'm going to be a little late this morning. I'll explain later when I get there."

"It's who?" asked Rebecca.

"Me. It's Gordy. Come on, my voice hasn't changed since puberty! When have you ever asked me my name?" The deputy could be heard chuckling in the background.

"Do I know you?"

Deputy Owens burst out in full laughter. "You're a funny lady, Rebecca! Anyway, if Urdano comes in before I get there, please tell him I need to meet with him right away. Try to keep him in the office until I get there, okay? Thanks, Rebecca!" Deputy Owens hung up before Rebecca could respond.

Rebecca just sat at the desk, holding the receiver in her hand for a minute. Then she glanced over at Deputy Smith, who was staring at her with his mouth wide open.

"The man said my name was Rebecca. He said his name was Deputy Gordy Owens. Do you know him?"

Deputy Ken Smith quaffed down the last few drops of coffee, then placed the mug on the desk. "The name sounds familiar, but I just can't quite place him."

9:45 am (Pacific Daylight Time)

While waiting for a sheriff's officer to arrive, Joe and Roger had each gulped down another thirty-six ounces of coffee. No one knew, including its manufacturers in Saudi Arabia, that an overdose of the tungis plant can cause a human being to fall temporarily into a comatose state. Depending on the amount consumed and the size of the person, it could last for twelve to twenty-four hours. But worse, upon wakening, memory loss would accelerate two or three times faster than normal. Joe and Roger had each consumed about sixty-four ounces in less than two hours. The biffy had been getting quite a workout.

"I don't know why," said Roger, "but I'm feeling a bit tired. You'd think after all this caffeine, I'd be awake throughout eternity!"

"I'm kind of feeling the same way. But you're still feeling the effects of being beaten up yesterday. That's why you're tired. I'm not sure why I am. Probably just overly exhausted. Go ahead and lay down on the couch for a few minutes. I'll wake you when the deputies get here."

Two minutes later, Roger was fast asleep. Five minutes after that, Joe was out cold, slumped down in the kitchen chair.

It didn't matter. Rebecca Grimm forgot to send an officer out to the house anyway.

10:00 am (Pacific Daylight Time)

The headline in the *Arizona Republic* read: *Sensor Accident Destroys Senso-McNamara.* The story goes on to say that every employee was killed in the blast, and although the cause is still being investigated, the likely reason for the tragedy was due to the improper handling of a laser sensor being tested to treat liver cancer. A second building, presumed to be a storage facility, was also destroyed. That structure most likely caught fire when flames spread from the headquarters building. Mesa fire chief, Branson Dooey, told news reporters that the information he was feeding them was merely his best-educated guess. Branson actually had no clue.

Gene Schultz approached Special Agent Earl Kelly, who had returned to the scene and was taking pictures from every possible angle. Deputy Sheriff Gordy Owens was standing next to him, taking notes.

"I think we found something, Agent Kelly," said Schultz as he handed the camera inside a plastic bag to him. He was wearing the helmet-cam on his head. "We checked out the vault, and sure enough, we believe a murder took place down there. Found this camera and lens, which we assume belonged to the killer. The SD card was missing. The man probably removed it to hide any evidence before he escaped. I'm guessing our lab can find some fingerprints and track down the serial number on the lens to find the owner. Unfortunately, we weren't very careful. Our prints might be on the camera, too. Anyway, I have a sneaking suspicion the murderer went down there to steal a laser weapon and energy packs and was confronted by a Senso-Mac employee. I think he killed the employee and blew up the buildings. Oh yeah, here's the helmet-cam. We got everything recorded from our investigation." Schultz handed the helmet to Kelly.

"A sneaking suspicion, is that right? What about motive? Why would this guy want to blow up Senso-Mac?" Kelly tried to keep the scorn from creeping into his voice, but it was becoming difficult.

"Probably some anti-American scuzzball who found out about our Homeland Security building and wanted to make a statement by destroying it. We have Homeland Security warning signs and an electric barbwire fence all around the perimeter, you know. He probably guessed we had a building inside."

"So, you're saying an anti-American scuzzball wiped out a laser factory and did the same with our Homeland Security building? That's your theory?"

"Yes, that's it. He most likely had some training on weaponry and killing; probably spent time in the military."

"Okay, we'll send the camera and helmet-cam down to the FBI lab and see what they come up with," said Kelly hiding his contempt.

He spent years separating truths from untruths, and he knew a good liar when he heard one. Schultz was borderline good.

Schultz and Schoenholtz departed. When they were out of sight and earshot, Deputy Owens looked at Kelly and said, "Are they for real?"

"I'm afraid they are for real, Gordy. And that's what scares me. We need to find out what they are up to. I'm going to take the camera, lens, and helmet-cam to the FBI lab and see what they find."

"What they will find will be what Schultz wants them to find," mentioned Owens.

"No doubt. And that's what raises my curiosity."

"I'm going to head over to the office and meet with Sheriff Urdano. I want to know what he was doing down in Ajo yesterday."

"Be careful," said Kelly. "You don't want to spook him."

"Don't plan to. I'm going to approach him cautiously and casually. Smile and tell a few jokes to ease his mind. I think our receptionist will help, too. I called her this morning, and she's in a strangely playful mood."

"A sheriff's receptionist in a playful mood? That's an oxymoron! Usually, they are stressed from dingbat callers that keep them on edge all day long."

"That's true. But Rebecca was full of jokes this morning. She pretended she didn't know me."

"She probably had too much coffee!" chuckled Kelly as he headed to the car. If he only knew.

Chapter 30

Wednesday, April 18, 2018
Sonoran Desert, Arizona
11:00 am (Pacific Daylight Time)

"You never had any plans to fly to Gila Bend, did you?" asked Donnor Colten to Rick Frye.

"No, as a matter-of-fact, I didn't," replied Rick. "But I didn't ask for you to come along, either." The two men were trying to figure out a way to repair a tire in the middle of the desert with no rubber patches or an inflation device.

Rick had flown the biplane in the same general direction as Mack Colten had earlier with the five teachers and two students. When he saw smoldering ash in the desert south of Ajo, Rick had a gut feeling Mack's Cessna had crashed. Flying with only the moonlight to provide any illumination, Rick tried to land on a nearby dirt road but was unable to keep the plane steady as the route curved in the darkness. The biplane came to a stop a few feet short of a giant saguaro cactus but had blown the front left tire.

After landing the plane, Donnor and Rick had climbed out and jogged the half-mile distance back to the burnt Cessna. They were in horror and shock thinking about the eight people on board, including Donnor's cousin and two kids from Gila Bend Charter. The Cessna's frame was charred but intact. The interior of the plane was demolished. They knelt and offered prayers, then sat in silence staring at the wreckage. Twenty minutes later they walked dolefully back to their biplane.

"We obviously can't repair the tire, Rick. Can we take off with it flat?"

"The tire will slow us down. We may not be able to gain enough speed and lift for takeoff before we hit a cactus or some other unique desert doohickey." Neither Rick nor Donnor had slept. Both were becoming cranky!

"What do you suppose Mack hit when the Cessna landed? It looked like he put down safely on the dirt road and then ran into something before he could stop."

Rick thought about that for a moment, then gave Donnor a concerned look. "You're right. Let's go back to the Cessna. I need to check something out."

"Check what out? What did I say?"

"Nothing. Maybe something, I don't know. Just come with me." Rick and Donnor jogged back to the Cessna crash site.

The fire was out, and all that remained was the scorched body of the aircraft. Rick tiptoed around, careful not to put his shoe on a hot, hidden metal fragment. That's when he noticed something peculiar and walked up to get a closer look.

"What is it?" asked Donnor. He was standing a few feet away, watching Rick.

"A small hole in the port side fuel tank," replied Rick. "It's what most likely caused the fire."

"I thought the crash caused the fire." Donnor was confused.

"So did I, but now I think someone shot a bullet through it from the ground."

"What?! You're kidding me! Please tell me you're kidding me!"

"And something else. If the plane had crashed, the frame wouldn't be intact. How stupid of me to not think of that!"

"So, what are you saying?" Donnor wasn't sure he wanted to know the answer.

"Was Mack a good pilot? I guess I should ask if he was a great pilot."

"The best," replied Donnor. "He could fly this thing upside-down to Hawaii if he wanted to!"

"Then my theory is that Mack landed this plane and ditched it. He may have even somehow caused the fire to incinerate the frame faster to make the appearance that everyone on board died. If someone had shot him down, the gunner might have gone to see if anyone was alive."

Donnor and Rick shielded the sun with their eyes and gazed around the desert. Donnor noticed it first and ran to a location about fifty yards from the crash site, then knelt to get a closer look. Rick followed and saw what Donnor was looking at.

"Footprints!" shouted Donnor. "Several shapes and sizes! I think they escaped and headed south into Organ Pipe National Park. The tracks are headed for Bates Well Road which is just a mile or so past that hill over yonder. That would be an easy path for them to follow in the night, assuming they had a flashlight. We need to follow them."

"What about our plane? We can't just leave it in the desert."

"The plane has a flat tire, Rick. You said it yourself. Chances are slim we could get enough ground speed to get it airborne. They took off from the airport late yesterday afternoon. Bates Well Road cuts southwesterly through Organ Pipe and ends about forty miles from here near the Mexico border. Assuming they walked through the night, it's possible they could be there by now. Just across the border is Los Vidrios, where they were planning on going to when they left."

"Forty miles is a long walk, Donnor. Where would they get water? How would they have enough stamina to make it?"

"Henry Gray owned several cattle ranches along that road, and each one has an underground well. Mack knows exactly where those are located. The ranches ceased operations in 1976, but the wells still contain water, and there are abandoned bunkhouses that can be used for shelter."

"How do you know that? Or should I ask, how does Mack know about that?"

"There's something I need to tell you, Rick, but we don't have time right now. We should follow the tracks."

"What do you think their plan is when they reach the end of the road—hope the border patrol can save them?"

"Well, no, it's more complicated than that. Yes, the area is swarming with border patrols, but Mack won't be going to them for help." Donnor looked away from Rick and down at the ground.

"You need to tell me Mack's secret first if you want me to go with you! What am I getting myself into?"

Donnor paused for a moment and stared at Rick. "I can't explain it. I wish I could. I need to show you instead. Somehow, we need to fix that tire."

Chapter 31

Wednesday, April 18, 2018
House of Lords, Palace of Westminster, London, England
1:00 pm Pacific Daylight Time
9:00 pm British Summer Time Zone

Lord Shaffer was suffering through another long session of Parliament where arguments surrounding Brexit somehow morphed into quarrels about safety and security during the Oxford versus Cambridge Goat Race. Someone shot and killed Oxford as the four-legged mammal mascot was about to cross the finish line ahead of his arch-rival in the annual race held at Spitalfields City Farm. The goat murderer was caught, and when questioned by police said he didn't want a "bloody Welch" beating a Scot once again. Oxford was born, raised, and grass-fed in Wales, while Cambridge hailed from a farm outside of Glasgow. In this case, the shooter claimed Oxford stood for the British exit from the European Union, while Cambridge symbolized the British remaining in the European Union. Now the House of Lords were embattled in an argument about how crazy Scots could terrorize any person or animal that epitomized the Brexit leave vote. But Lord Shaffer wasn't even listening, and he hadn't participated in any aspect of this ridiculous late-night session of Parliament. He was thinking about the phone call from Mesa, Arizona, and wondering if he had made the right decision to destroy Senso-McNamara headquarters and the Homeland Security building. And he was worried that he had made a mistake giving General Leonid Sokolov the green light to direct the laser death ray program eighteen months ago.

As the head of military aviation, Sokolov oversaw Roscosmos, the Russian space agency. Three Russian cosmonauts were currently on a joint mission to the International Space Station with three American astronauts. It was a yearlong quest that would end in May after a new crew was sent to replace them. That triggered an idea in Sokolov's dangerous mind. The space travelers return to earth was scheduled to land in Kazakhstan. He called NASA and asked to have the Soyuz TMA spacecraft landing changed to Edwards Air Force Base in California. NASA officials didn't know why but were thrilled to death to have them land on American soil. It would be good public relations.

In late January, NASA and Roscosmos gave a joint press release indicating the destination change for the Soyuz's return. It was buried on the last page of every periodical that decided to print it. Who cared about science when journalists were still busy trying to explain how Randall Thompson was elected president of the United States a year earlier? Thompson was a wealthy tycoon who rented a one-bedroom apartment overlooking the Niagara River in Buffalo but owned no real estate in the US. Instead, he heavily invested in foreign properties, mainly in Canada and Russia, and rumors were that he avoided paying US taxes by exploiting loopholes in the system. But, regardless of the rumors, American voters were fed up with politics-as-usual, and they thought Thompson would clean house in Washington, DC.

On February 1st, Sokolov called Russian President Vladimir Putin with a suggestion that could help boost his struggling image worldwide. Why not have him and his new friend President Thompson hold a welcome home ceremony for the space station cosmonauts and astronauts? Sokolov then suggested a fun surprise to end the celebration: Putin's presidential airplane, the Ilyushin Il-96 Command Point, would take off from Edwards and circle the airbase while Thompson's Air Force One became airborne. Then, as a gesture of solidarity between nations, they would perform a side-by-side flyby and wave their wings to the crowd on the ground. Putin liked the idea, and after a hotline call to Thompson, so did the American president.

Sokolov licked his chops! He planned to blow apart both planes in midair. Finally, after all the talking and testing, the death ray was going to happen! Lord Shaffer hesitantly agreed. It would be a significant step in the masterplan, and if successful, it would create a diversion from the Taste Of Arabia memory-loss scheme. News agencies would be overloaded for months reporting the presidential tragedy, and they wouldn't investigate anything else—for instance, the fading memories of coffee drinkers everywhere. It might just work! It would be very dangerous and risky, but the reward could be exponential!

Two years ago, Lord Shaffer had insisted on secretly relocating the laser weapon program to America from Sultan Tariq's palace in Arabia. Once exposed to room temperature, the useful life of the energy packs would be about one month, and it was too difficult to provide cold storage for transportation halfway around the world. KGB spies reported that Senso-McNamara Corporation of Mesa, Arizona, already produced the death rays covertly for the military. Only a handful of executives at the company were involved in the top-secret operation. Residents of Mesa believed that Senso-Mac was simply a harmless laser sensor and surgical equipment factory that also happened to make traffic speed guns for the police. But the Pentagon made a huge mistake when they set up the Senso-Mac facility to design and create the death ray. They allowed it to remain a publicly-traded company on the New York Stock Exchange.

Lord Shaffer amassed his wealth by being a corporate raider that preyed on unsuspecting companies whose assets appeared to be undervalued. Senso-Mac was one such corporation. Based on Sokolov's recommendation, Shaffer purchased seventy-five percent of the stock and, in reality, became its new owner. The Pentagon didn't even raise an eyebrow. The fact was they didn't even know the takeover happened.

A big selling point for Shaffer was that Senso-Mac was close to Gila Bend. The small town was an hour or so away and shaping up to become the American base for his Taste Of Arabia operations. He would keep the current employees at Senso-Mac to avoid suspicion as to what he really planned to do. But there was a glitch. Sokolov informed Shaffer that Homeland Security had built a secret outpost a short distance away. Lord Shaffer would need to eliminate that problem.

Shaffer moved his MI6 friend Bond to Mesa to head up operations. He had to give Bond a first name for obvious reasons, so Jim sounded like a good choice. Jim Bond, COO of Senso-Mac—it kind of had a nice ring to it! Someday, somewhere in a local pub, someone would put the number seven after COO just for laughs.

Russians Yury Glebov and Ruslan Kozar had earned gold medals in two Olympics for sharpshooting. They were the best marksmen in the world. But trying to convince them to give up training for a third medal to become presidential assassinators was a challenge. However, money talks. In March, Glebov and Kozar were smuggled into America under the guise of Harry Gleason and Kevin Karson, two nice Norwegian gents trying to make a buck as traffic speed gun testers for Senso-McNamara Corporation in Arizona. They would be assigned to an underground laboratory that most employees of Senso-Mac never even knew existed. But instead of firing speed guns, the Russian sharpshooters would practice their skills blasting away a hologram of Air Force One until the day they were called upon to complete the real task. Their bosses at Senso-Mac never knew.

President Thompson's national security director almost nixed the Edwards Air Force Base ceremony a few days before Glebov and Kozar had been hired by Sokolov. The NSA boss was in a tizzy after Thompson tweeted about it while the secret service was preparing for a decoy maneuver to protect him. Now the American public would know about the celebration months before it happened. Fortunately, the president didn't mention the flyby to end the ceremony.

As Parliament arguments labored on, Lord Shaffer was utterly off task. He was thinking about how his masterplan had unfolded so well to this point. Now that Senso-Mac and the Homeland Security office had been destroyed, there was no turning back. Shaffer sent Directorate Chief Yegor Bovnik to Arizona in the Gulfstream to get Schultz, Schoenholtz, Glebov, and Kozar out of there before they could screw things up and get arrested. He also needed to transport them and the laser weapons to California to satisfy Sokolov's wild hair idea. Killing two presidents on the same day! Would it work? He thought about everything that had happened over the past six years and rubbed his temples.

Lord Shaffer then stood up and announced in a loud voice so all his colleagues in Parliament could hear him, "Goat terrorists! We have been here for twelve hours, and now you want to discuss how one isolated goat killer could lead to the destruction of the British Empire. I won't be part of this, gentlemen. I'm leaving. Good night." With that, Lord Shaffer was the first to exit the Palace of Westminster. But he wasn't going home. He boarded his limo, and his driver dropped him off at the Savoy Hotel. There, in the Royal Suite overlooking the Thames River, General Leonid Sokolov and Sultan Tariq Nassar were waiting impatiently for him to arrive. The meeting had been scheduled for six o'clock. Directorate Chief Yegor Bovnik was on his way to Arizona, so Sokolov had to finish off a whole bottle of Black Cow vodka all by himself. Tariq had downed several glasses of apple juice and Perrier sparkling water by the time Lord Shaffer opened the suite door and stepped inside.

Sokolov looked at Lord Shaffer with bloodshot eyes. "Could we get this meeting started? This might take all night."

Chapter 32

Wednesday, April 18, 2018
FBI Laboratory, Phoenix, Arizona
2:00 pm (Pacific Daylight Time)

Agent Kelly sat patiently in the uncomfortable steel foldout chair as two FBI lab technicians completed their examination of the helmet-cam recorder. They were taking notes while watching the video on the tiny camera's screen and using an earphone splitter. When finished, they unplugged the earphones and nodded to each other.

"So, here's what we got," said Morris Radcliff, chief technician for the Phoenix FBI laboratory. "Schultz and Schoenholtz allegedly smell gasoline and claim there was a fuel leak in the vault. Schultz claims there was gasoline residue on the floor and zooms in on his hand, which is being used to rub the gasoline between his thumb and forefinger. He claims gas was spread around the vault to start a fire, but he doesn't know why it was not ignited.

"Then Schoenholtz notices the trap door is open and that the storage compartment contains two energy packs. He claims other energy packs must have been stolen. Schoenholtz theorizes that whoever splashed the gas was planning to destroy the vault with the energy packs but couldn't find a laser gun to use. So the perpetrator decided to ignite the place with the gasoline, but something 'spooked' him, and he ran before lighting the match.

"Schultz then finds a bat-shaped, cylindrical container lying on the floor. Schoenholtz believes it's a homemade atomic bomb.

Rather an ignorant hypothesis for someone who examined it with just a quick glance, wouldn't you say?"

The FBI agents all nod, then Radcliff continues, "Schultz then finds another open trap door on the far wall and a hidden compartment beneath. Schoenholtz finds blood on the floor at once, then sees a Canon camera and telephoto lens nearby. Strangely, Schultz then uses the word 'killer' as he suggests the camera most likely belongs to whoever that might be. I say strange because there is no body nor solid proof of a murder taking place. It could have been merely an accident. Schoenholtz questions him and Schultz then admits the blood could have been accidental, but it also could mean someone stole the energy packs, splashed gas around, and committed murder.

"They then bag the camera and lens and claim the serial number can be traced back to the owner, and the owner's fingerprints are most likely still on the camera. Then they seal the vault."

"Okay," replied Kelly, "what is your opinion?"

"My opinion is Schultz and Schoenholtz are bad actors. Not really anything in the physical evidence to support that, but my years interrogating witnesses leads me to believe they are hiding something. As for the fingerprints, there are none, which I find very unusual. Not many photographers use gloves when snapping pictures. Also, the SD card is missing, so we can't see any pictures that may have been taken. However, we do have the serial number, and I will have that traced as soon as possible."

"Sounds good, Rad. Now, what about the Apple watch I gave you yesterday. Find anything?"

"We're still working on the four-digit security code to turn it on. Apple folks can override the code to get in, but they are not willing to work with us. Claim it would ruin their reputation for protecting their customers' rights of privacy. But we'll get in—we've got one of our best software engineers taking a crack at it as we speak."

"What about the ring?" asked Kelly.

"Still in the bag. As soon as we finish with the watch, we'll deal with the ring."

Lab receptionist Alice Kaiser opened the door just enough to stick her head inside. "Rad, you almost done? That coffee salesman has been waiting over an hour out in the lobby. He's not being pushy, but he started telling me jokes, and I can't take much more of it."

Radcliff chuckled and smiled at Agent Kelly. "I get salesmen every day. Alice tells them I might be a while, so they wait for about a half-hour and then leave. This dude's persistent! But I guess he sells coffee, and I sure could use an afternoon wake-up call. Want one?"

"No, I'll pass," replied Kelly. "Actually, I could use a good night's sleep, but I doubt that will happen anytime soon! Call me when you have the results on the watch and ring. Thanks!"

Radcliff nodded as Kelly exited the lab. He passed through the lobby and got a good look at the coffee salesman who smiled at him. Kelly walked out through the main doors and paused.

"Something about that guy," he muttered to himself. "I can't place it."

2:30 pm (Pacific Daylight Time)

How was he going to get the watch and ring? That was the question James LeBron contemplated while fidgeting in the reception area for the past hour. The receptionist was too serious and didn't want to shoot the breeze, so he thought about telling some jokes to lighten the mood. He needed everyone to be relaxed when he made his presentation. He knew the coffee would have a long-term effect, but for this meeting, LeBron needed the watch and ring.

"Hello, sir, my name is Morris Radcliff. I understand that you sell coffee. Well, that's great, but Starbucks is just around the corner, so I think you are wasting your time." Radcliff shook LeBron's hand with a light grip and a dismissive frown on his face.

"If you will try just a cup of Taste Of Arabia, I can guarantee you will never spend outrageous money for a cup of joe at Starbucks again. Deal?"

Radcliff glanced at Alice, who was trying to hide a smile. "Okay, can you make this quick? I've got to get back to work."

"Yes, of course. But I just noticed that I brought the wrong Keurig brewer with me. This is the one I use for demos in Europe, and it's 220-volt. You don't happen to have a 220-volt outlet?" Lebron had guessed that this decoy might work while driving to the lab. He knew an FBI lab would most likely have both a 110-voltage and 220-voltage outlet. He was only hoping they didn't already have a Keurig somewhere in the reception area. It didn't appear that they did.

"They have a Keurig down in the work lounge," Alice said to Radcliff. "Want me to go get it?"

Radcliff thought for a moment, then shook his head no. "We don't have time. I have a 220 outlet in the lab we can use." LeBron's heart rate dropped back down. Radcliff motioned to the coffee salesman. "Okay, sir, follow me and bring the dang brewer with you."

Radcliff led LeBron to the outlet, and the coffee salesman plugged it in. "What's the name of that coffee again?"

"Oh, I apologize! I haven't had a chance to introduce you to myself. I'm very sorry. My name is James LeBron, and this here incredible coffee is Taste Of Arabia. You can't find it in stores because we are selling it exclusively door to door."

"Did you say James LeBron?" Radcliff broke out in laughter. "You know, if you switched your name around, you might be making millions playing pro basketball in Cleveland instead of pounding the pavement in Phoenix!"

LeBron laughed back. "I know! I get many jokes when I introduce myself for the first time. But, the coffee I sell is no joke. If you like it, I will give you a box of 200 for free that you can try out. I'll be back in two weeks to take your order for more. I guarantee you will want more!"

"I'll fill up your reserve tank with bottled water," said Alice. LeBron smiled and handed her the clear plastic container.

Before she left the room, Radcliff reached into his pocket and pulled out a piece of notebook paper. "Alice, wait! Here is a serial number of a camera and lens that I want traced. Give it to Agent Talbert on your way to the fridge. Tell him I need a name and address soon." He handed Alice the paper with the serial numbers scribbled on it.

LeBron pulled out two coffee mugs while Radcliff decided to check his notes, waiting for Alice to return. Radcliff turned his back on LeBron and walked to his desk. He picked up a clipboard and began flipping through pages. LeBron looked around the room, squinting to read the labels on the cupboards. He was trying to figure out where the watch and ring might be stored. Suddenly, he was stunned by a delightful surprise. On the laboratory table next to him were two plastic zip-lock bags. One contained the watch, and the other held the ring. They were five feet away. LeBron padded gently on the floor hoping Radcliff wouldn't hear him.

Staring at Radcliff to make sure he kept his back to him, LeBron picked up the watch and slid it into the inside pocket of his sports coat. But, when he grabbed for the ring, it slipped out of his fingers and landed on the floor. Radcliff turned and was flabbergasted to see LeBron at the table, then noticed the coffee salesman was picking the ring off the linoleum tile.

"Hey, what do you think you are doing?!" shouted Radcliff. He strutted towards LeBron. "Give me that ring!"

Lebron had to move fast. He backed away and stood opposite of Radcliff on the other side of the table. He reached into his coat pocket and pulled out the plastic bag with the watch. Radcliff tried to slide around the table, but LeBron shifted at the same speed and kept an equal distance away using the table as a barrier. Keeping his eyes glued on Radcliff, LeBron opened the plastic bag and shook the watch onto the table. Radcliff saw what was happening and dove onto the table, reaching desperately for the watch. He couldn't grasp it but was able to clutch LeBron's hand—the one that held the ring. LeBron yanked his arm, but Radcliff was too strong. He tugged again, and the ring slipped out onto the table, rolled a couple of inches from the watch, and stopped. Both men tried to seize the jewelry, and as they did, the ring touched the watch. A loud pop could be heard, and a strong current of electricity moved quickly through Radcliff and LeBron's interlocked hands, up their arms, and directly to their hearts. The hair on their heads, arms, and legs stood straight up, and smoke escaped from their eye sockets, noses, and mouths.

Alice opened the door, dropped the container of water, and covered her mouth with both hands as she watched her boss and the coffee salesman convulse and sizzle their way to the floor. The potent mixture of uranium, plutonium, and thorium atoms that were contained within a micro-sized hollow chamber inside the ring packed plenty of electrical punch. The wide-bandgap semiconductor could produce a high-amperage current for several minutes, plenty of time to provide a series of 1,000-volt electric shocks. The continuous internal tremors led to organ burns and stopped their hearts cold. Radcliff and LeBron never stood a chance.

Neither did the data that was stored in the now-internally-fried Apple watch.

Chapter 33

Wednesday, April 18, 2018
Falcon Field, Mesa, Arizona
2:40 pm (Pacific Daylight Time)

The Northwing Ultralight Rotax 447 engine sounded like a lawnmower on its last legs before it sputtered and killed at 2,000 feet. The pilot had pushed the range of the flying trike beyond its limits since stealing it from Max's Used Microlight Aircraft Sales at Falcon Field in Mesa. The Northwing was parked outside in the display area, and the pilot had hidden behind a dumpster waiting for an opportune time to thieve it. At noon, the two owners who were brothers stepped out for lunch, locked the front door, placed a *Will Return at 1:00 pm* sign in the window, and headed out for a couple of Bell Bottom Bacon Blues burgers at nearby Flancer's Restaurant.

The pilot hotwired the ignition system, hopped in, and rolled out onto Falcon Drive for takeoff. There was no midday traffic on the four-lane service road, and the trike only needed eighty feet to become airborne. Once he was above the treetop levels, he veered east to keep away from the airport runways. But the two air traffic controllers saw him and were agitated. A Learjet was on approach from Tucson and needed to land from the north. If the Ultralight continued to climb, there could be a problem.

The pilot was a highly-skilled veteran and immediately turned southwest towards Gilbert. He estimated the distance he needed to fly was about 125 miles, and he guessed the Ultralight had a range of about 60 miles. He knew he would have to kill the engine several times and use the thermals for gliding to increase the range. His destination was the burnt trash pile of helicopters and SUVs in Ajo, where the news was just beginning to form a day after the incident. The *Arizona Republic* was busy covering the Senso-McNamara disaster and didn't feel a priority to report whatever happened in Ajo yesterday. They would get to it when they got to it. But the pilot knew better; he believed the two events were linked and was determined to find out.

The Ultralight finally ran out of fuel as the pilot was descending north of Ajo. A strong westerly wind blew across the desert, and the pilot tried to maintain his course, but he was pushed south of the town and needed to find a place to land where no one would notice him. By now, the owners of Max's Used Microlights would have returned from lunch and called the police, and the air traffic controllers at Falcon Field could have plotted his probable course for them. He didn't want anyone to see him land. That's when he noticed something peculiar. He could see what appeared to be the wreckage of a small aircraft, perhaps a Cessna, and further down his line of vision was a completely intact biplane—with two men crouched down near the front left tire. It was possible that these men had witnessed the helicopter dogfight that took place yesterday and could provide some information. He glided the Ultralight towards the biplane and landed softly fifty yards away.

3:00 pm (Pacific Daylight Time)

A toolkit was built-in underneath the passenger seat of the Stearman biplane. Rick Frye hadn't noticed it until he started searching the plane for something to repair the flat tire. The wheel was thirty inches in diameter, and the front tires were originally solid rubber, but over the years, they were replaced by standard automobile-type tires with innertubes. Rick and Donnor thought if they could fill the tire with anything of substance, be it cloth, plastic, or pebbles, they might be able to take off. It was when they were about to peel the plastic from the cockpit floor that they found the toolbox. Among the usual contents of a toolbox was a half-used tube of superglue and a small bicycle tire pump.

Rick and Donnor stacked several flat boulders on top of one another to prop up the plane so that it was high enough to remove the tire. Donnor was barely able to lift the front axle sufficiently for Rick to scoot the top stone underneath it, but with a boost of adrenaline, he managed to raise it two inches. Removing the wheel from the frame was tricky. It was apparent that whoever changed the tire last tightened it too much, so the only tool in the kit that would work was an adjustable wrench. Taking turns pounding the wrench's handle with a rock, the two men were finally able to loosen the bolt. New cuss words were invented at the same time.

Using a screwdriver, Rick pried the tire from the rim. They were hoping and praying that the innertube had not blown, but instead ran over a nail or something that could be fixed. They got lucky; the plane had rolled over a cactus thorn that caused the puncture. With a pocketknife, Rick shaved off a patch of rubber from the sole of his tennis shoe. He removed the thorn, glued the piece onto the tire, and both men crossed their fingers and took a deep breath.

Miraculously, the patched-up innertube held the air from the bicycle pump. Rick placed the innertube back into the tire and reset it onto the wheel frame. He and Donnor kicked out the boulders from underneath the axles, and the wheel dropped to the ground. They both took turns pumping more air into the innertube. When finished, they wiped the grime from their hands onto their pant legs, then gave each other a high-five. It was time to see if they could start the engine again.

Suddenly, they were startled by an Ultralight gliding directly towards them.

4:00 pm (Pacific Daylight Time)
Mojave Desert, California

The Hummer H3 limousine jounced wildly on its last leg through the Mojave Desert as it approached Edwards Air Force Base. After operating off-road for almost 400 miles, crashing through numerous fences, and hurdling dried-up river beds, the driver was incredibly fatigued and wanted desperately for this journey to end. So did his passengers: ten ICE agents, two school kids, and one feisty teacher. The kids said absolutely nothing for the past sixteen hours while their teacher didn't shut up. The Hummer had made its way west through the Sonoran Desert, crossed the Colorado River south of Yuma without using a bridge, crisscrossed through a slice of Mexico, and then outran five border patrol SUVs by cutting across the sweeping dunes at Gordon's Well in southeastern California. From there, they headed northwest across Joshua Tree National Park to avoid all city traffic heading in and out of Los Angeles. The thirty-two-gallon gas tank needed one refueling stop, so in the middle of the night, the driver rammed through the chain-link fence surrounding the Imperial Sand Dunes Cahuilla Ranger Station and pulled up in between two park rangers' pickup trucks. Agent Bogdan Smirnov siphoned off gas from both vehicles while the other ICE agents stood guard. Fortunately for their wives, kids, and any other probable inheritors, the rangers didn't wake up.

There had been only one biffy break, a dusty stop in the middle of the desert east of the Salton Sea. It was a quick stop due to the rattles from snakes and howls from coyotes that could be heard nearby. Everyone tiptoed carefully over the starlit sand, then ran as fast as they could back to the limo. The kids decided it was safer to just wet their pants.

North of Big Bear Lake in the San Bernardino National Forest, the driver steered the Hummer onto a road for the first time since leaving Ajo. He got on California 18 and drove through Apple Valley, then turned onto the Antelope Valley Freeway and passed through Palmdale and Lancaster. A few minutes later, the four-wheel-drive stretch limo reached Rosamond, and the driver veered right onto Rosamond Boulevard. Needless to say, the Hummer got looks from everyone on the road. No one inside the limo, except perhaps the teacher and two students, wanted that kind of attention.

The limo pulled over for a moment so that Kurt Kellner, Isaac, and Zaira could be gagged and shoved onto the floor. Three ICE agents held a pistol to their heads and threatened them to keep absolutely silent. As the Hummer pulled up to the west gate of Edwards Air Force Base, two military police glanced at one another and came out of the guardhouse.

"Who the hell could that be?" said one guard.

"Another high-ranking VIP," replied his partner. "We see them every day."

"Why do you suppose their Hummer is dirty and dusty?"

"Probably an astronaut who wanted to have some fun in the desert before coming here."

"Yeah, you're probably right. Probably John Glenn. He could afford a Hummer limo."

"Is John Glenn still alive?"

The guards held their rifles by their sides with the barrels pointing up to the sky. Neither had a finger on the trigger. Whoever was in the limo had to be a VIP, which meant there was no imminent threat to the air force base.

The deeply tinted window did not allow for an outsider to see inside the vehicle. The Hummer stopped at the gate, and the driver lowered his window. The guard glanced inside and noticed eight or ten men in the back seats wearing ICE windbreakers. That answered a lot of questions. Immigration and Customs Enforcement regularly used Edwards to fly illegal immigrants back to their home countries. But the guards were curious as to why they arrived in a Hummer instead of a Chevy Suburban, their usual mode of transportation.

"A Hummer limo today," said the guard to the driver. "What's the occasion?" He was trying to be casual in his questioning so as not to offend the ICE agents, but his military responsibility dictated that he query anyone who might be suspicious. ICE agents arriving by a Hummer limo were definitely questionable.

"Sorry, Sergeant, confidential." The driver handed a letter to the guard who skimmed it then gave it back. He stood at attention and saluted.

"You may proceed, sir."

The Hummer entered and zipped past the Muroc Lake Golf Course, the Air Force Test Flight Museum, and the administration buildings. It headed directly to Runway Five on Rogers Dry Lake and stopped about a hundred yards away.

The Boeing C-32 was parked off to the side with a petroleum semi-truck pumping jet fuel into one of the five auxiliary tanks. The two-tone, powder blue and white plane would have looked lonely on the three-mile-long runway (five miles long if you include the lakebed extension on the north end) had it not been for the fifteen secret service men in their black suits watching over it like hawks. Each one of them noticed the Hummer approach and park some distance away, but none seemed overly concerned.

And even from a football field away, the letters printed on the fuselage could be read very clearly:

UNITED STATES OF AMERICA

Chapter 34

Wednesday, April 18, 2018
Sonoran Desert, Ajo, Arizona
4:15 pm (Pacific Daylight Time)

The Ultralight bounced around on the rugged desert floor and came to a full stop several yards from the biplane. Not knowing who they could trust, Donnor pulled out a hammer from the toolbox, and Rick waved the wrench high in the air. They wanted whoever was flying that trike to know that they were armed and loaded with garage weaponry!

The pilot climbed down and raised both hands. "Whoa, whoa, whoa, boys. I'm not here to cause you any trouble. My Ultralight ran out of gas, and I needed to land somewhere. When I saw you from the air, I thought you might be able to help me."

Rick and Donnor looked at each other, then laid down the tools.

"Sorry. We'd like to help," said Rick, "but obviously we're kind of stuck out here, too. Where were you headed?"

"To Ajo, I guess. After my engines died, I got caught in a strong wind that blew me down here."

Donnor gave the pilot a strange look. "What do you mean you guess? Either you were going to Ajo, or you weren't. Which one is it? And where did you take off from?"

"Okay, the truth is I was investigating a helicopter accident that happened yesterday. Two helicopters went down. Know anything about it?"

Donnor and Rick were speechless. They both had plenty to say, but they weren't sure they could trust this man. They needed to probe a little first. Rick was a master at Socratic questioning techniques because he used the strategy every day in his classroom. The concept was to answer questions with questions. It supposedly built critical-thinking skills in students.

"What do you know about it," asked Rick as he stepped towards the pilot. Donnor could tell Rick wanted to take control of the conversation, so he stayed put and just listened.

"I know that an Aerovictor chopper gunned down two other choppers. Has it been in the news?"

"Newspaper boys don't really deliver out here in the desert," replied Rick sarcastically. That wasn't like him, but he was tired, and it just slipped out. "I'm sorry. I shouldn't have said that. My apologies."

The pilot smiled. "No problem."

"I meant to ask," continued Rick, "how did you hear about the helicopters?" Socratic questioning at its finest!

"I think you're wondering who I am and what I'm doing out here in an Ultralight, right?"

"Would that help us all to understand?" replied Rick.

"I guess it would. Maybe I should ask what you two were doing flying a biplane? And are you aware that there's a downed Cessna several hundred yards from here?"

"Do you think we know about the Cessna?"

"Will you stop asking questions and just talk to me, damn it!" The pilot was having a Socratic meltdown. It happened with many frustrated students, too.

"What do you know about the—" Donnor grabbed Rick by the arm and stepped in front of him. He also had enough Socratic questioning.

"Yes," said Donnor. "The Cessna belonged to my cousin. Are you investigating that, too?"

"No," replied the pilot. He hesitated before adding, "I'm sorry to hear that. Is your cousin okay? I apologize again, but did he survive?"

"We don't know yet," responded Donnor in a very subdued way. "But the plane appears to have been shot down. It has bullet holes in the airframe."

"Shot down!" exclaimed the pilot. "Who would shoot down a Cessna?"

"That's what we would like to know. So, who are you? What kind of investigator flies an Ultralight?"

"I guess an underpaid one," the pilot answered and smiled. Donnor waited for him to continue. "Okay, I'm not an investigator. I guess that doesn't surprise you. But I am looking for answers to some urgent questions that I have."

"Who are you?" asked Donnor once again. "Why are you out here looking for answers?"

"My name is Cliff Bullard," replied the pilot. "I'm the one who flew the Aerovictor that shot down those two helicopters."

4:45 pm (Pacific Daylight Time)

After handshakes and introductions, Rick, Donnor, and Cliff forged a trust with one another. They really didn't have a choice. Danger had surrounded all of them for the past two days.

Cliff listened attentively and without interruption as Donnor told the story of the ICE raid on the charter school and how he had shot one of the agents. Then Rick detailed their wild escape to the Ajo golf course where they dropped off several teachers and two students at a hidden tunnel before zipping across the desert to Cousin Mack's apartment. Thanks to a train, they were able to get away from the five SUVs chasing them, but two helicopters were tracking them from above. Donnor then explained how he had blocked the underground parking area with his pickup and doused it with gasoline while the others ran for cover. The two helicopters closed in and lit up the truck with bullets, but Donnor managed to flee into the building. He talked Mack into helping them by flying the teachers and students out of harm's way to Mexico with his Cessna. While they were bolting from the parking garage to the airport on Mack's golf cart, they looked up and saw an Aerovictor helicopter shoot down the two choppers that had been chasing them.

"So that was you," said Rick to Cliff as he tried to process everything.

"Yeah, that was me. I guess I better do some enlightening of my own." Cliff then told the story of his eventful two days. First, he revealed his background as a retired air force pilot who flew Air Force One for President Bush. Trying to remain humble, Cliff did not mention his storied past but did say he was hired by Zefron to test Aerovictor helicopters. He explained how he watched as the two helicopters and five SUVs had been chasing a pickup truck, then noticed that the choppers had Russian insignia on them. When they began to fire on the pickup, he fired at them with warning shots. Then, the Russian helicopters chased him south but couldn't catch him. Instead, they turned back to Ajo and inexplicably blew up the SUVs. That's when he unloaded his ammo on them and headed quickly back to Mesa.

"Those were Russian helicopters?" asked Rick. He couldn't believe what he had just heard. "Why didn't you radio for help?"

"Yes, they were Russian, and no, I couldn't radio for help. My radio wasn't working. And I'm pretty sure those weren't ICE agents who were chasing you. Anyway, I got to Mesa just in time to witness two men blow up the Senso-McNamara building with a laser gun. They were riding on ATVs, and I followed them into the desert. I hesitated and left them momentarily, but when I returned, one of them shot me down."

"Shot you down?! Oh, my God!" Rick was beside himself with anger. "Why did you leave them in the first place?"

"Well, that's the thing. The ATVs they were riding were from Homeland Security. At first, I didn't want to mess with Homeland, so I stopped chasing them. But then I realized that Homeland Security wouldn't have opened fire on Senso-Mac, so I returned. Unfortunately, they were waiting for me."

"How did you get away?" asked Donnor.

"They assumed I was killed in the blast. But I was able to jump out before it crashed and burned. I was scraped up and exhausted, so I spent the night in the desert a mile or so away. This morning, I was going to go back to Zefron and tell them what happened, but quite frankly, I'm not sure who to trust anymore. Instead, I decided to head back to where I downed those helicopters in Ajo and see if I could make sense of any of this. I stole the Ultralight, but I plan to pay for it when I get back. Anyway, I ran out of fuel and saw the Cessna and your biplane, so I was curious and decided to land here."

"You must be right!" exclaimed Rick. "If those were Russian military helicopters that were chasing us, that means those ICE agents were fake. But why invade a charter school in Gila Bend? That part doesn't make sense."

"None of this makes sense!" responded Donnor. "There had to be something inside the school that those men wanted. They were probably only disguised as ICE agents to clear everyone out. They could hardly have arrested anyone because they wouldn't have any place to take them. No fake jails in Gila Bend!"

"But they locked Principal Perez up in handcuffs!"

"Only to make it look like the school was covering something up. And seeing they were dressed as ICE agents, they wanted people to think Perez was hiding illegal immigrants."

"A perfect misdirection! Everyone in town would be scrambling to get their kids home safely, especially those who were undocumented. Meanwhile, once the building was clear, no one would be watching whatever they were planning to do there. But you ruined their plans, Donnor, when you shot that agent and got away with us all!"

"That's it! Their simple immigration enforcement ruse was busted up when I killed that guy. That ended their scheme because they wouldn't have time to finish what they started. And they didn't want me or you folks or even the two kids who were driving the school bus talking to the police after that happened."

"But by then, what difference did it make?" asked Rick. "Sooner or later, the cops would figure out they weren't real ICE agents."

Donnor thought about that for a moment. "You're right. I'm not sure why they needed to kill us. After all, they did demolish their SUVs on purpose, most likely to destroy any evidence."

Cliff inserted, "I think their SUVs were going to be used to get away. After they did whatever they were going to do at the school, they would let everyone go and then just drive off. Who would bother following them? But after you interrupted their plans, they changed the blueprint."

"Drive off where?" asked Rick. "How would they get out of the country and back to Russia? Those helicopters maybe? Do you think?"

"Two helicopters wouldn't have done the trick. Not enough space inside for all of them, but if they flew the leaders to some predestined place, they could pick up the others later. That pickup point would have been in their masterplan. You said there were about twenty to thirty agents, right? They would need a private jet the size of a Dornier 328 or a Saab 340 to get everyone inside."

"I've never heard of either one of those jets, Cliff," said Rick. "But, how big of a runway would they need? If we knew that, we could narrow down possible locations they might be heading."

"They can take off on a runway less than a mile. That won't narrow it down much. And we don't even know what direction they went."

"You're right, but we know they most likely walked there," said Rick. "Unless someone picked them up."

"It's a long walk back to Gila Bend," said Donnor, "but I bet the airport's runway is at least a mile long. Wouldn't it make sense to go there?"

"I doubt they would risk going back to the scene of the crime," replied Cliff. "I think we're missing something." Cliff walked away from Rick and Donnor and was in deep thought. He stared at an isolated cumulus cloud hovering in the late afternoon sky.

"What is it? What are you thinking?" asked Donnor.

"I'm thinking about those two hulks that shot me down."

"What about them?"

"Not them so much. The ATV."

"And?"

"The insignia on the ATV said *Homeland Security*. As I said before, Homeland Security isn't supposed to blow up American buildings. And they certainly are not supposed to shoot down American helicopters."

"Okay, I get that," said Rick. "But don't you think those were simply two thieves who stole the ATV and laser gun from Homeland Security?"

"Well, that's what I thought at first. But now I'm wondering."

"Wondering about what?!"

"If those men actually worked for Homeland Security, perhaps not everyone employed by Homeland Security is above board."

"What are you saying?" asked Donnor. "I'm not following you."

"I'm saying our nation's security may have been compromised! Spies, infiltrators, you name it. If you want to destroy something powerful, the most effective way is to get inside and kill from within. Like cancer."

"But to penetrate Homeland Security would require a bad guy in a leadership role working on the inside, wouldn't it?" asked Rick.

"I would guess it would," replied Cliff, who once again walked away from Donnor and Rick in meditation. He looked down at the ground and scratched his forehead. Then he muttered softly to himself, "Can't be."

Rick heard what Cliff had mumbled, so he strutted up to him. "Can't be what? You need to tell us!"

"The vice president oversees Homeland Security. He's not the director, but the director answers to him."

"Are you saying you think the vice president had something to do with letting Homeland Security become compromised?"

"No, I can't be sure. But I think I can find out. I need to be very careful."

"What are you going to do?"

"I flew Air Force One for President Bush, and I know every inch of the details on that jet. Both Air Force One and Air Force

Two, the vice president's plane, have black boxes just like all commercial aircraft that record flight data and cockpit voice commands. But one thing Air Force One and Two have that the others don't is a GPS recorder that logs everywhere the planes have traveled for the past year. The GPS is continually activated, meaning their locations are constantly monitored, but they are also cloaked."

"What do you mean by cloaked?" asked Donnor.

"I mean that only strategic military personnel can get access to the GPS. That way, our enemies don't know where to find our president or vice president. Anyway, if I can locate the Air Force Two tracking device, I will know where to find the vice president. That would be a start. From there, if I could extract the black box from the plane along with the GPS recorder, it would go a long way in finding out if the vice president is involved in something terrible."

"Extract? You mean steal, don't you?" asked Rick. Cliff didn't respond to the obviously rhetorical question.

"Do either of you have a cell phone? Okay, sorry! That was a dumb question. Of course, you don't. We need to fly your biplane back to Mesa."

"Why Mesa?"

"My boss at Zefron may have access to the military GPS system, which includes Air Force Two. We need to fly back and find out. There's an airport a block away where we can land."

They pushed back on the plane and swung it around forty-five degrees so that it was facing the oncoming wind. Rick looked at Cliff and waved his hand palm side up at the cockpit indicating *after you.* Cliff shook his head no and said, "You flew this airplane just fine before, you can get us back to Mesa."

Rick smiled and said, "Thanks!" He climbed into the rear pilot's seat and pushed on the throttle knob to give it some gas while Donnor and Cliff spun the propeller. It started on the third spin. Donnor and Cliff climbed into the front passenger seats, and all three men fastened the leather coverings to their heads and placed the goggles over their eyes. As the nine cylinders rumbled like thunder, Rick leaned forward and tapped Cliff on the shoulder.

"We took off on an airport runway," he shouted, trying to be heard above the engine noise. "I'm a little nervous about the rocky desert. Any suggestions?"

"This biplane has a strong airframe, high lift, and good tires. It's designed to take off and land on unstable surfaces. Besides, with the wind blowing this hard, we should be airborne about 500 feet from here. Go for it!"

"By the way," yelled Rick. "I didn't tell you that the only gauge working is the altimeter. The compass, speedometer, and anemometer are all broke, as is the radio."

Cliff turned his head around stretching his neck the best he could to look at Rick. He lifted his goggles and winked. "That's the only way to fly!"

With that, Rick let off the brake, and the Stearman C3B bounced through the desert as the airframe reverberated with every stretch of metal. A few seconds later, they were airborne. Rick steered towards the city of Ajo that he could see in the distance, then followed Highway 85 as it wiggled past Gila Bend and turned gently northward towards Buckeye. From there, he followed Highway 303 as it looped around the northern suburbs of Phoenix, crossed over Interstate 17, and headed towards Carefree. Rick was purposely flying at a low altitude and away from commercial traffic that would be landing at Sky Harbor Airport. With the wind continuing to blow strongly from the west, Rick had to land at Falcon Field from the northeast. He snaked around the McDowell Mountains until he saw the Saguaro Lake Marina, then turned and tracked southwesterly following Bush Highway. Rick began a slow descent toward Falcon Field as the plane jounced through a turbulent wind draft between the flat-topped Red Mountain to the west and Four Peaks to the east.

The two air traffic controllers at Falcon Field were having a conniption! The Gulfstream G550 arriving from London City Airport was on approach when the radar spotted the biplane heading in the same direction. They frantically tried to hail the small plane on every frequency possible but to no avail. No one was answering.

When they ordered the Gulfstream to divert to Mesa's Gateway Airport, the pilot refused. He lied and claimed his jet was too low on fuel. Rick didn't notice the Gulfstream flying 120 feet above him until its draft pushed the biplane down towards the first hole fairway on Longbow Golf Course. He pulled up in time to scoot over the McDowell Road fence and touch down softly on Runway 22L as the Gulfstream was lurching to a stop 1,000 feet in front of him. Cliff pointed in the direction opposite the control towers, and Rick made a right turn. They wanted to park as far from the ATCs as possible.

Knowing the FAA would be called in due to the near midair disaster, Rick, Donnor, and Cliff deplaned quickly and jogged north towards Zefron. They climbed over the chain-link fence and dodged traffic as they crossed over McDowell Road. The sun was setting as they ran through the employee parking lot and headed toward the south doors. A sprinkling of cars meant that a few workers were still in the building. Zefron employees were well known around Mesa for putting in long hours.

Cliff hoped no one would recognize him at the south access portal. His usual entry doors were on the north side of the facility, closest to the factory. His five-digit code could get him in any entrance, and his badge gave him clearance past the security guards. Knowing it would be impossible to get Rick and Donnor inside, Cliff told them to wait in the parking lot.

Cliff punched in the code and heard the click followed by a buzz. He turned the handle, pushed the steel door, then walked ten feet to the security desk. He flashed his badge and headed down the hallway. The two security guards didn't think twice about Cliff or his dirty and ripped test-flight suit, nor the cuts and bruises on him from jumping out of the doomed Aerovictor into the Salt River. Paul Goldschmidt had just sent a Madison Baumgartner fastball into the seats at Chase Field, and the guards were high-fiving over the thirteen-inch TV as they watched the Diamondbacks take an early lead on the hated Giants. Cliff rolled his eyes and cracked a smile. Only in America!

*****

Barney Kinkel's office was in the center of the administration facility next to the other corporate vice presidents. He was technically in charge of the Foreign Sales and Service Division but was delegated many different tasks within the company. One job was to oversee the testing of Aerovictor helicopters before they were sold to other nations. Most of his work was classified as *Top Secret.* The president didn't want other countries knowing who our government was doing business with these days. That's why Cliff thought it was highly unusual that Kinkel's office door was wide open with no one inside.

Cliff hadn't known Kinkel for very long. A month or so ago, he had been hired as an Aerovictor test pilot, but Kinkel hadn't been in the interview. The human resources staff made the decision to hire Cliff based on his past successes flying for the Air Force. They were able to overlook his dishonorable discharge when they found out he was the fall guy for the accidental killings of citizens in Egypt during a secret mission to eradicate terror cells in the Sinai Peninsula. However, Barney Kinkel was distraught when Zefron hired Cliff. His best-laid plans could be given quite a test.

Cliff sat down in a leather chair opposite Kinkel's desk. He guessed his boss wouldn't be gone long, seeing the door had been left open. He was trying to think what he was going to tell Kinkel about yesterday and how he had crashed the Aerovictor in the Salt River. Cliff wasn't sure where to start. Kinkel was a busy man and liked his employees to speak succinctly, but the events of the past two days were too important to ignore any detail. If Kinkel was angry at him, he probably would be fired on the spot. Then Cliff would never find out where Air Force Two was currently located.

After five minutes, Cliff was becoming impatient. Why was Kinkel not back? He stood up and began pacing the room. He noticed Kinkel's computer was on with his internal email page opened. Cliff thought he would flip through a few emails to see if Kinkel had mentioned to someone that they were missing an

Aerovictor. That way, he would know better what to say when Kinkel came back to the office.

"How stupid," muttered Cliff to himself as he opened the first email. "He leaves his office with the door wide open and computer running. Anyone else but a VP would be fired."

The last email to arrive was a reminder from the information technology director to power down computers when employees left for the day. Running computers could be hacked. Cliff let out a quick burst of laughter.

The email before that was strange: *Arrival FF at 1900 hours. Bring S, S, G, and K. Dep for Edwards at 1930.* The time stamp on the email was *6:30 PM 4/19/18.*

Cliff assumed someone was flying into Falcon Field at seven o'clock and that Kinkel was supposed to meet him. Perhaps that's why he left in such a hurry without shutting down the computer or closing the door. Very careless, although at this point, it was Cliff's only theory. But what or who was S, S, G, and K? And could Edwards be Edwards Air Force Base? Cliff remembered that all Oracle missile tests were supposed to be done there in the Mojave Desert, which is why he had a problem with his own mission yesterday—to test the Oracles on grand ol' saguaros south of Gila Bend.

Cliff looked at his watch. The time read *7:25.* He glanced at the far wall and noticed several small security monitors that showed various locations in and around Zefron. One moveable camera appeared to be placed atop the air traffic control center at Falcon Field. Cliff discerned that the same Gulfstream that flew over their biplane was now at the end of the runway, ready for takeoff. Could whoever Kinkel was meeting have flown in on that jet? Cliff's heart was beginning to beat rapidly. He couldn't pinpoint it, but something was wrong, and he was running out of time.

He went back to the computer, clicked on the search icon, and typed in his name: *Bullard.* Eight emails referenced him, and they were all listed on the left side of the screen. He decided to start from the beginning and clicked on the bottom email. It was dated

February 23rd and was a short and straightforward memo from human resources: *Hired Colonel Cliff Bullard as a test pilot. File in our office if you want to take a look.*

The second email was dated the following Monday, February 26th. It was a response from the first email: *ABSOLUTELY DO NOT WANT BULLARD!!!!! I've reviewed his file!! Get rid of him!!*

Cliff read and reread the email, then plopped back into the chair with his mouth open in shock. He had no idea that Kinkel was opposed to his hiring. He leaned forward and clicked on the third email: *Too late, he signed a contract!*

The fourth email posted one minute after the third: *I'm the damn VP here, you know! I absolutely DO NOT WANT HIM! Now what??????*

The fifth arrived a minute after that: *Then catch him violating protocol and fire him! But we can't release him without cause. You know that, Barney!*

That's when Cliff realized why he was sent out to Gila Bend. He was being set up. Kinkel had him test the Oracle missiles in an area that was not allowed by the Pentagon. He had never been given written orders from Kinkel, only spoken ones that he couldn't prove. Kinkel must have rigged the radio so he couldn't call anyone either. All communications from an Aerovictor helicopter are recorded and stored on a vast database forever.

Cliff sat back once again in the chair. He was thinking about his conversation with Kinkel when his boss gave him his test orders. He remembered that he was surprised that Kinkel didn't come with him, seeing this was his first mission with the company since completing the training. At the time, Cliff didn't think anything about it. He was an experienced pilot and assumed Kinkel had faith that he could go solo even if it was his first time. Cliff also remembered that they needed to finish the test mission quickly to complete a sale to Turkey. Once again, this was only communicated verbally to Cliff; nothing in writing ever existed.

Cliff looked up at the ceiling in deep thought while nervously wiggling his thumbs. He recalled that almost all test flights took place near the Salt River, only two or three miles from the Zefron plant. However, he was sent to Gila Bend. If the Oracles weren't going to be tested at Edwards, it made sense for Kinkel to have them tested away from populated areas. Or was it? Did Kinkel really care?

Cliff had a bad thought pop into his brain that he tried to deny with all sorts of reasons, but he couldn't seem to make it disappear. Could it be possible that Kinkel had something to do with the destruction of the Senso-McNamara building? Was that why he sent him far away for that day? And if so, were the two goons he chased to the river working for Kinkel? Worse yet, did Kinkel order them to shoot Cliff down? He gazed wearily back at the monitor. The jet was storming down the runway.

"What the hell are you doing in my office?!"

Cliff felt the barrel of a .44 Magnum Desert Eagle resting on the back of his skull.

Chapter 35

Wednesday, April 18, 2018
FBI Laboratory, Phoenix, Arizona
7:30 pm (Pacific Daylight Time)

Officially recorded at 3:30 pm by the emergency room staff, FBI lab technician Morris Radcliff and coffee salesman James LeBron were pronounced dead on arrival at Banner Heart Hospital. Neither were recognizable as the skin on their faces had disintegrated, including their eyelids. Their black and burnt out eyeballs were staring straight up from skinless eye sockets as the receiving nurses rolled them in. The first doctor to reach them was completing his internship at the University of Arizona Medical School. He fainted at the sight of the corpses and was revived with a nearby oxygen mask. Perhaps he should have gone to law school like his father requested.

Meanwhile, during the mad scramble to secure the laboratory and try to make sense of how a coffee salesman and lead technician could die together from electrocution, FBI agent Steve Talbert had traced the serial numbers that Radcliff's receptionist, Alice Kaiser, had given him. The camera and lens were owned by a man named Joe Freeman, who lived in east Mesa. After the horrendous incident in the lab, a visibly shaken Alice called Homeland Security and asked for them to find Agent Kelly and have him return to the FBI lab. Kelly was awoken from a nap when he heard the shocking news. He fired up the Vette and was back at the lab as the sun was setting.

"What the hell happened?!" asked startled and frustrated Agent Kelly. "They were just going to have coffee!"

"All I saw was that Morris had the coffee man by his wrist," whimpered Alice. "They were electrocuted by something very powerful, and I'm not talking about the Keurig machine!"

Kelly walked over to Agent Talbert, who appeared to be the person in charge.

"Found anything?" asked Kelly. Talbert nodded.

"Maybe. We're sure that the ring and the watch you brought in earlier were the cause of the electrocution. The coffee salesman appeared to have grabbed them, and when the two items touched, it set off a high-powered electrical current. Morris looked like he had tried to stop the man without much luck. He was holding his wrist when the shock occurred." Talbert paused for a moment, then added, "They were fried, Earl. It wasn't pretty."

"You said you think you may have found something. What is it?"

"The data in the watch was destroyed, which means we can't trace the GPS and find out where it's been. However, on the inside back cover was an engraved serial number. We talked to Apple, and they were happy to tell us about it. The first two digits indicate the country code where it was manufactured. They happen to be the same as international telephone codes. In this case, the first two digits were zero and seven. Russia."

"Russia? Apple has a factory in Russia?"

"They have factories all over the world, my friend! Ever been to a country and not seen an iPhone? Anyway, to make a long story short, the watch was manufactured in Moscow. The guy from Apple said only watches are made there—no iPads, iPhones, or Mac computers. And Apple only allows manufactured products to be shipped to distribution centers—not to stores or individuals. Then he checked some sort of list he had and said something was odd. I asked what and he told me that the Russian-made products are only distributed to one location. Normally, Apple sends out their products to a multitude of distribution centers. Those centers are also coded within the serial number. This watch, and apparently all the watches made in Russia, are shipped to location 61142."

"Where is location 61142?"

"London. It's the code for a warehouse near Kensington Palace. Does that sound strange to you?"

"No, I don't know London that well. Why should it?"

"The Kensington W8 neighborhood of London is the most expensive area to live in all of the United Kingdom. The warehouse is tucked next to embassies and consulates from various areas of the world."

"How could anyone build a warehouse in a neighborhood like that?"

"Exactly! The folks at Apple gave us the address, and I called Scotland Yard. They just laughed."

"Laughed? Why's that?"

"They said there is no way that Apple would have a warehouse at that address. Impossible, they claim."

"Why not?!"

"The address is the home, or I should say one of the many homes, owned by Lord John Shaffer. He is a bigshot in the British Parlia—"

"Yes, yes, I know who Lord Shaffer is. So, obviously, Apple has the wrong address."

"Well, you wouldn't know that by talking to them! They are adamant that shipments from the Russian factory have gone to that address, and they have paid invoices to prove it."

"What's the name of the company that paid for the watches?"

"Well, this is where it gets weird. The corporation is called *Taste Of Arabia, LTD*. Bizarre name for an Apple watch distribution company, wouldn't you say?"

"Taste Of Arabia? That name sounds familiar, but I can't place it."

"I'll call Scotland Yard again and see if I can get any information on that company. Hopefully, I'll be able to understand them through their laughter!" Agent Talbert nodded at Kelly and turned to walk away. Kelly stopped him.

"Wait a minute. I think I remember where I saw that name before. The coffee salesman who was electrocuted with Radcliff."

"What about him?"

"I passed by him in the reception area as I was leaving. He was waiting to see Morris. He had a familiar face that I couldn't place, and he was holding a box of Keurig coffee in his hands. The box was marked *Taste Of Arabia.* I'm sure of it!"

"The Keurig machine is on the counter," said Talbert. "Let's go check."

Next to the coffee maker was a box of single-brew coffee containers. A picture of a palace somewhere in a desert wasteland covered the box's background, while a sultan flying through a cloud on a magic carpet was enlarged in the foreground. He was sitting cross-legged, sipping coffee with a speech bubble coming out of his mouth. Written inside the bubble was one word: *Heavenly!*

Kelly picked up the box and read the label: *Taste Of Arabia.* In small print on the bottom of the box was the address: *Taste Of Arabia, LTD, 4 Palace Gardens, Kensington, London W8, UK.*

"What do you make of that?" asked Talbert.

"I think we have a British lord who will always know when the time is right for a cup of coffee," replied Kelly sarcastically, emphasizing ***time*** and ***cup of coffee***.

"We may have an international conspiracy on our hands," stated Talbert, then added, "say nothing of murder." Talbert was thinking about his friend Morris Radcliff.

"Perhaps murders—plural," countered Kelly softly as visions of Gila Bend, Ajo, Senso-Mac, and the remote Homeland Security building flashed through his mind. "Keep this quiet. Tell no one—including your colleagues here at the FBI."

"Mums the word," retorted Talbert. "Oh yeah, one other thing. I know it's off the subject, but we traced the serial number of the camera and lens back to a man named Joe Freeman. He lives near the Senso-Mac headquarters in east Mesa. Well, I should say what used to be the Senso-Mac headquarters."

"Perfect! I'll get a search warrant right away. Meanwhile, assemble a team and have them ready to raid the house tonight."

"Why tonight? What's the rush?"

"I have a gut feeling that the deaths of Radcliff and the coffee salesman may be related somehow to this Joe Freeman guy."

"How's that?" asked Talbert curiously.

"When we're done, I'd like you to join me in my office at Homeland Security. I'll share my theory with you then. Also, I want you to help me find out more about Lord Shaffer. I'm going to ask Sheriff's Deputy Gordy Owens to join us. He's been working with me the past couple of days. And a heads up—this might take all night."

"Another all-nighter. The story of my life. Well, I might as well bring that Keurig machine and the box of coffee pods with me. We could use caffeine, right?"

Kelly smiled and replied, "Good idea. I haven't had much sleep myself lately." He turned and walked out.

Red Mountain Ranch, Mesa, Arizona
10:00 pm (Pacific Daylight Time)

Three black Chevy Tahoe SUVs with government plates cruised slowly down Ranier Street and pulled up in front of Joe Freeman's home. Agent Kelly got out of the first vehicle and motioned for one SUV to park a few houses north and the second a few houses south of Freeman's. The dim streetlights barely provided enough light for someone to walk safely down the sidewalk at night. Kelly was trying to be discreet and not wake up the neighborhood that housed mainly Phoenix commuters. Most snowbirds had shuttered up their homes and were well on their way back to the Midwest. But tonight, it was impossible for FBI agents to be inconspicuous following the horrific events at nearby Senso-Mac. Every nervous resident of Red Mountain Ranch was peeking out their windows at the first sound of a car passing by. When twelve agents emerged with weapons drawn into Freeman's front yard, then spread out so the entire property was surrounded, a crowd of snoopy onlookers stood mesmerized in their driveways. The cops were raiding their beloved neighbor, someone who would do anything for them at the drop of a hat!

Kelly kicked down the front door, and three agents rushed inside next to him wearing night goggles. They quickly swept the house with their Colt M4 Carbine assault rifles. The neighbors let out a collective gasp!

One agent found Roger Bennett snoring away on the couch. He tapped Bennett's shoulder with the barrel of his rifle, but Bennett didn't wake up. Kelly found Joe Freeman slouched down on a kitchen chair, he too was snoring to beat the band! Kelly saw a glass and filled it with tap water, then splashed it on Freeman's face. Joe grunted and slowly opened his eyes, then shaded them with his right hand as he squinted at two men with weapons aimed at his head. Instinctively, he raised his hands and sat up straight in the chair. "Don't shoot!" he screamed.

Kelly cuffed Joe's hands behind his back and pushed him to the living room. The other two agents had awoken Roger, and he was now sitting up with handcuffs tightened securely behind him too. Kelly pushed Joe down on the couch next to Bennett. Joe looked at Roger, and Roger looked back at Joe. They had a bewildered and fearful look on their faces.

Kelly went to the door and yelled to an agent who was standing next to a Tahoe. "Steve, bring me the bags! Ed, get the others and come search the house." All the agents left their posts and entered Freeman's house, then spread out into various rooms. They weren't sure what they were searching for because Kelly hadn't told them. "Look for anything that looks unusual or dangerous," said Kelly.

Agent Talbert brought in two thick transparent evidence bags and handed them to Kelly, who was back at the couch.

"Okay, first things first. Which one of you is Joe Freeman?" asked Kelly. Joe raised his hand meekly. "Good! So, do you own this house?"

"Yes. Who are you, and why are you here?"

Kelly pulled out his badge and flashed it at both Freeman and Bennett. "My name is Agent Kelly, and I'm with the local branch of Homeland Security. The rest of these men are with the FBI."

"But why? Have I done something wrong?" asked Joe timidly.

Kelly raised the evidence bags in the air to show Freeman, then asked, "Do these belong to you?"

"Yes, that looks like my camera and lens. Where did you get them?"

"I'll ask the questions, Mr. Freeman. Where did you last see them?"

"I don't know. I can't remember." Kelly and Talbert looked at each other and nodded.

"You can't remember. Okay, so the camera is missing its SD card. Do you know where that might be?"

"I have no idea. It should have been in the camera. No wait, maybe I took it out. I can't remember that either, sorry!"

Kelly was becoming frustrated and walked away momentarily to whisper something to Talbert. Agent Ed Garver came into the living room from the kitchen. "Nothing out of the ordinary in the kitchen," stated Garver. "Seems they were enjoying coffee and donuts today. I found crumbs on the floor next to the coffee maker. There was a Dunkin Donuts box in the trash and a wrapper for the coffee filter. I didn't recognize the brand name of the coffee. Taste Of Arabia—never heard of it."

"Well, that doesn't help us much. Go check out the garage." Kelly turned back to Freeman, then stopped and turned back to Agent Garver, who was heading towards the laundry room to the side entrance of the garage. "Wait a minute, agent! Did you say Taste Of Arabia?"

"Yes, sir. Why? Is that important?"

"Probably nothing, but put that wrapper in an evidence bag and place it in the SUV. Use gloves; I will want to dust it for prints."

"I can do better than that. There was a whole box of that coffee next to the brewer. I'll bag that too."

Kelly turned to Joe. "Where did you get that coffee?"

"What coffee?" asked Joe.

"The Taste Of Arabia coffee! Don't test me, Mr. Freeman! Do you understand?!"

"I don't think I ever heard of Taste Of Arabia. I'm sorry! I really am!" Joe was beginning to panic. He realized his memory seemed to be fading.

"Did you buy it in a store, or did some kind of salesman give it to you at work?"

"I'm retired, Agent Kevin. I don't have a place of work."

"It's Agent Kelly, damn it! So, you must have bought it in a store! Which one!" Kelly's face was turning red.

Just then, Roger Bennett spoke up. "I think I remember a man stopping by today who was selling it. Gave us donuts, too, I think."

Kelly hadn't spoken a word to Bennett yet. He was waiting to finish with Joe first. "And who exactly are you?"

Bennett thought for a moment, then shook his head no. "Uh, my name is—" He shook his head again.

"What is this?! What are you two hiding?!" Kelly stared furiously at Joe while pointing at Bennett. "Who is this guy?! Tell me now, or you're both under arrest for obstruction!"

Joe glanced at Roger, who was only two feet away, and shook his head. "I don't know. I've never seen him before in my life."

Chapter 36

Thursday, April 19, 2018
Love's Travel Stop Parking Lot, Gila Bend, Arizona
1:00 am (Pacific Daylight Time)

Cliff woke up with a bruise on his temple and a throbbing headache. He wanted desperately to rub it, but his arms wouldn't move. He was sitting awkwardly on a metal fold-up chair in the middle of a semi-trailer. One wrist was handcuffed to a panel on the inside wall of the truck and the other to the chair. Locked in the very same position next to him were Rick Frye and Donnor Colten. Cliff looked around and realized he was in a semi filled with boxes of coffee.

"Thank God you are alive," whispered Rick to Cliff. "We thought you may be in a coma."

"Where are we?" asked Cliff. "What happened?"

"Shhh, keep it down," said Donnor in a soft voice. "They are up in the cab of the truck."

"Who's in the cab—"

"Shhh! Not so loud!" repeated Donnor, slightly raising his voice.

"Who's in the cab?" whispered Cliff.

"Don't know," said Rick. "After you went into the building, we decided to walk around to the back to keep from being seen. That's when we saw a van that I recognized, which was very strange."

"What do you mean by strange?"

"It was a fifteen passenger Chevy van. The van was white with blue and gold letters stenciled on the door that read *Gila Bend Charter*

School. I recognized it, Cliff. It was the same van I had driven the golf team to our matches when I was coaching last year."

"Why would it be parked at Zefron?"

"That's what we were wondering. We walked up to check it out, and two security guards arrested us. They were dressed in Army fatigues and pointed assault rifles at us! They cuffed and blindfolded us and pushed us face down in the cargo hold of our school's van! A few minutes later, we heard the side door open and voices talking. The van bounced, and we could tell someone was being shoved inside. We didn't know it was you. Then the front doors opened and closed, and we drove off. I'm guessing we rode about an hour or so."

"Did you hear what anyone was saying?" asked Cliff.

"They didn't say much the entire trip, just a few words at the beginning. A guy in the middle seat was upset that the driver took so long to get here, and the driver told him he wasn't paid to be at his every beck and call. Then he wanted to know who you were. The security guards were in the van, too, but didn't say a word the entire trip."

Cliff paused a minute to think. Donnor broke the silence. "I'm guessing the school must have sold the van to Zefron, and they haven't had time to repaint it to cover up the letters."

"Wishful thinking," said Cliff.

Donnor and Rick looked at each other and then at Cliff.

"What do you mean by that?" asked Rick.

"I think what happened at your school today and the events that followed are all linked together, including us being locked up here in this truck."

"You think Zefron is involved in some kind of conspiracy?"

"No, not Zefron. But I think my boss is. I was standing in his office waiting for him to come back. He had left the office door open, so I assumed he hadn't gone far. His computer was on, and I got a little bit nosey and read some of his emails. The next thing I know he had a gun to my head, then he hit me with it. That's the last thing I remember."

"What was in those emails?"

Before Cliff could answer, the back doors to the semi opened, and Barney Kinkel climbed aboard using a metal ramp. Behind him was an older man dressed in a brown corduroy sports jacket, an egg-white Eton Calvary twill shirt, and a pair of Vetements faded blue jeans. He was smoking a cigar. Rick thought he looked like an old college professor trying his best to be young and cool again but failing miserably.

Barney and his guest pulled up two more metal chairs and sat down a few feet from Cliff. Barney shook his head like he was in disbelief, then pulled out a .44 Magnum from his belt and pointed it at Cliff's nose.

"All you had to do was follow orders—shoot up a few saguaros with Oracle missiles. Then I could have simply fired your ass. But no, you had to shoot down two helicopters and crash land our own Aerovictor in the Salt River. That means you owe us about thirty-six million dollars—and some change! And seeing you probably don't have that kind of cash laying around, I'm thinking about wasting another sixty-five cents by putting a bullet through your skull!" Barney waved the gun at Cliff like it was a toy.

"If you were going to kill me, Barney, why did you drag me all the way to wherever the hell we are? And what's with all the coffee?" asked Cliff. The semi was jam-packed with boxes of coffee labeled *Taste Of Arabia.* Cliff, Rick, and Donnor didn't know it, but the semi was parked at Love's Travel Stop near the intersection of Highway 85 and Interstate 8 in Gila Bend.

Barney laughed and tucked the gun back in his belt. "Relax! I'm not going to kill you unless you give me a good reason," said Barney. "Instead, I'm going to give you gentlemen a cup or two of the greatest coffee in the world. Now how does that sound, my friend?"

Cliff was startled by Barney's change of heart. A few seconds ago, he threatened to kill him, and now he wants to offer him coffee! Rather Jekyll and Hydish, he thought. "Your friend? This is how you treat a friend? How dead would I be if I was your enemy?"

"Ah, sarcasm will get you nowhere. Just relax, the coffee is being brewed in the cabin. It should be done in a few minutes."

"So, what's up with all the coffee?" asked Cliff. "I didn't know Zefron was going into the java business."

"You really want to know? Well, I might as well tell you. None of you guinea pigs will remember what I said come tomorrow or at the very latest the next day."

"What do you mean by that?"

"You boys have been selected by me to be experimental test subjects. Quite an honor, wouldn't you say?" Barney laughed at his own sarcasm. "Ever heard of tungis?"

Cliff looked at Donnor and Rick, and all three shook their heads. "No, why?"

"The prime ingredient of this coffee is crushed tungis leaves grown only in the Sarawat Mountains of western Yemen. Tungis mixed with coffee has the unique ability to make someone lose his memory, which is why, my dear friends, you won't remember a thing I'm telling you—including me calling you 'my dear friends!'" Barney laughed again as Cliff's facial expression became one of concern.

"What are you planning on doing with the coffee?"

"Well, that's a long story. How bout we talk over a few cups of the world's finest java?"

One of the security guards that had cuffed Rick and Donnor at Zefron came up the ramp with a huge thermos and three coffee mugs. Barney stacked two boxes of coffee to be used as a table for the cups and the gallon-sized thermos. The guard unlocked the handcuffs from the metal chairs so the three men could drink. Their other hands were still attached to the wall panel. Barney poured coffee into the mugs and smiled.

"Drink up and enjoy!" he smirked. "Sorry, I don't have any cream or sugar. I hope you like it black!"

No one touched the mugs. Cliff, Rick, and Donnor didn't know how coffee could make you lose your memory, and they certainly weren't eager to find out.

Barney shook his head and pulled the .44 Magnum from his belt. "Boys, boys, boys. You don't seem to get it. Right now, we are in the experimental stage of testing the effects of Taste Of Arabia on good ol' Arizona folks, and you have suddenly become my chosen ones. Should you decide to decline this historic offer, each one of you will leave this truck with a shiny bullet lodged in your brain, and I'll be out another two bucks. You don't want that now, do you?" He placed the barrel of the gun on Cliff's forehead.

Reluctantly, Cliff, Rick, and Donnor took a sip and then another. Each time they paused, Barney would lift the gun in the air and wave it at them. They kept drinking.

"Okay, just so you know, I'm just a tally mark on a lengthy list of treasoners! . . . Is that even a word?

"Anyway, it all started back in the sixties, if you can believe that! The Russians wanted badly to spread Communism throughout our wonderful Planet Earth! Their biggest hurdle was America. If they were ever going to put an end to the free world, they had to win the space race. But a man named John Kennedy got in the way. As you know, Lee Harvey Oswald assassinated Kennedy. What you don't know is that Oswald was working for a man named Yegor Bovnik. Ever heard of him?"

"Of course," replied Rick, "he's the directorate chief of the KGB. And a real son-of-a-bitch, I might add!"

"And you know this how?" asked Barney curiously.

"I teach history. Just get on with it!"

"Well then, let me introduce you to my friend." Barney turned and looked at his guest. "This is the honorable SOB, Yegor Bovnik." Rick's face turned bright red. Yegor pulled his chair closer to the three men.

Rick was thinking about the research paper he had done in college about the JFK conspiracy. He knew Oswald had lived in the Soviet Union, but he thought he had been run out of the country. This didn't make sense.

"You're saying Oswald was working for the Russians?" asked Rick to Yegor.

"Yes, son, he was. Enjoy your coffee, and we'll tell you about it."

Barney started, "My friend Yegor's first ingenious plot was to have his spies monitor the court-martial proceedings of United States soldiers. Those disgraced American veterans would be perfect recruits for espionage training in the Soviet Union. They knew US military secrets and could hunt. So, in 1958 when a KGB report indicated that a dishonorable marine who was an excellent marksman had just been kicked out of the service, he personally made a phone call to the man's New Orleans home."

"Oswald?" asked Rick.

Yegor answered, "Yes, Lee Harvey Oswald was an easy recruit. He was upset over his court-martial for having an illegal weapon and displaying violent behavior. Oswald wanted nothing better than to stick it to his home country. On the phone, I dangled a carrot and mentioned that I had planned several missions that could bring fame and fortune to the ex-marine. I told him I had a vision of him being on the cover of Petrograd's monthly journal, *Zvezda*, dressed in a men's Barguzin sable fur coat! That brought a smile to Oswald's face, but the clincher was when I threw in a pretty Russian wife as part of the deal."

Barney interjected, "Back in '58, neither Yegor nor Oswald knew that they would directly control the fate of a young Massachusetts senator who would soon occupy the residence at 1600 Pennsylvania Avenue. The plan to kill Kennedy came later."

Yegor continued, "I tested Oswald's marksmanship skills with his first assignment, a relatively easy assassination of popular Russian author, Pavel Kuznetsov. Using a fake pen name, Kuznetsov published a historical fiction novel that claimed Joseph Stalin murdered his predecessor, Vladimir Lenin, to gain control of the Communist Party of the Soviet Union. In Kuznetsov's story, Lenin's massive stroke was a cover-up of gigantic proportions. The novel was obviously banned in Russia and the Eastern Bloc countries, but copies were sold copiously throughout Europe and began trickling back over the Iron Curtain."

Rick was stunned. He remembered reading several chapters of Kuznetsov's book as a class assignment for World History. "You're saying Oswald killed Kuznetsov?"

Yegor nodded. "Oswald made sure Kuznetsov never wrote the sequel.

"As head of the KGB, I assigned Oswald to the assassinations of five other political dissidents, and he completed the tasks with speed and efficiency. So, to fulfill my promise, I selected Marina Prusakova to be Oswald's wife back in April of 1961. That was a big mistake. She was only supposed to be Oswald's toy, but he ended up falling in love with her. After her daughter was born, Marina wanted out of Russia at any cost. Oswald was content in his new role as a chief marksman and executioner for the KGB, but he adored Marina and wanted to make her happy. I only agreed to let the Oswald family leave the Soviet Union on one condition—he must return to the United States and complete one last mission. That mission would change the course of history for America.

"We created official documents for Oswald's departure, and he moved to Dallas, Texas, under the alias of Alek Hidell. Once settled into his new home, I shipped a .38 handgun, a sharpshooter rifle, and ten million Russian rubles to him. Neither customs nor postal officials bothered to inspect the large package that I sent from Minsk, which proved to be a fatal mistake of major proportions for your country! So, in the fall of 1962, Oswald began planning the execution of President Kennedy."

"What would you have done if Oswald turned against you?" asked Rick.

"I wasn't about to let Oswald run free in America and tell Russian secrets. I knew that Oswald must be forever silenced soon after his mission to assassinate President Kennedy was completed. Once Dallas was the selected location for Kennedy's assassination, I contacted my KGB agent, who was planted as a clerk in a book depository in the center of the city. The clerk's cousin owned a nightclub in Dallas and was the son of a Russian immigrant to America."

"That was Jack Ruby!" blurted Rick. "I remember reading about this. He was the oldest child born to Joseph and Fannie Rubenstein. He changed his name to disassociate himself from his alcoholic and abusive father and mentally ill mother. The book depository was the Texas Book Depository, wasn't it? How did your KGB spy talk Ruby into murdering Oswald?"

"He spent at least a couple of evenings as a patron in Jack Ruby's nightclub. One night after hours at the club, he laid out the assassination plan to Ruby. He explained that Oswald needed to be silenced immediately after Kennedy was killed. If Oswald talked, my grand plan to bring down America would be in jeopardy. Ruby ended up being an easy sell as Oswald's executioner."

"Why?" asked Rick. He was so consumed with this firsthand account of a significant historical event that he forgot his life was in danger. Without thinking about the effects, he took another sip of coffee.

"It would be good for business, that's why. The nightclub owner figured that all of America would be totally distraught over losing their beloved president, and he would end up a hero if he killed Oswald. In fact, he would slay him in cold blood on national television and walk away as an idol to every American man, woman, and child desperate for revenge. Ruby expected a ticker-tape parade in his honor shortly after the state funeral in Washington, DC. However, Texas authorities had a different idea; Jack Ruby had sold his last martini!"

"Yegor's plan played out to perfection," said Barney. "Kennedy was dead, Oswald was dead, and soon Jack Ruby would be dead."

"But Ruby died in prison," stated Rick. "From cancer, as I remember. Are you saying you had something to do with that, too?" He stared directly into Yegor's eyes.

"My Texas Book Depository spy-clerk sealed that deal the night Ruby agreed to be Oswald's executioner. He poured a dose of the carcinogen ethanol in his cousin's drink shortly before toasting Jack on his protagonist actions. Due to the slow-acting nature of the chemical compound, death was supposed to occur six to eight months after ingesting the poison. That way, Ruby would have time to kill Oswald and die himself before he could spill the beans about his Russian connection. But the carcinogen took a little over four years to form a lethal blood clot in Ruby's lungs, and I sweated every waking moment worrying the plan would be exposed!"

"Okay, so Ruby kept his mouth shut, but the Warren Commission that President Lyndon Johnson authorized cleared him and Oswald from any kind of conspiracy. Weren't you worried they would find out the truth and connect the Russians?"

"Yes, I was. When I heard about the Warren Commission being formed, I knew I needed to act. I blackmailed Senator Gordon Rothschild of Arizona into offering his services for the committee."

"Blackmailed! What do you mean blackmailed?! Senator Rothschild is a good man—he would never be blackmailed into anything!" Rick was beside himself. His parents and grandparents had voted for Rothschild. "What are you talking about?"

"I didn't have much time. President Johnson sanctioned the Warren Commission as his first executive order on November 29th of 1963, just seven days after Kennedy's assassination. They were to investigate and report their findings regarding the deaths of Kennedy and Oswald. Seven powerful politicians made up the original committee: Chief Justice Earl Warren for whom the commission was named, two United States senators, two United States congressmen, a former CIA director, and a former president of the World Bank. Then Johnson added Rothschild after the good senator offered up his services—at my demand."

"Your demand? How could you demand anything from Senator Rothschild?" Rick was confused and curious. "And how could he talk the president into putting him on the commission, for God's sake?!"

"Senator Rothschild was a star student of Lyndon Johnson's during the days Johnson taught public speaking at Sam Houston High School. He placed first in every debate and became the future president's pride and joy, so much so that Johnson hired him as his first campaign director. Later, Rothschild moved to Arizona and became mayor of Phoenix, state representative, governor, and US senator, all within a matter of ten years. There were no other politicians in Arizona that could match him in a debate. So, when he solicited his old mentor to become part of the Warren Commission, President Johnson couldn't say no."

"You've got to be kidding!"

Yegor chuckled and continued, "No one could say no to Gordon Rothschild, including Raisa Vasiliev, the daughter of Premier Alexei Kosygin's council of minister's chairman."

"What are you getting at?" The question was rhetorical. Rick, Donnor, and Cliff all knew what Yegor was suggesting.

"Gordon met Raisa during a state visit to Moscow in 1965 and began a secret affair that lasted only one week. The senator was a self-proclaimed happily married man and a fantastic father of four who had just turned the golden age of fifty. Raisa was a promiscuous teenager who liked hanging out with her daddy's high-profile friends. The baby was born on October 20th. Raisa's father was a friend of mine and asked to have Rothschild assassinated. I had a better idea—blackmail.

"I easily planted Senator Rothschild on the Warren Commission. President Johnson was bursting with excitement when he received the letter from Rothschild offering his services on the committee. Then the commission became eight. Rothschild's task was to create false testimony and dispel conspiracy rumors. It worked. In the end, the commission declared that Oswald acted alone in the presidential assassination, and Jack Ruby killed Oswald during an act of temporary insanity and rage caused by Kennedy's death."

"Well, it may have worked at the time," said Rick, "but the conspiracy rumors still exist today. Whatever became of Raisa and her baby? I'm assuming she put it up for adoption, right?"

"Miss Vasiliev and her four-month-old son moved to America in February of 1966 with the covert help of her senator-lover who finagled paperwork through the normally bureaucratic mess known as immigration."

"What?!" blurted Rick. "That's impossible!"

"Sorry to say it's not, son. He hid her in a small house on West Norma Street in your hometown, the tiny village of Gila Bend. She probably lives close to you! He visited her and his illegitimate son once a week. Raisa spoke no English when she arrived but learned it quickly by taking night courses in the basement of nearby St. Michael's parish. Her neighbors were more than a little bit curious as to how the nice young lady and her cute kid survived. Raisa had no job. The only visitor that neighbors ever saw was a gray-haired man who dropped in weekly wearing blue jeans, a t-shirt, tennis shoes, and a stocking hat that covered half his head. Strange man, wearing a knit hat even in the summertime when the temperatures were nearing 120! Must be her dad or grandfather, they thought! Then there was a second child."

"A second child! Are you serious?!" asked Rick.

"I still don't get it!" exclaimed Cliff. "You said blackmail. Even if Senator Rothschild was an adulterer and all that's true about Oswald and Ruby and whatnot, how did you use all that blackmail? The kids and the mistress were tucked away quietly in Gila Bend. I've never heard anything about a scandal involving Rothschild."

"And what the hell does any of it have to do with all this so-called memory-loss coffee we're drinking?!" asked Donnor.

Suddenly, everyone became silent. There was tension in the air as the three cuffed men tried to process what they were hearing.

"Senator Rothschild's illegitimate son is heavily involved in our plan to use this coffee to take down America. And he's all for it, so we don't even need any more blackmail."

"So what?!" said Cliff loudly. "So, you have some no-name bastard as part of your ridiculous plan that's sure to fail! Who cares?!"

"I'm not sure I would classify Senator Rothschild's bastard son as a no-name," stated Barney.

"What's that supposed to mean?" asked Donnor.

"Senator Rothschild's oldest illegitimate son is the vice president of the United States. He moonlights as a coffee distributor. We'll let you think about that for a while. Now, drink up boys! Director Bovnik and I need to get our beauty rest!"

2:00 am (Pacific Daylight Time)

"You need to get them out of the semi!" yelled the man outside the truck. Cliff, Rick, and Donnor all heard him; however, the sound was muffled. They were handcuffed to the well-insulated walls of the trailer, and the hundreds of Taste Of Arabia coffee boxes added to that insulation.

"Would you just shut up!" replied the second man. It sounded like Barney Kinkel. "If we wake up these other truck drivers, it won't be pretty! Bovnik walked down to the Space Age Lodge and is getting two rooms ready. He'll be back in a minute."

"How long before the coffee takes effect?"

"Well, they drank an entire gallon-sized thermos. That's over twenty ounces each. They should start to lose their memory by tomorrow night."

"What then?"

"We'll release them and keep an eye on them. We don't want a murder scene that could raise red flags. They won't know where they are or what happened anyway."

"Where are you going to store all the coffee. After the mess up at the school, it's too dangerous to try and unload it there."

"Bovnik said to send it to O'Connell's house. They've got 6,000 square feet of secluded storage space out in the country."

"But, they aren't part of our operation!" The man was raising his voice again. "Won't they be suspicious if we say we are storing hundreds of boxes of coffee in their house?!"

"Don't worry! If they get suspicious, we have two undercover security guards watching them day and night. They will end up having a very tragic accident!"

"What about Orlov and the rest of those idiots who screwed up the school op?"

"They drove across the desert and are in California now at the rendezvous point. And the Gulfstream dropped off Glebov, Kozar, and the laser weapons at the same place, but Shaffer needed the jet back in London right away. Said he didn't have time for it to pick up Yegor. So, now there is a slight change of plans. Vice President Garrett had already concocted some diplomatic meeting in the Middle East that the president luckily approved, and he'll be transporting everyone, including Yegor."

"How's Yegor getting to California?"

"He's not. That's the change of plans. They're picking him up at the Gila Bend Air Force Auxiliary Field."

"That runway is only about a mile and a half long! That could pose some problems when they try to take off."

"There's plenty of desert at the end of the runway, and the airplane is one of the best in the country. They'll have no problem."

"If someone in Gila Bend sees them, they'll be asking a lot of questions, you know!"

"That's why they are flying in the middle of the night. They should be on their way now."

"What about air traffic controllers at Sky Harbor? You don't think they'll be suspicious when they're asked to clear traffic away from Gila Bend?"

"Where that plane flies is always classified. Air traffic controllers are not to question the destination or reason. Just like you! I'm now to my limit answering your questions! After you take Yegor and me down to the airfield, we really don't need you anymore. So, go back to work in the morning, keep your mouth shut, and do your thing. Got it?!"

There was no response. Cliff, Rick, and Donnor had their ears pressed hard against the truck's interior wall and were able to make out most of the conversation.

"That man's voice, the one talking to Barney," said Rick. "I've heard it before, but I can't place it. The sound is too stifled."

"What plane in California do you think they are talking about?" asked Donnor.

"It must be Air Force Two," replied Cliff. "They were talking about Garrett getting some meeting in the Middle East approved by the president. Senator Rothschild's bastard son, the vice president, is on his way to Gila Bend, and somehow we need to be around to greet him."

Curley School Apartments, Ajo, Arizona
3:00 am (Pacific Daylight Time)

Principal Sebastian Perez and his small group of nine teachers had camped out in the tunnel by the Ajo airport on Tuesday night, then patiently waited all day Wednesday for someone to pick them up. If it wasn't going to be Mack Colten, then they thought Donnor Colten and Rick Frye would have returned. But the day dragged on, and the teachers were getting tired and restless. Some had dozed off for an hour or two, but most had laid around thinking bad thoughts. Just before midnight, Principal Perez made the decision for the group to hike to Mack's place at the Curley School Apartments. Three hours later, they were standing in the underground garage waiting for the elevator.

"How are we going to get inside the apartment?" asked Margo Litweiler. "Surely, Mack would have locked it."

"I'm surprised we can even get into the elevator without some kind of code," replied Perez. "These days, most places have airtight security!"

The elevator stopped on the second floor, and Principal Perez pointed down the hallway. "I think I remember which one was his. We were in a big hurry the last time I came."

The teachers and principal padded quickly to Mack's apartment. Perez turned the handle, and the door opened. The teachers stared in disbelief.

"I forgot," said Perez. "Mack trusts everyone and never locks his door. Now find a place to crash. I'll use his landline and call the police."

The problem was Mack had no landline. Who did these days? Perez looked momentarily around the kitchen, then walked down the hallway to the master bedroom. The door to the only other bedroom was closed. As Perez walked by it, he shouted to the others, "Here's a second bedroom or office or something. Some of you can sleep in there."

Margo led three teachers to the second room and tried to turn the door handle, but it was locked.

"Mr. Perez, weird thing," called Margo to her principal as he was entering the master bedroom.

Perez turned and asked, "What's that?"

"The door's locked. Why would Mack leave the front door open but lock this room?"

"He's a book illustrator. Maybe that's where he does his work."

"Still, why would he lock it? It's just a simple wooden door that can easily be kicked in. If someone walked in through the—" Margo stopped and put her ear to the door. "Shhh! I heard a sound coming from the room."

Perez hustled back to Margo as the other teachers stood and watched, not saying a word.

"It sounds like someone is moving in there," whispered Margo to Perez.

It was late, he was exhausted, and he had enough. Perez whispered back to Margo, "Move aside. I'm going to find out." The principal had been a placekicker for the Arizona Wildcats back in his college days. In fact, he held the NCAA field goal record for sending a pigskin sixty-six yards through the uprights. The door posed no problem. Splinters erupted near the small deadbolt as the door flew open. With their backs pressed against the opposite wall, Mackenzie, Riley, and Charlie O'Connell gasped as Perez glared at them with clenched fists. When he saw that the trio posed no risk, he looked around the room in bewilderment. There were test tubes, microscopes, chemical bottles, needles, and whatnot. Stacked on one wall were boxes of what appeared to be generic drugs. But all that and the O'Connells were nothing compared to what was pressed up against the closet—a very large man lying on a stretcher with intravenous tubes running into both arms.

Margo covered her mouth in astonishment and stared.

Perez looked dumbfounded at the man, and then muttered, "Sheriff Urdano? What … the … hell?"

Chapter 37

Thursday, April 19, 2018
Los Vidrios, Mexico
3:30 am (Pacific Daylight Time)

Mack tried his best for a soft landing, but the Cessna DC-6 touched down hard on the Ajo runway and bounced several times before coming to a stop. This was the first time he had flown from Mexico empty—no cargo on board. He had left the four teachers in one of Henry Gray's abandoned bunkhouses in Organ Pipe National Park and drove an Apollo 125cc dirt bike across the border to Los Vidrios. Dr. Sancho Gomez was happy to lend him the DC-6, although he didn't appreciate being woke up in the middle of the night. At the age of sixty-seven, the good doctor needed all the sleep he could muster.

*****

The plane was built in 1929 and had logged well over 100,000 hours. It had a maximum speed of 155 mph and a range of 600, which was all that was necessary for weekly flights from Los Vidrios, Mexico, to Ajo. Back in the 1930s, the high-wing aircraft was used to fly Arizona Republic *newspapers daily from Phoenix to Tucson until one day the pilot decided to steal the plane and live out the rest of his life on a beach in Guaymas. But the aircraft sprung a small fuel leak and ran out of gas just north of Hermosillo. The pilot landed in the Mexican Sonoran Desert and was never heard from again. Pablo Gomez found the plane in 1939 while searching for gold—a hobby he did every Sunday afternoon after mass. His son, Pedro, used two oxen to pull it back to the family ranch near Codorachi. There it sat in an equipment shed for five years until Pablo died.*

Pedro had a friend who flew missions for Fuerza Aerea Mexicana, the Mexican Air Force. Marcos Rivera had provided air support for the United States during the liberation of the Philippines and earned praise from General Douglas MacArthur and decorations from the US, Mexican, and Philippine governments. While on leave to his hometown of Codorachi, he taught Pedro how to fly. The oxen had smoothed out a landing strip in the desert, and Pedro would fly every weekend for pleasure. But the thrill of dipping and diving through the clouds ended when he had a heart attack in midair. His only son, five-year-old Sancho, had observed his father from the cockpit on every weekend flight—they were best buddies and did everything together. Little Sancho was able to safely land the DC-6 while screaming at his father to wake up. Pedro never did. Sancho's mother died from cancer the following year.

Sancho inherited the ranch but left it vacant while he was raised by his uncle. He graduated from the University of Guadalajara's medical school in 1974 at the age of twenty-four. After losing his father to heart disease and his mother to cancer, Sancho made it his mission in life to find a cure for both. By the time he was forty, Sancho had won six Doctoralia awards for being the highest-rated physician in Mexico. In 1999, Sancho left his career as a doctor to go into pharmaceutical research. His ultimate goal in life was to develop two drugs: one that would put an end to heart disease, the other to cure cancer.

In 2005, he created a synthetic substance that stopped irregular heartbeats in laboratory monkeys. The drug was in pill form and inserted into bananas that were digested by the simians. Sancho's discovery won him a Nobel Prize for physiology and medicine. With the financial assistance from Baja Biopharma, he formed a company in Tijuana to mass produce the drug for sale throughout the world. The factory was completed while the drug was waiting for approval from the United States Food and Drug Administration, but that approval never happened. They claimed there was no proof it would work on human beings.

Then a funny thing happened. A month later, AmCan Pharmaceuticals, the largest drug company in North America, purchased Baja Biopharma for ten times what the company was worth. A month after that, the FDA approved Sancho's medicine formula, and AmCan began selling his pills for $1,000 each. Because the drug virtually ended irregular heartbeats, doctors prescribed them for *all their patients who suffered from the disorder. Patients who had good medical insurance began to live happy, healthy lives. Patients who couldn't afford high deductibles and astronomical coinsurance often died from heart attacks. Dr. Sancho Gomez was appalled. His drug should be affordable to everyone who needed it. He was determined to do something about it, but he didn't know where to start.*

Sancho moved from his temporary apartment in Tijuana to his family's deserted ranch in Codorachi. He had made visits home periodically to fly the old Cessna. Soaring through the clouds like his daddy did was the doctor's opportunity to "get away from it all" and relieve stress. The fields that the oxen once plowed became overgrown with weeds and desert shrubs, and the house had been consumed by cobwebs. But through the years, Sancho ensured that the dirt landing strip was well maintained. Now, standing next to the shed that protected his airplane, he viewed out over the property. It was a mess. He would have to fix it up alone.

Sancho never had time to get married. Yes, there were always friendly and attractive possibilities during his college years, but those girls would leave him because he studied too long and too hard. He lost three girlfriends to a disease he told his buddies was called "forgotitis." He had been so focused on his research that he forgot that he had a date! That same disease carried over to his career years. By the time he turned forty, he simply gave up on women and spent his free time either flying or collecting art. Yes, he loved all kinds of art: paintings, illustrations, sculptures, and photography. As his income grew, he would fly his Cessna to art shows in Mexico and the United States. He appreciated Rembrandt and Picasso for what they accomplished, but his preference was for local artists who could tell a story with their creations that dignified the culture of northern Mexico and the American southwest. That's how he met Mack Colten.

Curley School Apartments in the obscure town of Ajo, Arizona, rented only to local artists. Sancho flew there one weekend in 2006 to visit their annual art fair. Each night while at home in Mexico, he would search the Internet looking to find out-of-the-way places that were having a festival and also had a small airport nearby. Ajo seemed to be a perfect destination. He landed at noon, called a taxi, and spent the rest of the afternoon in awe of the fascinating pieces of work displayed in tents on the front lawn. Sancho purchased something from each artist, and he soon became the most popular visitor at the fair. The last tent he stopped at was Mack's. Mack had sketched a colored-pencil drawing of Dr. Seuss placing one of Bartholomew Cubbins' 500 hats on the head of George W. Bush while the president sat on the lap of his mother, Barbara Bush, who was reading him a story. The location was a desert campsite, and the Bush's were perched on a sandstone boulder by a campfire as the sun set over a mountain backdrop.

Sancho was captivated and wanted the artist to explain the illustration to him. Because the festival was about to close for the evening, Mack suggested that Sancho and some other artists head down to the Estrella Restaurant for a burger and some cold beer. It was around midnight when the booze had loosened the doctor's tongue, and he told about his experience with AmCan's buyout of Baja Biopharma and how he would like to run them into the ground. The artists tapped their draft beer glasses in agreement. Sancho was invited to crash for the night in Mack's apartment. The doctor passed out in the car and, with help from Mack's friends, was carried to his couch. Mack checked the medicine cabinet for aspirin—they would need a bottle in the morning!

Working through a hangover of exponential proportions, Mack kept the coffee pouring while he flipped pancakes for his guests. All the artists in the building crammed into the two-bedroom apartment for Mack's weekly Sunday breakfast. Every week they picked a topic to chat and laugh about, always coming up with solutions to problems if they had the power. Today, the subject was the theft of Dr. Gomez's irregular heartbeat formula and the skyrocketing costs of medicine in America. Today's solution was to develop drugs and get them to people who couldn't afford to buy them. The artists and Sancho decided to meet again that night after closing the art festival for another year. They chose the Estrella Restaurant again, but this time they ordered Club Sodas with lemon.

Sancho had saved plenty of money through the years. He had always lived sparingly, never splurging on exotic food, movies, or girls. His only entertainment was flying and going to art shows. In 2001, he authored a simple book called "How To Live A Hundred Years." It was a worldwide bestseller, and the doctor netted over four-million dollars in royalties. He never spent a nickel; instead, he deposited it all with a financial planner who invested wisely and quadrupled the money every year for the past five years. Sancho was willing to use every penny of his wealth to help those in need get affordable medicine in America.

The owner of the Estrella Restaurant never kicked out customers at closing time, especially when the artists from the Curley School Apartments dropped in for dinner. That night, he let them stay however long they wished. He could see they were in some sort of in-depth discussion, and he didn't want to interrupt their conversation. He locked the doors as he left and told the artists to drink whatever they wanted from the bar and they could pay him in the morning.

The plan began to unfold and take shape. Dr. Gomez would build a factory and an airstrip in a secret desert location across the border in Mexico where he could develop generic drugs without being noticed by Mexican or American authorities. He already had friends who would supply him with raw ingredients: herbs and such grown on their farms and ranches. They would need two airplanes—one to import the natural elements and one to export the drugs to the United States. Mack had seen an ad for a used Cessna 172 on the Estrella Restaurant's community bulletin board that the owner was selling for $10,000 out at the airport. He was also selling his hangar for another $10,000.

The artists and Dr. Gomez then discussed the increase in border patrolmen in the area since the advent of Homeland Security. The border patrol was known to set up checkpoints near the roads leading into and out of the airport. Eventually, someone would get suspicious of trucks departing Ajo's rarely used landing strip with unknown supplies destined for unknown locations. If the artists could build a tunnel from the hangar to the golf course, there would be minimal traffic leaving the airport for anyone to see. The expense to build the tunnel and secure the hangar would be hefty, but Sancho thought it could be done. He knew where to find cheap labor.

Sancho and his new cohorts thought it would be necessary to have a backup plan in the event Mexican Federales discovered the Los Vidrios factory. Several of the artists camped at Henry Gray's abandoned bunkhouses near the border to paint during the chilly winter days. There, they could store dirt bikes and ATVs for quick getaways between the two countries. A small tunnel that ran beneath the barbed wire cattle fence signifying the international boundary had been dug years ago. Not by immigrants wishing to enter America illegally, but by an animal activist who wanted to give the endangered gray wolf a chance to roam free. He was a drifter who spent many nights in the abandoned bunkhouses and became friends with the artists.

Distribution became the most challenging concept of the plan to hash out. Doctors who worked in small, non-franchised hospitals would be targeted. Those were the only health care facilities left that gladly accepted patients who had no insurance. But the doctors would be skeptical of anyone who tried to offer non-approved generic drugs for free. Sancho said he would have to call on doctors personally and explain his mission before manufacturing his drugs. That way, he could also research the most necessary medications prescribed for their patients, then try to replicate them or make them better.

In the wee hours of the morning, the artists were Googling and creating a list of targeted hospitals and possible doctors to call on. The only thing that remained was how to keep out of prison. The plan was highly illegal, and if they were caught, their mission would end as fast as it started. Homeland Security would like nothing better than to discover an illicit border-crossing drug operation. If only the artists could find an influential person—a politician or lawman who would support their philanthropist quest to help those in need. He or she could accompany Sancho when he called on hospitals and assure the cynical doctors that what they were doing was making society stronger.

"Impossible!" said several artists in unison.

"Finding a politician who actually values people over money? You've got to be kidding!" said sculptor Cecil Markham laughing at the thought.

"Wait a minute," inserted Mack. "I may know someone."

Everyone stared at Mack with blank faces waiting for him to continue.

"Sheriff Urdano and his family have a history of health problems. If Sancho could help him, perhaps we could get him on our side."

"The man's an asshole!" chortled Cecil. "He hates Mexicans. Sancho would be locked up and deported the minute he went knocking on the sheriff's door!"

"It's worth a try," countered Sancho. "We've worked all night on this plan, and it's a good one. We can't give up because we're afraid to take a risk. What we're going to do is save the lives of many poor people in America. That alone is worth the risk!"

The meeting ended a few minutes before the cooks arrived for their day shift at the Estrella Restaurant. *The tired group of artists returned to their apartments and crashed. Dr. Sancho Gomez borrowed Mack's car and drove to Phoenix. Sheriff Urdano's residence was unlisted in the phone book, but his haters splattered the address all over the new social media company that was overtaking the Internet by storm: Facebook.*

The haters were encouraging all their friends to picket Urdano's house, and when Sancho arrived, he had to park several blocks away. Phoenix police officers were trying to keep people at bay. Sancho walked up to Officer Emilio Alvarez and asked to see the sheriff.

"He's not taking visitors," replied Alvarez rudely. "His son Everett is dying inside. The doctors up at Mayo sent him home. Said there's nothing left they could do. Gave him one week, two at the most. I don't like the sheriff personally for his prejudicial ways, but these picketers should leave him alone."

"At the risk of sounding conceited, I'm a Nobel Prize-winning doctor. I would like to see if I can help the sheriff's son."

"You're also Hispanic, doctor. I don't think he will let you in."

Sancho shrugged his shoulders and gave a look of optimism. Officer Alvarez thought about it for a moment, then nodded and winked. "But I guess I'll try. What's there to lose, right?"

The diagnosis for Everett Urdano was that he was dying from a rare form of stomach cancer known as a Gastrointestinal Stromal Tumor, or GIST. Sancho enlightened Sheriff Urdano with his medical credentials, and the sheriff agreed to let him see his son. His son was awake, but obviously in a great deal of pain. Sancho asked him a series of questions and then wanted to see the prescribed medication he was taking. It was Gleevec, a drug that targeted specific proteins and was supposed to keep tumor cells from growing and dividing. Gleevec was manufactured by AmCan Pharmaceuticals. Sancho had a hunch, but he needed to take a blood test to be sure. He asked Urdano if he would be willing to move Everett to Ajo General Hospital, a small, run-down clinic that needed repair. Urdano really didn't want to transport his son there, but he thought it would be an opportunity to detach himself from all the wicked people picketing his house. After getting a tearful okay from his wife, the sheriff loaded his son into his SUV that was parked in the garage, then backed out into the crowd of angry onlookers and drove off. Sancho ran to Mack's car and hurried back to Ajo.

The blood test indicated what Sancho had guessed: Everett was actually suffering from Celiac Disease, and the AmCan medication he was taking contained gluten. He had an immune reaction in his small intestine from the

Gleevec that was preventing the absorption of nutrients. During his illness, the only food that Everett had a taste for was soup, and his favorite was vegetable barley. Nurses brought him that daily for lunch along with a piece of buttered wheat toast. Gluten overload! The wrong diagnosis occurred when the oncologist mistook benign hyperplastic polyps for malignant GISTs.

Sancho immediately placed Urdano's son on a gluten-free diet and provided him with vitamin supplements that contained iron and calcium. A week later, Everett was out jogging the streets of Ajo, and Sheriff Urdano had a new lifelong friend—Dr. Sancho Gomez. That's when Sancho laid out his mission to help the poor who needed health care but couldn't afford it. The sheriff was all for it! He had become a changed man, somewhat like Mr. Scrooge had after visiting Tiny Tim's home in a dream. He agreed to do everything in his power to disrupt Homeland Security investigations and fend off talented Special Agent Earl Kelly.

A handful of doctors working in poverty areas of the United States had been compatriots with Sancho on the Latin America Council of the World Medicine Association. Ironically, their committee was often asked to provide recommendations for improving medical ethics in the healthcare industry. Sancho wasn't sure how the council would react to doctors importing nonapproved drugs into America. It was time to test the waters.

Three colleagues and friends from the WMA now practiced in small Arizona towns on Native American land: Sells, Tuba City, and Whiteriver. He started with them. Sancho flew his Cessna DC-6 into Gila Bend and was met by Sheriff Urdano. The sheriff not only took care of the doctor's customs and immigration paperwork, he personally drove Sancho around the state in his unmarked squad car. The three stops were a good distance apart, and most travel was on two-lane roads. The journey took three days and two nights to complete. It was during those nights that Sheriff Urdano began to complain about headaches. Sancho said he wanted to see him as soon as the trip was over. They would figure out a place later.

The meetings were an enormous success. All three doctors agreed to give Sancho a chance. They would start with his irregular heartbeat medicine that AmCan stole from him. If all went well and there were no investigations by the FDA, they would agree to treat other symptoms with Sancho's drugs. The doctors had three common diseases that the prescription medication sold by big pharmaceuticals had become too expensive for their patients: diabetes, liver disease, and depression. Sancho now had his research and development plan.

Three months later, his so-called "cheap labor" crew finished constructing a small medicine factory in an indistinct desert location near Los Vidrios that he purchased from the Mexican government for next to nothing. They also built him a runway and a hangar for his airplane next to the factory. The artists and their drifter friend enlarged the tunnel underneath the international boundary fence so that dirt bikes and ATVs could pass through it. Then they placed large pieces of plywood on both ends and decorated it with the prettiest camouflage scene ever created! You know artists—they're so dang picky and proud of their work!

While Sancho was developing his generic drugs, Mack and two other artists, Archie McCormick and Paul Killian, enlarged and redesigned the hangar they had bought at the Ajo airport. After chopping out the old concrete floor with a rented breaker, they purchased a used mini-excavator to dig a subterranean compartment underneath it. Then Mack contracted the services of Browning Corporation to secure the hangar with steel-reinforced concrete walls and a hydraulic vault door that would raise and lower into the underground section. No one from the Browning Corporation questioned what the artists were doing. They were making a lot of money and were paid on time.

In small communities, everyone seems to know everything about everybody. And what they don't know, they make up by starting rumors down at the local coffee shops. Because everyone in Ajo would know that a lot of digging was going on out at the airport, Sheriff Urdano had decided to use his influence to stop the tittle-tattlers from negative gossiping. He laid out Sancho's plan to Pima County sheriff, Mike Morton, and Morton appeared to be totally on board with the operation. He would gladly support the artists any way he could—after all, Sheriff Urdano was his mentor. He hired him as a Maricopa County deputy, trained him, then campaigned for him during the Pima County elections.

Morton notified the local newspaper that a rather large family of rattlesnakes had made their home somewhere underground between the golf course and the airport, and for the safety of everyone in the community, it was best to relocate them to an unpopulated area of the desert. He asked that people stay far away from the golf course during this time—upended pit vipers would be especially dangerous. Many deaths could occur! A few senior golf course members canceled their memberships the day after the paper published the announcement.

Rumors swarming around the coffee shop were that no one within a twenty-mile radius was safe! Time to permanently move back to Minnesota!

With help from the newly purchased mini-excavator, Sancho's construction crew took two months to finish the tunnel from the airport hangar to the golf course. That included the time spent framing the tunnel walls with wood and concrete blocks and running electric lights from one end to the other. The last step was installing a six-by-six-foot steel entrance door next to a massive boulder on the golf course. Like they did camouflaging the tunnel doors at the international boundary, the artists decorated this one to perfection!

Five months after Sancho had contacted the three doctors in Arizona, the plan was put into place and was an immediate success! With falsified customs and immigration documents provided by Sheriff Morton, Mack Colten would fly his 1951 Cessna to Los Vidrios, load up cartons of generic drugs, fly back to Ajo, and pull into the hangar. Two artists from Curley School Apartments would transport the containers through the tunnel to their golf carts that were sitting by the boulder on the fifth hole. They would drive the carts back to the apartments and transfer the drugs into an SUV parked in the underground garage. Each artist took turns delivering the medications to Sells, Whiteriver, and Tuba City—a monotonous trip if ever there was one! But when Dr. Lopez from Sells Indian Hospital was able to stabilize a patient's heart attack and save his life thanks to Sancho's free medicine, every mile driven was well worth it!

The three doctors began to tell their colleagues around the state about the free medicine. To avoid suspicion, Sancho told them to say a charitable organization was donating the generic drugs on behalf of patients who couldn't afford the name brands. Sancho had successfully created medications to treat diabetes, liver disease, and depression that were more effective than AmCan was producing. He had become a mysterious, unknown hero. But his bank account was dwindling. Sancho guessed he had enough savings to run the operation for another five to ten years, then he would be broke. That's when he met the O'Connells at the annual Curley School art festival.

That's also when Sheriff Urdano's headaches caused him to have trouble breathing.

*****

Mack taxied the Cessna up to the hangar and parked it a few feet from the secured steel door. He opened it up and walked around, but Principal Perez and the teachers were not there. He went below into the tunnel and flipped the light switch. Nothing. Where were they? Could they have walked through the desert back to Gila Bend?

Mack got back into the cockpit and taxied out to the runway. The Ajo airport runway gave a pilot only two options: take off and land to the northwest or take off and land to the southeast. Tonight, the prevailing winds were still blowing hard from the west, so Mack took off to the northwest. A few minutes later, he was airborne and turned the Cessna in a northeasterly course for Gila Bend.

Dr. Gomez had installed a new radar system in his aircraft several months ago that included a traffic collision avoidance system—better known as a TCAS. The radar could locate and track flying objects in front of the plane and display them on the moving map, then warn the pilot if he was in imminent danger of a mid-air collision. Shortly after Mack began a descent towards the Gila Bend airport, flashing red lights and a loud beeping sound startled him. On the digital screen blinked the words:

WARNING
ENTERING RESTRICTED AIRSPACE
TURN STARBOARD AND DESCEND!

Mack had flown into Gila Bend on many occasions and had never known there was restricted airspace. However, most times, he operated his own Cessna, which didn't have all the fancy radar equipment. Then he remembered; if the Auxiliary Air Force base south of town was being used, they would automatically generate an alert to prevent small aircraft from penetrating a five-mile radius around it. But why would they be operating in the middle of the night? It didn't make sense.

Mack turned hard right and cut the engine speed. As the DC-6 began to descend, he saw the reason for the warning: a large jet was circling and making an approach for landing from the north. Mack wasn't wholly versed in aircraft types, but he thought the plane was a Boeing C-32. Awfully big to be landing in Gila Bend! Luke Air Force base in Phoenix was designed for VIPs and military personnel. Why not land there? Mack was trying to think this through when the jet touched down and slammed on its brakes. It rolled to a stop just a few feet from the edge of the runway.

Mack decided to circle around the auxiliary airport and see if he could find any type of flag or insignia on the airplane. The warning light in the cockpit was still flashing, and Mack understood he was still in restricted airspace. He reached for the radio mic and dialed the emergency frequency. Nothing was going to stop him from checking this out.

"Mayday, Mayday, Mayday! November-six-niner-eight-Charlie-tango requests emergency landing!" barked Mack into the mic with a smile on his face. He wasn't sure he could pull this off.

Only one air traffic controller was on duty at the auxiliary airbase between midnight and 0800 hours. The assignment was rotated nightly between a group of nine Air Force officers stationed at Luke AFB. When it was his turn to be the controller, Senior Airman Frank Gustine would stop at Seven-Eleven and buy potato chips and a longneck Bud Lite, then wallow away the night playing solitaire. Rarely did an Air Force jet make a landing during those lonely hours. Never while Gustine was on duty. Until tonight. When it rains, it pours! First, he finds out the vice president would be stopping by, and now he's startled by an emergency hailing from a private airplane. And to top it off, Air Force Two is still on the runway!

"Six-niner-eight, what is your emergency?"

"Out of fuel!" yelled Mack in his best fake-panicked voice. Then he turned towards the runway and killed his engine. He didn't want the controller to think he could land elsewhere.

"Hold on! There is a jet on the runway, you can't land here!" Airman Gustine was having a tough time remembering protocol for this type of emergency. He grabbed his binoculars from the desk, knocking the beer bottle onto the floor in his haste.

"No can do! I have no engine power, and I'm gliding in. Leave that jet at the end of the runway. I should be able to stop in time." Mack was trying to maintain a serious inflection in his voice.

"Roger, six-niner-eight," Gustine hailed. "Alfa foxtrot two, maintain your position. Repeat—do not taxi!"

The Air Force Two pilot had been listening all along and was waiting for instructions. Meanwhile, the rear hatch door opened, and two secret servicemen using magnetic grips climbed on top of the fuselage. They unstrapped rocket-propelled grenade weapons from their backs and aimed them at the approaching DC-6. Mack would need to stop at least fifty yards from Air Force Two, or this would be his final mission.

As Mack touched down, he noticed the men on top of the jet with weapons locked on him. He braked the DC-6, diverted off the runway, and rolled to a stop near the control tower. He leaned back and took a deep breath of relief, then unbuckled his seat belt. The full moon lit up the night sky just enough for him to see the insignia on the jet's fuselage.

"What is the vice president doing in Gila Bend?" muttered Mack to himself. He thought he would go and find out, but as he stepped down from the cockpit, three men with pistols aimed at him were running from the vice president's gangway towards his plane. Mack froze in place and raised his hands.

Chapter 38

Thursday, April 19, 2018
Love's Travel Stop Parking Lot, Gila Bend, Arizona
4:30 am (Pacific Daylight Time)

The semi's spark plugs ignited, and its cylinders rattled to a start. The truck slowly pulled out of Love's lot onto Main Street, and two minutes later, it was parked next to the Space Age Lodge. Cliff, Rick, and Donnor could hear the two guards slam their doors shut and shuffle to the back door of the truck. They were talking to each other, but none of the three could make out what they were saying.

"I have a plan, and we have no time for discussion, so no arguments, okay?!" whispered Cliff to Rick and Donnor. They both nodded. "Fake like you are weary and have lost your memories. When we get to wherever they are taking us, we jump them."

"Those two guards are big guys, Cliff, I don't think—"

"He said no arguments!" gritted Donnor, sotto voce. "We can do this!"

The back door of the semi was opened, and the two mega men in fatigues entered. Cliff, Rick, and Donnor pretended to be fast asleep. The guards unlocked the cuffs from the truck panel but then decided to handcuff the three together. Cliff realized that if they were all re-cuffed to each other, there would be no chance to attack the guards. It was now or never.

Cliff rose quickly and jarred his head into one guard's chest, then bulldozed him to the floor. The other guard was stunned and immediately moved to help his comrade. Rick and Donnor both jumped up and rammed the second guard in the back, sending him face-first to the floor.

"I'll take care of this dude," said Donnor as he kneed the guard's spine and punched his head in a rapid flurry. "Go help Cliff!"

Rick moved quickly to Cliff. He and the first guard were wrapped in a bear hug and rolling around, trying to get the dominant position. When the guard spun on top of Cliff, Rick used a half nelson hold—he passed his right hand under the man's arm and locked it onto his neck. With his left hand, the one with the cuff still dangling from his wrist, Rick pushed down hard on the guard's head. With a hefty yank, he was able to pull the guard off Cliff. That same move won him the state wrestling championship in high school.

Cliff grabbed the keys to the handcuffs that had fallen to the floor and unlocked his wrist. Rick was trying his best to restrain the guard but was gradually losing his strength. Donnor had knocked the first guard unconscious and came over to help. As the guard tried to pull Rick's arms away from the half nelson grip, Donnor grabbed his wrists, and Cliff fastened one cuff. Then the three men pushed the guard to the truck panel and locked him to it. Next, they dragged the unconscious guard to the wall and cuffed him by his buddy. When they had gained control, all three collapsed on the truck's floor and tried to catch their breaths.

"Come on," coaxed Cliff. "We need to get this semi to the Auxiliary airport and keep Yegor Bovnik from boarding that plane!"

"If that is Air Force Two like you suggested, how do you intend to do that?" asked Donnor. "There will be secret service swarming the place!"

"If we can go fast enough, this rig can rip the landing gear right off the belly of the plane, and we can be out of the way before the fuselage collapses on top of us. Then we continue riding on through the desert. They won't know what hit them!"

"You realize that you are putting the vice president of the United States in harm's way, don't you," asked Rick. "They won't stop chasing us until they catch us, and when they do, they will probably shoot us on the spot. Knowing what we know, they would not risk a tell-all trial."

All three men paused to think about that for a moment.

"Well then, are you in?" asked Cliff.

"I'm in!" stated Donnor firmly.

"I'm in, too!" said Rick. "We might be the only hope to save this country."

4:45 am (Pacific Daylight Time)

"You made the decision on your own to let them live?!" grilled Vice President Sanders. "I should have you shot right where you are standing!" The vice president was sitting on his oversized leather recliner onboard Air Force Two. When he said the word shot, two secret service agents drew out their weapons and aimed them at Gene Schultz and Loren Schoenholtz.

Schultz looked at the agents and then at the vice president. "Tell them you're just kidding, sir. I think they think you're serious."

The vice president snapped his middle finger with his thumb, then pointed at Schultz and Schoenholtz. The agents took a step towards them and placed the gun barrels on their temples. Schultz and Schoenholtz stood side-by-side with their hands behind their backs, looking downtrodden and in fear that they might be shot. On the flight from Edwards Air Force Base, the vice president received a call from Lord Shaffer who was demanding answers for the failures that had taken place. During the call, he inquired about hiking photographer Joe Freeman and Senso-Mac employee Roger Bennett who had escaped the crime scene. This was the first the vice president had heard about them. Lord Shaffer wanted an update on their status and the whereabouts of the camera's SD card. After the call ended, Schultz and Schoenholtz explained what they did with Freeman and Bennett and why they let them live.

"You two will right your wrong now!" exclaimed Vice President Sanders. "Get off this damn plane and find them and kill them. Do you understand?!"

"And once we do that, how are we getting out of the country?" asked Schoenholtz. "Lord Shaffer wants us all to reassemble in Saudi Arabia before we head back to Edwards for our final mission."

"Throw a rope around a pigeon's neck or have some dolphin take you across the ocean! I really don't care how you plan to get there!" Sanders stood up, his face bright red, and pointed at the hatch. "Now get out of here!"

Air Force Two was still sitting at the end of the runway waiting for Yegor Bovnik to board. The two secret servicemen on top of the fuselage were watching closely as three other agents were questioning the pilot of the Cessna DC-6. Mack could be seen shrugging his shoulders as if he had no clue why he had flown with a low amount of fuel. Had the agents bothered to check his fuel gauge, they would have found it was half full. Airman Frank Gustine was watching with binoculars while talking to the Air Force Two pilot on the radio. Once the Cessna and its pilot were secured, he would give clearance for the vice president's plane to taxi and take off.

The van turned off Air Force Station Road and moved onto the runway. The driver was still steamed about the argument he had with Barney Kinkel at Love's, so he just drove and said nothing. He pulled up next to the Air Force Two gangway and put the van in neutral. The driver stayed put while Kinkel and Yegor got out and shook hands. Then Kinkel got back in the van as the directorate chief climbed up the ramp and boarded the airplane. He bumped into Schultz and Schoenholtz as they were about to exit the cabin.

"Where are you two going?" asked Yegor. "We need to leave as soon as possible."

Before they had a chance to respond, a secret service agent brushed past them and glided down the gangway. He sprinted to the van trying to catch Kinkel before he drove off. Kinkel saw him coming, so he waited and rolled down his window.

"Sir, Vice President Sanders would like to speak to you," said the agent.

Kinkel looked up at the fuselage, exited the van, then made his way to the ramp. The driver was very curious. He opened the van's door, stood up, and peered all around the Auxiliary airport as if he was searching for someone or something.

The vice president gazed down the cabin and yelled an order for Schultz and Schoenholtz to wait. The two Germans rolled their eyes and shook their heads in disbelief. "First, he tells us to get off his damn plane, then he tells us to wait," muttered Schultz loud enough for everyone to hear.

Vice President Sanders bumped past Schultz and Schoenholtz and gave them an evil look, then grabbed Yegor's arm while motioning for Kinkel to hurry up the gangway.

"We need to talk," said Sanders. Yegor and Kinkel followed Sanders through the cabin, but Schultz and Schoenholtz had remained at the hatch. The vice president stopped and glared back at the Germans, his face in flames. "You dingbats, too! Follow me!"

He led them all into a soundproof conference room near the front of the plane and shut the door. The vice president informed Yegor and Kinkel about the situation that took place with the photographer and the Senso-Mac employee. He said he had ordered Schultz and Schoenholtz to go back and kill them, but now he wanted to know their thoughts. There was disagreement between them about what should be done.

"If Schultz and Schoenholtz are caught," said Yegor, "they would be encouraged to talk, if you know what I mean!" Yegor knew when it came to terrorists, the FBI would use whatever method was necessary to get them to speak. Torture would be ignored by authorities all the way up to the president.

"If that hiker and other guy talk, it won't make any difference!" exclaimed Kinkel. "We need for them to die!"

"They ain't going to speak to no one," responded Schultz. "After drinking all that coffee we gave them, they will have no capacity to think. If we kill them, it will only raise suspicions."

"We didn't ask for your opinion," said Vice President Sanders firmly. "Shut up! You'll do as we order you to do!"

"What's it going to be, Yegor?" asked Kinkel. "We need to get this plane and everyone on board to Saudi Arabia as soon as possible. Lord Shaffer wants to reassemble Pavel's team at Tariq's palace to hash out a new plan with you and General Sokolov. Part two of the plan is still a go at Edwards in a couple of weeks. We're running out of time!"

"Yes, I know that, but he also wanted Schultz and Schoenholtz to be there, too!" Yegor paced the small room in deep thought, then said to Schultz, "Alright, go with Kinkel to Mesa. Barney, can you get them one of Zefron's private jets for transport to Saudi after they kill the hiker and his friend?"

"Not sure, but I'll think of something."

"Then, get going!" Yegor wasn't happy with this diversion, but he needed to make a quick decision and live with it.

Kinkel, Schultz, and Schoenholtz deplaned and climbed into the van. Seconds later, the driver gunned the vehicle down the same road from which it came. The three secret service agents who were questioning Mack ordered him to stand by his plane until Air Force Two was in the air. He had never served in the military, but Mack saluted them anyway. He was just thankful they let him go.

Mack looked up at the fuselage and gazed into the windows. He wasn't exactly sure what he was looking for; he just had a hunch that something was very wrong. When he looked at the last window near the tail section, something caught his eye. He nonchalantly climbed into the Cessna's cockpit and reached for a pair of binoculars, then peered back into the window. What he saw made his hair stand up. It was the young schoolgirl who had parachuted out of his own plane shortly before he crashed in the desert. He could see that her arms were not free to move—they were fastened to something. But her eyes were locked on Mack's and her mouth was moving as if she was lip-syncing the word "help!"

Next to her, in the same row, were the high school boy and the teacher. They, too, were unable to move their arms. Mack shifted his binoculars left and observed as the hatch was closed. He was hoping to see something inside but had no luck. Air Force Two circled around and headed to the other end of the runway, paused momentarily for clearance from Airman Gustine, then initiated a take-off roll.

Just then, a huge semi-truck and trailer smashed through a perimeter fence and barreled head-on towards the runway. Mack gaped in astonishment. If it picked up enough speed, the truck would clip the tail section as it rolled back for take-off and send Air Force Two crashing back to earth. Mack could care less about the vice president's life; it was the young kids and their teacher's fate that he feared for the most.

Chapter 39

Washington, DC
Thursday, April 20, 2017
8:00 am (EST) 5:00 am (PST)

The last semi-truck loaded with Taste Of Arabia coffee rolled into Washington, DC, two hours later than expected. The two drivers left the Port of Saint John, Canada, at 4:00 pm Wednesday afternoon, hoping to drive through the night to avoid heavy traffic, but I-95 had been slow from Boston all the way down to the nation's capital. The four other semis had all reached their destinations and were waiting for the okay from Directorate Chief Bovnik to proceed. One was in Chicago, one in San Francisco, one in Houston, and one in Phoenix. With falsified documents provided by Vice President Sanders, the trucks crossed into the United States from Milltown, New Brunswick, then followed Maine State Route 9 to Bangor. At the US Customs office on the border, there was minimal scrutiny over the truck drivers' documents or cargo; this was Canada, not Mexico, after all. Thus the reason Lord Shaffer paid three times the port charges to ship the coffee from Aden, Yemen, to Saint John rather than to the Port of Ensenada south of Tijuana.

Taste Of Arabia's amnestic testing and analysis was complete, and now it was time to go forward with the masterplan concocted several years ago by Lord Shaffer, General Sokolov, Sultan Tariq, and Directorate Chief Bovnik. Memory loss had successfully occurred on every test subject who unknowingly drank the coffee: Saudi Prince Javed and his eight sons, Sir Barrett Handly of Wales and his wife, and three magistrate judges from Moscow, one who was the great-grandson of Tsar Nicholas II. Prince Javed was deplored by Tariq, Sir Handly had refused to allow Lord Shaffer to hunt fox on his property, and the three magistrates had all soundly beaten Directorate Chief Bovnik in a marathon poker game during a snowstorm that had shut down operations at the Kremlin for a day. They all made perfect laboratory rats!

The only concern now was to find covert storage and distribution. The plan was for the coffee to be stored at inconspicuous locations, not in warehouses that could be easily raided. Following an intense brainstorming session, the group made the decision to use schools. Older schools always had abandoned areas that were off-limits to kids and ignored by administrators who didn't like to get their hands dirty. Those same schools all had vans and buses that could be used for distribution without anyone questioning why or where they were going. No one would suspect a school to be involved in deadly drug distribution. And most importantly, they all had disgruntled employees who thought they were underpaid and would do anything to make an extra buck. Finding an accomplice in a school would be easy.

The attempt to secure the Phoenix location at Gila Bend Charter School had failed. A new option would be necessary soon, seeing that the semi loaded with coffee was parked at Love's Travel Stop waiting for instructions. *Operation Memory Loss* was the title given to the scheme to whitewash the brains of American politicians, military leaders, judges, and as many civilians as possible by drinking coffee. The initial five cities were chosen based upon the number of political campaign donations that were reported to the Federal Election Commission.

Operation Executive Control was the title given to the second part of the plan. If successful, the leadership of the United States would be in turmoil. Hopefully, American democracy would be too. The premise of *Operation Executive Control* was simple—destroy Air Force One with the president on board so the vice president can take his place! That event would happen during a joint Russian-American celebration for the space station astronauts and cosmonauts. The laser weapons and energy packs would be tested in an underground vault at Senso-McNamara headquarters in Mesa, Arizona, before being transported to California and safely tucked away at Edwards. As soon as Air Force One exploded in midair, Vice President Garrett Sanders would become President Garrett Sanders.

It was mid-afternoon in London, and once again, Lord Shaffer couldn't focus on the Parliament discussions taking place around him. Do we really need an argument about whether to send money to Queensland to help clean up after Cyclone Debbie? After all, Australia was a founding member of the Commonwealth, and the Statute of Westminster clearly affirms British financial support for its nations that are struck by natural disasters. Stop dickering and send them the damn pounds!

Shaffer hadn't slept much this past week, and he was cranky while thinking about the plan. Both operations had been going well until a hiker and a Senso-Mac employee had witnessed, and even taken pictures of, Loren Schoenholtz destroying Senso-Mac and the Homeland Security Building. Although Bovnik was now in possession of the camera's SD card, and the two civilian stragglers were seemingly incapacitated from coffee, that part of the plan could become a problem.

Shaffer had just received a text from Yegor; He was aboard Air Force Two and almost ready to take off from Gila Bend Auxiliary Airport. Moments earlier, Yegor had given the okay for the truck drivers in Washington to unload at John Quincy Adams Charter School, which was across A Street SE from St. Mark's Episcopal Church and a block away from the Library of Congress. Most of the legislators' school-aged children attended JQA, as did three of the nine Supreme Court justices' grandkids. The school would be hosting its annual breakfast awards on Saturday, an event that had nearly one hundred percent attendance every year the school had been in existence. It was a good time for Republicans and Democrats to put aside their differences for two hours and revel in their kids' accomplishments. This year, they would enjoy scrambled eggs made by the kids, donuts imported from Mickey's Bakery down the street, and the best coffee in the world—Taste Of Arabia.

Student Council Advisor Zella Norris met the semi drivers at the school's receiving area in the back of the school. She was extremely nervous! Zella purchased many products for resale that would be used to raise funds for the student council but had never been involved in something illegal—and very dangerous! But she was eight months pregnant with her first child, and her husband had ditched her for a congresswoman from Wyoming. Her salary could hardly pay for the rent in her one-bedroom apartment near the Hechinger Mall and all the diapers she would soon be buying. Zella had sold her car and now walked the two miles to work each day to save on gas and parking expenses. She needed supplementary income, and Lord Shaffer's headhunter did an excellent job finding her.

"Stay in the cab until I make sure the coast is clear," order Zella on her cell phone to the truck drivers. "You were supposed to be here at six! What happened?!"

"Traffic, lady! Ever driven down the east coast of the United States?"

Zella ignored the sarcasm and looked around, trying to make sure any latecomers had already been given tardy slips and were now in their classrooms. School started at 7:30, and fortunately, no one was nearby. The administrators would be tied up with demanding parents wanting to know why their children were not being treated like the VIPs that they were. Even the Supreme Court grandparents would drop by without appointments to argue their grandkids' constitutional rights with the principal. A thankless job to say the least!

Zella was given an unused classroom on the first floor for student council meetings. Knowing that the coffee shipment would be arriving soon, she bought storage cabinets that would be attached to all the walls. The janitors would have keys to the door, but only she would have keys to the cabinets. The classroom was next to the receiving area in the back of the school. It took the drivers an hour to unload all the boxes, but there did not appear to be any suspicious activity taking place. Trucks were always delivering lunches and materials during the day. The tennis moms walking by saw the semi but never thought twice about it.

When the truck was fully unloaded, Zella panicked. She had filled all the cabinets, and now there were twenty or more boxes stacked in the middle of the room.

"I have no place to put these!" she exclaimed to the drivers. "Can you take them back?"

"Sorry, lady, our orders are to deliver these to you. End of story!"

"But if they get noticed, there will be questions! What am I going to tell people?!"

"Ain't our problem," replied one driver as they exited the door and headed for the empty semi. "But good luck anyway!"

Zella called U-Haul and got a quote for a local rental and a small storage unit. Then she forged the principal's signature on a purchase order she had stolen from his secretary. Zella told the janitors that she would be testing kids after school and asked them not to bother her by cleaning the room. She waited until the last car left the parking lot at six o'clock, then she walked as fast as an eight months pregnant lady could go to the U-Haul location a mile away. Luckily, they were open until nine, and Zella completed the paperwork and got the keys to the storage unit an hour before closing. She drove the truck back to school and told the night security guard that she needed to move some boxes to Lincoln Park for a student council sale next weekend. The guard helped her load the truck and wished her a pleasant evening. She drove back to the storage unit and unloaded the boxes, then left the rental in the lot and dropped the keys into a night box.

As she was walking home under a full moon, Zella went into labor.

Chapter 40

Thursday, April 19, 2018
Auxiliary Airforce Base, Gila Bend, Arizona
5:10 am (Pacific Daylight Time)

Air Force Two rolled down the runway full throttle with a sidewind blowing sixty knots from the west. There was only one runway at the Gila Bend Auxiliary Airbase, and unfortunately, it ran north and south. And even more unfortunately—it was only 8,500 feet long. The pilots had used the entire runway to land the jet. Taking off would require even more distance to become airborne. The runway end safety area extended the reach another 500 feet, and if needed, there was hard desert soil after that. Chances were good that the vice president's plane could rip through the barbwire and chain-link perimeter fence to achieve flight. The pilot and copilot knew it was going to be touch and go, but they believed the Boeing C-32 could do it. That was until they saw a semi-truck and trailer crashing through the fence and barreling at them head-on.

The pilot waited until the last second to rotate nose up, but he could only hope he had enough lift to avoid colliding with the truck. If he got airborne, he would turn immediately west into the wind to increase drag. It didn't happen that way.

The truck's trailer clipped the jet's starboard landing gear and shattered the locking mechanism, then scraped and dented the tail end of the fuselage as the plane took off. It was precisely what Cliff, Rick, and Donnor had hoped for when they saw Air Force Two roll down the runway. If they had driven too slow, the jet would simply fly over them unharmed. If they had driven too fast, the plane and semi would have exploded into a million pieces. The timing had to be exact to take out the landing gear, and it worked to perfection!

Cliff, Rick, and Donnor had wanted to duck down and cover their eyes as the jet approached them, but they were frozen with fear inside the cab. They knew if a collision happened, death would be instantaneous—and hopefully, painless! There was structural damage to the roof of the trailer, but the semi's cab and engines were in excellent working order. They continued on, crashing through the north perimeter fence, then turned west on 307th Avenue heading for Highway 85. The three men pulled over and watched Air Force Two continue to climb, but they knew some damage had been done. If the vice president's jet couldn't land, what would they do? Mack Colten had watched the whole incident happen from the ground, and he thought the same thing. He had no idea that his cousin was driving the truck! Airman Gustine was awestruck by the entire episode. He was ready to call his superiors up at Luke Air Force Base, but a harrowing thought occurred, and he hung up the phone. He would be held responsible for not ensuring the safety of the vice president and would most likely be dishonorably discharged and possibly court-martialed. There's no way he was going to rot away in a military prison! He looked up and saw Air Force Two seemingly flying okay. No harm, no foul—right? He would just keep his mouth shut, and if someone questioned him in the future, he would play dumb. No sir—that didn't happen on his watch!

*****

"Starboard side landing gear has been hit, Jack," said Copilot Fritz Parker. "It retracted, but the warning light says it's inoperable. But worse, we have a leak in the hydraulics system that effects the landing gear and wheel brakes. Unless we try an emergency landing right now on one rear wheel, we might not have enough fluid left to lower the port side landing gear later. The wheel brakes would also be useless."

"So, we're either going to land this plane now with a broken leg or later using only the fuselage belly," stated Pilot Jack Carter with no sign of panic in his voice. He was an Air Force vet who enjoyed a challenge. "Do you want to ask Sanders which he prefers, or should I?"

"You're the captain, Jack. In an emergency, it's your decision, not his."

"Well then, let me go get his opinion. He'll want to know about our bumpy takeoff anyway." Carter unstrapped himself and walked back to Vice President Sanders, who was in a serious conversation with Yegor. Neither looked happy as the pilot stood next to them.

"What happened on takeoff?!" Yegor demanded. "I thought I was on a roller coaster!"

"We hit a semi-truck," replied Carter. He wasn't going to offer more unless asked.

Yegor unbuckled his seatbelt and stood nose to nose with the pilot. He was furious, and spittle was splashing out of his mouth. "What the hell do you mean we hit a truck?! What was a truck doing on the runway?!"

"Not sure. But here's the deal. The truck clipped our right-side landing gear, making it unusable. It also caused a leak in our landing gear and wheel brake hydraulics system."

"What!" exclaimed Vice President Sanders and Yegor at the same time.

"Relax!" said Carter firmly as he motioned for Yegor to sit back down. "I will land this sucker safely one way or another. I have two options for you to consider. Right now, we have enough hydraulic fluid to retract the wheels, but only the left side will lock into place. It would be a tricky landing, but I could do it. Or we could try a belly landing in the Sahara somewhere near Morocco. We were going to refuel in Casablanca anyway."

"What kind of options are those?!" yelled Sanders. "We can't make an emergency landing in the United States without every reporter in the country swarming our jet, say nothing of a thorough and lengthy investigation by the FAA and FBI! With Yegor and all these Russians on board?! And what about the two kids and the teacher we kidnapped?! Are you kidding me?! If we land on our belly in Morocco, we'll never be able to take off again! Then the CIA will be involved! Those are no options, you fool!"

"So what do you propose, sir? One way or another, we're going to make an emergency landing. We don't have enough fuel to make it to Saudi Arabia."

"Landing in the United States is out of the question!" replied the vice president. "How long before we run out of hydraulic fluid?"

"Not sure. I don't know the size of the leak, but I'm guessing we don't have much time. We could divert to Mexico and try to put down there on some obscure airfield, but if you don't want the authorities knowing about it, we can't use a main airport. That means we won't have radar guidance. But the sun is rising, and visibility should be clear down there."

"What is safer—landing on one wheel or a belly landing?"

"They're both dangerous, sir."

"Then let's get as far away from here as possible and go for a belly landing. But you need to put down in the middle of nowhere and not declare an emergency. Just cloak the damn plane and land it! What about Greenland?"

"We'd be landing on ice in Greenland. The desert sand dunes would be better and softer."

Yegor interrupted, "We can refuel in midair on this jet, right?"

"Yes, sir. We have a spigot above the cockpit. Why?"

"If we refuel, we could make it to Saudi and land on the Arabian desert, right?"

"Yes, but how can we refuel without notifying the Air Force?"

"We can't notify the United States Air Force. But we can notify the Russian Air Force. General Sokolov heads up Air Force operations for our country. I will have him deploy an Ilyushin refueling tanker immediately. Where should I direct him to meet us?"

"We're about ten hours flying time from here to Casablanca. It will take that long for Sokolov to get the Ilyushin airborne and to the African coast. I would suggest refueling over the Atlantic to avoid Moroccan airspace, somewhere between Funchal and Safi."

"Excellent! Then I will make the call!"

"Fine. I will set a course for Funchal, and you have Sokolov instruct his pilot to do the same. When we get closer, I will need you to join me in the cockpit. I don't speak Russian and probably wouldn't be able to understand the Ilyushin pilot's English!"

"Okay, will do," said Yegor with a hint of confidence in his voice. He got up to make the call in the privacy of the conference room. Pilot Jack Carter was making his way down the aisle back to the cockpit, then stopped abruptly, turned, and faced Yegor.

"I wouldn't get your hopes up. You realize we might all die in the Arabian desert, don't you?"

"Not a chance, Captain Carter. You're the best. You even said so yourself!" Yegor smiled and locked himself in the conference room. Carter smiled back. Yes, he was the best, and he knew it.

*****

"What now?" asked Rick. He, Donnor, and Cliff were standing outside of the parked semi with their hands shielding their eyes from the rising sun. They watched as Air Force Two banked right and then circled around to the east.

"Do you think we did any damage?" asked Donnor.

"I'm almost certain we accomplished what we set out to do—ram their landing gear useless and hopefully damage their hydraulics," replied Cliff.

"What now?" asked Rick again.

"This truck is loaded with evidence," said Cliff. "I think we should leave it at the airfield. There had to have been an air traffic controller in the tower who witnessed us trying to cause harm to the vice president. I'm sure he's already called it in, and a team will be coming from Luke Air Force Base to look for us. We need to explain the situation to him before they arrive."

"The situation, as you call it, is rather complicated. Where do we begin with the story?"

"I'm not sure, but trying to run and hide from the military police and the FBI in a semi doesn't sound too promising. Get back in the truck, okay?"

A minute later, the semi pulled onto the airfield's entrance road and turned toward the control tower. Two men were talking and looking at the sky in the direction of Air Force Two's contrail. When they saw the semi heading towards them, the man in a military uniform pointed at it.

"Look! That's the truck!" howled Airman Gustine. "It's coming back! They must think we were witnesses; let's get the heck out of here!" He turned to run, but Mack grabbed his arm.

"Hold on!" shouted Mack. "There's three of them in the cab, and I know them. The driver is my cousin."

Airman Gustine shook his arm free from Mack's grasp and took a step back.

"Who are you?! Who are they?! I thought you were some ordinary idiotic pilot who forgot to fill his airplane up with gas before taking off! Now you're telling me you know these criminals!" Instinctively, he grabbed Mack from behind and locked arms, then turned him towards the semi.

Mack looked over his shoulder at his captor. "Seriously? You're going to use me as a shield against a semi-truck?!"

The semi stopped a few yards from the control tower. The three men in the cab looked at each other and nodded. They were shocked to see Mack standing there, and even more surprised to see him locked in a wrestling hold.

"I don't see a gun," whispered Rick. "Do you think the man has one?"

"I'm not sure," responded Cliff. "But I'm going to find out." He reached for the door handle.

"Stop!" demanded Donnor as he glanced at Cliff. "He's my cousin. I'll do it." Donnor opened his door and climbed down with his hands raised over his head.

"Don't shoot!" yelled Donnor. "I just want to talk peacefully. I don't have a gun!"

"Don't worry, Cuz, he doesn't have one either," responded Mack. He turned and looked over his shoulder again. "Now, would you let me go so we can explain all of this to you?"

Cautiously, Airman Gustine released the hold, and Mack almost slipped backward. Cliff and Rick jumped down and walked over. The five men stood in a circle and looked at each other. No one knew what to say first.

"How much time before the authorities get here?" asked Cliff to Gustine. The airman dropped his head and looked at his feet, then kicked nervously at some gravel.

"There are no authorities scheduled to come," replied Gustine in a soft voice.

"What do you mean by that?!" responded Cliff incredulously. "Certainly, you called your superiors and the FAA, right?!"

Gustine looked at Cliff with a look of embarrassment. "No. I'm ashamed to say it, but I was worried that if they knew I let Air Force Two take off with a semi-truck barreling down the runway straight at it, I would be locked up in a military prison the rest of my life. If it was flying okay, I assumed no one would ever find out."

"What about me?" asked Mack. "You knew I was watching."

"That's what I was going to talk to you about when I came down. I was hoping to make a deal. I wouldn't report you to the FAA for violation of airspace and disobeying an order not to land if you would just walk away and keep your mouth shut." Gustine looked at everyone in the circle. "I guess this now changes everything."

"Maybe not," said Cliff. "Is there someplace we can go to chat for just a few minutes? There's something we need to tell Mack that you should hear, too. Afterward, we could use your technical skills to solve a problem. If you help us, we will promise to keep all this a secret. Deal?"

"I can't make a deal unless I know what's happening," replied Gustine. "But we can use the control tower to talk. I'm the only one on duty until six o'clock. You'll have to be miles away when my replacements get here."

"Fair enough. We don't have much time. Let's make this quick." They all hustled into the tower and up the steps.

Chapter 41

Thursday, April 19, 2018
Homeland Security, Phoenix, Arizona
6:00 am (Pacific Daylight Time)

Homeland Security Agent Earl Kelly, FBI Agent Steve Talbert, and Maricopa County Deputy Sheriff Gordy Owens had spent the night in Kelly's office going over the events of the past couple of days and had called Scotland Yard trying to get information on Lord John Shaffer. They were inquiring as to why his home in Kensington doubled as an Apple watch distribution center. Kelly thought he had a theory, but information from London didn't fit. Kelly and Owens only had short cat naps during the past forty-eight hours, and they were exhausted. To keep awake, all three men relied on the coffee they brought over from the FBI lab. By the time dawn had broken, they were all high on caffeine and wide awake. Each had consumed six cups of the world's finest coffee—Taste Of Arabia.

"According to the information in our database, Lord Shaffer is the second richest man in the world. He has personal assets just over one hundred billion dollars." Agent Talbert was referring to the FBI laptop computer he brought with him from the lab.

"Okay, this may be a stupid question, "said Kelly, "but why is Lord Shaffer in the FBI database?"

"Based on his profile, he's been investigated by us on several occasions."

"For what? According to Scotland Yard, he's an upstanding member of the House of Lords."

"The first time was many years ago when he tried to ship a gift to a friend in the United States, and it was confiscated by customs in New York. It was a stuffed Bengal tiger. Seems the good Lord is an avid hunter, but the Bengal tiger is on the IUCN endangered species list. So, the custom's director reported it to the FBI. We, in turn, reported it to MI5 in London."

"What did they do with it?"

"The report says they followed up and met with Lord Shaffer in his office. He apologized and said while on a hunting trip to India, he had come across the tiger in the jungle. According to Shaffer, the tiger had supposedly died from natural causes, and he didn't want it to be devoured by scavengers. So he sent it to his personal taxidermist for mounting. Case closed."

"Case closed? That was it?"

"As I said before, Lord Shaffer is highly respected in England. They believed him."

"Does it say who he was shipping the tiger to?"

"Hold on, let me look." Talbert scrolled down the page. "Here it is. Well, huh, isn't that interesting?!"

"What's interesting?!"

"In 2013, it was shipped to Senator Rothschild's estate in Phoenix."

"You mean it was supposed to be shipped, right?"

"No, I mean that the custom's director in New York released the tiger and shipped it on to Arizona."

"Now wait a minute. Gordon Rothschild died in 2008. I remember because it was during the Super Bowl that was played in Glendale. He had a heart attack after the Giant's David Tyree made that incredible leaping one-handed catch off his helmet near the end of the game. His funeral was played on national TV a couple of days later."

"What's your point," asked Talbert while Deputy Owens looked at him inquisitively.

"Why would Lord Shaffer ship a dead tiger to a dead senator's home?"

"Maybe as a museum exhibit. Rothschild didn't have any kids, and his wife had passed several years earlier, so the county turned his house into a museum in honor of the late senator."

"You're saying the county owns the house? Did he will it to them?"

"I'm not sure. I only know it's a museum now because my wife and I visited there last year."

"Can that fancy computer of yours find out if the county owns it, and if not, who does?"

"Maybe, let me check." Talbert punched in a few keys, scrolled down, then punched in a few more.

"Well, no, the county doesn't own the house. So, get this—Rothschild's estate is owned by the Smithsonian Institute! Paid for by a grant from the State Russian Museum! The grant stipulates that the Smithsonian may only use the endowment to purchase the Rothschild estate!"

"You've got to be kidding me!" exclaimed Agent Kelly. His fatigued mind was now on overload! Deep in thought, he began pacing the room. Deputy Owens and Agent Talbert just stared at him with their mouths wide open.

"Okay, let's review what we know," said Kelly. "Please take notes while I think aloud.

"John Shaffer is a respected member of the British House of Lords. He is also the second richest man in the world. One of his investments, Russian manufactured Apple watches, is distributed out of his basement in Kensington under the corporate name Taste Of Arabia, LTD. We know Taste Of Arabia to be coffee because we have been drinking it all night!"

"Damn good java, I might add!" interrupted Owens. He lifted his cup as if to give a toast.

"Yeah, right. Anyway, a fake team of ICE agents raided Gila Bend Charter School on Tuesday. We know they were impersonators because of the false insignia on their windbreakers, and because the agent they left for dead wasn't one of ours. That same fake team wreaked havoc on the school, and two onlookers decided to help defend the students and teachers from the intruders. According to witnesses, a Gila Bend resident identified as Donnor Colten used a rifle to kill the agent, then loaded up his pickup with teachers and took off. It's believed that they followed a school bus to Ajo that was being driven by two kids. Then, the fake ICE team chased them to the Curley School Apartments in five SUVs, and they also had air support from two helicopters. The pilots destroyed Colten's pickup truck before being chased away by an unidentified Aerovictor Defender. According to witnesses, those same helicopters returned and torched the five SUV's before the Aerovictor blasted them into pieces! And all those pieces landed directly on top of the vehicles! We are assuming the fake ICE agents escaped into the desert."

Agent Kelly paused for a moment and took another swig of coffee.

"The preliminary report is back on those choppers," inserted Agent Talbert. "They were identified as Russian Mil Mi-17s, manufactured by Kazan Helicopters in Tatarstan. There are none for sale anywhere outside of Moscow. And the five Chevy Suburban SUVs were manufactured at the General Motors plant in Hamburg, Germany."

"Can you find out who owns them and how they got to the States?" asked Kelly.

"It will take a few minutes. Go ahead with your summary. I can multitask with the best of them!"

"Owens and I found an Apple watch that was distributed by Lord Shaffer's company on the dead fake ICE agent back at the school. We sent it to the FBI lab, and it was there where the watch exploded, killing Morris Radcliff and the coffee salesman.

"While all that was going on in Gila Bend and Ajo, our secret Homeland Security facility and the Senso-McNamara building next to it were both blasted to smithereens. Our two employees who worked out there, Loren Schoenholtz and Gene Schultz, believe that a photographer named Joe Freeman killed a Senso-Mac employee, ditched his body, and then stole laser weapons and energy packs from an underground vault that he used to blow up both buildings. We have Freeman and an unidentified man in custody, but they seem to be playing games with us. They claim to have memory loss, which is typical of guilty people. The thing is there's no motive. We have no idea why Freeman would do it. Hopefully, we can find out later this morning when we question them again.

"It's just a hunch of which I have no firm evidence to support, but I'm guessing there is a definite link between the Gila Bend and Mesa incidents on Tuesday. The Apple Watch was made in Russia, the pistol the dead ICE agent had on him was a Soviet semi-automatic TT-30, the helicopters were Russian, and now we know that an ex-US senator's house is indirectly owned by the State Russian Museum. My theory is our country is under some sort of Russian invasion, and the common denominator appears to be the Honorable Lord Shaffer."

"And do you remember, Earl, what we found out while we were investigating the Mesa blasts?" asked Deputy Owens.

"What's that?"

"Senso-Mac's holding company is based in London. This is becoming way too coincidental!" Owens was now doing the pacing while Kelly drank a few more sips of coffee. "So, this Lord Shaffer distributed the watch that was used to kill an FBI lab technician, and he also supplied Senator Rothschild's museum estate with an illegal Bengal tiger, a museum that just happens to be owned by Russians. The obliterated Senso-Mac corporation is owned by a holding company in London, the city where Lord Shaffer rules the roost!"

Owens looked at Agent Talbert, who sat frozen in thought as he stared at the computer screen. "Any chance you could find out who owns that holding company, Steve?"

"Already did. It's a partnership of five sires."

Agent Kelly was confused and irritated. "Five sires?! Are you on the *Comedy Central* website, or what?! We've been here too long—just get to the point!"

"The official names on the holding company's corporate register are Sire Shaffer, Sire Bovnik, Sire Sokolov, Sire W. Nassar, and Sire T. Nassar."

"So, Shaffer didn't use a fake last name, which means the others are probably actual names as well. Why do you suppose Lord Shaffer and the rest of them would do that? If they're involved in something illegal, wouldn't they want fictitious names?"

"British law requires a thorough background check for all individuals who have applied for incorporation. Also, banks in England would need identification to open an account. It would be less risky to incorporate using actual names than to jeopardize themselves by getting caught using fake ones. Only last names are required on documents, which means they probably used 'sire' to disguise their company."

"Okay, so we know Lord Shaffer is a partner in Senso-Mac's holding company. You said the FBI has investigated him for other things. What are those other things?"

"Since the tiger incident, he has been on our radar every time he sets foot in America. That's not unusual; we flag anyone who enters America with a suspicious past. Usually, it's just a computer thing, and there is no human intervention. The flagged person flies into the USA and goes through customs. Their passport number is logged into the database along with the destination they filled out on the immigration card. Because it was flagged, it's forwarded to our system where it's stored forever. The red flags are perused by FBI agents who look for unusual destinations, but quite frankly, we don't have enough agents to look closely at everyone. So, we target those who are considered 'the most suspicious' due to their backgrounds."

"I'm assuming Lord Shaffer never reached that level of suspicion because, well, because he was a lord. Who messes with a lord, right?!"

"Actually, no. Lord Shaffer was targeted for a different reason. He never flew commercially into the United States; he always used a private jet and landed at small, private airports that lacked customs and immigration personnel."

"That's legal?!" asked Deputy Owens. He had been in law enforcement for quite some time and had never heard of that.

"Technically, no, but de facto, yes. Corporate jets from other countries must either file an overflight permit or land at an airport that does have an immigration staff. Lord Shaffer has flown into America many times and never filed for a permit or stopped at a larger airport first. That's why he was flagged."

"How did the FBI find out?"

"Every international flight that enters US airspace is picked up on radar, and they must identify themselves or risk being shot down by our Air Force. Once identified by call letters, they are logged permanently into the FAA database. The FAA notifies us of any questionable flight plans for follow-up because they are not a law enforcement agency. Evidently, no one followed-up on Lord Shaffer's red flags."

"Why not?"

"According to our database, it was because he had received clearance from the White House. When that happens, no one in our agency asks questions."

"You're saying the president must sign off every time a diplomat enters the US? That must be time-consuming!"

"It must either be the president, vice president, or chief of staff. Their actual signatures are not required—a rubber stamp will suffice. Some secretary will get the request and take care of the paperwork."

"Because Lord Shaffer is a member of the British Parliament, I can understand why he was given clearance without ever stopping at customs. So why is he still red-flagged in your system?"

Agent Talbert looked at the computer screen and saw a notation typed in by an agent. "Based on this note, I think I can guess. Seems Lord Shaffer has received multiple diplomatic visas to enter the United States. However, he has never flown into Washington, DC, or any state capital city. Why would he enter the US claiming to be on a diplomatic mission, but never fly into any government center?"

"Where has he flown to?" asked Kelly.

"Get this—most of his flights have landed at either Mesa's Falcon Field or in Gila Bend!"

"You think it's another coincidence that Lord Shaffer does most of his business in the two places we have been investigating the past couple of days?!" asked Kelly rhetorically. "That holding company of his; can you check your fancy database and see if it has any other real estate transactions in Arizona besides Senso-Mac?"

"Sure, but I probably could just Google that one." Talbert punched a few keys into the FBI database and waited. "Okay, I have your answer. The holding company owns a nursing home in Gila Bend and a 6,000 square-foot private mansion north of town that is currently occupied by three molecular geneticists."

"Why a nursing home? Does that make sense to either of you?" Both Talbert and Deputy Owens shook their heads no. "And a huge estate for three molecular geneticists?! I don't get it! Those other 'sires' listed on the holding company—what are their names again?"

Agent Talbert looked at the screen. "Bovnik, Sokolov, and two Na—"

"Bovnik!" exclaimed Kelly. "Could that be Yegor Bovnik, the directorate chief of the Russian KGB?! And Leonid Sokolov, a general who oversees military aviation in Russia?!"

"You may be right. Let me check something." Talbert typed and waited, typed again, and then scrolled down. He leaned close to the screen and read for ten minutes. After working all night, his eyes were red and glazed. He rubbed them with his fist and was about to say something, but then stopped and stared at the far wall.

"What is it, Steve? What did you find?"

"I'm guessing you're right about Bovnik and Sokolov. And I think I know the other two. They are most likely Wasim Nassar and Tariq Nassar. I checked our Middle Eastern database. Wasim was a Yemeni prince and fighter pilot, and Tariq is his uncle. Tariq's brother is Ra'id Nassar who was the governor of the Al Mahrah district of Yemen. Anyway, Wasim and Tariq disappeared several years ago, and there is no known address for them. The partnership lists a London flat as their business location."

"Hmm, interesting. And what about the SUVs that were at the Gila Bend school? Did you get any information on them?"

Agent Talbert looked back to his computer screen and scrolled down. "Yes. They were shipped from Hamburg to the Port of Saint John, Canada. They entered the US from Millstown, New Brunswick, which borders—" Talbert stopped abruptly.

"Which borders what? I'm assuming you were going to say Maine."

"Yes, no, I mean yes. It's not that. I just found something."

"What is it?"

"The dock and unloading facility in Saint John is owned by our friend Lord Shaffer, which I guess is no longer a surprise. But this might surprise you."

"What?! Come on, Steve, just tell us!"

"The vehicles were registered to the Maricopa County Sheriff's Department!"

"You don't say?!" said Agent Kelly with a look of surprise. Deputy Owens appeared to be in severe shock. Kelly looked at Owens, and the deputy knew exactly what he was going to say. "I think it's time we pay your boss, Sheriff Urdano, a visit. The photographer and his friend are being held there, so maybe they will have gotten over their 'memory loss,' and we can question them again. Then we'll check out the nursing home and Lord Shaffer's grand estate in Gila Bend."

All three took one last gulp of coffee and headed for the door. The box of Taste Of Arabia coffee pods were all gone.

Chapter 42

Thursday, April 19, 2018
Loop 202 Freeway, Mesa, Arizona
6:15 am (Pacific Daylight Time)

"I told you we needed to finish them right then and there in the photographer's house!" barked Loren Schoenholtz as he glared at Gene Schultz in the backseat of the van.

"Shut up, you worthless nincompoop! You're the idiot who let the guy in the vault live in the first place!"

"Yeah, but we could have easily knifed him and the hiker over at that house and left them in the desert for coyote food. Death by coffee! You're a foolish man!"

Schultz and Schoenholtz were riding in the middle seat of the stolen Gila Bend school van. Barney Kinkel turned around abruptly from the front passenger seat with a gun in his hand. "You both shut up! We need to figure out how we're going to kill them. If we can't find a way to do that, then there will be two fewer men on Lord Shaffer's payroll. You got that?!" Kinkel pointed the gun at Schultz first, then Schoenholtz.

"I tested the laser weapons and blew up Homeland Security and Senso-Mac!" bragged Schoenholtz defensively. "I did my damn job! What have you done?!"

"You blew up Homeland Security and Senso-Mac?" asked the van driver. "What's that all about?"

"None of your business!" howled Kinkel. "Just drive! Once we're finished in Mesa, you're done, and you can go home and live your life. We won't need you again!" The van driver knew about the coffee scheme, but nothing else. He had seen the news and heard about the blasts and fires near Senso-Mac, but he didn't realize his two passengers had anything to do with it.

The van driver looked in the rearview mirror at Schoenholtz and asked, "You used a laser weapon to blow up those buildings? Why?"

"I told you to keep out of it!" shouted Kinkel. Now he was pointing the gun at the driver.

"Had to make sure those death rays were potent enough to kill a president!" laughed Schoenholtz. Kinkel put down the gun and stared out the window. As much as he wanted to, he knew that he couldn't shoot Schoenholtz. The idiot's next assignment was to create world havoc and complete the mission. Taste Of Arabia coffee would begin to brainwash American citizens and politicians alike, while at the same time, the struggling nation would mourn the death of their president!

The van exited the Loop 202 freeway at Power Road, then headed north towards Red Mountain Ranch. The turn into the golf course community was a little over a mile away, but for some reason, the van picked up speed and ran a red light as it raced across Thomas Road. Cars coming out of the Las Sendas subdivision slammed on their brakes and honked up a storm.

"What the hell are you doing!" yelled Kinkel to the van driver. "Slow down! Our turn is just ahead!"

"I can't!" said the van driver. "The accelerator is stuck!"

The van rolled on faster, zipped past the Redmont Street turn, and raced down the hill over a hundred miles per hour. Kinkel placed his hands on the dash while Schultz and Schoenholtz braced themselves for impact using the backside of the front seats. Their eyes were wide open, but no one said a word. At the bottom of the hill, there was a seventy-degree right turn. The strikingly beautiful Red Mountain with its signature flat-topped notch jutting out was going to be the last thing the four men ever saw. The speedometer on the van was now buried past 120.

The van flew down the short entrance road to Granite Reef Recreation Area and dodged the concrete toilet facility before the driver lost complete control. It flipped side-to-side several times, crunching mesquite trees and brush, then landed in the Salt River upside down. A kayaker who was out for an early-morning paddle up the usually serene stream dove into the river to avoid the hurdling van, while wild horses on the opposite side stopped their grazing and watched intensely. The wheels disappeared underwater, followed by bubbles, then nothing again but serenity. The kayaker resurfaced, climbed out on the shore, then ran to his pickup truck to get his cell phone. But instead of dialing 9-1-1, he phoned his twin brother.

"Hey, Bro, did I wake you up?"

"Naw, I'm getting ready for work," replied the brother. "Where are you?"

"Down at Granite Reef. You wouldn't believe what I just saw. A big passenger van came storming down Bush Highway like a bat out of hell and couldn't make the turn. It flipped about twenty times and landed in the river! It sank like a ship's anchor, Bro!"

"Did you call the police?!"

"Nope, and I ain't gonna! Serves them right. Damn van just about killed me! They must be high on something. They got to be dead anyway. No one could have survived that crash! And besides that, my kayak is loaded with marijuana—and I'm not talking the medical kind if you know what I mean!"

"Hey, I don't blame you, dude. So, I'll see you tonight. Bring some pizza home for dinner, okay?"

A few more bubbles surfaced on the river.

Chapter 43

Thursday, April 19, 2018
Gila Bend Charter School, Gila Bend, Arizona
6:20 am (Pacific Daylight Time)

The decision to reopen Gila Bend Charter School the following Monday was the wish of the local school board, not the parents. The board thought getting the kids back as soon as possible would begin the healing. But how could it? The principal, sixteen teachers, and two students who escaped in Donnor Colten's pickup truck were still missing and feared dead. No one knew the whereabouts of Assistant Principal Ted Sanderson or Athletic Director Cyrus McCool. When questioned how the school was going to find enough substitute teachers, School Board President Abe Fitzgerald said he and parent volunteers could work until the teachers returned. Eyeballs in that meeting were rolling like marbles on Teflon!

Calls from Fitzgerald to Maricopa County Sheriff's Office went to voicemail or were answered by a receptionist that sounded like she was living in a dream world. The four cops who made up the local police force appeared to be the only ones investigating, but their factfinding skills were limited by their lack of training. There was never enough money in the city's budget for CSI workshops, so instead, the mayor purchased a big screen TV and DVDs of *Law and Order* and *Chicago PD* that he required them to watch. Since the incident took place, the four officers had been searching the desert on ATVs for any sign of the missing people, but the scope of their investigation was very limited. The school bus had been found in

Ajo along with Donnor's bullet-ridden and charbroiled pickup truck, but the Ajo police said the Gila Bend police wouldn't be allowed to probe outside of their jurisdiction. That was an order from Pima County Sheriff Mike Morton.

The raid on the school by ICE agents, the rifle slaying of a federal lawman by Donnor Colten, the death of parent Pablo Hernandez in his car, and the escape of the sixteen teachers, principal, and two students made only one headline in the *Arizona Republic*. Reporter Smitty Douglas had snooped around and asked many questions on the day of the incident, then written a superb article for the daily journal, but he was never seen again. Locals assumed he was reassigned to cover the Senso-McNamara demolition in Mesa, which had become national news. Investigators there were beginning to believe that a laser death ray gun blew up the company, and the FBI and Homeland Security were involved in an intense probe of the vicinity. CNN, NBC, CBS, ABC, and Fox were now swarming the area like bees on honey.

Now it was early morning, and Police Captain Ned Segura wanted Abe Fitzgerald to meet him at the school. Seems a jogger had almost been run over by a Gila Bend Charter School van out by the turnoff to Dead Cow Road. Segura knew that Principal Perez and Assistant Principal Sanderson were still missing, so he wanted Abe to come down and fill out a report. Abe was complaining that it was awfully early, and he hadn't had his breakfast or coffee.

"It won't take long," said Segura. "And besides, I will have all the coffee your good heart desires when Sergeant Ruben gets here."

"What do you mean by that?" asked Fitzgerald.

"Pete called in and said he found an abandoned semi out by the Auxiliary airport. It was filled with boxes of coffee called *Taste Of Arapahoe*, or something like that. Anyway, he's going to join us and said he'd bring a box with him. There's a Keurig machine in the office. Stop at Seven Eleven and bring some Little Debbies, okay?"

Chapter 44

Thursday, April 19, 2018
Maricopa County Sheriff's Office, Phoenix, Arizona
6:30 am (Pacific Daylight Time)

Kelly, Talbert, and Owens entered Maricopa County Sheriff's Office and stopped abruptly just inside the door. Receptionist Rebecca Grimm was sound asleep at her desk—her head resting on her two crossed arms. But that was just a minor shock to Kelly, Talbert, and Owens. The major tremor was the sight of Deputy Ken Smith sitting in a chair next to her with his head also resting on Grimm's desk. He was snoring.

Deputy Owens was low on sleep and high on coffee. He was disgusted with his two coworkers. He walked over and pounded his fist on the desk.

"Wake up!" he yelled. That didn't seem to work, so he shook both of them hard.

"Wha, wha, what is it?" asked Rebecca as she began to awaken. Her head stayed on her crossed arms as her eyes surveyed the room. Then she noticed three men standing in front of her with their hands on their hips. She sat up and gazed at them. When she saw Deputy Smith next to her, she jumped up.

"Who is this man?!" she exclaimed, then glared at the others. "And who are you?! What do you want?! Where am I?!"

Deputy Owens walked up to Rebecca cautiously and touched her shoulder softly. "Relax, Becky, you're just waking up. It's alright. You're at the office."

Rebecca jumped backward and examined the room but didn't say a word. Meanwhile, Deputy Smith woke up and looked around. From his seat, his eyes caught Deputy Owens' eyes, and he stood up slowly. Kelly, Talbert, and Owens looked at each other—speechless!

"Can I help you?" asked Smith to Owens and the others. Then he looked again at Owens. "Don't I know you from somewhere?"

"Jeff, don't talk to them!" shouted Rebecca to Deputy Smith. "They have guns! I think they're a gang of criminals coming to rob us!"

"I'm not Jeff!" yelped Smith to Rebecca. "My name is Ben! And who are you again? He called you Becky."

Kelly, Talbert, and Owens looked at each other again. They knew this wasn't a joke. Something was wrong, very wrong!

Deputy Owens unholstered his gun and placed it on the desk, then raised his hands over his head. "It's okay, we're not going to hurt you. Are you sure you don't know who I am?"

Both Smith and Rebecca shook their heads no.

"My name is Gordy Owens, and I have worked with you for many years. We are friends." He turned and pointed to Kelly and Talbert. "These two gentlemen are with me, and we're here to help you. This is Agent Kelly from Homeland Security. You both know him. And this is Agent Talbert of the FBI."

Before Smith or Rebecca could respond, out walked Joe Freeman and Roger Bennett from the hallway leading to the holding cells. Instinctively, Owens grabbed his gun from the desk and pointed it at Freeman and Bennett, who both froze. Agent Kelly grabbed Owens' handcuffs from his belt and cuffed Freeman's right wrist to Bennett's left one.

"Why are these two not locked up?!" shouted Kelly at Deputy Smith. The deputy shrugged his shoulders.

"They are very nice people, that's why," replied Smith. "Some men dressed in FBI windbreakers brought them in last night and asked us to lock them up. But they were really friendly, so we knew the FBI must have made a mistake. The four of us played cards most of the night. Janet cheated and won all the money." Rebecca smiled and nodded.

"The two night crews—where are they?!" Deputy Owens was panicking.

"What night crew?" asked Smith.

"Six officers work the four to midnight shift and another six work the midnight to eight shift. Where are they? And why are you and Becky still here? Your shift ended at four o'clock last night! I know you usually work late, but this is ridiculous! What happened to the night crew, damn it?!"

"Oh, I sent them home as soon as they walked in the door," inserted Rebecca. "They shouldn't be working on Christmas. That's a time to be with your family, which makes me wonder why you are here."

"Christmas?!" blurted Deputy Owens. "It's not Chr—"

"Those officers—they left?!" interrupted Kelly. "They just went home? No questions asked? I find that hard to believe!"

"We lied a little bit," said Deputy Smith. "Told them the sheriff was going to pay them triple time to be at home with their families. They laughed but didn't want to argue! That's for sure!" Smith chuckled.

"What's the sheriff's name again?" asked Rebecca. "I keep forgetting. Nice man, though!"

"Fitzgerald!" shouted Joe Freeman. "Larry Fitzgerald. That's his name. On Sundays, he does play-by-play broadcasting for the Cardinals."

"Who are the Cardinals?" asked Roger Bennett.

"Enough of this nonsense!" yelled Owens. His face was bright red. "You're all under arrest! I'm locking you up!"

Owens took a step forward, but Agent Talbert grabbed his arm to stop him. Then he motioned for Owens and Kelly to move backward out of earshot of Rebecca and Smith.

"This isn't an act," whispered Talbert. "They are losing their memories. All of them!"

"What are you saying?" asked Kelly.

"Is there a common denominator? Is there something Rebecca and Smith ate that Freeman and his friend also ate?"

Kelly looked around the reception area while Owens checked the lounge. A minute later, Owens stuck his head out the door and shouted. "Donuts! There's an empty box in the trash can. I bet they all ate donuts."

Rebecca sat down in her chair and laughed aloud. "Those donuts are a couple of days old! We wouldn't feed our guests stale donuts on Christmas, you fool!"

"There are a few crumbs left," yelled Owens. "Steve, do you want to take them back to the lab and check out the ingredients?"

"Hold on," said Kelly. "Where are the donuts from?"

"The box says Rainbow Donuts. I've been there many times. It's up on McDowell and Fourteenth Street."

"Is there a freshness date on the box?"

"A freshness date? Are you kidding me?"

"No, just look." Owens turned the box upside down and read a label stuck to the bottom.

"Says they were made on April 17th. That was three days ago. Says *eat or freeze by April 19th*."

"Then Freeman and the other guy didn't eat them."

"Why not? I'm not following you."

"A box of donuts brought in on Monday morning would be devoured by lunch. You work in a sheriff's office—tell me it isn't so!"

"Now's not a good time for stereotypes, Earl!"

Agent Kelly and Agent Talbert walked down the hallway to join Owens in the lounge. "That's not my point. My point is those two didn't eat them here. But there may be a link with the donuts. Coincidently, we found an empty box of Dunkin' Donuts at Freeman's house when we arrested them last night."

"You think Rainbow and Dunkin' use the same ingredients? Same sugar company, perhaps."

"Could be. We'll need to get that box of crumbs from Freeman's house and compare them with the crumbs in this box. That might tell us—" Kelly stopped in midsentence and dashed for the countertop by the fridge.

"What is it?" asked Owens and Talbert at the same time.

"Coffee. Boxes of coffee, both for automatic drip and Keurig machines. A whole bunch of coffee!"

"Okay, but I don't get it," said Owens. "Every sheriff's office in the country has coffee. It's what keeps the night shift from falling asleep on the job!"

"But they don't all drink this brand of coffee." Kelly raised a box in the air to show Owens and Talbert. "This is Taste Of Arabia, Lord Shaffer's contribution to the caffeinated world we live in."

"Are you thinking what I'm thinking?" asked Talbert.

"The coffee salesman who died in the FBI lab was selling it. We also found it at Freeman's house. Yes, this could be our link. Can we get this analyzed along with the donut crumbs?"

"Yeah, sure. No problem. I can do that. But, Earl, we have a different problem."

"Yeah, I know what you're going to say."

Owens looked at Talbert, then at Kelly. "What are you going to say? Would one of you tell me?!"

Talbert paced the room slowly. "If the coffee is the common denominator for the memory loss experienced by those four out there, then we've got bad news!"

"Come on!" yelped Owens. "What bad news?!"

"The three of us have been drinking that same brand all night long!"

Kelly, Owens, and Talbert all sat down on a metal chair in the lounge and didn't say a word. They needed to sort things out but were having difficulty brainstorming ideas. Lack of sleep can do that to you. So can Taste Of Arabia coffee.

Kelly's stress was becoming more agitated. He picked up a business card that had been lying on top of several boating magazines and was nervously tapping it on the Formica table. Then he noticed it. Right there, smack dab in front of his nose was a significant piece of this complicated puzzle.

"Steve, what was the name of that coffee salesman who was electrocuted?"

"Well, that one is easy! I don't even need to look it up. Who could forget a name like that—James LeBron!"

"James LeBron?!" chuckled Deputy Owens. "You're kidding me—right?!"

"Wish I was!" chortled Talbert. Then he caught on and glanced quickly at Agent Kelly.

Kelly was nodding as he handed the business card to Talbert and Owens.

The card was light beige with a picture of a sultan on a flying carpet off to one side. The name on the card was embossed with gold letters:

James LeBron, Sales Representative,
Taste Of Arabia Coffee Company

"Where do we go from here?" asked Talbert. He and Owens watched as Agent Kelly paced the room.

Finally, Kelly spoke up. "Okay, here's what we need to do. Steve, go get the donut crumbs and coffee analyzed as soon as possible. Then, I need a picture of James LeBron from the morgue. We can send it through our database and see if he's wanted anywhere."

"That won't work, Earl. He was fried to the bone. The only place you would find his picture would be on a poster advertising Halloween masks." Talbert shook his head. "Sorry, that was out of line."

"What about DNA?"

"Yep, we can get a DNA sample."

"Priority one, please. If this coffee is causing people to lose their minds, we don't have much time."

"Will do!"

"Gordy, you'll need to stay here and get your men back on duty. Call an ambulance to transport your secretary, Deputy Smith,

Freeman, and the other guy down to the University of Arizona research hospital in Tucson."

"Their research is limited to cancer and other common diseases. I'm not sure they would know where to start with those four."

"They contract out to some of the best specialists in the world. Hopefully, they can find a molecular geneticist or someone to help them."

"Where are you going?"

"First, I'm going back to the office and find out what goods have been shipped through Shaffer's piers at the Port of Saint John. Canadian customs should have a cargo manifest record on file. We know he sent the SUVs through there; I'd like to know what else he has shipped and where it was sent. Then, I'm going to check out his properties in Gila Bend, both the nursing home and his estate out in the foothills."

Just then, Rebecca walked into the lounge. "Are you boys still here? Would you like some coffee?"

Chapter 45

Thursday, April 19, 2018
Auxiliary Air Force Base, Gila Bend, Arizona
7:00 am (Pacific Daylight Time)

Mack was leaning on the wall in the Gila Bend Auxiliary Air Base control tower. He was stunned and alarmed at the same time. Rick and Donnor had finished telling him and Airman Gustine about being held prisoner in the semi and Yegor Bovnik's plans to wipe out the memories of Americans with coffee. He couldn't believe that the vice president of the United States was the illegitimate son of Arizona's ex-Senator Gordon Rothschild and a Russian girl from a prominent family in the Politburo.

"He grew up in Gila Bend?!" asked Mack, repeating what he just heard. "Why don't we know this?! How was that covered up all these years in a tiny town of 2,000 people?! And who do you suppose is the second son? You know, the vice president's brother?"

"I have no idea, but we need to let the FBI know," said Rick.

"You're right, but we don't have the time," responded Cliff. The others looked at him inquisitively. "To call them and explain all of this will take most of the day. Rick and I just drank a gallon of that coffee. If Yegor and Kinkel were telling the truth, our memories would begin to fade by nightfall. We overheard Kinkel and the truck driver arguing outside when we were locked up over at Love's. They said that Air Force Two would be going to the Middle East for some sort of meeting. Your teacher friend and those two kids are on board, and they are in grave danger."

"What are you trying to say, Cliff?" asked Mack. "We can't fly my jalopy to the Middle East in time to stop them!"

"No, you're right. That's not what I had in mind." Cliff glanced at Airman Gustine and wanted to say something, but hesitated.

"What is it, Cliff?" asked Gustine. "Spit it out."

"What's parked up at Luke these days?"

"Why? The Air Force won't transport you without authorization from the Pentagon, and the odds of that happening are about zero to none! And even if they did, it would take longer than simply notifying the FBI and letting them handle it."

"You didn't answer my question."

"There are twelve F-16s and two F-15D two-seater Eagles that will be tested tomorrow. I'm acting as copilot on one of them. But like I said, you have no—wait a minute! You're not planning on—"

"Stealing them?" interrupted Cliff. "Is that what you were going to say? Absolutely not! But perhaps I could borrow one for a couple of days. What do you think?"

"You're crazy!"

"Do you have the code for the cockpit doors?"

"Of course, but I'm not giving them to you! You need a different plan!"

"Can you think of a better one? The vice president of the United States is involved in an international crime syndicate that could wipe out the minds of every American who drinks coffee! With an F-15, we could stop him and save our country! But time is running out, Airman Gustine. You need to make a fast decision. Are you with us or not?"

Gustine briskly paced back and forth in the control tower. His thought process was a chaotic mess. If he allowed this to happen, there's no doubt he would eventually be caught. He would face a court-martial and spend the rest of his life in prison. But if the plan worked, he would be a hero, and the court-martial would be suspended. Moments later, Gustine's consciousness kicked into high gear. Before deciding, he wanted one question answered satisfactorily.

"How are you going to assure that the teacher and two kids are safe? You can't shoot down Air Force Two without killing them."

"I have no plans to shoot down Air Force Two—just follow them and try to stop them on the ground. How I'm going to do that I haven't figured out yet. We need to accomplish three goals: save the kids and their teacher, apprehend the bad guys, and force those sick bastards to give us the antidote for the damn coffee poison!"

"You can't do that all alone!" exclaimed Mack. "It's a two-seater F-15. I need to go with you!"

"Rick or Donnor should go with me. If there's an antidote for the coffee, they both need it." Cliff looked at them both arbitrarily. "I have no preference boys; it's your decision. But even if we find the antidote, chances are slim that we'll survive. We're not sure exactly where we are going, we're outnumbered, and we're flying over other countries' airspace without permission. If I were to estimate the probability of dying, I'd say the safer bet is to stay here and see a doctor for an antidote."

"I'll go," said Donnor. "It would give me immense pleasure to whip those SOBs!"

"No," said Rick. "I need to go. Kurt Kellner is a good friend of mine, and those two students were in my classroom when all this started. It's my fault they are in danger. I didn't keep an eye on them at the time."

"I just thought of something," said Mack. "It's too long of a story to tell you now, but I may know a trio of molecular geneticists who could help find an antidote. It may be a shot in the dark, but right now, it's all we've got. They are back at my place in Ajo. Donnor can come with me."

"Who are these geneticists?" asked Donnor. "Do they live in your apartment complex? I thought only artists lived there."

"They don't live there. But they have a lab there."

"Where?"

"In my guest bedroom. Like I said, it's a long story."

Cliff looked at Airman Gustine. "We need an answer, Frank. Are you in or not? Rick and I will need a ride up to Luke either way. We're going to give it a try with or without your help."

Gustine punched a few numbers on the computer keyboard. "Air Force Two can't make it to the Middle East without a refueling stop. If the semi damaged their landing gear on take-off, they would need to make an emergency belly landing somewhere in Morocco or Spain—unless they refueled in the air. But, considering their covert mission and the passengers who are on board, who would they get to help them?"

"Easy!" replied Cliff. "The damn Russians! So, are you in?!"

"Okay, I'm in, and I've got an idea. You can take my car up to Luke Air Force Base. I don't know how you plan to get inside, but you're an ex-colonel, so I'm assuming you have an idea. I'll give you one hour exactly to get there, then I'll call my superiors and tell them I have an emergency on my hands and that I'm requesting their immediate assistance. If they ask, I'll tell them the control tower has been surrounded by terrorists threatening to blow it up. I'm certain everyone on duty will come to help. That would be your diversion."

"Yes, but they will call Homeland Security and the Pentagon before they leave. What are you going to say when everyone arrives at a false alarm? That will end your career."

"I'll make up something! Don't worry about me. But here's what must be considered: you'll need a refueling stop. I can contact Lajes Base in the Azores and have it ready before anyone can stop me. You'll be flying at 1,800 miles per hour, so figure only a couple of hours to get there, but you may be riding on fumes. You'll be stretching the F-15's range to the max! Same goes for the next flight to Arabia if that's where Air Force Two is headed. Their GPS tracking code is cloaked, but I can find it for you on this computer, and you can punch it into the F-15. The Gila Bend Auxiliary control tower is on frequency 277 and is not monitored by anyone else unless requested. Stupid, I know, but that should work to your advantage. Call me when you are in the cockpit. Hopefully, I'll know the GPS code by then. Remember, I'll give you one hour before I phone in my emergency. That will give me some time to come up with a good story! Now, get going!"

Cliff nodded at Mack and Donnor, and the cousins ran down the control tower's steps to Dr. Sancho Gomez's airplane that they would take back to Ajo. Cliff looked at Rick, who gave him a thumbs-up. Finally, he embraced Airman Frank Gustine in a bear hug.

"You're the best, my man!" uttered Cliff. "You're a hero!"

"No, just a man who loves his country," replied Gustine.

"Enough to risk going to prison for the rest of your life? No, sir, you are a great hero!"

Cliff stood at attention and saluted the airman, then he and Rick headed briskly for the stairs.

"Hold on!" shouted Gustine, and the two men stopped and turned. "One-two-zero-seven-one-nine-four-one."

"What's that?" asked Cliff.

"It's the code for the F-15's cockpit hatch. You'll need it to get in."

"Okay, thanks! I forgot to ask!"

"It's also the date that will forever live in infamy. Use it proudly!"

Rick caught on first and smiled. After all, he was a history teacher.

Chapter 46

Thursday, April 19, 2018
Curley School Apartments, Ajo, Arizona
8:15 am (Pacific Daylight Time)

Mack and Donnor touched down in Ajo after a fifteen-minute flight from Gila Bend, then called a cab to take them back to Mack's apartment. They were startled to find a Pima County Sheriff's car parked in the Curley School underground garage. They were even more surprised to see several Gila Bend teachers crashed on Mack's couch, chairs, and floor. When he heard the door open, Principal Perez came out of the guest bedroom along with Sheriff Mike Morton.

"Mack and Donnor, you're back!" yelped Perez. "Thank God! Where's Rick?! Did you make it to Gila Bend in the biplane?! And where are the others?! Are they okay?!"

"At this point, I believe everyone is okay except Mr. Kellner, Isaac, and Zaira. They have been kidnapped and are in serious danger. Rick is on his way to find them. It's a long story, but first I need—"

"Kidnapped!! How—what happened?!"

"We were shot down in the desert. Kellner and the two kids parachuted but were apprehended by the shooters when they landed. The shooters happened to be the ICE agents who had been chasing you. Obviously, they weren't ICE agents! The other four teachers are safe—holed up in some abandoned bunkhouses down by the border."

"What about Rick?! You said he's out looking for them! Where?! And you didn't answer my question—did you make it back to Gila Bend?! Did you call the police?!" Principal Perez was frantically trying to sort things out, but nothing made sense. Mack was going to transport the teachers and kids to Mexico to get them out of harm's way, while Rick and Donnor were supposed to be flying the biplane back to Gila Bend to get help. How did Mack and Donnor find each other?

Sheriff Morton stepped in to calm down the principal. The dozing teachers now were all wide awake and listening intently.

"Relax, Mr. Perez," said Morton softly. "One question at a time. Let Mack tell us what he knows."

"Rick never had any intention of going to Gila Bend," interrupted Donnor. "When Mack hadn't returned to pick up the next group of teachers, we went searching for them. We landed in the desert and found their wrecked airplane. A retired Air Force pilot—"

"We don't have time for this!" shouted Mack. Everyone became still and stared at him. "We will tell you the whole story later! Right now, we need their help!" He pointed down the hallway at the three molecular geneticists. Mackenzie, Riley, and Charlie O'Connell were standing by the doorway of the guest bedroom listening to the conversation.

Mackenzie walked into the living room. "What's up, Mack? What can we do to help?"

"It's Donnor," replied Mack as he pointed at his cousin. "He's ingested a type of coffee that supposedly causes memory loss. It's a long story, but we thought you might be able to help."

"Taste Of Arabia. Is that the brand?"

"Yes!" interjected Donnor. "That's it! Have you heard of it?"

"Yes, we have," replied Mackenzie. "And that's a long story, too. When did you consume the coffee, and how much did you drink?"

"Around midnight or early this morning—I'm not entirely certain. Rick and I were being held hostage in the back of a semi, and we were forced to drink it. We probably had about a gallon, I'm guessing."

"Rick? Who's this Rick?"

"Rick Frye. He teaches at Gila Bend."

"I overheard Mack say he is on his way to find the kids and that other teacher. Where did he go?"

"Saudi Arabia. He's with a retired Air Force pilot named Cliff who rescued us in the desert. The biplane blew a tire when we landed it and—"

"Donnor!" interrupted Mack. "We don't have time for the whole story! So, here it is in a nutshell. This Cliff guy and Rick are planning to steal an F-15 Eagle from Luke Air Force Base and fly it to Arabia."

"Why Arabia?" asked Sheriff Morton.

"Because that's where we think the plane the kidnappers were on was headed!"

"They were kidnapped on a plane?! Can you give us a description of the kidnappers or the airplane?"

"I can do one better! I can tell you who kidnapped them! But you won't believe it!"

Just then, a large man limped out of the guest bedroom, wearing only a hospital patient's robe. He was bleeding from the intravenous tubes that he had yanked out of his body. He stepped forward towards the living room and stumbled. Charlie O'Connell caught him and helped him back to his feet.

"I know you're in a hurry, but you need to slow down and tell us everything," asserted Sheriff Urdano. "I will help you, but I need to know all the details."

The sheriff was guided to a kitchen chair, and the others sat down as well. Sheriff Morton pulled a miniature voice recorder from his pants pocket and turned it on. Donnor spoke first and told about his encounter with Yegor Bovnik and Barney Kinkel while handcuffed inside the semi with Rick and Cliff. Amazement, disbelief, and stunned silence filled the apartment. You could hear a pin drop when Donnor paused to think. However, when Donnor told them that the most famous politician from Arizona had an affair with a young Russian girl that resulted in the birth of the nation's current vice president, the atmosphere of the room turned to anger. Senators Barry Goldwater and John McCain were heroic statesmen, but Senator Rothschild was one step short of deity on the stairway to heaven. Vice President Garrett Sanders was assumed to be from a hog farm in Iowa. *Wikipedia* would never make a mistake, right?!

The kitchen was amassed in conversation. Everyone had a theory as to how this could happen in America and a prediction of what was to come—most were teachers, after all! Sheriff Urdano was slumping down a bit in his chair, and his face was turning a whiter shade of pale. It was apparent that he didn't have much time left. Sheriff Morton brought him a glass of water.

"How do you know they are going to Arabia?" muttered Urdano, but no one could hear him over the intense discussions going on. So, with all the gusto he could manage, the dying sheriff repeated it a few decibels louder. "How do you know they are going to Arabia?!" The room fell silent again, and everyone looked at Donnor and Mack.

"We thought we heard them say that there was going to be a meeting of some sort in Saudi Arabia," replied Donnor. "But we were chained inside the semi, and their voices were muffled, so we're not sure."

"And if you think about it, the coffee says Arabia right on the box," added Mack. "We were hoping they could find an antidote for the coffee drug while they're there. We need to find some kind of cure and fast! There's a chance many others have drunk the coffee and are in peril as we speak!" Mack looked pleadingly at the O'Connells. "Do you think you can help find a remedy?!"

"Rick and Cliff won't be finding an antidote in Saudi Arabia," replied Mackenzie somberly. All three O'Connells looked at Mack and Donnor with grave expressions.

"Why not?!"

"There isn't one over there," said Riley O'Connell.

"You know about the coffee drug?!"

"Lord Shaffer sent us back to the United States from Yemen so we could study the effects of a hallucinogen called tungis. He lied and said his researchers thought it might help cure Alzheimer's. We didn't want to leave the country that we believed to be our life mission, but we were offered five million dollars each and a huge estate to live in near Gila Bend. As we look back, we're all ashamed of what we did for the sake of money, but now we're going to right our wrongs." The O'Connell siblings all nodded. So did Sheriff Urdano. He knew their story, and he knew it was important for them to tell the others.

"Tell them," said Urdano. "They need to know. Then all of us together can stop this sinister plan!"

Another half-hour passed while the O'Connells told their story to a stupefied audience. They explained that they first went to Yemen on a mission to help the poor and needy find solutions for congenital diseases that had plagued their people for ages. The O'Connells found cures and saved many lives, and even though they were molecular geneticists and not physicians, the locals called each one "Doc." Then one day Anwar Abadi, the owner of a local coffee roasting plant, and his teenage employee Dawud came to the hospital with complete memory loss. The O'Connells did brain scans and biopsies and found one commonality with the two patients: each had a small bubble on his basal ganglia that was restricting their memories. Although the trio of sibling geneticists could not determine the cause with absolute certainty, they all hypothesized the problem stemmed from the new coffee they were manufacturing—Taste Of Arabia.

It was while conducting tests on Mr. Abadi and Dawud that they met Lord Shaffer, who happened to be a business partner of Abadi's. He was personable, a member of the British Parliament, and seemed to be an honest man. With a great deal of money as a carrot, he convinced them to relocate to his nursing home in Gila Bend which doubled as a memory-loss research facility. When Shaffer requested that the O'Connells focus on the causes of Alzheimer's and other memory-loss diseases rather than a cure, they became suspicious of his intentions.

One night, after returning to their estate from the nursing home, they were startled to find an unknown, rather large and muscular man sitting on their couch. He flashed a CIA badge with the name *Special Agent Marv Cullins* printed in bold letters. The agent motioned with his finger on his lips to whisper. Agent Cullins quizzed the O'Connells and quickly made the determination that they were not knowingly involved in Lord Shaffer's deadly plan. For their safety, he decided to tell the O'Connells what the CIA knew. After explaining Shaffer's grand scheme to wipe clean the memories of American coffee drinkers, the outraged trio of geneticists wanted to fight back!

Agent Cullins warned them to not say anything, or they could suffer grave consequences. He explained that a small, covert CIA team of five men and women were thoroughly investigating Lord Shaffer under the authority of the CIA director . . . and ONLY the CIA director. When the O'Connells questioned why the president had not been notified, the agent replied that the team wasn't sure who all the players were yet—or who in Washington could be trusted. That night, the O'Connells saw two men hiding in their yard watching the house, and the same two followed them to work the next morning.

At that point, Mack cut in and explained how he met the O'Connells at the annual art fair in front of the Curley School Apartments. After a few Coronas in the beer tent, Mack's alcohol-induced loose tongue started spilling secrets that should have been undisclosed. He realized that the O'Connells would gladly do anything they could to help with the mission.

"What secrets?! What mission?!" asked Principal Perez. He and the other teachers now knew about the Taste Of Arabia plot but were oblivious to Mack's clandestine operation. Yes, because of the airport tunnel, they guessed he was involved in illicit activity, but they didn't know what.

Mack laid it out in detail—Dr. Sancho Gomez's courageous plan to develop low-cost medications and give them to patients in America who couldn't afford them. He mentioned the secret factory across the border, which happened to be where Mack planned to provide a safe haven for the fleeing Gila Bend teachers. He then explained how Dr. Gomez saved Sheriff Urdano's son's life. And lastly, he revealed why the sheriff was now here and being treated by the O'Connells. Based on their superior intellect and experience saving lives, the O'Connells were the best option to find a cure for Urdano's headaches and respiratory problems that were slowly killing him.

After two hours of discussion, everyone had questions, but no one was asking them. All of them knew something had to be done quickly, but they sat in Mack's apartment paralyzed in deep thought. Finally, Charlie O'Connell stepped forward and took the lead.

"We need to get Sheriff Urdano and Donnor back to our lab in the nursing home. We've got more materials to work with up there than our makeshift lab in the guest bedroom! Mack, we could use Dr. Gomez's help. Can you fly down to Mexico and bring him back to Gila Bend?"

"Yes! Definitely! Good idea!"

"Principal Perez, can you and the teachers wait here? This will become our operations center. Write down everything you heard this morning. It will take a few hours to get everyone to the nursing home. We'll call the FBI and Homeland Security once Dr. Gomez gets there, then we'll call you. If something happens to us, you'll need to share your notes with them." Charlie heard Urdano groan after he said it. He turned to the sheriff. "Are you okay?"

"Homeland Security. In Phoenix, that would be Agent Earl Kelly. Can't stand the man! He's been a pain in the butt my whole life!"

"What about Marv Cullins—that CIA agent you met in your home?" asked Principal Perez. He looked at Riley. "We should call him instead. Did you get his name and phone number?"

"No, he didn't give us a number. He said he would be in touch. But he did tell us in an emergency where we could find him. He said he has coffee at six sharp every morning at the Space Age Restaurant. He said to sit down in a booth and not make eye contact. If no one was watching, he would approach us."

"Okay, let's get moving!" yelled Principal Perez. "There's no time to waste! Sheriff Morton, do you have enough room in your squad car for Sheriff Urdano, Donnor, and the O'Connells?"

"Yes, I can squeeze them in," replied Morton.

Mack called a cab for a ride to the airport. Perez helped Sheriff Urdano down to Morton's squad car while the O'Connells packed up items they needed at the nursing home.

Donnor was confused as he watched everyone moving all at once.

"Where am I going again?" he asked meekly. "I forgot."

Chapter 47

Thursday, April 19, 2018
Luke Air Force Base, Glendale, Arizona
10:15 am (Pacific Daylight Time)

Cliff pulled Airman Gustine's black Lincoln Town Car up to the main gate at Luke Air Force Base and rolled down the window. It wasn't Gustine's personal car; it was owned by the United States Air Force. Twenty old Town Cars were on loan at the base for junior officers' business use, and six new Lincoln Continentals parked there for colonels and generals. The vice president had authorized a new Continental for Luke each year since the Town Cars had been discontinued in 2011.

Cliff had wrongfully been dishonorably discharged from the Air Force two months ago. He was the fall guy for a mission in Egypt that killed eighteen citizens near Bir el-'Abd. Cliff was a distinguished veteran pilot who was once assigned to fly Air Force One for President George W. Bush. A few weeks before the unfortunate incident in the Sinai region, Cliff led a team of Thunderbirds on a flyover of US Bank Stadium in Minneapolis to kick off the Super Bowl. But oddly, when he received his walking papers, no one asked for his credentials to be returned. He was still carrying his ID card. The guard saw the Luke sticker on the windshield, and after Cliff flashed his ID, the soldier stood at attention and saluted. A colonel driving a Town Car and not a Continental had thrown the confused guard for a loop.

"At ease, lieutenant," said Cliff. The guard ended his salute and bent down to look inside the car. He found it strange that the colonel was wearing torn and dirty civilian clothes, and his passenger looked like a school teacher who spent the day on the playground playing with the kids. Cliff saw the guard's eyes and knew what he was thinking. "I understand that you have two F-15 Eagles that are due for testing tomorrow. This is Airman Frye. We have orders to check out the landing gear and taxiing mechanisms today before the pilots test their flight capacity tomorrow. If you're wondering, that's why we are dressed in these greasy civvies."

Rick almost burst out laughing but was able to keep a straight face. Check out the landing gear and taxiing mechanisms! Oh my God—that was the best he could come up with after having the last hour to think about it? He noticed Cliff's face was turning red. Even the retired colonel was embarrassed by his own statement!

"I will need to check, sir," stated the guard. "Can you please give me a minute?" He stepped into the guard gate and picked up the phone.

Cliff glanced at Rick and whispered, "If Gustine didn't make the call, we're probably screwed. Get ready for a fast exit!"

Just then, a red light began flashing in the guard shack, and the lieutenant hung up the phone and picked up the hotline next to it. The guard nodded, then hit a switch that lifted the gate.

"I think we're in business," blurted Cliff anxiously. The guard rushed back to the Town Car.

"We have an emergency, sir! Could you please pull in and park your car over by Hangar 19? The two F-15s are inside. I'll send someone over to check out your orders in a few minutes."

"Certainly!" responded Cliff. "And where is Hangar 19?"

"Make the first left turn and head to the runway service road. Hang a right and go to the end. You can't miss it!"

"Thank you, lieutenant!" Cliff drove quickly through the gate, turned left, and pulled over to the side to avoid an onslaught of vehicles whizzing toward the exit. Three Continentals led the charge, followed by five military Humvees and a troop transport truck. The truck was loaded with airmen carrying assault rifles.

"Looks like Airman Gustine's timing was just perfect!" exclaimed Rick.

"Now, let's hope he is a great storyteller!" added Cliff. He gunned the accelerator, and the Town Car sped towards the service road.

10:30 am (Pacific Daylight Time)

Luke Air Force Base looked like a resort for F-16s. Cliff drove past a line of fourteen Vipers perched menacingly on the tarmac like the venomous snakes for which they're named. He glanced at them, then chortled and drove to the end of the service road.

"What's so funny?" asked Rick.

"There sits $280,000,000 of taxpayers' money. Over a quarter-billion dollars parked in the space the size of a football field. What do you suppose Lockheed Martin's cut is, my friend?"

"How much?"

"Don't know. Only the CEOs and our president know for sure. Then, add another $10,000 or so for each hour they are in flight, and they become quite an expensive flying machine. But they are amazing if I do say so myself!"

Cliff slowed down as he approached Hangar 19. As expected, the airbase was in a tizzy. He couldn't begin to imagine the panic taking place among the officers' think tank inside the headquarters building. Terrorists attacking the Auxiliary field in Gila Bend was something they had not planned for, nor was it something the high-ranking brass at the Pentagon would easily forgive Brigadier General Meade Morgan, the commander they placed in charge.

The general was a perfectionist! Because of that, he had lived his life as the world's worst worry wart! He had only one child, Jim, who was his pride and joy. Morgan's wife had died giving birth. Jim was a successful rancher in Gila Bend. Some say he sold the planet's best salsa!

General Morgan had a duty to his country to defend and protect Luke and its Auxiliary base at all costs. But, he had an even higher personal commitment to his family, both living and dead. He was named after his great, great, great, great grandfather, George Meade, the Civil War general who defeated Robert E. Lee at the Battle of Gettysburg. Valor was in his blood! And that made him apprehensive every single day!

A successful terrorist attack at Gila Bend Auxiliary Air Force Base could mean a demotion—or worse yet, a dishonorable discharge and a lasting stain on the Morgan name. If that happened, Jim's salsa business would tank, and he would leave town disgraced! General Morgan was not going to lose to a bunch of cowards! The airmen stationed at Luke were given orders to assemble within their squadrons and prepare for battle. A battle inside America's borders—that was incomprehensible!

Four airmen assigned to Hangar 19 ran to a Jeep and stormed off down the service road to their preassigned squadron location. Cliff and Rick peered around the perimeter of the building and could see no one. The airmen scurried out in a hurry and left the vast hangar doors wide open. Cliff and Rick walked inside unnoticed and stared up at the three F-15 Eagles that looked like they were ready to soar. Each one had a portable ladder leading up to the cockpit hatch.

"Which one do we take?" asked Rick. "We have the code, but Gustine didn't tell us which jet."

"The code will work for every hatch on every jet stationed at Luke," replied Cliff. "They need to be ready to deploy quickly in an emergency, and too many codes would be confusing."

"Was the date of Pearl Harbor Day used on purpose, or was that just random?"

"Every air base uses a code that symbolizes great moments in Air Force history."

"As a history teacher, I could argue that Pearl Harbor wasn't such a great moment!"

Hanging on the wall were a variety of G-suits and helmets with a range of sizes. Rick and Cliff hustled over and found one that fit. This was Rick's first time using sub-atmospheric flight garb, and he struggled to get inside. He wasn't sure he had fastened everything correctly, but time was of the essence, so he did the best he could and left it at that.

Cliff pointed at the nearest jet fighter, climbed the steps, and punched in the code: one-two-zero-seven-one-nine-four-one. The hatch lifted automatically. Cliff slid into the pilot's seat with ease; Rick clambered awkwardly into the copilot's seat directly behind him. Cliff fired up the jet's engines and checked the fuel gauge. Full tank! Then he grabbed the mic and punched in frequency two-seven-seven into the radio's digital display.

"Eagle Ten here waiting for instructions." Cliff was told that only Gustine would be monitoring the communication, but he decided to play it safe anyway.

Airman Gustine picked up at once. "Eagle ten, this is Gila Bend Aux. Please identify yourself."

"Colonel Bullard, USAF." He used his actual name, knowing it would be recorded by the control tower in Gila Bend. He knew there was a good chance that this could be his final mission, and he wanted history to show that it was him that tried to end the scheme to take over America.

"Eagle Ten, based upon the GPS tracking device in the target jet, it appears they are setting a course for Casablanca, Morocco."

Cliff turned and looked back at Rick, who just shrugged his shoulders. Could they have gotten misinformation? Could the Taste Of Arabia operation be headquartered in the Sahara Desert, not the Arabian Desert?

"Gila Bend Aux. Are you suggesting we are ultimately heading for the Sahara Desert?"

"No, sir, probably not. The target will need a refueling stop, and I believe Casablanca is it."

Airman Gustine reached down and turned off the recording device.

"Cliff, I've disabled the recorder. We need to speak bluntly. I hacked the computer and was able to bypass Air Force Two's cloaking device. Their GPS is now locked into Sat Seven, co-owned by the United States Air Force and NASA. You will be able to identify their aircraft on your radar screen as W67X. I've also contacted Lajes Air Force Base. They were hesitant to allow you to land on my orders, but they gave the okay. After I called in the emergency, I notified the airmen in Luke's control tower that you were authorized to take off and provide air support over Gila Bend. They believed me—reluctantly. They didn't want to interrupt the officers who were scrambling to figure out what was happening down here, so they didn't bother to get verification. Bottom line, get out of there fast, but beware of what's behind you at all times! If the Pentagon finds out that they have a rogue F-15, they'll chase you and take you down in a heartbeat!"

"I'm Air Force, Frank. I know that! What are your plans?"

"As soon as we hang up, I'm going to shoot up the walls inside the tower, then shoot myself in the leg and lay down on the floor. When the guys from Luke arrive, I'll tell them the terrorists tried to enter the tower, and we exchanged gunfire. I'll say that I hit a couple of them, so they got scared and fled in Jeeps into the desert without blowing up the tower."

"I like that!" said Cliff grinning. "You'll end up being a hero."

"If I bleed out before they get here, I'll be a dead hero. Hopefully, Vice President Sanders and his entourage will be arrested before the Air Force finds out that I was lying to them. Good luck, Cliff!"

"And good luck to you, Frank. If Rick and I don't find a cure for this coffee poison, then we may never remember these crazy last few days. But somewhere in the depths of our gray matter, you may rest assured we will know that you were a champion!"

Five minutes later, Eagle Ten was airborne and had climbed to an altitude of 85,000 feet. Cruising beyond Mach two, Rick was not prepared for the g-force and was not sure he was wearing his G-suit correctly. He began to get dizzy and thought he was losing consciousness. But Rick was not going to tell Cliff. He was determined to see this mission through to the end, whatever the end might be.

"You okay back there?" asked Cliff. He knew Rick wouldn't be used to flying faster than the speed of sound.

"Roger that, General Bullman!" replied Rick.

Colonel Bullard was worried. Was it the coffee or the altitude getting to Rick?

11:15 am (Pacific Daylight Time)

Airman Gustine was lying on his back in a pool of his own blood when Brigadier General Morgan and the support troop from Luke Air Force Base arrived at the auxiliary airfield. Gustine's gun hadn't been fired. He had taken four nine-millimeter slugs from a Luger pistol to his face and another two to his heart. The door leading from the stairwell into the control tower was open, a clear sign an intruder had entered and killed Gustine before the airman could get off a shot.

The computer had suffered and died, as well. The shooter destroyed the screen and fired at least ten shots into the hard drive. There were no terrorists at the airfield or in the surrounding desert. General Morgan assumed Airman Gustine's death had hastened their exit. One by one, the troops entered the control tower and were shocked to see their fellow comrade dead on the floor. Two airmen collapsed to their knees, two more vomited, and the rest grasped each other's hands and said a prayer.

"Get the MPs from Luke down here right away, Sergeant," ordered Major Ben Willis to a soldier standing next to him. "Captain, call Mortuary Affairs down at Davis-Monthan Air Force Base in Tucson and have them send a team."

General Morgan was standing next to Major Willis and staring down at Airman Gustine. His mouth was stuck in an open position, and his face was as white as a ghost. Major Willis was waiting for him to give the troops a directive, but the general was frozen in his tracks.

"I'll notify the Pentagon and Homeland Security," muttered Major Willis to General Morgan. For several minutes there was complete silence. Everyone was waiting for the general to take the lead. Finally, without looking at anyone except dead Airman Gustine, General Morgan gave a firm, yet straightforward, command. "No!"

"No?" whispered Willis dubiously.

"Yes, Major, I said no! Don't call Mortuary Affairs, don't call the MPs, don't call the Pentagon, and don't call Homeland Security. We'll clean up this mess ourselves and transport Airman Gustine to the mortuary at Davis-Monthan. They will do an autopsy and notify the next of kin. Then I'll make all the necessary calls when we get back to Luke. Is that understood, Major?!"

"Yes, sir. I'm sorry if I overstepped your authority, sir. I was only trying to—"

"I know what you were trying to do, Major! Thank you, but as I said, I'll take care of the phone calls."

"Yes, sir," replied Major Willis. Then he looked at Captain Dick Royce and ordered, "Captain, take what's left of the computer hard drive and drop it off at tech services. Hopefully, they can see what Airman Gustine was working on and why it was so important for the terrorists to shoot it up."

Before Captain Royce could acknowledge the command, General Morgan cut in. "No, Captain. I'll take the hard drive with me. Could you please extract it from the casing?"

Major Willis bit down hard on his lip to keep from saying something he might regret. A few minutes later, Captain Royce slipped the hard drive into a protective plastic bag and handed it to the general.

"Thank you, Captain. And Major, I'm going to get some coffee over at the Space Age Lodge. When you're finished here, you may head back to Luke. I'll find my own way back."

"Sir? Your own way back, is that what you said? May I ask how?"

"There has to be at least one Uber driver in Gila Bend, don't you think?"

"Uber? To Phoenix?" Major Willis was trying to hide his apprehension. The last thing he wanted was to disrespect his commanding officer. "Yes, sir, I suppose there is."

1:00 pm (Pacific Daylight Time)

"You said no one would be killed!" shouted General Morgan into the payphone outside of the Space Age Lodge. Only a handful of those antiquities were left in the world, but many immigrants couldn't afford cell phones, so this one saw plenty of action. The general was careful not to use his own traceable mobile device. "Airman Gustine was a good man! He didn't have to die!"

"Our semi was hijacked, and Justine witnessed it trying to take down Air Force Two on the runway, General," said the voice on the other end of the line. "He would have reported the incident."

"So then you leave the damn hard drive in the computer?! You kill Gustine because he knew too much, then you turn around and leave evidence in the room?! Are you kidding me!" The general was turning red. Workers at the auto body shop across the street could hear him screaming into the receiver but couldn't make out what he was saying.

"Calm down, General. I shot up the computer and thought that would take care of it. Where are you calling from? Can anyone hear you?"

"I'm at a damn payphone! And yes, most likely someone can hear me! That's usually what happens when someone is yelling! I just walked five miles to get here, and I'm done with all this foolishness!"

"What did you do with the hard drive?"

"I threw it in the dumpster! Now, I'm going back to Luke, and I'm done with you. Is that understood?"

"I doubt that, General. You need to stay in the game until I tell you we don't need you anymore. And I'm holding an ace, and you know that I'm not bluffing! I'll be in touch." The voice hung up. General Morgan ripped the cord off the payphone and threw the receiver onto the roof of the hotel. Then he pulled out his cell phone and called a cab.

Chapter 48

Thursday, April 19, 2018
Nursing Home, Gila Bend, Arizona
2:00 pm (Pacific Daylight Time)

Mack and Dr. Sancho Gomez jogged through the hallways of the nursing home and headed towards the steps that would take them down to the basement laboratory. There was a nurse's station that doubled as a reception area near the entrance, but at the moment it was unstaffed. The residents perked up a bit at the sight of two healthy men running in their establishment, especially the older man who was carrying a leather physician's bag.

"My, my, aren't you a cutey," blared an elderly woman sitting in a wheelchair. "Are you in the Olympics?!"

"No, ma'am," said Sancho as he smiled at the lady. "But, thank you anyway!"

In the laboratory, Sheriff Urdano was resting comfortably on a stretcher. Intravenous tubes were back in his arms, and he was falling in and out of consciousness. Donnor, on the other hand, was sitting in a chair with a cotton ball taped around his left bicep. It had been an hour since Mackenzie O'Connell had extracted a pint of blood, and he was starting to get over his lightheadedness.

The three O'Connells were busy working with their microscopes. They had made several dozen slides with drops of Donnor's blood on each one. A variety of liquids sat in hermetically sealed miniature jars on the countertop next to them. They heard Sancho and Mack come in but were too focused to greet them.

"Mack told me about the coffee and explained what you are doing," said Sancho as he approached the counter. "Have you found anything?"

With her left eye hovering over the microscope's outer lens, Mackenzie responded. "Maybe. I believe we have found the Tungis plaque. There are abnormal protein clumps similar to those we've found in Alzheimer's patients, except they are black instead of blue. The plaque is growing at an alarming rate right on the slide! I can't imagine how fast it's multiplying while contained within the warmth of the human body! Donnor's white blood cells are attacking but to little avail. The clumps are regenerating faster than the lymphocytes can create new antibodies and the eosinophils can attack them."

"What chemical solutions have you tried?" asked Sancho.

"Virtually everything we know that shows promise on Alzheimer's: the cholinesterase inhibitors Donepezil, Rivastigmine, and Galantamine. None have slowed the breakdown of acetylcholine. We've also tried a combination of Memantine and Donepezil without luck."

"Would you mind if I tried something?"

Mackenzie lifted her head from the microscope and grinned at Sancho. Then she stepped back from her stool and motioned for the doctor to take a seat.

"Be my guest," she said.

Sancho opened his bag and took out a brown bottle with a cap that had a dropper attached. He reached for a new slide that contained Donnor's blood and placed it gently into the holder. Mackenzie switched on the forty-three-inch overhead monitor and the projector so everyone could watch what was happening underneath the microscope. Sancho unscrewed the cap and dropped a minuscule portion of the liquid onto the blood, then moved the holder into its locked position. Under the lens, the substance appeared to be a light green color. It immediately bypassed the red blood cells and attacked the black protein clumps, much the same way white blood cells act as antibodies to attack bacteria.

Within a few seconds, the black plaque began disappearing into thin air! Whatever Sancho had in that brown bottle was working like pool acid on algae. The laboratory was filled with stunned silence! Even Sheriff Urdano was now wide awake and watching the monitor intensely.

"What is that stuff?!" blurted Charlie O'Connell. "Where did you get it?!"

"I have been trying to find a cure for Alzheimer's since I opened our facility in Los Vidrios. The spouses of three late-stage Alzheimer's patients gave me permission to use samples of blood from their loved ones. I tested hundreds of chemicals and drugs with no luck—until I found this." Sancho lifted the brown bottle up. "Although it was not approved for medical use by the Mexican government, it didn't take much for the three spouses to give their consent to try it out on their husbands. The wives had nothing to lose—their husbands had all lost both long-term and short-term memory."

"What happened to them?" rasped a voice from the back of the room. Sheriff Urdano was now sitting up.

"They are all cured. They've regained complete memory functions. I believe I have found the answer to that horrible disease!"

Dead silence filled the room once again. Then the O'Connells began high-fiving each other. Their lifelong dream was to end Alzheimer's. It didn't matter to them that they weren't the ones to find the cure. What mattered was that a successful remedy was found in their lifetime.

Sancho stopped the celebration before it could even begin. "Hold on. This stuff may work for Alzheimer's patients, but that doesn't mean it will heal the victims of this coffee fungis problem. Sure, it may appear to have worked using one test slide, but that certainly doesn't mean it will be successful as an antidote. We should give it several more tests, then try it out on some laboratory mice before administering it to a live patient."

"I don't think my cousin has the time for all those tests, Doc," said Mack. "I think we need to try it on him—now."

Everyone was staring at Sancho, and they could tell he was hesitant. Donnor was still sitting in his chair, also listening to every word that was spoken. Then he stood up and approached the group huddled around the doctor. He tapped Mack on the shoulder. Mack turned around and saw the confused look on Donnor's face.

"I think I understood all that," he said to Mack. "Just one thing. Who is this cousin you're talking about?"

3:00 pm (Pacific Daylight Time)

"Hold it right there! Hands in the air where I can see them!" shouted Agent Kelly. He was pointing a Glock 22 at Sancho, Mack, and the trio of O'Connells. Donnor was lying on a stretcher with a tube in his arm running from a plastic bag hung on a portable stand. Sancho was about to deliver the mixture of his herbal remedy and saltwater into Donnor's bloodstream. "What is going on down here? This is supposed to be a nursing home. That man surely doesn't look elderly!"

"Put the gun down, Earl," croaked a voice from the side wall. Kelly quickly turned his weapon and took aim at Sheriff Urdano, who was lying down again on his stretcher. "Or shoot me. Whatever!"

"Urdano, what the hell are you doing here?!" Kelly hesitated momentarily, but then realized no one in the room was going anywhere, so he put the gun back in its holster.

"Let me guess," replied the sheriff in a hoarse voice. "You're wondering why Lord Shaffer of the marvelous British Parliament owns a nursing home in Gila Bend, right? We're one step ahead of you, Earl. Sit down, we have quite an amazing story to tell you."

"And I have an important question for you," stated Kelly; however, he couldn't remember what it was, just that it involved several SUVs. His mind was starting to slip from the effects of tungis. "But first, who are all of you? What is going on in this lab, and what is wrong with that man?" Kelly walked over to the group. Their hands were still raised above their heads. "Okay, put your damn hands down! I just need some answers. Let's start with a simple question: do you all work for Lord Shaffer?"

Charlie O'Connell shook his head an adamant no, but Riley O'Connell was nodding a firm yes. Mackenzie O'Connell looked at her siblings and rolled her eyes, then glanced at Agent Kelly.

"Sort of," she said.

"What do you mean by sort of? It's an easy question: yes or no?"

"We were hired by him under false pretenses. We thought he built this lab underneath the nursing home as a research center. We thought we were going to find a cure for Alzheimer's disease, but instead, found out we were helping him develop a coffee product that could wipe out the minds of everyone who drank it!"

Agent Kelly stared at Mackenzie with his mouth wide open. He didn't know where to begin. "Was the coffee product called Taste Of Arabia?"

"You know of it? Well, that's a relief! Anyway, we're here now because we may have found an antidote. This man has consumed about a gallon of the coffee, and we were just about to try it out."

Agent Kelly looked at the man. "What's your name, sir?"

"David, or Donny, I think," replied Donnor.

"His name is Donnor Colten," said Mack. "He's my cousin."

Kelly looked at Mack. "Donnor Colten? By any chance, did he drive a pickup truck loaded with teachers to get away from the Gila Bend school a couple of days ago?"

"Yes, that would be him. But the men chasing them weren't ICE agents, they were—"

Kelly cut him off. "Yes, I know they weren't ICE agents. Where did he drink a gallon of that coffee?"

"I will tell you everything, Agent Kelly, but first, please let us try and see if this antidote will help Donnor!"

Kelly looked at Sancho and did a doubletake. "I know you from somewhere." Sancho didn't say a word. "You're Dr. Kildare, aren't you? You're a Nobel Prize winner, right?"

"Well, you're partially correct," said Sancho. "My name is Dr. Gomez, and I did win a Nobel Prize. Do you read medical journals?"

"No. You are on the Homeland Security watch list. That's how I know you."

"Watch list?! Me? Why?"

"AmCan Pharmaceuticals reported you to the FBI as a drug smuggler, and they sent a picture of you to our office."

"Well, they are correct, Agent Kelly. I am a drug smuggler. And I will gladly tell you the whole story if you will first allow me to help this man."

Kelly saw Donnor's confused state of mind and realized that he would soon be like him. There was no reason not to give the antidote a try. "Go for it!" exclaimed Kelly.

Sancho opened the IV container, and the solution began to flow through the peripheral catheter into a vein on Donnor's left arm. The O'Connells were fixated on the digital monitor that displayed his heart rate and other vital signs. Less than a minute later, his blood pressure dropped to 89/59 while his heart rate jumped to 235.

"Doc, he's going into hypotension!" shouted Charlie.

"But his heart rate is climbing too fast! Now up to 240!" said Riley.

"It's okay," assured Sancho. "The solution is causing him to dehydrate, which is lowering his BP. The rapid pulse is his heart trying to compensate. If the BP doesn't come back up in the next five minutes, be ready to inject one-tenth milligram of fludrocortisone into his other arm."

Mackenzie filled a syringe with the drug and attached a hypodermic needle. Seconds later, Donnor passed out. Mackenzie stepped forward to administer the shot, but Sancho held her back.

"Hold on," commanded Sancho. "It's his low blood pressure. He fainted; it's natural. Give him another three minutes."

Mack came close and whispered in Donnor's ear. "Come on, Cuz, you can do it! Make this happen!"

Then it did happen. Gradually, Donnor's heart rate dropped below a hundred, and his blood pressure began to stabilize. But he remained unconscious. Everyone stared at him in silence.

"What's wrong?!" asked Mack. "Why isn't he waking up?!"

"The tungis seems to bypass other organs and goes directly to the brain," stated Sancho. "The antidote is now fighting the plaque in his head, and it's restricting oxygen flow, which in turn is causing a syncope. We need a thrombolytic medication ready in case a clot forms."

"Would you speak English, Doc!" yelped Agent Kelly. "I need to know what's going on!"

"The antidote may cause a stroke, Agent Kelly. We need to be ready for that."

Seven minutes after his pulse and blood pressure returned to normal, Donnor opened his eyes. He moved his head back and forth, looking at everyone in the room gaping at him. "Why are you all ogling me?" The concerned looks quickly turned into smiles, and another round of high-fives began taking place.

"What's your name," asked Sancho.

"Donnor, of course! And you are Dr. Sancho Gomez. Why are you asking me that?" More high-fives and grins. Mackenzie gave Sancho a long, firm hug!

After the mini-celebration concluded, Agent Kelly asked, "What is this antidote, Doc? There are people I sent to the medical center in Tucson who need it soon! And so do I, I'm afraid to say."

The antidote is an herbal remedy that I discovered in my Los Vidrios laboratory. I have enough with me for you and your friends in Tucson, but that's all I'm going to allow for now."

The entire celebratory group became silent again. Did Sancho say what they thought he did?

"Allow for now—what is that supposed to mean?" asked Kelly.

"Your government is allowing the medical industry to gouge your own citizens in the name of corporate profits. Who knows how many people have drunk Taste Of Arabia coffee thus far? Tens? Hundreds? Thousands? And if tungis works in coffee, it won't be long before Lord Shaffer decides to use it in other products. Like ice cream or cookies or cake, things Americans can't seem to resist. Even if you catch and close Shaffer's operation, who knows what evil person will discover tungis next? The bottom line is this: I will not allow only the wealthy in your country to be able to afford the antidote. If you want this remedy to save your nation, then it and all pharmaceuticals sold in America need to be affordable so that everyone who needs them may readily obtain them, including the poor!"

"Are you saying that you are holding the United States hostage in order to secure the antidote? That's crazy, Sancho, and you know it! Sooner or later, someone will find a cure!"

"How much time do you have to find one? Once memories are totally lost, they can't be recovered. Not even my antidote can do that. In the meantime, do your senators and congressmen drink coffee?"

"What are you implying?"

"Lord Shaffer may be targeting your government. Attack the leadership and who will lead? Your democracy will crumble, leaving the door wide open for a revolution and perhaps a hostile takeover by your enemies!"

"He's right, Agent Kelly," said Donnor, who was now leaning on his elbows and listening intently. The effects of tungis were wearing off quickly. "Does Barney Kinkel, a bigshot at Zefron, ring a bell? How about Yegor Bovnik?"

This was the second time Yegor Bovnik's name had been brought up in the past twelve hours. Agent Kelly perked up. "Barney Kinkel—no. Yegor Bottleneck—he's the directorate chief of the Russian KGB. Yes, I know of him. Why?"

"Bovnik, not Bottleneck, sir!" said Donnor. "A retired air force pilot, a teacher at Gila Bend, and I had a not so pleasurable meeting with him while handcuffed to the interior of a semi-truck last night. Would you like to know what he had to say?"

"You're saying Bovrich was in the United States?" Kelly remembered that the Taste Of Arabia company was owned by a holding company that he believed Bovnik invested in. Donnor could be telling the truth. "Okay, it's possible. But I find it hard to believe."

"Would you like to know what was in the truck?" asked Donnor.

Just then, Agent Kelly's cell phone rang. It was from his secretary who had followed-up on Kelly's request to find out what had been unloaded at Lord Shaffer's dock in Canada besides SUVs.

"Damn! Where was the truck headed?" Kelly said into the phone. All eyes in the room were on him. "That was the destination on the manifest? You're sure? Okay, thanks."

Kelly hung up and looked back at Donnor. "Let me guess. The truck you were locked in was loaded with Taste Of Arabia coffee?" Donnor nodded.

From the back of the room, Sheriff Urdano coughed, then asked in a gravelly voice, "The phone call, Earl—who was it?"

"My secretary Je, Jel, Ja—I can't think of her name right now. Anyway, it seems there was a cargo ship full of Taste Of Arabia that was unloaded just recently at Lord Shaffer's pier in Saint John."

"Where was it headed?"

"JQA Charter School in Washington, DC." Kelly began pacing the room. He realized that Sancho's crazy idea about a revolution and takeover may not be so outlandish. "Okay, tell me about last night, Connor, and what happened on the truck with Gregor Povnickle."

Everyone glanced at Sancho. Here we go again! They were all thinking the same thing.

"He will tell you everything, Agent Kelly," said Sancho. "But first, you need to lie down on the stretcher. You need a few drops of my antidote."

Chapter 49

Thursday, April 19, 2018
Lajes Air Force Base, Ponta Delgada, Azores
4:00 pm Pacific Daylight Time (Thursday)
11:00 pm Coordinated Universal Time (Thursday)

Air Force Two circled Lajes Air Force Base three times at an altitude of 50,000 feet with the cloaking device engaged. Air traffic controllers on the ground were panicked. A large, unknown jet was circling overhead that they were unable to identify. A secured hotline ran between the airbase and Portuguese Prime Minister António Costa's residence next to São Bento Palace in Lisbon. The airbase was a joint Portuguese and American operation of the Azores Air Zone Command; thus, English was required for all communications. Costa had just gone to bed and decided not to answer the call. He was tired, and it could wait until morning. A few minutes after the secured hotline in his office stopped ringing, the unsecured cell phone on the nightstand started buzzing. Reluctantly, he picked it up and touched the green answer button.

"Yes, who is this?! It's late, and I would like to rest!"

"Lajes Air Base here, sir," stated Corporal Uffe D'Souza. He was the highest-ranking officer staffing the air traffic control center on the island of Terceira. "Sorry about interrupting your sleep. We have an unidentified aircraft that is circling overhead at an altitude of 50,000 feet. It appears to be a Boeing 757, but I'm unsure."

Standing next to Corporal D'Souza was United States Air Force Lieutenant Ray Monson of the 65th Air Base Group in Europe.

D'Souza and Monson were both listening carefully for Prime Minister Costa's orders.

"Could it be a passenger jet that has lost its communication and is trying to signal you by circling?" asked Costa.

"We thought about that too, so we checked the registered flight plans of every transatlantic commercial jet flying tonight. All have been accounted for, sir."

"Circling at such a high altitude suggests either reconnaissance or possible bombing attack, Mr. Prime Minister," inserted Lieutenant Monson. "I believe we need to take precautions."

"Who the hell wants to spy on the Azores or bomb them?!" blurted Costa into the receiver. He'd had a long day that now appeared would become a long night. "Very well! Send up two F-16's and have them wave their wings. If the jet waves back, guide it into Lajes. If the jet appears hostile, try to scare it away. However, I'm giving permission for the pilot to use deadly force if the other two options don't work. His call! Understood?"

Cliff Bullard had tracked W67X across the Atlantic on his radar screen. Traveling faster than twice the speed of sound, it appeared that he and Rick had caught up with Air Force Two. But the emergency flashers in the cockpit had been blinking for the past five minutes; their F-15 was about out of fuel. That's when he intercepted the unsecured call from Lajes Tower to Prime Minister Costa. Cliff listened carefully and then slapped his helmet. He had gradually been losing cognition during the flight, and hitting himself was his way to try and stay alert.

"Something's changed, Rick. Air Force Two has interrupted its flight path to Casablanca and is circling overhead. That means their landing gear might be okay, and they are planning to refuel at Lajes. But, if the gear is damaged, maybe they're contemplating a belly landing here or even a water landing nearby. Regardless, because they are cloaked, the airbase doesn't know who they are! They think the jet may be hostile, and the Portuguese Prime Minister has given his blessing to take them out, if necessary!"

"What is Lajes again?" asked Rick. The extreme altitude had slowed his and Cliff's memory loss, but the effects were gradually coming on, and they both knew it.

"The airbase where we need to refuel," replied Cliff. He stared at the radar again and saw two unidentified blips moving across the screen. The blips were somewhere near Gibraltar heading towards the Azores. Just then, Air Force Two broke out of its holding pattern and set a course directly at the unknown planes. Cliff caught on at once. "Aerial refueling!"

"What is aerial refueling?" asked Rick.

"My guess is that one plane is an Ilyushin Il-78 tanker that Yegor Bovnik ordered from Russia to gas them up in midair! The other one is probably a Sukhoi Su-35 fighter jet used to protect the Ilyushin. Air Force Two was only circling Lajes in case they needed to make an emergency landing. There's nowhere else to do that in the middle of the Atlantic!"

"What do we do now?!" asked Rick.

"We have no choice. We need to refuel because we're out of gas, too." Cliff switched the radio over to the Lajes frequency. "Lajes Tower, this is Eagle Ten. Colonel Bullard here requesting landing clearance."

"Who is Eagle Ten?" asked D'Souza to Monson. He punched a few keys on his computer. "I don't have a flight plan for them!"

Lieutenant Monson remembered speaking to Colonel Bullard a few hours ago when he reluctantly gave permission for a refueling stop. But right now was not a good time! He grabbed the mic from D'Souza.

"Eagle Ten, we have a possible emergency on our hands. Advise you proceed to Casablanca."

"Lajes, if you don't let us land, you will definitely have an emergency on your hands! We are out of fuel!"

"Just what we need!" blurted D'Souza. "When it rains, it pours!"

Monson nodded, then said into the mic, "Roger, Eagle Ten. Wind is at twenty-five knots from the north-northwest. You'll need to circle and come in from the east. I have a lock on you now."

"Roger that, Lajes. We thank you!"

Cliff circled, descended, and landed uneventfully. He and Rick let out a gasp of relief. That comfort didn't last long, though. As he taxied towards the hangar, two F-16s were being fueled and serviced for takeoff. A voice crackled on the radio.

"Unidentified aircraft has moved out of its holding position and is heading east towards Africa," stated D'Souza into the mic. "Finish fueling and get to the runway! Hold on takeoff until we get orders from the prime minister."

Cliff pulled up to another refueling tank and shut down the engines. He opened the cockpit window and glanced down to see an airman standing on a ramp. Within seconds, the airman had hooked up the hose and was already beginning to pump gas. He saluted Colonel Bullard, and Cliff returned the salute. "Wow! They are fast here! I feel like I'm in the pits at the Indy 500!"

He flipped the radio back to the unsecured frequency he had been listening to earlier. Prime Minister Costa was speaking once again into his personal cell phone.

"We know they are not a commercial jet, so they must have been reconnaissance!" exclaimed the prime minister. "But what country would do that to us? By not identifying themselves and acting as a threat to our national security, they have violated the rules of the Geneva Convention! Blow them to smithereens!"

Cliff glanced a shocked looked at Rick. "Damn! We can't let that happen! Not with your teacher friend and those two students on board!" He grabbed the mic and shouted, "Lajes Tower, Eagle Ten here. Overheard your orders from the prime minister, and I strongly advise you allow the unidentified jet to proceed unharmed. They are no threat, I assure you!"

D'Souza and Monson looked startled and confused. Then D'Souza became angry.

"Eagle Ten, you are interfering in a private military conversation—one that is highly classified, I might add! Turn off your damn radio! That's an order!"

"Who the hell was that?!" yelled Prime Minister Costa.

"Sir, your cell phone is not a secured line. Please hang up and use the hotline, sir!"

"Wait! I'm heading to my office. Call me in two minutes! This is unbelievable!" The prime minister was fuming as he climbed out of bed and padded to his office.

Cliff leaned out the cockpit and yelled at the airman, "Shut her down, airman! We need to leave!"

The airman wasn't sure he heard correctly. He looked up at Cliff and shouted, "Do you want me to stop refueling, sir?"

"Yes, now, please!"

"But you're only half full, three-quarters at the most, sir!"

"I realize that son, but I'm ordering you to shut it down. We need to go now!"

The airman finished while Cliff closed the cockpit. They both gave each other the "thumbs up" sign, and Cliff taxied quickly to the runway.

"Eagle Ten, where are you going?!" shouted D'Souza into the mic. He and Monson watched as Cliff headed for the takeoff area. "You are directed to return to the hangar and shut down. Do you hear me?! I said that's an order, Colonel!" Cliff turned off his radio.

The second F-16 was now on its roll with the nose wheel rising upward. Cliff slammed down the throttle and rotated early to avoid as much wake turbulence from the F-16 as he could. D'Souza and Monson were both yelling frantically into their mics, commanding Cliff to stop. They wondered how he could refuel so fast, but more incredulously, why he was disobeying orders and taking off without their clearance!

As soon as Cliff was airborne, the chase was on. By now, the Air Force Two pilot would see them all coming, but what would he do? What could he do?!

Behind his visor, Rick was sweating bullets.

"What do we do now, Ken?" he asked Cliff.

"Have you ever heard the idiom *play it by ear*?" responded Cliff rhetorically.

"What's an idiom?"

"You're a teacher, Rick! You don't know what an idiom is?"

"I'm a teacher? Since when?"

4:30 pm Pacific Daylight Time (Thursday)
11:30 pm Coordinated Universal Time (Thursday)

A moment later, the starry, cloudless night sky was lit up with two enormous bursts of flames, like a pair of volcanoes erupting simultaneously. Cliff saw it coming a split-second earlier and took evasive action—a displacement roll followed by a nosedive that almost bulleted his F-15 into the dark and cold Atlantic. That's what he wanted anyone watching to think—that his jet was sitting on the ocean floor. He leveled off only a few feet above the ominous waves in time to see the black troposphere morph into a bright orange inferno.

The Su-35's Irbis-E array radar is capable of tracking up to 30 targets simultaneously and can engage up to eight at the same time. The Russian captain had locked on three enemy aircraft, but fortunately for Cliff and Rick, destroyed only the two Portuguese F-16s. Cliff continued an eastbound course at an altitude of ten feet above sea level. He could see the Sukhoi on his radar screen, but the Russian fighter pilot couldn't see him. Their incredible guidance system could find everything in the atmosphere—everything flying above fifty feet, that is! The Russian assumed the American F-15 had crashed in the ocean and would soon rust away into oblivion. Cliff was banking on that assumption and had guessed right.

By the time the Sukhoi had returned to the Ilyushin that it was assigned to protect, the refueling tanker was flying over Air Force Two, and its extracted hose was being secured into the receptacle on top of the fuselage—an arduous task to carry out in the dark. They were flying at an altitude of 25,000 feet and gently drifting eastward at 300 knots. The Sukhoi circled the Ilyushin several times, dipping and diving and even performing a few barrel rolls to keep the bored pilot awake! It looked like a kitten trying to coax a couple of lazy basset hounds into some playful action.

Cliff was looping in a giant circle beneath Air Force Two. He had to slow down, which was making him anxious and nervous. In the darkness, he wouldn't be able to see a giant wave if it happened to push upward from the volatile ocean, and it would spell doom for him and Rick if it did. Cliff knew that as soon as the Ilyushin was finished refueling, it and the Sukhoi would head back home to Russia. He just had to wait it out a few more minutes. He turned the radio back on to try and listen to any communication going on between the Ilyushin and Air Force Two. What Cliff heard instead alarmed him! He hadn't thought about that!

"Beja Air Base, this is Lajes. Per orders from the prime minister, we are requesting any assistance you may be able to provide. A rogue American fighter jet was aiding an unidentified reconnaissance spy plane and shot down two of our F-16s. The American jet appears to have crashed into the Atlantic, but the spy plane's whereabouts is unknown. We have no radar signal on it, but it was bearing east. We are sending up ten F-16s from the rear and request that you set up a frontline barrier. We need to trap the unknown aircraft."

"Copy, Lajes. We should have ten ready to go in five minutes."

"They think we shot down their F-16's!" exclaimed Cliff. "That's bad news, Rick!"

"Did we?" asked Rick. He couldn't remember.

Chapter 50

Friday, April 20, 2018 (4-Shaban-1439)
Sultan Tariq's Palace, Rub' al Khali Desert, Saudi Arabia
6:30 am Arabian Standard Time (Friday)
7:30 pm Pacific Daylight Time (Thursday)

Bassam Bashir had seen enough. Shaking his head in disgust, he jogged away from the crowd that was still cheering the stoning death of Sultan Tariq's eldest wife. Allegedly, the sixty-eight-year-old mother of twelve daughters had been caught cheating on the sultan with one of his cooks. It was a bald-faced lie! At the time of the alleged act, Bassam was playing a game of backgammon with the cook who was a close friend. For several months, the sultan had been trying to weed out the wives in his harem who could no longer satisfy his needs or who talked back to him. His eldest wife fell into both categories.

Every Friday after the Fajr prayer time, it seemed another wife was stoned for some sort of capital offense. Two weeks ago, a fourteen-year-old wife was charged with witchcraft and condemned to die. Last week, a twenty-six-year-old wife was sentenced to death for blasphemy. Both were stoned because it was Tariq's preferred method for executing women. Men received a different form of punishment, better known throughout Tariq's desert oasis as chop-chop.

Bassam ran faster to disengage himself from the women's high-pitched, tongue ululations and the men's whooping and hollering. Tariq required everyone in the sultanate to attend executions, so Bassam couldn't go far. He hid near a palm tree on the edge of the oasis as the masses moved from the stoning pit to the chopping block. Moments later, Bassam heard the distinct sound of sword metal snapping neck bones. The roar of the crowd was deafening.

Bassam pounded the tree with his fists and angrily screamed, "No!" Then he dropped to his knees to offer up a prayer to Allah for his friend. A friend who was beheaded for being a scapegoat.

Nursing Home, Gila Bend, Arizona
8:00 pm Pacific Daylight Time (Thursday)

As a side effect of Sancho's antidote, Agent Kelly and Donnor were both extremely tired and falling in and out of sleep on twin beds in the Gila Bend nursing home. Gladys Wagner had passed away yesterday only minutes after her roommate Maude Byerson died. Both had suffered from Alzheimer's, neither had family in the area, and both were looking forward to eternal life in heaven. Father Kent was at their bedside to help make that happen. The O'Connells had tried investigational medications on Gladys and Maude but to no avail. Now they were at peace. And now Agent Kelly and Donnor were recuperating on their empty beds. Sancho's antidote had worked, but it had made them sleepy.

As the sun set out of the west window and darkness surrounded the tiny town of Gila Bend, Agent Kelly and Donnor were finally waking up and becoming alert. Riley and Charlie O'Connell were monitoring their vital signs while Mack dozed on the chair. Suddenly, Kelly sprang up in his bed.

"Where's Dr. Gomez?!" he blurted. "I can't stay here! I need to find Deputy Owens and the others!"

"Sancho is downstairs with Sheriff Urdano and Mackenzie. The sheriff's health is rapidly deteriorating."

Kelly had now regained complete memory functions and was perhaps sharper than ever before. "Urdano! I need to question him about the five SUVs and why they were registered to the Maricopa County Sheriff's Office!"

Just then, Mackenzie walked into the room, followed by Sancho. Both had a forlorn expression on their face and tears were rolling down Mackenzie's cheeks. "You won't be questioning Sheriff Urdano," she said. "At least not in this life. He died a few minutes ago."

Kelly collapsed back down on the bed and stared at the ceiling. "Now what?" he muttered to himself softly. "What do I do next?"

Mackenzie pulled out a voice recorder and placed it on the medical cart between the beds. "The sheriff had something he wanted to tell you before he died, Agent Kelly. He recorded it for you to hear."

Gila Bend Charter School, Gila Bend, Arizona
8:30 pm Pacific Daylight Time

The carton of Little Debbies had been devoured, and ripped cellophane wrappers were lying all over Principal Perez's conference room table. School Board President Abe Fitzgerald was alone and sound asleep in a comfortable leather chair. It had been a long day. First, he met Captain Segura and Sergeant Ruben at daybreak to answer questions about why a Gila Bend Charter School van would be driving recklessly in the early morning hours near the airport when school wasn't even in session. A jogger had almost been hit and had called the police. Fitzgerald said he would follow up as soon as Principal Perez or Assistant Principal Sanderson returned to work.

At dawn, Sergeant Ruben had located an abandoned semi with a damaged roof out by the auxiliary airfield that was loaded with a brand of coffee he had never heard of—Taste Of Arabia. After filling out the report, Abe and the two police officers brewed a pot of the coffee and chatted about the events of the past week. The coffee paired with Little Debbies was heavenly, so they drank a second pot. After Segura and Ruben left, Abe decided to stick around and begin phoning for substitute teachers to work on Monday. The coffee was the best he had ever tasted, so he brewed a third pot all for himself. He managed to secure one teacher for Monday—Philomena Hayes, the owner of Philly's Flower Shop downtown. She had an associate degree in Horticulture from South Mountain Community College and was dying to try out her pedagogy skills in the classroom. Least that's what she told Abe. She wasn't sure what pedagogy meant, but she overheard two teachers talking about it while shopping for roses in her store. She would look it up before Monday.

Abe told Philomena that she would be teaching science and asked her to come to the school that afternoon so he could show her the classroom. He said he would also be subbing on Monday and thought they could do some long-range planning together; Abe wasn't sure when the regular teaching staff would return.

Abe was still making phone calls when Philomena came in late in the afternoon, so he unlocked her classroom, which was the science lab, and went back to the principal's office. Something was wrong, but he couldn't pinpoint exactly what it was that was bothering him. By six o'clock, the tungis in the coffee had kicked in. He thought he saw someone walk down the hall, but he guessed it was Philodendrum, no wait, Philoberto, no—oh whatever, it was probably the new substitute teacher heading for home.

Abe got up to go lock the classroom door. Then he remembered what was bothering him before; who locked the science lab door in the first place? No one had been in the building since the raid last Monday, and in their haste to exit the building, the teachers didn't have time to lock their classrooms. Abe sat back down to think about it but fell asleep instead.

The phone on the desk kept ringing and ringing. Abe opened his eyes and wondered why anyone would be calling the school at nine o'clock at night. He decided to pick up. It was Philomena's husband, Ralph.

"Hello, this is Gabe Fitzsimmons, I mean Fitzpatrick," said Abe, who wasn't really sure what his name was. "Who is this?"

"I'm Ralph Hayes, Philomena's husband. May I speak to her? She left a note saying she was going to work at school this afternoon. We don't do much business with the school, so I'm wondering why she went over there?"

"I don't know a Philomena—sorry. You say she's here now?"

There was momentary silence on the other end. "Don't play games with me! Are you having an affair with my wife?! What did you say your name was—Gabe Fitzpatrick? I've lived in Gila Bend all my life and have never heard of you! Is that a fake name, or are you some hotshot from Buckeye or something?! I'm coming down there right now!" Ralph slammed down the receiver, picked up his car keys, and marched for the garage.

Abe vaguely remembered calling a substitute and unlocking the science lab for her, but that was about it. What was happening to his memory? Getting old was worse than he thought! Abe walked down the hallway and noticed a familiar classroom. "This must be it," he mumbled to himself. He turned the key, flipped the light switch, and walked into the science lab.

There were sinks, lab carts, Bunsen burners, Petri dishes, test tubes, microscopes, Kevlar gloves, and all sizes of glass beakers. In the back of the room was a storage closet for chemicals and other items that kids shouldn't be using without supervision. The door was always supposed to be locked, but now Abe could see that it was open a crack. As he got closer, he could smell an overpowering odor coming from the closet. Cautiously, Abe stepped inside and turned on the light. Bottles of liquids were stacked three-deep on the shelves, and nothing seemed out of place, but the odor was getting stronger. In the back of the closet was another door that was labeled *Darkroom-Knock Before Entering.* The science teacher hosted a photography club after school. Abe walked slowly to the door and turned the handle.

Philomena was lying on the floor with her face in a tray full of an intensely odorous liquid chemical, and it was not photographic developing fluid. The empty bottle next to her said *Sulfuric Acid.* She had been strangled by a coat hanger that was still around her neck.

Lying next to her was a man with a coat hanger also around his neck. He, too, was face down in a tray of sulfuric acid. He must have been there much longer than Philomena because there was no skin or hair left on his skull. Abe rolled him over on his back, then gagged and vomited all over the faceless dead man. When he recovered, Abe saw that the man was wearing a lanyard around his neck. Afraid that the man might be a zombie ready to pounce, he carefully reached and turned the ID around to read it.

Next to a photo of what the man once looked like was his name: Smitty Douglas, *Arizona Republic.*

*****

Mackenzie pressed play on the recorder. Everyone listened intently as Sheriff Urdano's final words were spoken in a rough, broken voice:

"Earl, this is for you. I know I'm down to a few breaths. This shouldn't take long."

Several guttural coughs were heard.

"Dr. Sancho Gomez is a good man. I support his efforts to make pharmaceuticals affordable for all Americans. If you can help him to keep importing his medications, please use your power at Homeland Security to make it happen. That's enough about that."

More coughing.

"Sooner or later, you are going to find out that I have connections to some bad people. This is my one and only chance to tell you that—"

A wheezing sound followed by another cough.

"Tell you that I'm not a bad person. I'm not one of them. I was only trying to stop them."

A gasp of breath and a long pause. Everyone in the room looked at each other. Was that it? Was that the end? Then the tape continued:

"My father wrote me a letter that I found only a few months ago with details about me that I didn't know. He was ashamed, and so am I, which is why I wanted to do something about it. But now I'm too sick to go on, so I'm asking you to finish the deal."

Another gasp and another long pause.

"I knew about the raid on the school. I thought it was a chance for me to catch red-handed a person my father told me about so I could throw him in jail and throw away the key. I was told nobody would be injured, say nothing of being killed. It got out of hand."

Six raspy coughs and a deep breath. Everyone knew it wouldn't be much longer

"The fake ICE agents were only supposed to clear out the school so they could store poisoned coffee inside and then go back to Russia where they came from."

Another cough and gasp.

"But, when Donnor Colten killed one of their men, the plan blew up."

A long pause. The sheriff's voice was becoming softer and his breathing lighter.

"I registered their imported SUVs. I didn't know they were also bringing in choppers."

A delicate cough and a gentle breath of air.

"My father's letter is in the glove compartment of my squad car. You will know my father. His name is—"

The voice-activated tape recorder stopped. Everyone in the room was stunned. Out of respect for Sheriff Urdano, they bowed their heads, and no one said a word. But they were all thinking the same thing; who was the sheriff's father? They needed to find the letter!

Chapter 51

Friday, April 20, 2018 (4-Shaban-1439)
Sultan Tariq's Palace, Rub' al Khali Desert, Saudi Arabia
8:30 am Arabian Standard Time (Friday)
9:30 pm Pacific Daylight Time (Thursday)

"He's dead. I'm very sorry, Sultan, about your nephew." The man held the satellite phone receiver to his ear, waiting for a response. He could hear what sounded like a soft whimper. A moment later, the Sultan's grief turned into rage.

"You're sure? You've seen him?!"

"I just left the morgue in Phoenix. Yes, I'm sorry to say it's him."

"Who's to blame for this! I demand to know! There will be justice!"

"Things didn't go as planned here in Arizona, your highness."

Lord Shaffer and General Sokolov sat in lush velvet chairs inside Sultan Tariq's office. They had just arrived at his palace a few minutes ago and were waiting for Yegor Bovnik and Vice President Sanders to land. The mess up in Arizona required a Plan B to be drawn up, and it would take place in this room. "You're damned right it didn't go as planned! My nephew has died, and I will seek immediate revenge! I want names!"

"Pavel Orlov, who was using the alias name Sergeant Bill Clemons, was in charge of the Gila Bend mission. Things got out of hand, and his men tried to escape through the Sonoran Desert. He destroyed the evidence—five SUVs and two helicopters. A short time later, they shot down a small airplane, but a teacher and two students parachuted, and Orlov captured them on the ground.

Ironically, the same two students happened to have escaped Gila Bend Charter School by stealing a bus. To make a long story short, the stolen bus may have started the chaos that ultimately failed the entire operation. The teacher and two students are being held prisoners on board Air Force Two. The man and boy would make good servants. Or perhaps executing the teacher would meet the 'eye for an eye' requirement of the Qur'an? But one student is a young Muslim girl who we thought would make a lovely wife for you!"

"My nephew is a prince and worth the lives of all three of them! As soon as they land, they shall all be executed! Today is Friday, execution day! They will be put to death before midnight!" Sultan Tariq slammed down the receiver. Lord Shaffer gave him a stern look and shook his head.

"Wayakun alaistirkha," said Shaffer. *Be relaxed.* Despite all his travels to the Middle East, the lord's Arabic wasn't the best. The sultan spoke perfect English, so Shaffer tried again in his native tongue. "You should calm down, Tariq," said Shaffer. "High blood pressure can kill you! There's no need to execute those three people. Do as Pavel intended: make the man and boy servants and enjoy another young wife for yourself!"

Tariq waved his hand in the air as a brushoff of Lord Shaffer. Then he glanced at Sokolov, who had sat there listening but hadn't said a word.

"What about you, General? My nephew worked for you, too!"

Sokolov thought about it a moment, then nodded. "Go ahead, kill all three of them. Then you won't have to feed them!" He snickered and winked at Lord Shaffer.

Sultan Tariq called for his assistant. Within seconds, a man appeared at the door and waited until Tariq motioned him to come in.

"Make a declaration to the people that we shall have three more executions this afternoon that will require their attendance. Two shall be by the sword, and one shall be by stoning!"

"Yes, your highness, I will do that. However, we have another problem, your royalty!"

"What's that?"

"Air Force Two. Our air traffic controller confirmed Mr. Bovnik's previous communications. They have no landing gear and will need to attempt a belly landing."

"Very well. That should pose no problem. They are the most skilled pilots in the world! And even if they run out of runway, there's a gigantic sand dune that will stop them! I am confident they will survive!"

"Yes, your highness. Thank you!" Tariq's assistant turned and departed quickly, then jogged down the hallway and out of the palace. General Sokolov stared at Sultan Tariq and smiled.

"Perhaps your executions won't be necessary," said Sokolov. Then with a good deal of sarcasm, he added, "Your highness!"

Skies over the Rub' al Khali Desert
9:30 am Arabian Standard Time (Friday)
10:30 pm Pacific Daylight Time (Thursday)

"They're descending, Dick," said Cliff. "They're coming down."

Rick himself wasn't sure he was Dick or Rick or anyone else at this point. He had totally forgotten his own name! Both he and Cliff had bits and pieces of their memory left, but they were fading fast. They had flown thirty feet above the earth's surface since leaving the Azores and were able to stay under Air Force Two's radar, but they were almost out of fuel again. They left Lajes Air Base in a hurry and hadn't been able to fill the tanks.

Cliff had maneuvered over the Atlas Mountains in the middle of the night using moonlight and the F-15's enhanced sensors. Rick thought he was a participant in a new video game! The fighter jet blew a line of sand through the Sahara Desert until it reached the Nile River near Luxor, Egypt. Cliff was nervous as the plane approached the Hejaz Range of western Saudi Arabia. American Airborne Warning and Control System (AWACS) radars attached to Boeing E-3 Sentry planes roamed the coastline from Yanbu to Jeddah and inland to the holy city of Mecca. The F-15 would be an easy target for surface-to-air missiles from the altitude it was flying. Fortunately for Cliff, Air Force Two banked in a southeasterly direction and followed the Red Sea towards the Gulf of Aden before turning left and bearing northeast towards the desolate Rub' al Khali. Cliff was skimming the tops of sand dunes fifty miles behind Air Force Two when the fuel gauge started flashing red again.

"Where are you going to land, you bastard?!" Cliff was watching Air Force Two through the blowing sand and talking to himself. He felt the F-15 jerk as it began to misfire. "Come on, just a little bit further!"

"What's our plan?!" asked Rick frantically.

"They don't have wheels, remember? If they are landing out here in the middle of nowhere, they need to put down on a flat surface. I was hoping we could find a road to land on near them, but that doesn't look like much of a possibility!"

"We can't see anything from this altitude, Ralph. We need to go higher to see what's out there, don't we?" Cliff didn't respond, so Rick asked again. "Don't we, Jeff?"

A minute later, Air Force Two dropped below Cliff's horizon line. "They're landing somewhere up ahead, damn it!"

Just then, an emergency voice responder in the cockpit activated along with a siren. "Pull up! Pull up!" The F-15 vibrated violently and rolled back.

Cliff throttled up, then shouted in his receiver to Rick. "Hold on! I'm climbing to 200 feet, and then we're ejecting! Brace yourself!"

Seconds later, Cliff yanked the lever, and the cockpit window blew. To avoid tangling the parachutes, the ejection mechanism was programmed to eject the rear pilot's seat first, then the front seat three seconds later. Rick shot upward like fireworks on the Fourth of July, but Cliff's failed to deploy. The F-15's engines ran out of fuel and stopped. Cliff tried to keep the nose up, but he couldn't avoid the mountain of sand directly ahead. The jet blasted straight through the middle and out the other side, then hit the ground sideways and flipped several times before coming to rest upside-down. Cliff wasn't in it. He had been swept out of the cockpit as the jet ripped through the dune.

Rick's parachute opened perfectly, and he drifted back to earth slowly as the wind carried him into the side of a dune five miles from the doomed fighter jet. He unstrapped himself from the seat but was unable to gain footing, and he rolled all the way down to the bottom of the bank. He sat up for a moment wondering where he was, why he was here, and worse yet, who he was! He couldn't remember. He laid his head down on the sand and closed his eyes.

*****

"Brace for impact!" shouted the Air Force Two pilot. Everyone on board tugged tightly on their seat belts, then lowered their heads and covered them with their forearms. The pilot had been dumping what remained of his fuel for the last ninety miles and slowed down to 175 knots. He was now aiming towards the middle of Tariq's private runway. The crosswinds would be tricky.

A mile from the airfield, Air Force Two's landing flaps were deployed. Ten seconds before touch down, the pilot cut the engines to stop the flow of fuel and leveled the wings. One second before landing, he lightly pulled up and the plane gently caressed the dusty tarmac. Sparks flew madly as Air Force Two slid off the runway and stopped a few feet from an inauspicious sand dune. The passengers let out a gasp. The pilots high-fived and wiped the sweat from their foreheads. Then they deployed the emergency slides.

Tariq didn't have a fire department or ambulance or even a hospital. If it was Allah's will that you should have an accident, then it was Allah's will if you should live or not. The Sultan had his own personal doctors who he would allow his people to use, but only if he desired them to be healed. He really didn't like the sick or the injured, so most simply cured themselves or died. One less mouth to feed.

But Tariq had plenty of sentries, guns, and ammunition. And while the vice president of the United States and the directorate chief of the KGB were ushered to Tariq's palace by a host of zealous servants, Kurt Kellner, Isaac Martinez, and Zaira Tahan were escorted to the executioner's holding cell by five guards with AK-47s.

Chapter 52

Friday, April 20, 2018 (4-Shaban-1439)
Sultan Tariq's Palace, Rub' al Khali Desert, Saudi Arabia
12:50 pm Arabian Standard Time

Sultan Tariq completed the midday Dhuhr prayer in a private room inside his private mosque inside his private palace. No one entered any of those locations without his consent. The palace was only used for the sultan's cloistered comforts, business matters, entertaining guests, and celebrations within the oasis community. The mosque was used for religious ceremonies the Sultan ordered, but the isolated room at the back of the mosque was the Sultan's personal prayer space. No one except him had ever entered the room.

At 12:25 pm, which was one minute before the midday call to prayer sounded, Sultan Tariq commanded all faithful Muslims to include an invocation of forgiveness for the royal executioner who would be ending the lives of the three Americans who were guilty of murdering Tariq's nephew. The Sultanate's devoted followers had already said a prayer for the master slayer before the execution that took place earlier that morning.

The stoning would take place first. Many men wondered why the Sultan would not keep the young lady as part of his harem instead of having her put to death, especially when Tariq found out the girl was Muslim. Under her blouse was a gold necklace with the Arabic inscription: الله أكبر—Allahu akbar! God is great! However, the women of Tariq's harem were delighted with the Sultan's decision. One less young, beautiful wife to replace them!

"You must join me," said Tariq to Lord Shaffer, General Sokolov, and Directorate Chief Bovnik. "I am extending to you the honor of being at my side to witness the executions. To reject my offer would be disrespectful."

"There was no trial, and those three harmless souls had no chance to tell their side of the story!" rebuked Lord Shaffer. "I will not attend your outrageous ceremony! Besides, we have a lot of work to get done today. We waited for you to complete your midday prayers out of deference to your religion, but that's as far as it goes. Time is of the essence to finalize a Plan B strategy! Go ahead and make your royal appearance, but we're not waiting for you!"

"You are bordering on blasphemy, my dear Lord Shaffer!" responded Tariq harshly. "I could have you executed, too!" Then Tariq glared at everyone sitting in his conference room. "This is my kingdom, you are my guests, and you shall all treat me with the dignity and esteem I so richly deserve!" He slammed his fist on the table and stormed out of the palace.

While the others in the room looked dumbfounded, General Sokolov chuckled. "Seems a bit stressed, wouldn't you say? Tariq could use some fine Russian vodka if you ask me. Now let's get to work, gentlemen."

2:00 pm Arabia Standard Time (Post-Midday Dhuhr Prayer Time)

Lying face down in the scorching, gritty sand, Rick opened his eyes, tried to blink, and realized he was suffocating. A thick, guttural cough loosened the crud in his throat, and he raised his neck just enough to spit out the disgusting filth that was blocking his air passages. Crawling out of the repulsive muck-covered saliva was a dung beetle. The scarab had been feasting on a feces dinner dropped from the back end of a camel, and based upon the damp moisture content, not all that long ago. But as Rick discharged what was left in his oral cavity, his first thoughts were filled with bewilderment. Where was he, or even more important, who was he?

Rick's lips were severely chapped, and pain caused by the rough parachute landing was edging down his neck into his torso. He wanted to get up, but the agonizing sting forced him back to the earth. He glanced around at the desert wasteland that surrounded him. Where was he? Who was he? Why couldn't he remember?

Rick could feel an extreme heat sensation sizzle over his entire body. He was desperate for water! The hot, arid atmosphere coupled with blowing sand was miserable, and Rick needed to find answers soon. Despite the sharp twinge in his neck, he managed to roll on his back. The wind and sand had dulled the sun's brightness, but the intense rays were piercing through the dusty air with little trouble, scorching whatever living thing that was foolish enough to get in its way. Rick bent forward into a sitting position and saw what looked to be the tops of several palm trees about 200 yards away behind a sand dune ridge. Only the palm fronds were visible as the trunks hid below the crest. In the distance beyond the trees were more dunes that appeared to be small mountains on the horizon. The wind was blowing very fast, and grains of sand were cutting at his face and eyes. Rick's only chance for survival was to find water and shelter soon.

Steadying himself with both hands pressed against the blistering earth, he pushed himself into a wobbly stance and moved cautiously toward the palm trees. Ascending the steep dune proved more complicated than he imagined, and as he neared the peak, he stumbled. To keep from losing ground, Rick dug his fingers into the sandbank. He inched his way to the top of the dune.

As his head emerged above the apex, a wave of optimism surged through his blood. Glancing downward, Rick caught an image that appeared to be a small lake or pond perfectly surrounded by lush greenery. On the far side of the water was a domed marble building that resembled a miniature mausoleum. Could this be a mirage? Was a horrible hallucination eating away at what little remained of his sanity?

Believing he was alone in this empty wasteland, Rick once again scrambled to his feet and hastened down the dune towards the pond.

He wanted to quickly quench his terrible thirst. But as he descended, he caught a glimpse of movement beyond a cluster of palm trees in the distance to his left. Then he heard the faint sound of a drum. Rick ducked back down to keep out of sight and observed black stumps of all sizes that seemed to be alive and marching in a circle to the whistling wind.

Rick slid down the embankment and clambered behind a group of shrubs. Squinting through the brittle branches, his eyelids and mouth opened wide at the sight of what was unfolding beyond the palm trees. The black stumps were human, and he could make out a faint chant coming from the circle. Aching with every silent step, Rick crept slowly around the shrub toward the alien congregation. To keep from being heard, he concealed his awkward movements behind the desert foliage.

He was no more than twenty yards away now, and as he squinted through the relentless sun and commanding wind, he could see several women in black abayas walking in a circle. Each was carrying a rusty, tin bucket of rigid stones the size of baseballs. Their faces were carefully veiled behind a thin black cloth with gold lace trim, and only the dim shadow of their lips, nose, and chin could be seen through the wispy material. As they were walking, the women would glance up at the sun and unload terrifying shrieks and clicking sounds; then, they would look down into the circle and chant in low-toned, sickening voices. Goosebumps appeared on Rick's arms beneath the red, scaly patches of dry skin. Suddenly, the women stopped their circular parade, and together in unison they each lifted their veils to reveal pairs of dark, uncertain eyes. Rick stared intensely at the fatigued faces of the Arab women through the slight openings in their niqab, and as unlikely as it seemed, he could swear those eyes told a story. A story of sacrifice, servitude, fear, and hopelessness. But why were they carrying buckets of stones, and why were they moving in a spiral direction?

Then he saw it. In the center of the circle was the head of a young Arab girl. Rick was confused. The girl looked familiar, but he couldn't remember when or where he had seen her before. She could be no older than fifteen; her black, curly hair was partially covering youthful dimples and tearful eyes of fright. The girl's head was moving frantically back and forth. Sand covered her body to the top of her shoulders, trapping her in this horrifying position. She was unable to move her extremities even the slightest bit.

The chant abruptly ended. Each Arab woman genuflected and offered praise and glory to Allah, and then each took a stone out of her bucket and gripped tightly. A stout gal, whose worn and wrinkled forehead made her appear many years older than her actual age, raised a jagged rock and aimed at the sobbing girl's face. Her throw was weak and missed by two feet. The young girl began to scream in broken Arabic that sounded as if it were a second language; it was a panicked call for forgiveness that needed no translation. Once again, Rick was sure he recognized her voice but couldn't seem to remember. Within seconds the next woman launched a solid, grapefruit-sized stone that was so heavy it required an arcing trajectory to reach the target. It landed directly on the girl's upper forehead causing cranial bones to crack. The human circle of black cloaks turned away momentarily, several covering their mouths with their hands, as the girl blasted a curdling scream of terror.

Rick was covered in a cold sweat and frozen in time. His pain was unconsciously stored somewhere outside his body. A sweeping mixture of fear and anger over what he was witnessing replaced the soreness. Could he possibly save this girl, or was the situation hopeless? A brave attempt at heroics might cost him his own life by tortuous means that he could not even begin to imagine. What had a seemingly innocent child done to deserve this type of death?

Before he could gather his thoughts, a third stone hit the girl on her fragile temple, sending a gushing flow of blood down her chin and neck. The next rock was the last one. The impact forced the girl's head backward, and a wicked snap echoed through the desert.

Sultan Tariq's personal doctor, Sachit Laghari, walked up to Zaira and placed two fingers on her carotid artery. She was unconscious, and blood was oozing down her cheeks and neck, but there was a pulse. Dr. Laghari turned towards Sultan Tariq, who was perched on a portable throne still fuming from his run-in with Lord Shaffer but enjoying the stoning nonetheless. "She's still alive, your highness!"

Tariq stood up and stamped his feet like a spoiled brat who didn't get his way. Then he put his hands on his hips and glared at the women stoners who were shocked that the young girl had not been killed. "Well, pick out a bigger rock and get back in your circle! I command that you finish what you started!"

The ladies stared at Tariq and didn't move. They stood frozen in place as they gaped at their husband. Some covered their mouths and let out a gasp. Tariq didn't know why they weren't doing as they were told! He was about to repeat his command when he heard footsteps running up from behind. He turned just as a sword crushed his Adam's Apple and sliced entirely through vertebrae, tendons, and skin. The sultan's head landed on his foot while his torso remained standing, blood shooting up from his neck like a geyser in Yellowstone Park. Dr. Sachit and Tariq's bodyguards watched in awe. They didn't see their boss's killer coming. It all happened so fast no one could react in time to save the Sultan.

After murdering Tariq, Bassam Bashir dropped the sword and ran like a gazelle towards the sand dune that marked the western boundary of the sultanate. Tariq's harem of women dumped their buckets of stones and prostrated on the ground, their high-pitched ululations sounding like a hen house being raided by a coyote. The sultan's bodyguards gave chase but knew they would never catch the fleet-footed Bassam. They would need to use their AK-47s before he reached the top of the dune. Dr. Laghari, now free from Tariq's cruel authority, stooped down next to Zaira and tried to stop the bleeding.

Rick had seen everything unfold. Now the sword-wielding murderer was running right at him, and he saw the eight bodyguards kneel and take aim. Rick jumped out from behind the shrub and tackled Bassam a split second before bullets whizzed harmlessly over their heads.

"Come on!" yelled Rick as he let go of his grip on Bassam. "Stay low and crawl fast!" Bassam didn't understand English very well, but he certainly knew what this man who had saved his life wanted from him! They bent low and scampered up the sandbank as a deluge of shots rang out.

Suddenly, Rick collapsed to the ground face first. Simultaneously, he had been hit in the triceps of his left arm as well as his right hamstring. Bassam paused and turned to assist his new friend, then saw the eight bodyguards racing towards them. The top of the dune was only ten feet away, but Rick would never make it. Bassam thought about running, but leaving the man who saved his life would be cowardly. So he stood up and raised his arms high in the air to surrender. Chances were slim that Tariq's bodyguards would merely arrest him; most likely, they would execute him on the spot. But by giving himself up, perhaps he could return the favor and save Rick's life.

Tariq's bodyguards chose the killing option. All eight formed a line, then the leader shouted out his orders in Arabic.

"First, the traitor, then the other man! Fire on my command!" he exclaimed. He paused momentarily while the sultan's bodyguards took aim. The other man appeared to be American. The leader thought it would be wise to issue a proclamation in English before executing the two conspirators.

"In the name of Allah, you are both sentenced to death for the murder of his royal highness, Sultan Tariq! Would you like to offer a prayer of forgiveness before I order your—"

From a crouched position with his Heckler & Koch MP5A3 submachine gun resting on his shoulder, the man pulled the trigger, and within seconds all eight bodyguards fell to the ground. Spraying ammunition left and right, the man had managed to hit each one in the heart.

Bassam dropped his arms and turned quickly to see who had fired the shots that, for the second time, had saved his life. Rick was losing blood, and his memory loss was taking a toll, but he raised his head as the man dashed over the ridge and knelt beside him.

"Rick, are you okay?!" asked the man as he ripped off his own t-shirt to try and stop the blood coming from Rick's bullet wounds.

Rick turned his head and looked at the eight dead bodies resting peacefully a few yards away. Then he looked up at the man who had killed them and was now trying to give him medical attention.

"I know you from somewhere," he murmured softly. "Don't I?"

Chapter 53

Friday, April 20, 2018
Curley School Apartments, Ajo, Arizona
3:00 am (Pacific Daylight Time)

After Sheriff Urdano died, Donnor borrowed Emile Forester's 1966 Cadillac DeVille to drive back to Ajo. He was going back to Mack's apartment to get the letter out of the sheriff's glove compartment and bring it to Agent Kelly. Emile was a 103-year-old lifelong bachelor, a resident of the Gila Bend nursing home, and his one and only prized possession was the shiny apple red convertible that he won playing a nickel slot machine at Caesar's Palace in Las Vegas on the day the mega-casino opened for business. The mint condition vehicle was now parked under a tree in the nursing home lot. Emile couldn't drive it anymore, but he spent hours in his rocking chair looking out the window at the car reflecting on the good old days. Emile had been Donnor's high school auto mechanics teacher, and Donnor had been Emile's favorite student. He had no problem loaning the Caddy to Donnor for the day.

Mack helped load Sancho and the O'Connells into Sancho's airplane. It was a four-seater, so Charlie crammed himself into the luggage area in the back. They flew from Gila Bend to Los Vidrios, Mexico, so that Sancho could pack up the plane with more of the herbal tungis antidote, then they all flew to Tucson. The O'Connells caught a cab to the University of Arizona Hospital and began administering the remedy to deputies Gordy Owens and Ken Smith, receptionist Rebecca Grimm, photographer Joe Freeman, and Senso-Mac employee Roger Bennett. Roger had left his wallet at

Joe's house and had no form of identification; however, once the antidote kicked in, he remembered his name.

Agent Kelly had driven his Vette back to the FBI lab to see if Agent Talbert had received the results from coffee salesman James Lebron's DNA. Talbert's memory had faded to the point where he couldn't remember Kelly's name or position with Homeland Security, but he had the results on a printout and handed it to Kelly. Kelly read the report, then reread it again just to be sure. The news was shocking, but now things were beginning to make sense. The letter written by Sheriff Urdano's father might help tie up loose ends. He was about to call Mack and Donnor to set up a rendezvous point when his cell phone rang. It was Donnor calling from Mack's apartment in Ajo.

"Urdano's car is gone!" huffed Donnor. He was with Principal Perez and the teachers who had helped him search the garage and several blocks around the Curley School apartments. He put the phone in Mack's apartment on speaker for all to hear.

"Gone?! You had his keys! You're saying someone broke in and hotwired the car?!"

"I don't know, but I know the car isn't here anymore. What should we do?"

"A stolen sheriff's car shouldn't be hard to find! Call Sheriff Morton and—wait a minute! Where is Sheriff Morton?"

Donnor looked at Principal Perez and the teachers. They all shrugged their shoulders.

"I'm not sure. The last time we saw him he had driven Urdano, the O'Connells, and me to the nursing home in Gila Bend. My memory wasn't the best at the time, so I don't know where he went after dropping us off."

"Okay, then I need for you to drive over to Morton's office and see if you can find him. He can put out an APB for Urdano's squad car."

"Agent Kelly, it's the middle of the night. He's probably not going to be in his office."

"Then find out where he lives and wake him up, damn it! We must get that letter! I have some new information, but I need the letter to confirm some things."

"What new information?"

"It's too long of a story to tell now. I need for Mack and Dr. Gomez to meet me as soon as possible. Let me know what Sheriff Morton has to say!" Agent Kelly hung up and phoned Mack. He asked him to fly Dr. Gomez to Mesa as soon as possible, and then he and Agent Talbert headed for the Falcon Field airport.

Falcon Field Airport, Mesa, Arizona
4:25 am (Pacific Daylight Time)

Mack planted the wheels of the Cessna DC-6 down lightly on the Falcon Field runway. One air traffic controller was working the night shift, and he appeared to be the only living soul awake in east Mesa. Starbucks would open in five minutes, and soon Zefron employees would be arriving for work. They would bring their coffee into the lounge and talk about the mysterious disappearance of their boss Barney Kinkel.

"This is your airplane, Doc?!" exclaimed Agent Kelly. Mack had taxied the old Cessna to an airplane parking cove outside the *Steak and Stone* restaurant, which was closed for the night. The area was out of view from the control tower. "You fly around in that jalopy, for God's sake?!"

Sancho gave Kelly a somber look before responding. He glanced at Kelly's Corvette that the Homeland Security agent had maneuvered onto the airfield's taxiway and was now parked next to him. Agent Talbert was asleep in the front seat.

"This babe's been flying for nine decades with nary a sputter!" announced Sancho. "How will your pistons be holding up in the year 2100?!" Agent Kelly smiled and nodded. Good answer!

"Here's the deal," Kelly said. "Seems Sheriff Urdano's squad car has gone missing along with the mysterious letter from his father! Donnor and the teachers are trying to find Sheriff Morton and locate the car. But there's urgent news that I must act on right now. Agent Talbert received a fax from the Canadian authorities at Lord Shaffer's dock in Saint John. A shipment of Taste Of Arabia was shipped from Aden, Yemen, to Canada. Five semis loaded with the coffee left the pier and crossed the border into Maine. Thanks, or I should say no thanks, to Vice President Sanders, customs officials just waved them through. Sanders had provided the drivers with signed papers allowing them free passage into America. Port documents say the trucks are headed for Washington, Chicago, San Francisco, Houston, and Phoenix."

"Where are they going in those cities?" asked Sancho.

"Obviously, we know about the one in Phoenix, and thanks to Donnor stealing their semi, that one isn't going anywhere. The FBI is heading there now to seize the truck. But, the paperwork was very vague—no specific delivery addresses were given for any of the cities. The bigger question is 'why' were those cities chosen?"

"What's your guess, Agent Kelly?" asked Mack.

"I think that the people in those cities drink a lot of coffee! Where else could Shaffer do the most damage?"

"That makes sense!" said Mack enthusiastically. "So why are we here? What's your plan?"

"I'm assuming the most coffee drinkers out of those five cities are in San Francisco," responded Kelly. "At this point, I still don't know who to trust, so I don't want to requisition a Homeland Security jet. Mack, I would like you to fly me to San Francisco in this plane."

Mack looked at Sancho, who nodded yes. It was the doctor's plane after all.

"Sancho," continued Kelly, "Agent Talbert is in desperate need of the tungis antidote. You may use my office to administer it. Take the Corvette; the address is saved on my GPS." Sancho nodded again but didn't say anything. He rubbed his temples and was clearly focused on something else.

"What's the matter, Doc?" asked Kelly. "You're not saying much."

"San Francisco. That's what's bothering me. I believe your theory of shipping the coffee to cities that drink a lot of coffee is not correct." Sancho paused and looked up at the sky. The others could see he was deep in thought. No one spoke.

Kelly finally broke the silence. "Why do you think I'm wrong, Doc?"

"A few days ago, I was researching how to best drum up support for lowering the cost of medication in the United States to make it affordable for everyone. I realized that America needed fresh, open-minded politicians who could change laws and make new ones. My thought was to solicit activists that would bring the issue to the forefront during the next national elections. I Googled the areas of the country that donated the most money to political campaigns." Sancho paused again.

"And?!" Agent Kelly couldn't wait any longer!

"And ironically, that's where I've seen those cities listed before. They are the locations that the highest political campaign donations in the US come from. I'm sure of it!"

"So, you're saying Lord Shaffer wants to influence our voters?"

"No, if the voting public all lose their memories, they wouldn't know who to vote for! What I'm saying is that Lord Shaffer wants to put your political arena in chaos! And chaos could cause a revolution!"

"That's insane!" shrieked Kelly. Trying to wrap his head around it, he began to pace in a circle. "No! That's impossible! A revolution?! You've got to be kidding me!"

"After all that's happened this week, I don't think anything is impossible!" inserted Mack.

Sancho and Mack were silent as they watched Agent Kelly walk to his car and pound his fist on the hood. The sound and vibration were loud enough to wake up Agent Talbert in the front seat. Kelly turned back and approached them.

"If you're right about chaos and revolution," stated Kelly, pausing before finishing, "then we need to get to Washington before that semi delivers its contents! Congressmen, senators, and even the president—they all drink a lot of coffee!"

"You need to call and warn somebody!" exclaimed Mack.

"The vice president is part of this scheme. What if some congressmen are also involved?! I can't take the chance. It would put all of you in danger if someone came after me! I can't risk anyone knowing my whereabouts right now, which is why I can't take a commercial jet out of Sky Harbor."

"But It will take us twenty hours to get there in the DC-6! We will need two or three fueling stops, and our top cruising speed is only 150 knots!"

"Then we need to get a move on it, wouldn't you agree?!"

Chapter 54

Friday, April 20, 2018 (4-Shaban-1439)
Sultan Tariq's Palace, Rub' al Khali Desert, Saudi Arabia
3:30 pm Arabian Standard Time

The CIA agent who saved Rick and Bassam pulled Rick back over the ridge of the dune and laid him on his side. He wanted to ensure that Rick's bullet wounds didn't touch the sand. Seconds later, the agent ducked down and pulled Bassam to the ground with him. The agent rolled onto his belly, grabbed the submachine gun, and aimed it towards the palace using only his right hand. With his left, he tossed a canteen to Bassam. There was mass hysteria on the oasis. People were screaming and scattering in all directions!

"Give him a drink, but stay down! Keep your heads below the ridge!" The CIA agent made gestures while he spoke. He wasn't sure how much English the young Arab understood.

Rick groaned in pain. Bassam was wiping the sweat from his forehead with his shirt, but now Rick was getting the chills.

"Sir, we need to get him to Sultan Tariq's personal doctor, or we'll lose him!" Bassam was panicking. He'd seen enough deaths for one day.

"Where is this doctor?!" The agent stopped gesturing. It was obvious Bassam was somewhat fluent in English.

"Down there—look! He's the one putting the sultan's head next to his body!"

The CIA agent observed everyone scurrying away from the site of the beheading except for the man Bassam claimed to be Tariq's doctor. He didn't see any more bodyguards other than the eight he had killed. He had to make a quick decision.

"I'll be right back!" the CIA agent yelled at Bassam, then jumped up and dashed down the opposite side of the dune. Halfway down, he lost his footing in the soft sand and tumbled end-over-end to the edge of the oasis, but he managed to hold tight to his gun. He got up quickly and sprinted to the doctor. Doctor Laghari saw him coming and instinctively stood and raised his arms above his head. The CIA agent stopped a few feet from the doctor and took aim at his heart.

"Up the dune! Now! Move it!" The CIA agent pointed to the ridge where he had come from, and Laghari jogged as fast as he could, but he was out of shape and needed to stop to catch his breath. The agent poked him with the gun barrel. "Not here! Keep moving, damn it!"

With his wobbly legs about to give out near the top of the dune, Laghari glanced at the dead bodyguards. His fear caused an adrenaline rush, and he managed to make it to the ridge, but then collapsed face down on the other side—his feet sticking over the top. Bassam dragged him a few feet, turned him over, then clenched his fists like he was going to punch Laghari in the face. The agent grabbed Bassam and yanked him to the ground.

"What are you doing?! We brought him up here to save a life, not hurt him!"

"I'm sorry," replied Bassam. "But he's a bad person! Anyone who helps Sultan Tariq deserves to die!"

"We'll deal with him later! Right now, he needs to take care of this man's injuries!" The agent grabbed Laghari by his shirt and pulled him into a sitting position. "Fix him! Do you understand?!"

Doctor Laghari nodded and slid next to Rick. He didn't have his medical instruments, but he had a Swiss Army knife and a cigarette lighter. He looked frantically at the CIA agent and muttered, "I need to remove the bullets, but you need to know that this might make him bleed to death."

The agent thought about it for a few seconds, then nodded. "Go ahead! Do it!"

Bassam removed his shirt to give Rick something to lay on, then rolled him on his stomach. Laghari pulled out the smallest blade and sterilized it with his lighter. While the flame was torching the knife, Laghari glanced at Bassam.

"Do you have any tungis on you?" The doctor guessed that Bassam still smoked the leaf every chance he could, but Bassam was shocked by the question. He was surprised anyone knew!

"Yeah, maybe, but it's only because I was going to use it in the next batch of coffee!"

"Bassam, you murdered the sultan! Who is going to care if you were toking on the side?!"

"Why do you need it?" asked the CIA agent.

"I will place it on the wounds once I remove the bullets. It will help stop the bleeding and prevent infection."

"How do you know it will work?"

"I've tried it before. Mixing tungis with coffee is a terrible thing, but the plant also has benefits. I cut myself a few weeks ago, so I put a leaf on the wound, hoping it would work like *aloe vera.* My injury healed within a day! I never told Sultan Tariq. I was planning on escaping soon and hoped to manufacture the leaf as a pharmaceutical drug."

Bassam was speechless. How many others in the sultanate had planned to bolt? He reached into his pocket and took out a plastic bag filled with leaves. He always kept it full and carried it with him wherever he went!

The blade was hot, and Rick gasped in pain before losing consciousness. Laghari removed both bullets, but the makeshift scalpel left gaping holes that were bleeding profusely. Using water from the canteen, the doctor washed the wounds the best he could. Then he placed tungis leaves on each hole and wrapped strips of Bassam's t-shirt tightly around Rick's arm and leg.

Moments later, the first of ten Mi-8TV helicopters landed in the valley opposite the oasis. The cavalry had arrived.

6:00 pm Arabian Standard Time

By sundown, it was all over. Sultan Tariq's palace had been turned to rubble. Lord Shaffer, Yegor, and Sokolov all heard the submachine gun being fired and could see Tariq's bodyguards lying dead on the dune. Yegor commanded Pavel Orlov, aka Bill Clemons, to gather as many hostages as they could get their hands on and drag them back to the palace. Surely, whoever was out there wouldn't harm innocent people, would they? But, as soon as Orlov's squadron stepped outside, they were immediately showered with 7.62 mm projectiles. No survivors.

The men and women of the sultanate who had been ordered to watch the executions all took off running after Bassam beheaded the sultan. While scrambling away, they watched in horror as someone with a machine gun fired his weapon at the bodyguards. They didn't return to their tent homes nestled between the palm trees where some lived, nor the underground cement huts where others resided. They just ran in every direction imaginable!

The CIA agent guessed that the palace was only occupied by international criminals—including the vice president of the United States. He attempted to call NSA Chief Martin Calhoun on his satellite phone, but atmospheric interference was preventing that from happening. The agent had to make a snap decision, or everyone inside Sultan Tariq's residence might escape. He directed the ten choppers to destroy the palace, making sure the underground Taste Of Arabia factory was also demolished. Twenty S-5 rockets hit the royal mansion and leveled it within minutes, then the Mi-8s hightailed it towards the Omani border. This was a top-secret mission, and they needed to be out of the country before the Saudi Air Force spotted them.

The CIA agent swept the oasis with the scope of his gun, looking for survivors. Something caught his eye. The executioner had dug up Zaira from the stoning pit and was dragging her on the ground. She appeared to be alive, but the CIA agent wasn't sure. He followed along with his scope until the executioner laid her next to Isaac

Martinez and Kurt Kellner. The teacher and Isaac were lying face down on a cement slab, arms and legs chained to the ground. Zaira's wrists had been tied behind her back, the customary way to bury someone for a stoning. The executioner knelt, prostrated, and kissed the ground. He was offering a prayer to Allah.

A moment later, the slayer stood up and reached for his sword. The CIA agent zeroed in but was afraid to shoot. His weapon was not completely accurate from this distance. He might accidentally kill the kids or the teacher—or all of them!

Bassam had been watching raptly. He saw the executioner begin to raise the sword over his head and take aim on the neck of the teacher. "Shoot! Shoot him!" Bassam cried out.

Time for another snap decision. The CIA agent aimed high to keep stray bullets from hitting Zaira, Isaac, and Kurt, then pulled the trigger and emptied his magazine. He missed. The executioner paused with the sword lifted at its peak and glanced up to the ridge. The agent could not reload! It was over! The executioner brought the sword down with all the force he could muster.

The momentary hesitation had given enough time for a bullet shot from the opposite direction to enter the back of the executioner's skull and emerge through his eye socket. The jolt caused the sword's arc to deviate slightly and come slicing down on Kurt's shoulder blade. The executioner wobbled and fell, his knees crashing down on Kurt's back. He laid dead on top of the teacher like a heavy blanket. Kurt's scapula was crushed, and blood was spurting from the wound, but he was alive thanks to a man who was standing thirty feet away and lowering his gun.

It was Cliff Bullard.

Chapter 55

Friday, April 20, 2018 (4-Shaban-1439)
Sultan Tariq's Private Runway
Rub' al Khali Desert, Saudi Arabia
6:30 pm Arabian Standard Time

Doctor Laghari's private clinic inside the palace was blown to pieces along with any type of medical equipment or drugs he needed to help the injured. However, the CIA agent guessed that Air Force Two probably had some sort of sickroom onboard, and he was right. The residents of the sultanate were long gone by the time Zaira, Isaac, and Kurt were rounded up and moved to the airplane.

Once everyone was on board, the CIA agent jogged back over the ridge to his ATV, then hurtled his way over three more dunes until he reached the heavy-lift Mi-26T helicopter he had flown in on. His pilot had been told to wait for him, and when the agent arrived, the pilot was helping thirty or more of Sultan Tariq's refugees load up. The pilot had seen the frightened men, women, and children running away from the oasis towards certain death. The Rub' al Khali wasteland would have eaten them alive!

The chopper was capable of transporting eighty passengers and up to twenty tons of cargo. NSA Chief Calhoun had requisitioned one for the task force, and ironically Vice President Sanders signed off on it because the president had not been available. Sanders hadn't asked any questions; the helicopter only cost $10,000,000—a drop in the bucket for US taxpayers! The powerful whirlybird had been waiting for Calhoun to pick it up from the factory in Krasnodar, Russia, where it was built, but until now, the NSA chief hadn't had the time. Instead, its first mission would originate right from the Russian plant and fly directly to Sultan Tariq's compound along with five CIA and five KGB attack helicopters. Calhoun had given the order to destroy the palace and everyone inside leaving as little collateral damage as possible. He had no plans to arrest anyone—long, drawn-out international trials would be frustrating for him. Kill all of them now and answer questions later.

The Mi-26T lifted off and within a few minutes landed on Tariq's private runway next to Air Force Two and its unfixable landing gear. The CIA agent boarded the vice president's plane while the helicopter pilot stayed with the terrified escapees. The last place they wanted to be was back on the sultan's oasis!

Dr. Laghari treated Zaira first. Rocks had broken four of her cranial bones and three facial skeletal bones. She was suffering from a concussion and had several lacerations. Laghari placed tungis leaves around Zaira's face and bandaged her head. Next, he ministered to Kurt's wounds. He applied the rest of Bassam's tungis leaves to the sword cut, and the bleeding stopped at once. There was nothing he could do for Kurt's broken scapula other than to immobilize it with a sling. Miraculously, Rick's gashes were already healing with no infection in sight. The only thing Dr. Laghari couldn't seem to fix was Rick and Cliff's memory loss, which was getting worse by the minute. Without treatment soon, they would have irreparable amnesia. Unfortunately, no one knew of a cure.

But then, with his hands supporting his head and looking at nothing but his own two feet, Cliff muttered two words, "Donnor Bolten."

Chapter 56

Friday, April 20, 2018 (4-Shaban-1439)
Homeland Security, Phoenix, Arizona
8:00 am Pacific Daylight Time

Agent Steve Talbert suddenly opened his eyes and stared up at the ceiling. He was lying on a cot in Earl Kelly's office at Homeland Security in downtown Phoenix. Talbert was tired and had an excruciating headache, but he felt more alert than ever before. He glanced at an unknown man sitting at a desk punching keys on a computer. That was the same man who had injected something into his arm a few hours ago. Talbert's memory was coming back. Then the office door opened and in walked a man wearing a beige sports coat and a massive sunburn followed by a young lady in a gray business suit.

The man glanced at Agent Talbert as he moved towards the desk. The young lady stood in the doorway. Sancho saw him coming and stood up.

"I'm Special Agent Bob Billings, and you must be Dr. Sancho Gomez," said the man in the sports coat. He turned and motioned at the lady. "And I believe you've already met Gretta Paulson, our receptionist. She got the message from Earl that you would be using his office, but he didn't say why. I'm supposed to be on vacation this week, but Gretta said it was urgent that I came in. Perhaps you could tell us what you're doing here?" Agent Billings shook hands with Sancho using a grip that the good doctor thought would rearrange his metacarpals!

"It's a long story that would best be told by Agent Kelly," said Sancho. "But I need for you to get me to London as fast as humanly possible! Trust me when I say that Earl would approve."

"London?!" Are you kidding me?! And why would I trust you?!"

"Earl said to do what we can for Dr. Gomez," inserted Gretta. "He said he would fill us in as soon as possible."

"Did Earl know the doctor would want to fly to Europe?! I've been on vacation all week! I need some more information!"

"If I had the time, I would tell you everything, but I don't!" said Sancho frantically. Then he took a deep breath to control himself. "Look, I understand why you wouldn't trust me. But, you have been hired to protect this country. I can assure you that this is a matter of national security! Please just gamble and roll the dice!"

Agent Billings was angered by that remark, but he refrained from responding. He needed a moment to think about it. Gretta piped in again. "Earl's our chief, Bob. His words to me were to give carte blanche to Dr. Gomez. I think we need to do it."

"Alright, alright, damn it! I need to get on the phone to Vice President Sanders' office for approval to requisition a jet. We don't have any readily available for our immediate use. It will take just a few—"

Sancho cut in, "No! You can't call the vice president!"

"What do you mean by that?! He oversees Homeland Security. I can't get you an airplane without approval from his office!"

Sancho wasn't sure what to say. Chances were slim the agent would believe him if he told Billings that Vice President Sanders was involved in an international crime organization. He decided to try a different approach.

"Perhaps this will explain some things." Sancho turned the computer screen around and turned up the speaker volume so everyone could hear the video that was playing. Homeland Security monitored the Al Jazeera Media Network closely for breaking news out of the Middle East that could pose a threat to the United States.

The reporter was broadcasting live from Al Jazeera headquarters in Doha, Qatar:

"... not sure exactly, but because it has happened to three men, authorities are not ruling out foul play.

"If you just joined us, we have breaking news out of London. Three ambassadors to England, including Saudi Arabia's Mohammed bin Nawwaf bin Abdulaziz Al Saud, have been hospitalized with what doctors are calling transient global amnesia. None have sustained any visible injuries to the head, which has baffled hospital researchers. Ironically, the three embassies are all located on the same block in London's Kensington W8 neighborhood. Scotland Yard is investigating the possibility that the ambassadors have been poisoned, but they are not confirming that the poisoning was malicious. Other residents of the wealthy neighborhood have been notified and asked to have an immediate examination to determine if they may have been poisoned. The most prolific resident of the area is Lord John Shaffer, who is away on a retreat to an undisclosed location; however, his personal secretary expressed extreme shock and promised that Lord Shaffer would happily assist Scotland Yard in any way that he could.

"In other news ..."

Sancho looked up from the computer screen, and his eyes met Agent Billings. "I can help those ambassadors, and I believe I'm the only one who can. If they don't have treatment soon, they will suffer permanent memory loss."

"Okay, I believe that you possess some power or whatever to help those men, but they are in England," responded Agent Billings. "How do they pose a threat to our national security?"

Just then, a demanding voice came from the cot. "Get him a jet," stated Agent Talbert firmly. "Time is of the essence. I will fill you in on what's happening! Just get him a jet now!"

Agent Billings wasn't happy about everyone giving him orders, but if this is what Agent Kelly wanted, then he decided to go with it. "Okay, I will requisition a plane. Gretta, call someone in Sanders' office and get approval while I—"

Talbert cut in, "No, don't call the vice president's office! I know this is out of the ordinary, but I will explain as soon as we get Dr. Gomez on his way."

Agent Billings was about to respond when the Al Jazeera reporter stopped him in his tracks.

"More breaking news! This just in from the prime minister's press office in Lisbon: a Boeing C-32 aircraft that had entered Portuguese airspace over Lajes Air Force Base in the Azores early this morning has been lost somewhere in the Rub' al Khali desert. Portuguese officials believe the jet was Air Force Two, which is Vice President Sanders' personal airplane. When the American C-32 didn't respond to communications from Lajes Air Command, a fighter pilot was summoned to protect Portuguese airspace. The pilot caught up with Air Force Two near the Red Sea and noticed that the Boeing aircraft was being followed by an unknown US fighter jet flying at an incredibly low and dangerous altitude, presumably to avoid detection by Saudi AWACS planes. It appeared that the US fighter jet may have inexplicably shot down Air Force Two somewhere near the Yemeni or Omani border. The US plane, believed to be an F-15, disappeared from the Portuguese pilot's view and is presumed to have crashed along with Air Force Two. The exact location of the accident is unknown at this time, and there is no word whether Vice President Sanders was aboard the aircraft. Portuguese Prime Minister António Costa has contacted President Randall Thompson; however, the White House has refused to comment until they receive confirmation of the crash. Saudi Arabian search and rescue teams have been deployed to the area, but they fear it could take some time to locate Air Force Two in the harsh and desolate desert. Stay tuned for more information as it comes in. This is Haniya Nader reporting."

Everyone in Agent Kelly's office was stunned and speechless. Then Agent Billings looked at Talbert and Sancho and asked, "Does this have something to do with you not wanting me to call the vice president's office?"

Chapter 57

Friday, April 20, 2018 (4-Shaban-1439)
Sultan Tariq's Private Runway
Rub' al Khali Desert, Saudi Arabia
7:30 pm Arabian Standard Time

"What did he mean by that?" asked Dr. Laghari. "Donnor Bolten."

Rick glanced at Cliff with a puzzled look on his face. He seemed to remember something. "No, I think he means Holten, not Bolten." Then he stared at the CIA special agent for a moment. "And I know you from somewhere, but I can't place it! What's your name?"

"I'm Special Agent Marv Cullins."

"No," replied Rick meekly, scratching his head. "That's not it. I don't think I know a Marv Cullins."

Special Agent Marv Cullins ignored Rick and glanced at Cliff. "Do you mean Donnor Colten?"

Cliff looked up and smiled at him. "Yeah, I think maybe that's his name. But I can't remember why I said it."

Rick was perplexed. How did the CIA agent know Donnor Colten? He wasn't sure how he knew Donnor! But he remembered something. "Donnor drank coffee with us in that truck."

Cliff responded, "What truck?"

"The one in Gila Bend. Something about that truck and Gila Bend! What is it?!"

Bassam was standing nearby and was listening. "Gila Bend is in Arizona, in the USA."

Agent Marv Cullins shot Bassam a baffled glance. "How do you know about Gila Bend?"

"The O'Connells. I think they were triplets, but maybe just siblings. They were some sort of chemists that worked here for a while but then were sent to Gila Bend. Who could forget that name?!"

Dr. Laghari added, "Yes, that's right! Lord Shaffer moved them to Gila Bend to do research on memory loss. They might know a cure for the amnesia these two are suffering from! And I have their cell phone numbers stored on my satellite phone."

"Yes, the O'Connells," said the special agent to himself. "Why didn't I think of that?!"

University of Arizona Hospital, Tucson, Arizona
8:45 am Pacific Daylight Time

Mackenzie O'Connell was dozing on a couch in the lounge at the University of Arizona Hospital when she received the call from Special Agent Marv Cullins. A TV connected to the wall was tuned to CNN, but the volume had been muted. It had been a long couple of days, and all the O'Connells were exhausted. They had administered the antidote to Rebecca Grimm, Gordy Owens, Ken Smith, Joe Freeman, and Roger Bennett. All seemed to have regained their memories and were now recovering from severe headaches and fatigue. While she touched the green answer button on her iPhone, breaking news was scrolling on the bottom of the television screen. Mackenzie read it, but the words didn't register right away. She was still trying to wake up.

"Mackenzie, this is Special Agent Cullins. I don't have time to explain, but I have a couple of questions. Have you three found a cure for the Taste Of Arabia toxin?"

"Why?" asked Mackenzie groggily. She was trying to regain her faculties. "Where are you?"

"I'm at Tariq's palace, or I should say what's left of Tariq's palace. Long story! Anyway, please answer my question. Two men with me have been infected, and I need to make sure they don't permanently lose their memories. Like I said, I'll explain later, but I need to know!"

"Yes, there is an herbal remedy that works, but we didn't find it. A doctor named Sancho Gomez created it."

"You're sure it works?!"

"Positive! We've now tested it on several people; it definitely works!"

"How do I get in touch with this Dr. Gomez?"

"Do you know a man named Earl Kelly?"

"You mean the director of Homeland Security in Phoenix?"

"Yes."

"I know of him. We've never met."

"He has been investigating the same thing you have. Dr. Gomez is with him. I'll get you his phone number. Hold on." Mackenzie switched to her phone contact list and wrote down Kelly's number. She was about to switch back when the breaking news byline caught her attention. She was stunned and stared at the TV screen, then remembered Agent Cullins was holding on the other line.

"Here's the number: 480-626-3000."

"Okay, thanks! I'll be in—"

Mackenzie cut him off. "Are you aware that Vice President Sanders' plane is missing in the Rub' al Khali and has presumably been shot down by a US fighter jet?!"

"I need to go! Sorry!" Cullins was about to hang up when Mackenzie shouted into the receiver.

"He's there, isn't he?! The vice president is with you!"

Mackenzie's line went dead. She stared back up at the screen. Goosebumps covered her arms and legs.

*****

The news of Air Force Two missing in the Rub' al Khali was now being broadcast globally. And worse, the story was wrong; Air Force Two hadn't been shot down by a US fighter jet. Soon the Saudi military would be swarming the area searching for the vice president's plane. Cullins wasn't ready to explain to the world why a joint mission of the Russian KGB and the American CIA was taking place in Saudi Arabia. He decided that he needed to get the Mi-26T chopper full of Tariq's refugees out of the country before the Saudi's found them. The Saudi's would end up transporting the exiles to Riyadh, and the CIA would never have the chance to question them. The attack helicopters that blew up the palace were safely back in Russia. The transport chopper was now in flight to the same destination.

The call from Agent Cullins to Agent Earl Kelly's cell phone had been forwarded to his office and picked up by his receptionist, Gretta Paulson. She said Kelly was flying to Washington, DC, and had no cellular reception on board his plane. Gretta also refused to tell Cullins why Kelly was flying to Washington. That was top secret, and only Kelly could reveal the reason. When Cullins asked the whereabouts of Dr. Sancho Gomez, she slipped and told him he had taken off for London an hour ago with Agent Bob Billings on a chartered Learjet.

The Learjet was one of three owned by SBSNN Corporation that was located at Mesa's Falcon Field. They always had one pilot assigned to the office for emergency purposes. The other two pilots each owned a condo in Scottsdale and could be at Falcon Field with an hour's notice. Homeland Security had no jets of their own, so when agents needed to fly on business, they used SBSNN. Over the years, Agent Billings and Agent Kelly knew the pilots well and even formed friendships. Poker games were held once a month.

"You've been flying with us for several years, but I don't remember taking you to London, mate," said Pilot Gary Peters. Agent Billings was sitting in the copilot's seat, which was rarely used unless flights lasted over six hours. Billings was a certified multi-aircraft aviator, so when he was traveling on long trips, he named himself the copilot.

"Never been there, my friend," responded Billings.

"If you have some extra time, I'll show you my hood." Gary was from London and still had a strong British accent.

"How did a chimney sweep fella like yourself end up landing a job in America? Shouldn't you be flying Mary Poppins around on an umbrella or something!" Billings laughed at his own humor, something he was very good at.

"Aye, matey, wish I could live back home! I miss dancing in the fog! But at least my paychecks are still in pounds and not dollars."

"What do you mean by that?"

"SBSNN is headquartered in London, not the US." As soon as he said it, Peters wished he hadn't. The trivial chitchat had gone a bit too far. He let that one slip.

"SBSNN is headquartered in London?" responded Billings curiously. "Now that's strange. Why would Homeland Security use a foreign company for transportation when there are plenty of American companies they could use? Taxpayers would scream if they knew that!"

The radio beeped. Pilot Peters was thankful for the interruption.

"Yeah, I don't know. Uh, let me get this." He put on his headphones and switched on the receiver. "Okay, just a minute." He took off the headphones and handed them to Billings.

Special Agent Cullins identified himself as the caller and immediately insisted that if there was anyone on board the Learjet within earshot, including the pilot, Billings should not repeat anything nor ask any questions. Cullins said what he was about to tell him was "beyond" top secret! For the next ten minutes, Billings just nodded and uttered a few yeses.

Then Billings switched off the receiver and handed the headphones back to Pilot Peters. "Change in plans, Gary," he said. "Set a course for Saudi Arabia."

"May I ask why?"

"Sorry, I can't tell you, ol' chap. We're headed for an unmarked landing strip in the Rub' al Khali. I have the GPS coordinates. You'll have to make an extra refueling stop. I'll let Dr. Gomez know there's a change in plans."

Agent Billings walked out of the cockpit and into the cabin. Sancho glanced up, and Billings put a finger to his lips. He didn't want the pilot to hear what he was about to say. Then Billings whispered a succinct version of the conversation he just had with Special Agent Cullins. Sancho nodded.

Meanwhile, Pilot Gary Peters used his Russian-made Apple watch to send a text.

Tariq's Private Runway, Rub' al Khali Desert, Saudi Arabia 8:30 pm Arabian Standard Time

Special Agent Marv Cullins hung up the satellite phone, sat down, and nervously twiddled his thumbs. He pondered what he should do for the next fifteen hours before the Learjet arrived. Would Rick and Cliff last that long? Dr. Laghari suggested giving them more Taste Of Arabia coffee. He hoped doing so would keep their minds active and avoid permanent amnesia from settling in until the antidote arrived. He guessed the recovery time would be much longer, and the side effects much more severe. It was an extremely risky maneuver; an overdose of the active tungis in the coffee could cause the brain to completely shut down, and death would then occur within minutes. Cullins reluctantly gave the okay.

Chapter 58

Friday, April 20, 2018
Gila Bend Charter School, Gila Bend, Arizona
10:30 am Pacific Daylight Time

Ralph Hayes' lifeless body was lying face down in a tray of sulfuric acid next to his wife, Philomena, and *Arizona Republic* reporter, Smitty Douglas. The murderer could have used a bullet and ended Ralph's life quickly, but the acid had more entertainment value for him. Ralph had stormed into the school the previous night to confront his wife and school board president, Abe Fitzgerald, who he assumed were having an affair. As Ralph walked inside the front door, he was knocked unconscious by a baseball bat, then dragged to the photography darkroom inside the science lab.

Meanwhile, Abe had been tied to a leather rolling chair in Principal Perez's office. The killer had drugged him with Ambien, and he immediately fell asleep. The next morning, after a long evening filled with dreadful nightmares, Abe groggily looked up to see a man pointing a gun at him.

"You still don't know me, do you?" asked the man holding the pistol. Abe shook his head no. He smelled something foul and looked down. There was dried vomit on his pant legs, but Abe couldn't remember how it got there. Then he gave a strange look at the computer screen in front of him and realized the web page was open to his own Gmail account. Abe had no recollection of signing in. Neatly typed on the screen waiting to be sent was a suicide note that he didn't remember typing, which was because he hadn't typed it! The man holding the gun had done it for him. Fitzgerald read the email and gasped:

To Whom It May Concern:

I have failed as the president of the school board, and I can no longer live with myself! After receiving low test score results from the Department of Education, Principal Perez and I conspired to blame the illegal immigrant children instead of ourselves. They were smart kids, but we never gave them a chance to succeed. So, we called in ICE to raid the school, but things fell apart, and Pablo Hernandez was shot and killed in his car while trying to stop them. Pablo was a nice man, but he was an illegal, too!

Principal Perez escaped with some teachers who think he is innocent, but he is not. Hopefully, he will be arrested! As for me, my pride and reputation have been destroyed, so I am taking my own life by setting the school on fire with me in it.

Goodbye forever!

Abe Fitzgerald

"None of this is true!" yelled Fitzgerald as he struggled to loosen the ropes wrapped around his body and the chair. "At least I don't think they're true! I don't even remember what Principal Perez looks like, but I remember he was an honest man! Why are you doing this?!"

While Abe was asleep, the gunman had grabbed two five-gallon cans of gasoline from the bus barn and poured a trail of the flammable liquid throughout the school hallways. Now, with Abe wide awake and eyes bulging in fear, the man clicked *Send* on the computer screen. The email was sent to the police station and to the other four members of the school board.

Then the gunman poured a chemical on a cloth handkerchief and stuffed it into Abe's mouth. The board president gagged and passed out. The man untied Abe, lit a match, tossed it on the gasoline, and walked calmly out the front door to the parking lot. He waved at Myra Adams, who was getting in her car across the street. She smiled and waved back.

Captain Ned Segura heard the ding and looked at the computer screen. He and Sergeant Pete Ruben had returned to the police station after drinking coffee with Abe Fitzgerald yesterday morning. As the day wore on, so did their minds. Both forgot to go home last night; instead, they slept at their desks in the stationhouse. The ding woke Captain Segura from a long stupor.

Segura looked over and saw Sergeant Ruben sitting with his head lying sideways on the desktop calendar pad. He was gently snoring. Then Segura looked back at the computer screen. He vaguely recalled that if he moved that thing called a mouse and clicked it on the email byline, it would open. It worked! He skimmed over the words, then did a double-take and re-read it carefully. Segura got up and shook Ruben until he awoke.

"Huh?! What's the matter?!" muttered the startled sergeant. He looked at the man who was standing over him but couldn't quite place who he was.

"We've got a problem, Corporal Tubby!" replied Segura. "Take a look at this." He motioned for Ruben to look at his computer screen. Ruben didn't even realize that he wasn't a corporal. Nor did he realize that his name wasn't Tubby. The sergeant read the email.

"It's a suicide note," said Ruben as he studied the email trying to grasp what it meant. He checked the time on the bottom of the screen. "And it was sent a couple of minutes ago."

"Who is this Fitzgerald guy?" asked Segura.

"I think it's the man I had coffee with yesterday. Weren't you with me? He's like the janitor or something at the school. I wonder why he cares so much about the test scores?"

"Good question. But if he just sent this email, we should get over to the school right away before he starts the fire."

"You're right, Andy!" Ned wasn't sure that was his partner's name, but then again, he wasn't sure it wasn't! Ruben and Segura started for the door, but then both stopped and gave a confused look at each other.

"Where's the school?" they blurted at the same time.

Chapter 59

Saturday, April 21, 2018 (5-Shaban-1439)
Sultan Tariq's Private Runway
Rub' al Khali Desert, Saudi Arabia
1:45 pm Arabian Standard Time

The tiny infirmary aboard Air Force Two was made for two patients at a time. A couple of cots were attached to the fuselage wall and could be pulled down when needed. Today, Zaira, Isaac, and Kurt were moved to comfortable seats in the cabin that folded down into beds. They were sore but recovering. Rick and Cliff had been drinking more coffee trying to keep their minds alert to avoid permanent comatose, but both had fallen asleep on the cots an hour before Sancho and Agent Billings arrived.

Dr. Laghari had medically prepped Rick and Cliff using intravenous tubes and had kept them hydrated while waiting for Sancho to land. He also hooked up a device to monitor their vital signs. The Learjet landed on the private runway and stopped just a few yards short of the crippled Boeing C-32 plane. While the midday sun scorched the desert, Sancho was hustled on board Air Force Two.

Quickly, Sancho administered the antidote and waited. He leaned against the wall and kept a close eye on his patients' heart rhythm and brain voltage patterns. As Sancho discussed the effects of tungis with Dr. Laghari, Agent Cullins and Agent Billings stood a few feet behind the doctors listening carefully and taking notes. Dr. Laghari's description of Sultan Tariq's surreptitious venture was mindboggling!

As if connected by the same heart, both Rick's and Cliff's blood pressure dropped to 65/35, a clear sign of extreme hypotension. Dr. Laghari increased the flow of crystalloid through the intravenous fluid resuscitator while Sancho prepared for shock treatment. Then amazingly, the diastolic and systolic readings slowly rose to a normal range. A few minutes later, Rick and Cliff opened their eyes at the same time and rubbed their temples hard with their fists. A throbbing migraine would be minuscule compared to the pain they were now feeling.

Agent Marv Cullins let out a sigh of relief, and with a huge smile, he took a step towards Rick. Sancho stepped in front of him.

"A bear hug right now is not what the doctor, or I should say doctors, have ordered!" Sancho was grinning. Kurt, Isaac, and Zaira overheard the commotion and hurried to the infirmary. So did Bassam.

Rick looked wearily around at all the faces, and his memory was returning slowly. He still couldn't remember his own name but strangely was able to recollect who the man Sancho was holding back. It was the CIA special agent that just saved his life.

"Cyrus? Is that you? What in the world are you doing here?"

"Right now, trying to make sure you live to teach history in Gila Bend for many more years to come, my friend!"

"You two know each other?!" Sancho was confused. So was Agent Billings. Meanwhile, Dr. Laghari gave Rick and Cliff ice packs for their headaches.

Rick smiled at Sancho and remarked, "This man is Cyrus McCool. He's the band conductor at the school where I work."

Cyrus, Kurt, Isaac, and Zaira all laughed. Kurt, Isaac, and Zaira found out a few hours ago that their beloved athletic director, Cyrus McCool, was working undercover for the CIA using the alias Marv Cullins.

"Actually, I'm the AD, Rick, but I've been known to toot my own horn like a band conductor!"

Rick recognized Kurt, Isaac, and Zaira in the back of the room. He smiled, then noticed Zaira's injuries, and he sprang up in the cot and gasped. Rick remembered seeing the girl being stoned and realized that it had been his own student. He glanced at Kurt who just nodded. It was all coming back fast.

Seconds later, Cliff lurched forward, and everyone looked at him.

"What's that?! Listen!" he yelped.

"The Learjet!" shouted Sancho. "It's taking off!" He and Agent Billings dashed to the open door of Air Force Two's fuselage and watched as the Lear's belly soared above them. Gary Peters was a friend of Billings, but Billings had been curious when the pilot told him that the company they used to fly Homeland Security agents was based in London. That didn't make sense. Now he knew Peters and the charter corporation were frauds.

"This isn't good," said Billings gravely.

*****

There was no election process and no quibbling about the outcome. Cliff Bullard was in charge. Agent Billings and Cyrus McCool (aka Special Agent Marv Cullins) both knew the ex-colonel had more experience during times of crisis than anyone else onboard the inoperative Air Force Two jet. They needed to get out of Saudi Arabia quickly if Sancho's antidote were to save America. If the Saudi search party found them, they would be detained indefinitely while answers were being sorted out. But was Colonel Bullard back to full capacity? Because Cliff and Rick had drunk more coffee to stay awake, Sancho said to give it another hour or so for the effects of tungis to wear off.

The nervous group sat quietly in the cabin, no one wishing to speak. They were all exhausted, but it was impossible to sleep. The young man from Yemen stood up to address them but dropped his head to avoid eye contact. He was ashamed.

"Taste Of Arabia," uttered Bassam. Everyone stared at him. "I'm to blame for everything! I was the one who mixed the tungis plant with the coffee beans in Sadah to hide it from the religious police! I didn't know it would make people lose their memories—I really didn't!"

"Where is Sadah?" asked Agent Billings.

"It's in Yemen near the Sarawat Mountains. We, the kids there mostly, smoke tungis to get high. I was working as a coffee bean roaster when the mutawa raided the place. I ditched the tungis into the roasting oven with the coffee beans. The taste was sensational, but right away, three doctors from the United States who volunteered in the local hospital figured out that something in the coffee was causing memory loss."

"O'Connells," inserted Cyrus. "Their last name is O'Connell, and they are siblings. They're molecular geneticists—not doctors."

"Yes, that's right! You know them?"

"Yes, I do but go on."

"Well, in a nutshell, a man name Lord Shaffer bought our little factory and found out that tungis mixed with coffee created a chemical reaction that caused memory loss. He also found out that I was the one who first roasted the mixture, so he brought me here to the oasis. He and Sultan Tariq were partners. Tariq was the devil! He was a monster, I'm telling you! We had executions of innocent people every week!"

Bassam paused for a moment and looked up at the sky, seemingly saying a short prayer. Then he muttered in a low voice, "Which is why I murdered Sultan Tariq."

Rick was listening but having a difficult time following along. The pain in his arm and leg was excruciating, and his headache was intense. He glanced at McCool.

"Cyrus, obviously you told Kurt, Isaac, and Zaira, but tell me. Why are you here?"

"I'm not who you think I am, Rick. My AD job is a cover for my real job. I'm with the CIA. I head up a small task force of twenty men who answer only to National Security Chief Martin Calhoun. No other CIA agents even know we exist! Our task force is assigned to monitor America's political power structure to prevent and rid our nation of treasonable acts by unscrupulous people."

"Wait," said Rick. He taught history and knew about politics, but he was struggling to remember specifics. "Doesn't the national security chief answer only to the president? What if the president is involved in treason?"

"Good question, Rick. Even the president doesn't know about our task force. Calhoun wants to keep it that way. Not that he doesn't trust the president, just that he doesn't want to start a leak."

"You are obviously here because of the coffee, right? Why did the CIA place you at Gila Bend Charter School? Strange, aren't you from Gila Bend?"

"Yes, born and raised there. That's only a wild coincidence, though. Calhoun received a tip from his KGB counterpart in Moscow that Directorate Chief Yegor Bovnik and General Leonid Sokolov were secretly involved in a coffee business with Lord Shaffer of England. The KGB created their own task force to investigate and found that Shaffer had been making frequent calls to Vice President Sanders on his private line at the White House. Thus, the reason for the tip. Our task force found out that Lord Shaffer made several flights to Gila Bend without filing flight plans, which sparked curiosity about what he was doing in our tiny town. I was already in Gila Bend investigating another possible crime, so Calhoun ordered me to switch and see if I could find out what Shaffer was involved in. The CIA and the KGB would monitor all of Shaffer's flights out of London, so when it appeared he was headed for Gila Bend, they gave me a few hours' notice.

"Twice, I followed him from the Gila Bend airport to the nursing home. He would call a taxi and have the driver wait. He never stayed long. The next time he landed, I was waiting for him in our Gila Bend school van. I pretended I didn't know who he was, but I offered him a ride into town. He took me up on it, and I quickly befriended him on the drive to the nursing home. I offered to drive him back to the airport, and he said yes. We stopped at Sofia's for some homemade tamales and a couple of margaritas, then he offered me a job. He asked if I made a lot of money working for the school district, and I said no. He wanted to know if I was interested in driving part-time for him. He would pay me $10,000 a week, and I could keep my AD job. The only thing was I couldn't tell anyone what I was doing. I said sure, and one thing led to another, which is how I found out about the tungis-laced coffee.

"Rick, I was outside the semi-truck you were handcuffed in at Love's."

It was starting to come back to Rick. He could only recall bits and pieces, but as each minute passed, his mind was becoming clearer. "You were arguing with someone! I remember!"

"His name was Barney Kinkel, a big shot at Zefron in Mesa." Cliff perked up when he heard his boss's name.

Cyrus continued, "I wasn't arguing—I was just pretending to be angry. I was asking probing questions to see if he would tell me something he shouldn't. That's how I pieced together everything—by listening closely while transporting these crooks around the state."

"You said you were placed at Gila Bend for something else. What other problems does our small town have that needs the help of the CIA? You said you investigate political corruption, so why Gila Bend? We don't have any politicians down there."

"Yeah, I'm afraid we do, but no one in town knows about it." Cyrus then went silent.

Then Rick's memory of being handcuffed inside the semi returned. He nodded. "Senator Rothschild's illegitimate son is Vice President Sanders. That's what you were investigating, wasn't it?"

Cyrus nodded back at Rick. But his mission wasn't complete, and he wasn't sure how much to tell the others. Then Rick thought of something. "What happened to Barney Kinkel and those two tough guys with German accents?"

"I drove the school van into the Salt River with them in it! Fortunately, I escaped. They are either rotting away on the bottom of the river or washed up on shore and now food for the rattlesnakes. After hibernation, those gorgeous reptiles are always very hungry, you know!" There was no love lost for Kinkel, Schultz, and Schoenholtz.

Cliff was regaining his memory quickly. "How did you know where to find us?"

"We intercepted communication from the Portuguese Air Force and pinpointed an approximate crash zone. We flew a CIA jet to Krasnodar, Russia, which was where our joint mission began. Then we teamed up with the KGB, destroyed Tariq's palace, and hustled the refugees out of the desert."

"Who's we?" asked Rick. "How many agents do you have in the Gila Bend area?"

"Only one you may know," replied Cyrus.

"Who is it?"

"Sheriff Morton from Pima County down in Ajo. He's a double agent like me. And he is also the pilot who flew the Mi-26 helicopter with the refugees on board."

"You've got to be kidding!"

"One other thing you all should know." Cyrus looked at Kurt, Isaac, Zaira, and Rick, but hesitated to continue.

"What is it?!" yelped Rick. Everyone became silent, waiting for Cyrus to speak.

"Your assistant principal." Cyrus paused again. He knew what he was about to say would be a shock. "Ted Sanderson is really Ted Sanders. He is Vice President Garrett Sanders' brother. He, too, is the illegitimate son of Senator Rothschild. Mr. Sanderson was running the Taste Of Arabia coffee operation out of the school."

"You've got to be kidding!" exclaimed Kurt, Rick, Isaac, and Zaira in unison.

Chapter 60

Saturday, April 21, 2018
Dulles International Airport, Washington, DC
6:00 am Eastern Standard Time

After refueling stops in Tucumcari, Joplin, and Louisville, Mack landed the Cessna DC-6 at Dulles International Airport in the wee hours of the morning. It wasn't easy. To be close to the city, they wanted to land at Ronald Reagan National Airport in Washington, but it had been closed for security reasons. Until Air Force Two could be found wherever it went down in Saudi Arabia, and the many questions surrounding its disappearance could be answered, all three airports serving the DC area were closed. The two military airfields weren't an option either; Andrews Air Force Base was on high alert and sending medical personnel to the Middle East, while Langley was deploying reconnaissance jets to try and locate Air Force Two. They weren't about to let an old high wing airplane built in the 1920s interfere with their operations. Fortunately, Homeland Security had an office at Dulles Airport, and Special Agent Earl Kelly talked the supervisor into opening a small runway for the DC-6 to land. He said it was a matter of life and death but gave no specifics.

The supervisor let Agent Kelly use his personal 1965 royal blue Ford Mustang with the assurance that Earl brings the car back in the same condition it was in when he left. Kelly said he had a red Corvette back in Arizona he would use as collateral, and the supervisor grinned and wished him luck, even though he didn't know what Earl was up to. Mack hopped into the passenger seat, and they were off.

"Where are we going?" asked Mack.

"To the US Customs and Border Protection office on Ninth Street. They should have a record of license plate numbers and the cargo being hauled for trucks crossing the border in Maine. Destinations and amount of cargo dropped off at each location is also required, as is a signature from a person at the drop off who received the cargo. Those signatures are permanently kept in a database at the Ninth Street office."

"That's a ton of signatures!" exclaimed Mack.

"It's a humungous hard drive!"

Kelly floored the accelerator, and the blue Mustang roared down Highway 267 at speeds topping 120 mph. With the airport closed and the sun still tucked under the horizon to the east, the road was almost free of vehicles. But that luxury ended when the 267 merged with Interstate 66 in Falls Church, and the speedy Saturday rush hour traffic suddenly morphed to a thudding halt. All Virginia roads within a five-mile radius of the Pentagon had just been closed as a security precaution. No one was moving because the detours hadn't been established. Kelly pounded the steering wheel in frustration. Mack pushed his seat back and decided to take a nap. He couldn't remember the last time he slept.

7:30 am Eastern Standard Time

Every major news network in the world was now reporting the disappearance of Air Force Two and the unknown condition of Vice President Sanders. The mood was grim as parents pulled into the parking lot at John Quincy Adams Charter School for the annual breakfast awards program. Senators, members of Congress, and even three Supreme Court justices had either children or grandkids who attended JQA. Usually, the breakfast had perfect parent attendance—it was the one time of the year kids were more important than political wrangling. And today, President Thompson was the guest speaker.

Student Council Advisor Zella Norris wasn't going to miss this event. She had given birth to her first child a little over twenty-four hours ago, and her obstetrician wanted Zella to stay in the hospital until Sunday. But the breakfast awards were always the school's main attraction, and her student council students would be making scrambled eggs once again. A pediatric nurse offered to watch the newborn if Zella agreed to return at once after the program and stay the night in the hospital. Zella called an Uber and stopped at Mickey's Bakery to pick up some donuts, then hurried to the school cafeteria to start brewing coffee. She had plenty of java—her classroom was full of boxes of a new brand called Taste Of Arabia! She didn't think that the man from London who was paying her a fortune to secretly store the coffee would mind if a few boxes were missing. Zella had no idea why he wanted to keep it at JQA school, but she wasn't about to turn down the thousands of dollars he paid her to do it. There was so much coffee that she had to rent a storage unit next to U-Haul to stockpile everything that didn't fit into her room.

The program went off without a hitch. Every student received some sort of award. The politicians and judges momentarily forgot about the plight of Air Force Two as they proudly watched their kids and grandchildren walk across the stage. President Thompson arrived in a limo near the end of the ceremony surrounded by secret service agents. He was supposed to kick off the awards presentation but was unable to come early enough due to the situation with the vice president. Thompson gave an impassioned ten-minute speech that addressed patriotism and encouraged the future JQA graduates to pursue careers where they could serve others. Then he joined the parents for a cup of coffee. Because the coffee was delicious, he decided to have a second cup. Then a third. By the time the breakfast ended, over one hundred legislators and three Supreme Court justices had drunk enough coffee to keep them wide awake for several days!

By noon, the parking lot was empty except for the student council parents who were waiting for their kids to clean up. By then, Zella was long gone. Right after the program ended, she had locked her room and called another Uber. Her hungry baby was delighted to see her!

12:00 pm Eastern Standard Time

"I found it!" said Agent Earl Kelly as he touched the computer screen. "Five trucks owned by SBSNN Corporation out of London picked up a shipment of coffee originating from Aden, Yemen, at their private dock in Saint John. All of them crossed the Maine border from New Brunswick a couple of days ago. The terminuses were logged as Washington, Chicago, San Francisco, Houston, and Phoenix. The semi headed for Washington had only one destination: John Quincy Adams Charter School. The signature on the customs form looks like Zella Norris. It doesn't say what her position is at the school."

Agent Kelly and Mack hadn't moved for three hours from where they had come to a dead stop on Interstate 66. Traffic had been detoured on local roads to McLean, where drivers could use the Beltway north to cross the Potomac. Inching along at a snail's pace, they arrived at the US Customs and Border Protection office at 11:30 am. Being Saturday, only a small staff was working, and unfortunately, the director was attending his son's breakfast awards ceremony at a local charter school. After verifying Agent Kelly's credentials, a staffer reluctantly allowed him access to the mainframe computer.

"Where is the school?" asked Mack.

"According to Google Maps, it's two miles away near the Library of Congress. We can be there in ten minutes. But there's one other thing."

"What's that?"

"There is a notation on the truck's entry form that I need to print out before we leave. I believe it's very incriminating, and I may need it for evidence."

"What does it say?!"

"Seems Vice President Sanders has given free access for any trucks owned by SBSNN Corporation to enter the United States with minimal documentation. It's a PDF copy of a White House permission letter clearly signed by the vice president. SBSNN Corporation is also the London-based company that sent SUVs to Sheriff Urdano."

"Any chance I could drive the Mustang?" asked Mack. Kelly ignored him and shut down the computer. "Please!"

12:30 pm Eastern Standard Time

Agent Kelly flashed his Homeland Security badge at a janitor who was putting several bags of trash into the dumpster in the back of John Quincy Adams Charter School.

"Is there a Zella Norris who works here?" asked Kelly.

"Sure! Nice gal!" the janitor exclaimed. He was in a good mood. The student council let him finish off the remaining coffee from the morning's awards breakfast. "She supervises the student council. Just had a baby, too!"

"I know it's Saturday, but we would like to look in her room if we could. Would that be possible?" Agent Kelly smiled politely. He preferred to influence the janitor with kindness rather than position power.

"Yes, I guess that would be okay." The janitor led Kelly and Mack into the school and unlocked Zella's classroom door. "I'm sorry, but I have to run. I have tickets for the Nationals' game this afternoon. Would you mind making sure the doors are locked when you leave?"

"Yes, certainly!" responded Kelly. The janitor quickly left the building while Mack and Kelly gaped at the boxes of Taste Of Arabia sitting in open cabinets around the room. In Zella's rush to get back to the hospital, she had forgotten to lock them up.

"What do you suppose the student council advisor is doing with all this coffee?" asked Mack. "Are you guessing she is working for Lord Shaffer?"

Agent Kelly was confident that Shaffer somehow employed Zella. But he didn't realize there was a breakfast ceremony held at the school earlier that morning. Kelly didn't know that gallons and gallons of Taste Of Arabia had been consumed by senators, congressmen, and Supreme Court justices. And he definitely was unaware that the president had downed three cups all by himself!

So instead of trying to find Zella and confiscate the plunder, Agent Kelly decided to park on the street and stake out the school. He called the Homeland Security supervisor at Dulles and explained the situation but asked him not to say or do anything until he heard back from him. Kelly said it might take a few days, and the only response from the supe was to make sure the Mustang was shined up before he returned it!

Agent Kelly and Mack took turns watching the school in two-hour shifts. While one kept a close eye on the comings and goings, the other either slept or ran to the Seven Eleven for a biffy break and to stock up on prepackaged processed goodies. Saturday turned to Sunday and Sunday to Monday without any suspicious actions taking place near the school. Moms dropped their kids off in their Lincoln Navigators, Infiniti QX80s, and BMW X6s, then raced away to the health clubs. Kelly and Mack passed the time listening to the news reports on the radio surrounding Air Force Two and the Vice President's whereabouts.

While the clock was ticking away the seconds, the tungis-corrupted memories of America's political leaders were fading away.

Chapter 61

Monday, April 23, 2018 (7-Shaban-1439)
Sultan Tariq's Private Runway
Rub' al Khali Desert, Saudi Arabia
6:00 pm Arabian Standard Time

Fifteen agents from the British Secret Intelligence Service (MI6) located Air Force Two a few hours before sunset. MI6 agents used a Russian-made transport helicopter, Mi-26, to enter the Rub' al Khali and extract the castaways. It was strange that US reconnaissance jets and Saudi military personnel couldn't locate the small group, but the British found them easily. The group was escorted from Air Force Two to the transport helicopter with assault rifles pointed at them as they were strapped into a seat using a locked buckle. Not one word was spoken.

Cyrus McCool and Bob Billings were pleased they were rescued, but they had plenty of questions. They weren't sure why they were locked into their seats; however, they assumed MI6 needed answers for the crippled Air Force Two jet before they could trust anyone. McCool had no way to prove he was with the CIA. Because he worked undercover, he wasn't allowed to carry official identification. Billings handed his badge to the MI6 leader to show he was a Homeland Security agent. McCool and Billings knew something was wrong when the leader tossed the ID into a wastebasket.

The helicopter lifted off and flew only a few feet above the desert dunes. The propellers kicked up a cloud of sand in every direction. Cliff was sitting next to Cyrus looking out the window. He leaned over and whispered to the CIA agent.

"We're going south. That's a problem."

"What are you talking about?!" responded Cyrus a bit too loudly. The MI6 leader turned his head momentarily to see who was whispering, then continued to punch away on the keypad of his laptop computer.

"Any direction but south!" Cliff was trying to emphasize in a quiet voice. "We should be going to a friendly location, either west towards Jeddah, north towards Riyadh, or east to Abu Dhabi. The only place south is Yemen. Not so friendly!"

"You're right! And I assume we're flying low to avoid radar surveillance."

"No doubt. We need some answers, Cyrus!"

"That ain't gonna happen anytime soon, fellas." The voice came from the cockpit via the intercom system. Apparently, someone up front was monitoring everything spoken in the cabin.

Cyrus sat up and opened his eyes wide in disbelief. He thought he recognized the voice.

Al Jazeera News Headquarters, Doha, Qatar
8:00 pm Arabian Standard Time

An anonymous and untraceable call to Al Jazeera News Media was picked up by a reporter who almost hung up thinking it was a hoax. Whoever made the call said they found Air Force Two, and they gave the exact GPS location. The caller also lied and said he witnessed several US fighter jets annihilate a civilian outpost on an oasis near where Air Force Two was resting on a makeshift runway. He said there were no survivors. Then the call abruptly ended.

The location wasn't all that far from Al Jazeera's home base in Doha, so the megamedia company flew a corporate helicopter into the Rub' al Khali and touched down at midnight on the runway next to Air Force Two. Now the question was should they call the authorities immediately or report live to the world? It was a no-brainer; option two would catapult the news agency's ratings well above those of CNN Worldwide and BBC International.

Technicians quickly propped up flood lamps all around the scene. A generator onboard the chopper provided all the necessary power, and a small satellite dish delivered clear audio and visual to stunned listeners all around the globe. Especially those who were watching the transmission from 1600 Pennsylvania Avenue in Washington, DC.

*****

"Reporting live from southern Saudi Arabia, this is Irfan Toma. We have incredible breaking news! What you see behind me is Air Force Two sitting on a private runway in the heart of the Rub' al Khali desert. The Boeing C-32 aircraft appears to have attempted an emergency landing with nonfunctioning landing gear. To my left is what remains of an oasis community that has been devastated by explosions. Al Jazeera received a call from an eyewitness who claims that US fighter jets destroyed the outpost. We are speculating that the American pilots knew that Vice President Sanders was in the area when they fired their missiles.

"As you know, Al Jazeera first reported that a rogue US fighter jet was seen chasing Air Force Two last week before both planes went missing. Although it's just speculation at this time, it appears Vice President Sanders was the target of a covert assassination attempt that most likely has been successfully carried out in a foreign country along with massive collateral damage to an Arab community. President Thompson will have some explaining to do!

"This is Irfan Toma reporting. We will be providing further reports after the Saudi search and rescue team arrives. Stay tuned!"

*****

Two minutes later, a call was placed from Al Jazeera's headquarters in Doha to King Salman bin Abdulaziz Al Saud's palace in Riyadh. Two hours later, Saudi paratroopers were descending upon what had once been Sultan Tariq's secret oasis. And before he began his Fajr prayer, the king ordered all American expatriates and military personnel to be arrested, and any US jet flying in Saudi airspace to be shot down.

It was crisis time.

Chapter 62

Tuesday, April 24, 2018
John Quincy Adams Charter School, Washington, DC
10:00 pm Eastern Standard Time

The stakeout at JQA Charter School had ended abruptly when Special Agent Earl Kelly's phone beeped. It was a curious call from his receptionist, Gretta Paulson, back in Arizona. She said the White House was ordering him to attend an emergency meeting tomorrow at 7:00 am sharp in the Situation Room. All Homeland Security lead agents from across the country were expected to be there.

Kelly and Mack's efforts to find any cagey activity or observe the movement of Taste Of Arabia boxes in or out of the school had proven fruitless. Earlier in the day, Mack posed as a student council advisor from a neighboring school. He asked to speak with Zella Norris but was told she was taking maternity leave until the end of the school year. After receiving the late-night call from Gretta, Kelly and Mack broke into the school and loaded the coffee into a school bus that was out back. Then Mack hotwired the bus, drove it to Union Station, and locked it up in the Colonial Parking lot. He and Kelly would deliver the contents to Homeland Security sometime in the morning and return the bus to its rightful owners.

Kelly followed Mack to the train station, then picked him up and drove back to Dulles Airport to return the Mustang. That's when they heard the news about Air Force Two being shot down by US fighter jets. Kelly now knew the purpose of the White House meeting. He and Mack took a cab to the JW Marriott Hotel on

Pennsylvania Avenue, which was within walking distance of the White House. They had time for two hours of sleep and a quick shower.

Chapter 63

Wednesday, April 25, 2018
White House, Washington, DC
7:00 am Eastern Standard Time

"Why are we here?!" asked President Thompson to those sitting at the long table and along the walls of the Situation Room. The cabinet members were huddled in the basement of the White House West Wing. Everyone looked at each other, and a few eyelids were raised. Was the president kidding, or was this merely a rhetorical question to get everyone thinking?

The White House Chief of Staff, Henry Gable, knew the president wouldn't be joking around at a time like this. Director of Homeland Security, Roy Leland, was visibly upset that his immediate boss, Vice President Sanders, was presumed dead. And the chairman of the Senate Committee on Armed Services, Gilbert Russell, shrugged his shoulders. He had no idea why they were holding a meeting. All he could think about was how proud he was when his son won the top math (or was it reading?) award at Saturday's JQA Breakfast Program. He also remembered toasting the president with a cup of that incredible coffee!

After a couple of minutes of total silence, Gable decided to speak up. "Sir, Air Force Two has been found in Saudi Arabia at the site of an unknown oasis community. Al Jazeera reporters are saying Sanders' plane was shot down by our own people, and the outpost was bombed. They are reporting the vice president is missing and presumed dead. There was plenty of collateral damage, and the king has arrested every American working in Saudi. We are on the brink of war, sir!"

"Really?!" responded President Thompson. "I vaguely remember hearing about that."

There was a loud, angry grumbling in the room. What was the president up to? Yet, no one dared to confront the leader of the free world. Except for Special Agent Earl Kelly. He recognized the symptoms at once.

"The president is under the influence of a drug known as tungis. I'm not sure where or when, but he must have drunk coffee laced with it. His memory will fade until an antidote is provided. It is imperative that you remove him from office straightaway and swear in Senator Demmel!"

Speaker of the House, Dave Demmel, was next in line for the presidency due to the disappearance of Vice President Sanders. However, he too attended the breakfast program at JQA Charter School. Agent Kelly was still unaware of the ceremony on Saturday.

Roy Leland stood up and turned to his lead agent from Arizona. "Agent Kelly, you've overstepped your authority! What in the world are these myths that you are talking about!"

Before Kelly could respond, NSA Chief Martin Calhoun interrupted.

"He's right!" stated Calhoun. The NSA chief wasn't sure how Kelly knew about the coffee. He had no idea that someone other than his own team members had been investigating the vice president. Kelly was even more surprised; he didn't know that the CIA also had knowledge of Taste Of Arabia.

Calhoun continued, "Agent Kelly is very much correct. I have CIA operatives in Saudi right now. I presume they are trying to take care of a criminal mess that Vice President Sanders started." He paused for that last statement to sink in. "Yes, you heard me right—Sanders is involved in treasonable acts, one which is the use of tungis in coffee to overthrow our president and eventually our entire government!"

"That's preposterous!" yelped President Thompson. "Overthrow me with coffee?! Absurd, I tell you! I haven't had coffee today! In fact, I haven't drunk coffee since the breakfast program at JQA Charter School last Saturday!"

"What?!" exclaimed Kelly. "You drank coffee at JQA?!" He was beginning to understand, but angry at himself for assuming that the coffee in Zella Norris' rooms hadn't been consumed!

"I most certainly did! I think the name was Taste Of Babylonia or something like that. Exceptional java, I might add!" He smiled at the group, forgetting once again why they were gathered there.

Calhoun glanced at Agent Kelly. The NSA chief was shocked that the coffee had been distributed so quickly and had already been ingested. By the perplexed looks of everyone in the room, Calhoun realized that he needed to provide some answers soon!

"Let me explain," he said. "Sanders is working for—" Calhoun's iPhone rang, and he paused to look at the caller ID. It was from Special Agent Marv Cullins, better known to colleagues and students at Gila Bend Charter School as Cyrus McCool. He excused himself for a moment and walked into the hallway to take the call. Once again, there was mass chaos in the Situation Room. President Thompson wasn't sure if Agent Kelly's theory of tungis terrorism was correct, but he did remember drinking more coffee than usual at the JQA ceremony. It was so good—how could anyone forget that taste!

A few minutes later, Calhoun returned with his cell phone call on hold. He looked at everyone in the Situation Room and said glumly, "Gentlemen, we have a problem."

Then the NSA Chief placed the iPhone on the table and pressed the speaker button.

7:30 am Eastern Standard Time

The voice wasn't Agent Cullins; it was a synthesized vocal resonance that sounded like a robot. But the words were unequivocal and straight to the point:

"By now, you should know the nature of the crisis you face. Not only is your president afflicted by a drug called tungis, but many of your nation's senators, congressmen, and Supreme Court justices are also under the influence. Tungis will first destroy your memories and eventually your minds. Washington, DC, is not the only metro area contaminated; four other major US cities are also infected. However, you are not alone. Leaders of Great Britain and Russia have also consumed tungis, and their government is going to crumble right along with your own!"

"Who are you!" screamed Chief of Staff Gable from across the room. NSA Chief Martin Calhoun motioned for Gable to calm down. He knew the complexity of what they were dealing with, and he also knew that negotiations were necessary to resolve the conflict.

"Who we are is of no concern to you!" responded the synthesized voice. "We are holding captive several US citizens and two doctors from other countries. Our prisoners include an ex-Colonel in your esteemed Air Force, a Homeland Security special agent, and a CIA operative. Those three are not cooperating and will be the first to die. There is also a teacher and two students. Everyone will be released if our demands are met, except for a young Yemeni man who will remain with us. That is unfortunate for him!" A synthesized chuckle came through the speakerphone. No one else was laughing, especially Bassam.

"What is it that you want?" asked President Thompson.

"Alaska. Your forty-ninth state, that's all. You don't need it anyway. It's nowhere near the rest of your states, it's cold and overrun by polar bears! If you agree to give us Alaska, once we have established ourselves as a sovereign country, we will agree to end the distribution of tungis. And we also have a special bonus. I understand that one of the doctors we have detained has discovered an antidote for tungis. If you make this deal quickly, you will have him back in time to save your people who have already been affected, including yourself, Mr. President!"

"America will not be held hostage!" shouted Gable furiously. "We don't negotiate with terrorists!"

At that moment, Speaker of the House Dave Demmel entered the room. He had been summoned a few minutes earlier and happened to be in the White House waiting to chat with the president.

"What's this all about?" asked Demmel. He looked around the room. "You all look familiar, but I can't place your names." Everyone cringed. The Speaker of the House would not be an option to succeed Thompson. That meant the president of the Senate was next in line. But who's to say if he had drunk coffee at the JQA Breakfast Awards Program last Saturday?!

"What's it going to be, Mr. President?" asked the robotic voice. Everyone in the room held their breaths while the president paused to think. It was impossible to remove him from office without a psychological evaluation and a signed medical doctor's decree of incompetence. That wouldn't happen anytime soon. After a tense minute passed, the president leaned forward so he could be heard easily by the techno-voice.

"Where exactly is this Alaska you are referring to?" he asked.

Chief of Staff Gable looked despondently at President Thompson, then at Speaker Demmel. He shook his head in acquiescence and muted the phone. All eyes were on him as he opened his mouth and hesitated momentarily before muttering in defeat.

"It's time to make a deal, gentlemen!"

Everyone nodded yes.

Chapter 64

Thursday, April 26, 2018
US Capitol Building, Washington, DC
9:00 am Eastern Standard Time

The people of the world watched and waited and were awestruck at the expediency of the United States Congress. The bill to relinquish Alaska to a group of unknown insurgents passed both houses on the first go around. There was little need for discussion. Ninety-six congressional representatives and twelve senators drank Taste Of Arabia coffee at JQA Charter School, and none of them had any idea what they were voting on. Their colleagues were firsthand witnesses to the slaughter of minds taking place around them. Without the antidote soon, a good chunk of Congress would be vegetables, as would President Thompson.

The president had been in no condition to deliver a statement to the American public, so Chief of Staff Gable stepped in for him. As ridiculous as it sounded, there was no other alternative. Support for ditching Alaska came in droves from Chicago, Houston, San Francisco, and Phoenix, where residents of those cities had no idea if they had been affected or not. Alaskans were given the opportunity to exile to the lower forty-eight, but only a few decided to leave. Living in a new country sounded like an adventure for them, which is why they settled near the Arctic Circle to begin with!

The Alaskan military bases, jets, weapons, and ammunition would stay—another demand from the radicals. Members of the armed services would need to evacuate within twenty-four hours or risk imprisonment. The rebels apparently had their own military personnel to man the bases.

And while America was on the brink of despair, so was Russia. They had received notice from the rebels that many members of the Politburo, and President Putin as well, had drunk Taste Of Arabia and their minds were starting to fizzle. Amid the turmoil, Russian politicians quickly gave in to the demands of the insurgents and gave them the sparsely populated far eastern region of Siberia known as Chukotka. None of the 50,526 residents exiled because they had nowhere to go. The new country was taking shape better than expected. The rebels now controlled the entire Bering Sea, and their most dangerous weapon was coffee!

*****

After transporting Sultan Tariq's refugees to Krasnodar, Russia, in the Mi-26 helicopter, Sheriff Morton (aka CIA Special Agent Morton) disappeared. He reemerged stupendously as a guest of King Salman's royal palace in Riyadh. While the United States Congress was negotiating a way to protect its citizens at home, Morton was negotiating a way to protect US citizens abroad. No one knew about the secret meeting between the CIA agent and the king until it was announced that the American expatriates would be released and allowed to return to the states or continue in their Saudi jobs.

The media was focused 24/7 on the loss of Alaska and the formation of a new hostile country that bordered the North Pole's ice pack; however, the reports out of Saudi Arabia provided for a bit of relief from the unpleasant news regarding the inimical takeover of the forty-ninth state. The threat of war in the Middle East had ended, and American lives were saved. Sheriff Morton returned to the states as a brave protagonist and an international hero. War in the Middle East at this turning point in history could have proved apocalyptic!

Chapter 65

Saturday, April 28, 2018
Juneau, Alaska
10:00 am Alaska Standard Time

Lord Shaffer hung up the phone with Yemen president Abdurabu Mansur Hadi and sat down in Governor Bill Walker's comfortable leather chair at the capitol building in Juneau. He clasped his hands behind his head and stretched his legs on top of the desk. Shaffer smiled at the ceiling, amazed he was able to pull this off. He was now the self-appointed ruler of the world's newest country. Governor Walker had vacated the office and moved to Seattle while the other Alaskan officials scattered to various locations throughout the US. Some even settled in Canada and retired.

While the joint mission of the CIA and KGB was blowing up Tariq's sultanate, Shaffer, Directorate Chief Yegor Bovnik, General Sokolov, and Vice President Sanders dropped down into an underground bombproof vault below the palace and hid. The vault was the same design Shaffer had installed near Senso-Mac Corporation in Mesa. Had Sultan Tariq not lost his head, literally, he would have been saved too. While Special Agent Marv Cullins and the others waited in the cabin of Air Force Two, Shaffer's personal pilot Gary Peters flew the lord and his retinues to Yemen in the Learjet. Peters had texted Shaffer while on approach to the Sultan's private airfield and advised him that his passengers were becoming suspicious.

Shaffer had recruited the fifteen best British MI6 agents that the secret service had to offer. It had cost him £10 million for each man and a promise to build each one a vast estate on the Kenai Peninsula where they could fish for salmon and hunt grizzly bears the rest of their lives. But, the money hadn't come from his usual endless pot of investments. Lord Shaffer was a close friend of the crown jeweler at the Tower of London, and for a nice cut of the action, he agreed to steal Edward the Confessor's coronation regalia for him. Shaffer sold the objects for £500 million to a ruthless dealer of stolen goods in the Falkland Islands, who, in turn, would eventually sell them back to the royal family for a mere £1 billion. A homeless man that slept in Trinity Square Gardens was arrested and identified as the person the crown jeweler witnessed running away with the irreplaceable items. Lord Shaffer's accomplice pocketed £10 million, as well, and retained the keys to Jewel House.

Shaffer had no plans to form a democracy, so he decided to become Premier Shaffer. Vice President Sanders was now Prime Minister Sanders, and Yegor Bovnik assumed the role of Military Director. General Sokolov had been diagnosed with melanoma a month ago and did not want a role in the new government. His doctor said the skin cancer appeared to have developed a while back and grew slowly, a result of an extended period in the sun without protection. Sokolov didn't tell the doctor about the camel ride through the Rub' al Khali with Wasim years ago. Now he wanted to die in peace, somewhere a long way from hot weather. He passed into the afterlife on the bush plane flight taking him to his new home outside of Nome.

Bassam Bashir was forced to continue overseeing the production of tainted coffee. Premier Shaffer's first alliance was with the Yemeni government, who would gladly allow tungis and arklundis shipments to Alaska in exchange for military protection and money. Arklundis was another plant grown only in the Sarawat Mountains region of Yemen. A few days before Sultan Tariq's palace was leveled, one of his researchers discovered that arklundis also created memory loss, and if mixed with tungis and coffee, would be immediate and irreversible. An antidote could stop it, but chances were slim the remedy could be administered fast enough to do any good. The name of the coffee needed to be changed and the product would need to be exported using a fake certificate of origin. Goods coming from Alaska would not be allowed into the United States.

Yemenia Airlines carrying the released hostages touched down at Baltimore-Washington International Airport at 2:05 pm and were met by a horde of secret service vehicles. Doctors Gomez and Laghari were raced to John Hopkins Hospital where the president, 108 members of Congress, and three Supreme Court justices were waiting. None of the politicians knew where they were or why they were there, and worse yet, who they were. The rest of the captives were taken to the George Bush Intelligence Center in Langley, Virginia, for debriefing.

John Hopkins Hospital, Baltimore, Maryland
7:00 pm Eastern Standard Time

Sancho and Dr. Laghari finished administering the antidote to President Thompson and everyone who had ingested Taste Of Arabia at the JQA Charter School breakfast awards program. Sancho's assistants at the factory in Los Vidrios had worked around the clock to package the herbal remedy and ship it to Washington, DC, as fast as possible. The antidote was trucked over the Mexican border to the Gila Bend Auxiliary Airfield, where it was flown to National Airport on an F-16. Now the nation could only wait and see if their elected leaders regained their memories. It had been a week since the coffee was consumed.

Chapter 66

Monday, April 30, 2018
White House, Washington, DC
10:00 am Eastern Standard Time

President Thompson needed a new vice president, and this time he wanted someone he could trust. Thompson was back in office and beginning to think clearly again even though his headaches lingered. Speaker of the House, Dave Demmel, assumed he would be next in line for the number two job, but he was wrong. Thompson wanted to restore a positive public image in the Oval Office that had dissipated this past week. He wanted a great American hero, someone the US citizens would be proud to call their vice president. Thompson selected Sheriff Mike Morton to be his righthand man. After all, the undercover CIA agent from Arizona had saved many American lives in Saudi Arabia and may have stopped World War Three from beginning!

The first act of Congress on Monday morning had nothing to do with the loss of Alaska or how the United States would form any type of diplomacy with the new country. Instead, Congress did something that would eventually spark the economy: it regulated the cost of health care in America. Dr. Sancho Gomez was appointed chief of the new American Medical Regulatory Commission, which was set up to control the cost of insurance premiums, deductibles, provider fees, and pharmaceuticals. His first task would be to ensure health care was affordable for all Americans. Congress theorized that if people spent less on medical costs, they would have more money to spend in stores, which in turn would generate more sales tax revenue, and no doubt, lower the unemployment rate. Plus, the United States would be a healthier nation!

Before the week was over, Sancho merged the Food and Drug Administration with the World Health Organization to open global commerce and force American pharmaceutical companies to compete with their international counterparts. Dr. Sachit Laghari was appointed director of the new agency. He would ensure that if generic drugs were proved to be safe by the lofty standards of the WHO, they would be allowed importation into America, regardless of their origin. Sancho also decreed that exploratory surgical procedures and experimental medicine would be covered by insurance if a physician believed it would save the life of his or her patient.

After seeing how Sancho singlehandedly saved Washington, the politicians fully believed in his vision to improve America's health care system. They were even more impressed by his oratory skills and leadership ability. The Nobel prize-winning doctor from Mexico spoke to the United Nations about the need to recruit, educate, and retain top-quality doctors, and he had a plan for that, too. If the United States was going to regulate the costs of medical care, then they wanted to ensure doctors and pharmaceutical companies continued to be fairly compensated for their important work. Sancho knew that the United Nations owned gold, diamonds, and other precious resources throughout the world that were being stockpiled for future use in the event a global conflict broke out. The General Assembly was so impressed by Sancho's passion for improving the health care system that they offered to fund liability insurance premiums for doctors and medical companies that had been approved by the World Health Organization. Excellent physicians and the pharmaceutical industry would no longer have to pay astronomical insurance costs to protect themselves from lawsuits. It was a win-win for everyone.

Chapter 67

Tuesday, May 1, 2018
Gila Bend, Arizona
6:00 pm Pacific Daylight Time

The Gila Bend Charter School board meeting was moved to the football field to accommodate the throngs of people in attendance. Everyone in the community wanted to know what was going to happen next. Most didn't even have kids in school; they were just curious, like the elderly folks from the nursing home. The school had burned to the ground, and members of the community had perished. The first order of business was to memorialize the lives that were lost. The mood was somber.

Two heroic citizens were not at the meeting: Captain Ned Segura and Sergeant Pete Ruben of the Gila Bend Police Department. They were hospitalized in Phoenix, recovering from the side effects of the tungis antidote treatment. By the time they were diagnosed, it was almost too late. Shipments of the herbal remedy arrived via FedEx quickly, but doctors believed the officers may have suffered some permanent memory loss. Meanwhile, they were also being treated for burns and smoke inhalation sustained when they broke into the burning building and saved the life of board president, Abe Fitzgerald.

Abe started the meeting, which was actually a ceremony, with a prayer. He still was suffering from a severe headache following his antidote injections for tungis, but he was going to battle through it. He needed to eulogize those who had died and thank the heroes from Gila Bend who may have saved the country. As each person's name was read, a large framed portrait was raised which would be placed in the new school that was beginning construction tomorrow. Mack Colten had sketched the pictures in his apartment in Ajo. He was one of the heroes, but he refused to accept that fact and did not draw a portrait of himself.

First came the eulogies. Abe began the commendations with Pablo Hernandez, the father of Lucas, who was killed as he drove his AMC Gremlin at the fake ICE agents in the parking lot. The next plaudit was for Philomena and Ralph Hayes. Abe told how Philomena offered to take a few days off from her florist job to help out by substituting at the school. He didn't mention that Ralph was a jealous husband who thought Philomena was having an affair with him! And finally, Abe paid tribute to *Arizona Republic* reporter Smitty Douglas. The local Boy Scouts troop then lowered the flag on the football field to half-mast.

Abe followed the eulogies by giving testimonials for the living heroes. Their portraits would be placed in a small museum inside the new school. The first accolade was to Donner Colten for his bravery in helping Principal Perez and several teachers to escape. The next was for Principal Perez himself, followed by teachers, Rick Frye, and Kurt Kellner. When Abe told the story of Athletic Director Cyrus McCool's heroics and his work as a double agent for the CIA, the crowd was stunned and silent. Then they began applauding so loud that the sound could be heard a mile away. When students Isaac Martinez and Zaira Tahan were introduced, everyone stood, clapped, hooted, and hollered! The standing ovation lasted over ten minutes! Perhaps an undocumented immigrant from Mexico and a young Muslim girl would change the face of racism in America! The cab of the school bus they took to escape would be placed in the museum with wax figures of Isaac and Zaira displayed at the helm.

The next item of school board business was to apologize for hiring Ted Sanderson as the school's assistant principal a few years back. Gila Bend had been the focal point of the world's stage this past week as news of Vice President Sanders' acts of treason came out into the open. It was now confirmed that he was the illegitimate son of Senator Gordon Rothschild, and his brother was none other than the beloved assistant principal Ted Sanderson. Both were born in Gila Bend, both were integral players in Lord Shaffer's coffee scheme, and both are now number one and two on the FBI's most-wanted list. It was reported that Garrett Sanders now held the position of Vice President in Shaffer's newly -formed country, but Ted's whereabouts was a mystery.

Teacher Kurt Kellner had identified Assistant Principal Sanderson as the "man in charge" who he saw in the desert after parachuting from the small Cessna with Isaac and Zaira. The three had been captured by the fake ICE agents, and when Kurt's blindfold was removed, he saw Sanderson barking out orders to the others. Then they were forced aboard Air Force Two to be Sultan Tariq's slaves. The FBI had traced a multitude of cell phone calls from Sanderson's iPhone to SBSNN Corporation in London. Most had originated within a two-mile radius of Senso-Mac headquarters in Mesa. Myra Adams was the last person to see Sanderson. She waved at the always-friendly assistant principal as he calmly left the school after setting it on fire.

During investigations, it was discovered that Sanders and Sanderson never attended school and had very few friends. They lived on West Norma Street in Gila Bend and were tutored at night by Emile Forester, their next-door neighbor who was also the auto mechanics teacher at the high school. Emile needed gambling money for his jaunts to Vegas, and moonlighting as a tutor helped pay for gas in his 1966 Cadillac DeVille convertible. He had won the shiny red beauty playing a nickel slot machine on the night Cesar's Palace opened. All of Emile's students loved him, and they still visited him in the nursing home. At 103, he was the oldest resident of the community, and he enjoyed chatting with the FBI agents about the good ol' days!

Turns out that Sanders held a bogus master's degree in political science from Harvard while Sanderson had a phony master's in educational leadership from Purdue. Seems Senator Rothschild had friends at both universities who falsified transcripts in exchange for substantial fees. On paper, both kids were "A" students and graduated Phi Beta Kappa. Forged letters of recommendation touted each brother as having extraordinary moral character. Senator Rothschild was listed as a reference on job applications, and prospective employers never bothered to call anyone else after the great American statesman gave the boys exemplary accolades. But every human resource director wondered how Sanders or Sanderson knew Senator Rothschild well enough to have him sing their praises!

Now that the serious stuff was out of the way, Abe focused the board meeting on next year. The new school would be open by the first day of classes in the fall thanks to Gila Bend residents, including undocumented Mexican immigrants, who offered up their free time to volunteer for the massive construction effort. The crowd gave another standing ovation when Abe said that Kurt Kellner would be promoted to assistant principal, and Cyrus McCool would sever ties with the CIA and return as athletic director. Retired Air Force Colonel, Cliff Bullard, was offered Kellner's math teaching position, but he politely turned down the proposition. Then, with deep sadness, Abe told the crowd that Rick Frye had resigned.

Cliff and Rick had decided to move to northern Arizona and become trout-fishing guides.

*****

Following the conclusion of the meeting, four uniformed Air Force soldiers approached board member Jim Morgan. Two were military police investigators, and two were high-ranking officers who asked to speak to him in private. Jim was a prominent rancher who owned the highly-successful Morgan's Southwestern Salsa and Chili Company. Jim's friends knew he hired illegal immigrants to work his fields; however, they also knew Jim always paid his undocumented hands equal wages to that of the US citizens who worked for him. It wasn't about cheap labor to increase profits; it was about finding industrious employees who would put out an exemplary product.

Morgan's Southwestern Salsa and Chili was the best! But Jim knew that the Air Force wasn't interested in his spicy comida.

Jim asked the investigators to follow him to Sofia's Restaurant, where they found a table in the back. The lead detective got right to the point. Jim's dad, Brigadier General Meade Morgan, was nowhere to be found. The Air Force put out a warrant for his arrest after he went AWOL following a fake terrorist attack at Gila Bend Auxiliary Airfield. Major Ben Willis and Captain Dick Royce explained to Jim that his father was acting very strange at the time and appeared to try and cover up the brutal murder of Airman Frank Gustine. They said the general was going to take an Uber back to Luke Air Force Base! But no one had seen him since.

Jim knew it was time to protect his father's legacy. After all, his dad had risked his career to protect him.

"I don't know where dad is now, but I received a phone call from him shortly after Airman Gustine was killed in the control tower. He was outraged! At first, when the call came into Luke Air Force Base from Auxiliary control tower, dad thought it could have been a real terrorist attack. But as soon as he saw Airman Gustine dead and the computer shot to pieces, he knew it was Lord Shaffer's doing." Jim looked away. He was embarrassed that his father was involved in something illegal for his sake.

"Lord Shaffer?" asked the lead detective. "You mean the same son-of-a-bitch that just overthrew Alaska?!"

"Yes, but it wasn't Shaffer who murdered Gustine. He just ordered the hit."

"Who killed the airman?" asked Major Willis.

"Ted Sanderson, the assistant principal at the school who is Vice President Sanders' brother. The one everyone is looking for right now."

"And your father knew about it?!"

Tears started forming in Jim's eyes. He muttered softly, "Yes, sir."

"So why didn't your dad say something to us?!" barked Captain Royce. "We could have arrested Sanders and the others before they ever left the United States! All this crap could have been prevented, damn it!"

"For me," replied Jim weakly. "He was covering for me."

"For you?!" asked Royce loudly. "What do you mean by that?!"

"As the assistant principal, Sanderson knew that I was employing undocumented laborers from Mexico. It was obvious. The workers' kids had no proof of citizenship when they enrolled in school. He threatened to spill the beans to Homeland Security unless I did something for him." Jim paused, not sure he wanted to continue without having a lawyer present.

"What something?" asked Major Willis calmly. He was playing good cop while Royce was playing bad cop. "Tell us now, Jim, and we can make this as easy as possible for you and your father. Okay? Tell us."

"I was to dedicate ten acres of my ranch to growing tungis. Yes, the same tungis that has caused memories to collapse from here to Washington, DC! But I didn't know that tungis could wipe out your brain, I really didn't! Sanderson said it was some sort of hallucinogen that was milder than marijuana and non-addictive. It would only be sold to adults. I knew it was wrong, but I was assured that tungis was safe. Because I didn't want my illegal employees to be arrested and forced back to Mexico, I took the deal.

"I told my dad about it, and he had a fit! He said I could lose everything that I worked so hard to get. Then, to protect my investment and my family, he reluctantly got involved. When Lord Shaffer found out that my dad was a brigadier general at Luke, he smelled an opportunity. Shaffer blackmailed my father, but Airman Gustine's death was the final straw. Dad told me on the phone that he couldn't work for Shaffer anymore. Then, he advised me to tell the truth if I were caught. He also said somehow, someway he was going to make amends for what he did. That was the last I heard from him."

"Jim, your secret is safe with us," said Major Willis. "Burn the tungis. And if your dad calls you, please have him turn himself in. We will do everything in our power to help him, too!"

Chapter 68

Homeland Security, Phoenix, Arizona
Wednesday, May 2, 2018
8:00 am Pacific Daylight Time

Special Agent Earl Kelly brought a box of Rainbow donuts and plopped it down on the conference room table at the Homeland Security office in Phoenix. Special Agent Bob Billings reached for a French Cruller and huffed it down. Then he winked at Kelly and receptionist Gretta Paulson who were both amazed Bob could devour the donut without taking a breath!

Gordy Owens was excited to be reunited with Kelly. Yesterday, the governor appointed him interim sheriff of Maricopa County. He would serve in that role only until a special election to replace Elliot Urdano could be held. Gordy selected Ken Smith to be his temporary assistant, and Ken was also sitting at the conference table, as was the sheriff's receptionist Rebecca Grimm. Ken and Rebecca had politely declined the offer for a cup of coffee. They decided that they would get their caffeine fix from tea and cocoa from now on!

President Thompson had ordered NSA Chief Martin Calhoun to form a covert team of law enforcement personnel in each state who would be responsible for identifying foreign intruders and stop them before they could disrupt government systems. Internal spies, you might say. Picking the unit from Arizona was a no-brainer; who better to lead that team than the players who may have saved the United States from complete collapse? Kelly and Billings would leave Homeland Security and become the owners of *Earl and Bob's Specialty Cars*, a new dealership on Bell Road that would sell high-end and classic automobiles, a perfect business to trap wealthy foreigners who may have questionable intentions. Taxpayers wouldn't know they were footing the bill for the covert operation; however, all the profits from the sale of cars would be reinserted into the nation's revenue system. Calhoun placed an agent at the IRS who would ensure the details were never discovered.

After Owens and Smith completed their temporary duties at the sheriff's department, they would become the owners of *Gordy and Ken's Outfitters*, a new hunting and fishing shop in Flagstaff. Gretta would relocate to the car dealership, while Rebecca would assume the same role at the outdoor sporting goods store. Cyrus McCool offered to be a consultant for the group; however, he let Calhoun know that his first priority was being the athletic director at Gila Bend Charter School.

While Agent Billings was wiping the crumbs off his shirt, the phone rang. Gretta punched the speakerphone button so everyone could hear. President Thompson and NSA Chief Calhoun briefed the Arizona team on their mission, then wished them well.

*****

The three O'Connell molecular geneticists had seen enough crime and evil acts for a lifetime. They all decided to retire from research and pursue their love of sports. They accepted Dr. Laghari's offer of becoming advisors to the World Health Organization, but only on a very limited basis.

Once a year, the O'Connells would reunite and travel to far corners of the world to help the sick and needy by providing health care and building clinics.

*****

Preparations were in the works to transform Ajo into a national historic site. Donner and Mack Colten were heroes, and the town showed their appreciation by selecting Donner to fill the role of sheriff, which was vacated when Mike Morton became vice president. President Thompson chose Mack to head up MACAS, the Mexican American Cultural Appreciation Society that would have its national headquarters in the Curley School apartment building. An art museum would be built next to it, and visitors could watch the artists draw, sculpt, paint, whatever, right on the premises.

The makeover of Ajo would also include preserving the tunnel from the golf course to the airport. To entice young kids, a pair of tracks would be laid over a new cement floor with fancy side-by-side go-carts on top. Children could safely drag race the mile course while their parents played golf on the new Trent Jones designed links. Sancho's old Stearman C3B biplane was returned from Dulles Airport to its new home at the Ajo airport. Tourists could fly a scenic route over Organ Pipe Cactus National Monument to Los Vidrios and visit Sancho's factory. The three-hour roundtrip tour would cost $200, and proceeds would be donated to MACAS.

*****

The Mexican government stood firmly with the Americans throughout the political disaster that had transpired. They sent troops to the states of Washington, Idaho, Montana, North Dakota, and Minnesota to secure the northern border. Who knew if Lord Shaffer had plans to attack the US someday? But if he did, America would make sure an attack via Canada would be impossible.

Plans to build a wall on the southern border between Mexico and the United States were scrapped. The Mexicans were obviously our allies, and it was time to build upon that friendship rather than shut the door. Border Patrol agents were reassigned to Spokane, Billings, Minot, and International Falls. President Thompson signed into law an amnesty agreement: all illegal immigrants would now be free to pursue US citizenship without the risk of deportation.

Then an interesting thing happened: many of them joined the Armed Services to fight for American freedom and democracy—the pillars of their new nation!

Chapter 69

Friday, May 4, 2018
Red Mountain Ranch, Mesa, Arizona
8:00 am Pacific Daylight Time

Joe Freeman returned from a sunrise hike in the desert behind his house. It was the first time he, or anyone not working for Homeland Security or the FBI, was allowed on that land since the explosions had leveled Senso-McNamara. The mess was bulldozed and would soon become a new housing development, much to the chagrin of the residents of east Mesa who had gradually watched their one-time paradise neighborhood turn into a cement jungle over the years.

Joe grabbed the cup from the Keurig tray, walked to his office, and booted up the computer. His morning caffeine now came from *Café Escapes Chai Latte* tea pods instead of coffee. The added sugar might kill him, but at least he would remember drinking it!

Joe returned from the hospital in Tucson with a severe headache, just like all his counterparts who had drunk Taste Of Arabia. Like most Americans, Joe had been locked into the news day and night since coming home. He couldn't believe he happened to wander across the worst crime in United States history since the attacks on the Twin Towers and the Pentagon. What was this world coming to?!

A memorial had been placed in Red Rock Park, a few blocks away from Joe's house in Red Mountain Ranch. The names of Senso-Mac employees had been engraved on a bronze plaque attached to a miniature marble obelisk. The obelisk would be a hindrance to flag football players, but residents of the community didn't care. Many of their friends and neighbors had worked for Senso-Mac, and everyone was still in a state of mourning. The monument would forever honor the victims of the senseless tragedy. Joe had snapped a picture of the stone on his way home from the hike.

He pulled the SD card from his camera and slid it into the reader on his computer. All the gorgeous desert pictures from a few hours earlier appeared in small squares displayed on the screen. As soon as he finished his tea, Joe would touch them up and file them away. As he sipped the last drops, Joe clicked on the picture of the memorial and relaxed in his chair. He wanted to reflect upon the lives of friends whom he had lost.

Joe was about to close the photo when something occurred to him. There was a name missing. The explosion killed everyone who worked at the factory, and because of that, the engravers used an employee list to ensure everyone's name was included on the plaque. Granted, the record was released from SBSNN Corporation after the Brits had seized Lord Shaffer's now-defunct company, but there was no reason to believe it was not correct. Shaffer had employed only a handful of his own men and planted them there, but they were not included in the directory. Only the innocent underlings' names who had no idea that Senso-Mac was a coverup for the manufacture of Shaffer's laser weapons and energy packs were given to the engravers.

"That's odd," muttered Joe to himself as he placed his cup down and rolled closer to the screen. "Why isn't Roger Bennett's name on the memorial?"

Nursing Home, Gila Bend, Arizona
8:00 am Pacific Daylight Time

"You're saying this letter is from my grandpa?" asked Everett Urdano. "This is all too crazy! I never even knew I had a grandfather. What should we do with it?"

"I think they got one of them fancy new gadgets called a shredder at the nurse's station," replied Emile Forester. "I say rip the damn letter to pieces. Then your grandmother and me can go to our graves knowing our secrets are safe. In a hundred years from now, no one will know any different. I'm just glad Bruce got to your dad's squad car before Donner Colten got there. Bruce Gledich never moved that fast when he was in my class! It's beyond me how he ever became a police officer in Ajo, I tell ya!"

"I still can't wrap my head around this!" Everett looked at the lady who was holding hands with Emile. Two hours earlier, he had met this energetic centenarian for the first time—and he also met his grandmother, someone he never knew even existed. When he received the call from the old man saying he had vital information about his recently deceased father, Everett was curious and couldn't resist. "Why didn't dad know about this? He was a sheriff, after all! How could he not know the truth?!"

"All this is water under the bridge," said the man sitting in the corner, a distant blood relative of Everett's that he also just met. "But I think the letter should go public. Clear the air. It would give people some answers so they could start to make sense of what took place the past couple of weeks."

"It would hurt me," said Raisa to the man as tears flowed down her cheeks. "I invited you here to meet Everett, the son of your half-brother. It was important for me to do that before I die. The world knowing about my infidelities is not something I would be proud to have in the history books!"

Roger Bennett stood up, walked over to his mother, and gave her a hug. They were in Emile's room at the Gila Bend nursing home. He and Everett glanced at each other but said nothing. They were profoundly pondering Raisa Vasiliev's last statement. This was a touchy subject!

A couple of weeks ago, Emile had lent his Cadillac DeVille to Donner Colten so he could retrieve an unknown letter in the glove compartment of Sheriff Urdano's squad car. Emile had guessed what was in the letter, so to protect his mistress of almost a half-century, he called Officer Gledich to move and hide the automobile. Like Donner, Gledich was once a student in Emile's auto mechanics class and would happily do anything for his beloved teacher. He also hand-delivered the letter to the nursing home in Gila Bend for Emile.

After Emile read the letter, he asked Raisa to come over. Years ago, after Emile went into the nursing home, Raisa sold her home on West Norma Street and moved into Emile's house next door. Although he was thirty-three years older, he was her comfort on those nights that Senator Rothschild wasn't around. And when the senator was on assignment as temporary ambassador to China and didn't see Raisa for over a year, Emile became even more of a comfort! That was when Roger was born.

Roger was only a month old when he was sent to Raisa's family to be raised in Russia. If Senator Rothschild ever found out that his mistress was unfaithful, there would be problems. Emile and Raisa visited Roger once a year during Emile's summer vacation. Roger grew up knowing his parents lived in America but wasn't quite sure why.

Roger joined the KGB after graduating from high school. A few years later, he was assigned to a team that was investigating possible acts of treason by Directorate Chief Yegor Bovnik and General Leonid Sokolov. Roger was thrilled to be placed in an undercover espionage position at Senso-McNamara Corporation in Mesa, Arizona. He would be a short drive away from his hometown of Gila Bend and his parents. But Roger never knew that he had three step-brothers until this morning. All that information was jotted down in the letter from Senator Rothschild to Sheriff Urdano that he was now holding in his hand.

Senator Rothschild fathered three children by Raisa: ex-Vice President Garrett Sanders, ex-Assistant Principal Ted Sanderson, and ex-Sheriff Elliot Urdano, who happened to be Garrett's twin brother. The senator knew that Raisa would have her hands full raising twins, so he moved the future sheriff of Maricopa County into his housekeeper's apartment a few miles down the road from his vast mansion in Phoenix. His housekeeper, Marilyn Urdano, was a gal who desired to be a lifelong bachelorette, yet always wanted a son to call her own.

Until the sheriff read the letter a few weeks before he died, he never knew that Senator Rothschild was his father or that Russian immigrant Raisa Vasiliev was his mother. He also never knew that the vice president of the United States was his twin brother, and the assistant principal of Gila Bend School was his little brother. And he went to his grave not knowing that he had a half-brother who worked for the KGB.

Roger took out a lighter from his pocket and lit it. Then, holding the letter over an ashtray, he set it on fire.

"You're right, mother," he said. "The world will never know. Your secret stays in this room."

Chapter 70

Saturday, May 12, 2018
Edwards Air Force Base, California
12:00 pm Pacific Daylight Time

Sharpshooters Yury Glebov and Rusian Kozar had patiently waited the past two weeks for word that part two of Lord Shaffer's plan was still going forward. After all that had happened, would President Putin and President Thompson continue with their plans to hold a welcome-home ceremony at Edwards Air Force Base for the astronauts and cosmonauts who had just completed a yearlong mission aboard the Soyuz TMA spacecraft? It had been General Sokolov's idea to blow up Air Force One and the Ilyushin Il-96 Command Point to wreak havoc on world order. First, the tungis would wipe out minds, then a laser death ray would wipe out leaders! Glebov and Kozar had trained for months by firing upon holographs in the underground vault at Senso-Mac in Mesa. They were ready and itching to go!

Putin and Thompson agreed that the ceremony would be a technological sign of strength for two countries reeling from a collapse of power caused by coffee! Perhaps this would be a start to ending the embarrassing image recently portrayed by the global media. They would take off from Edwards within seconds of each other, then circle the airbase and wave their royal wings to the cheering crowd below! What they didn't know was that things were about to get even worse.

Lord Shaffer made the call to Washington, DC, on his cell phone. Before he gave the go-ahead to Glebov and Kozar, the new premier wanted to make sure his crucial player was ready to assume a new position.

"Good morning Vice President Morton!" exclaimed Shaffer. "I'm assuming that you are still basking in the glory of being a great American hero, are you not?"

"I most certainly am, Premier Shaffer!" replied Morton with a grin from cheek to cheek.

"Then, I'm also assuming that you are now ready to become commander in chief of those wonderful forty-nine United States?" Shaffer put a strong emphasis on *forty-nine.*

"Of course! If the American people only knew how stupid Thompson was to select me as his vice president! Or how clueless they were to believe that I talked King Salman into releasing the expatriates to prevent World War Three! It didn't take much negotiating, just a nice little carrot in front of his nose. By the way, when are you planning on telling the world that the king now owns Denali and every moose that roams around that massive mountain?!"

"I didn't want to give up North America's highest peak, but it was all worth it! By the end of the day, you will become the president of the United States. Then you may start negotiating a fake peace plan with my new country!"

"Have you picked a name for your country?"

"I believe so! Beginning next week, we will be known as Gila Curva, the Spanish translation for my favorite destination in America! Goodbye, Mike, or should I say, President Morton!"

*****

Lord Shaffer hung up with Morton, then called Glebov.

"It's a go. Do your thing. I'll be watching!" Shaffer didn't wait for a response. He put down the phone and turned on the TV, then kicked back on a comfortable leather couch in his new office. A moment later, he was startled as Yegor Bovnik barged in without knocking.

"When the door's closed, would you mind knocking?!" The premier's new military chief was standing next to him with some sort of microchip in his hand. "What is it, Yegor?"

"I think we have a problem!" Yegor wasn't about to say sir or premier or even lord to Shaffer. In his mind, they were equals and always had been. He picked the microchip off his palm and waved it in the air as if it were a lizard, and he was trying to break its neck. "I never had the time to look at what's on this until now!"

"What the hell is it?"

"It's the SD card from that photographer's camera in Mesa. I just looked at the pictures."

"So, what's the problem?"

"The last few pictures are from the far end of the compartment underneath the vault."

"Who cares?! We have the SD card, and the vault was plowed over during the cleanup of the area. When Putin and Thompson are shot down, there's no concrete evidence that we had anything to do with it. People may assume we did, but it will be hard to prove!"

"I don't care about the evidence, John! The last picture is what concerns me!"

"Pray tell, my friend!"

Yegor and Shaffer moved quickly to Shaffer's desk. Yegor placed the card in the reader slot on Shaffer's computer and zoomed in on the picture in question.

"In the background, you can see the man who Schoenholtz failed to kill."

"Okay, so what? He was just a low-level Senso-Mac employee. Even though he survived, he wouldn't know there was a connection to us."

"That's where you're wrong, my friend. I recognize him. His name is Roger Bennett, and he works for the KGB. My only guess is that the KGB was tipped off about Sokolov and me being part of this conspiracy, and someone sent him to Arizona to investigate!"

"Are you saying what I think you're saying?!"

"Bennett knows about the plot to take out Thompson and Putin. He would do whatever it takes to make sure that our plan doesn't succeed. I know him. He is a good man. He's also Garrett's half-brother, but Garrett doesn't even know it!"

"Why are you just telling me all this now!?"

*****

Yegor joined Shaffer on the couch, and they stared up at the TV. A live CNN feed was coming from Edwards Air Force Base, where Putin and Thompson had finished making speeches to honor the astronauts and cosmonauts, and now they were headed back to their planes for the surprise flyover. It would all be over in a few minutes. With all the security surrounding the base, it was doubtful that Roger Bennett would be allowed close enough to interfere and save the presidents.

Prime Minister Garrett Sanders knocked on the door, and Lord Shaffer shouted for him to come in. Sanders was holding two shot glasses of vodka that he handed to Yegor and Shaffer.

"I thought you two might want to toast the end of America and Russia as we know it!" Shaffer was nervously watching the events on TV, but he smiled and lightly tapped Yegor's crystal tumbler. Both men gulped the vodka down in one swallow and smacked their lips. A tasty Russian treat, for sure!

Air Force One rolled down the runway first and lifted off. The Russian Ilyushin Il-96 Command Point followed a few seconds later. President Thompson's face was pasted to the window as his plane circled the base in a clockwise direction. President Putin also stared out his window as the Ilyushin veered counterclockwise. Led by the recently honored astronauts and cosmonauts, a throng of well-wishers cheered from the ground.

Simultaneously, the planes began waving their wings. Those with binoculars could see Putin and Thompson giving a thumbs-up signal from their windows. CNN, ABC, NBC, CBS, BBC, Al

Jazeera, and the Russian RT network zoomed in. The entire world was watching! It was time for some good news again!

Lord Shaffer and Yegor stood up and approached the TV to get a closer look.

"Now!" shouted Shaffer at the television screen. "Shoot them now, damn it!"

Then Shaffer's and Yegor's knees buckled at the same time, and they collapsed, both hitting their foreheads hard on the floor. With difficulty, they rolled on their backs and stared upward, grabbing their throats with their hands. They were choking and couldn't breathe.

Prime Minister Garrett Sanders crouched down and smiled only a few feet away from Shaffer and Yegor's dying faces. Then he let out a shrilled laugh that pierced the room and echoed off the walls.

Sanders didn't mix tungis with the vodka. Instead, he used arsenic. Very potent arsenic, at that! He sat down on the couch, picked up the remote, and turned the volume up on the television.

AUTHOR'S NOTE

"Ladies and gentlemen, the story you just read is true. The names were changed to protect the innocent." Those of you baby boomers just raised an eyebrow, right? Sounds a bit like the introduction to the *Dragnet* television series you watched on your black and white Motorola back in the day, huh? The only difference in my book is that it's a flat-out lie! The names were not changed. Many of my fictional characters are actually friends and family who blindly requested a role in *Gila Bend* after reading my first novel, *Seminole Bend.* In that mystery thriller, the lead villain is none other than my good friend Oliver Harwas who wouldn't harm a soul.

So, here's my appreciation list of friends and family who volunteered their reputations for one shot at publication immortality. None knew what character he or she would portray:

Lord John Shaffer is Dr. John Shaffer, a professor of geography at Scottsdale Community College and a past colleague of mine. He's not as wealthy as the infamous British parliamentarian. However, he does own a share of the Green Bay Packers' stock, which makes him a full-fledged cheesehead from Arizona!

Rick Frye was the best man in my wedding. He has never been an educator, but he did try to teach me how to win at three-card poker in Las Vegas. Try is the key word here. Several hundred dollars later, I still consider him a friend.

Mackenzie, Riley, and Charlie O'Connell are my fun-loving, kind, and wonderful nieces and nephew! Enough said!

Loren Schoenholtz is a good friend from my days in Saudi Arabia. He is affectionately called "The Animal" for his extraordinary softball homerun-hitting abilities!

Gene Schultz is my avid-reading brother-in-law. He is an ex-Marine, private pilot, and a Harley Davidson road hog. He's a perfect model for a character in a thriller novel!

Principal Perez is Isaac Perez, and his role is very similar to that in the book. As a one-time principal in Gila Bend, he made a valuable impact on the lives of many kids, faculty, and community members. Hat's off to an exceptional lifelong educator!

Joe Freeman is a friend who retired from his role as a technology expert with Mesa Public Schools for one simple reason—to harass me on the golf course each week. It can be dizzying!

Roger Bennett is another good friend from Saudi Arabia who I consider to be a fantastic family man, a wine connoisseur, and an expert mechanic. In fact, I drove from Arizona to Georgia one time so he could replace my wiper blades!

Randall Thompson is my Canadian friend and fellow cruiser. Now that he has tasted the power of American politics as president, he longs to be a Prime Minister. A short move to Ottawa could be in the works!

Lastly, *Gila Bend* is a work of fiction. But discrimination and disrespect throughout our world is a fact. My appreciation list extends to everyone who stands up by words or actions for equality, human rights, and treating others with dignity. Please keep up your exhausting fight for decency and decorum, and rest assured that you are making a difference!

ACKNOWLEDGMENTS

My sincere appreciation goes out to the entire community of Gila Bend, Arizona, for the hospitality shown to me during two years of visits to the friendly rural town an hour south of Phoenix. I would like to offer a special thanks to Isaac Perez, the high school and elementary school principal, who was an exemplary role model for his students, staff, and parents during his brief time employed by the public schools. Also, if you are ever traveling on Interstate 8 through the desert southwest, a stop at Sofia's Mexican Restaurant for lunch or dinner would be a pleasure to your palate!

Having lived the past twenty-four years in the Red Mountain Ranch subsection of Mesa, I can genuinely say the residents there are wonderful, and the area is beautiful! Red Mountain itself is stunning, especially if you view it from all angles, which you can easily do while hiking or biking the multitude of trails that extend into the Tonto National Forest.

Boeing Corporation (Apache Helicopter Division) employs many workers who live in Red Mountain Ranch. The company strongly supports local education and business partnerships. Boeing is highly respected and actively involved in making Mesa a special place to live. They are a true pillar of the community!

The events in the novel that took place in the Rub' al Khali desert of the Arabian Peninsula are pure fiction. I'm appreciative of the chance to experience the Arab culture firsthand during my three years living in Dhahran, and for the lifelong friendships I've made as a result.

A special thanks to Luke Hansen for exceptional website photography and the creative design of the cover! The Luke Hansen Media drone logged many air miles between Gila Bend and Ajo.

Thanks also to Mary Reppe Raisleger for your marketing assistance, and more importantly, for your words of encouragement. It's nice to have you in my corner.

And finally, thank you to my wife, Meg, for scrutinizing several rough drafts, posing tough questions, and providing excellent advice.

ABOUT THE AUTHOR

Tom Hansen is a native of New Richmond, Wisconsin. He holds a BS from the University of Wisconsin-River Falls and an MS from Nova Southeastern University. Tom has lived in or traveled to seventy-two countries and all fifty states. He is currently a resident of Arizona. Tom has dedicated most of his life to the field of education as a teacher (Dhahran, Saudi Arabia, Okeechobee, Florida, and Orlando, Florida), principal (Hazel Green, Wisconsin and Mesa, Arizona), educational consultant (State of Arizona), college professor and administrative director (Scottsdale, Arizona). This is his second novel.

APPENDIX ONE: CAST OF CHARACTERS
Alphabetized by Last Name & Chapter First Appeared In Book

FIRST	LAST	REFERENCE	CH
Anwar	Abadi	Owner of Taste Of Arabia factory in Sadah	7
Myra	Adams	Witnessed ICE raid on Gila Bend School)	15
Bassam	Bashir	Teenager from Sadah (mixed tungis with coffee)	8
Roger	Bennett	Senso-Mac Employee (works maintenance in vault)	23
Bob	Billings	Special Agent at Homeland Security (Phoenix office)	56
Jim	Bond	MI6 Agent (British Secret Intelligence Service)	6
Yegor	Bovnik	Directorate Chief of Russian KGB	6
Leonid	Brezhnev	General Secretary of the USSR	6
Cliff	Bullard	Ex-Air Force Colonel (fired after 18 civilians died)	18
Martin	Calhoun	National Security Agency Chief	54
Bill	Clemons	ICE Sergeant (led raid on Gila Bend School)	12
Donnor	Colten	Gila Bend Resident (escapes with teachers in pickup)	14
Mack	Colten	Artist (Donnor's cousin - lives at Curley School Apts)	19
Marv	Cullins	CIA Special Agent	46
Smitty	Douglas	Arizona Republic Reporter	43
Abe	Fitzgerald	Gila Bend Charter School Board President	43
Emile	Forester	Retired Auto Mech Tchr (now in GB nursing home)	53
Joe	Freeman	Professional Photographer (discovers vault)	23
Rick	Frye	History Teacher at Gila Bend Charter School	14
Yury	Glebov	Russian Olympic Sharpshooter (works in Senso vault)	31
Bruce	Gledich	Ajo Police Officer	19
Sancho	Gomez	Mexican Doctor (Nobel Prize winner)	37
Rebecca	Grimm	Receptionist at Maricopa County Sheriff's Office	13
Frank	Gustine	Senior Airman (air traffic controller at GB Aux AFB)	37
Philomena	Hayes	Owner of Philly's Flower Shop in Gila Bend	50
Ralph	Hayes	Husband of Philomena Hayes	50
Pablo	Hernandez	Parent who drove AMC Gremlin into the ICE agents	14
Kurt	Kellner	Math Teacher at Gila Bend Charter School	20
Earl	Kelly	Special Agent in Charge of Homeland Security (PHX)	15
Barney	Kinkel	Vice President of Foreign Sales (Zefron Enterprises)	18
Ruslan	Kozar	Russian Olympic Sharpshooter (works in Senso vault)	31
Sachit	Laghari	Sultan Tariq's Personal Doctor	5
James	LeBron	Taste Of Arabia Coffee Salesman	13
Margo	Litweiler	Girl's PE Teacher at Gila Bend Charter School	27
Isaac	Martinez	Gila Bend Charter Student (steals bus to escape)	14

Cyrus	McCool	Athletic Director at Gila Bend Charter School	14
Ray	Monson	Lieutenant assigned to Lajes Air Force Base	49
Jim	Morgan	Owner of Morgan's Southwestern Salsa & Chili	14
Meade	Morgan	Brigadier General assigned to Luke Air Force Base	47
Mike	Morton	Sheriff of Pima County	19
Kevin	Myers	Ajo Fire Captain	19
Haniya	Nader	Reporter for Al Jezeera News Agency	56
Tariq	Nassar	Sultan (brother of King Ra'id & uncle of Wassim)	4
Wasim	Nassar	Prince of Al Mahrah (nephew of Sultan Tariq)	2
Zella	Norris	Student Council Advisor (JQA Charter , Washington)	39
Charlie	O'Connell	Molecular Geneticist	10
Mackenzie	O'Connell	Molecular Geneticist	10
Riley	O'Connell	Molecular Geneticist	10
Gordy	Owens	Deputy at Maricopa Sheriff Office with Ken Smith	15
Gretta	Paulson	Receptionist at Homeland Security (Phoenix office)	56
Sebastian	Perez	Principal of Gila Bend Charter School	14
Gary	Peters	British Lear Jet Pilot for SBSNN (based in Mesa)	57
Morris	Radcliff	Head FBI Lab Technician	32
Gordon	Rothschild	Senator from Arizona	36
Dick	Royce	Captain assigned to Luke Air Force Base	47
Pete	Ruben	Sergeant at Gila Bend Police Department	17
Garrett	Sanders	Vice President of the United States	39
Ted	Sanderson	Assistant Principal of Gila Bend Charter School	14
Loren	Schoenholtz	Homeland Security Agent (works near Senso-Mac)	12
Gene	Schultz	Homeland Security Agent (works near Senso-Mac)	12
Ned	Segura	Captain of Gila Bend Police Department	17
John	Shaffer	British Parliamentarian and Wealthy Businessman	5
Bogdan	Smirnov	ICE Agent (2nd-in-charge) during raid on GB Charter	12
Ken	Smith	Deputy at Maricopa Sheriff Office with Gordy Owens	13
Leonid	Sokolov	Russian General of Military Aviation	2
Dawud	Tadros	Teenager from Sadah (works coffee factory)	8
Zaira	Tahan	Gila Bend Student (steals bus with Isaac to escape)	14
Steve	Talbert	FBI Agent (works with Morris Radcliff in lab)	32
Elliot	Urdano	Sheriff of Maricopa County	13
Everett	Urdano	Sheriff Urdano's Son (misdiagnosed for cancer)	37
Raisa	Vasiliev	Russian-born mistress of Senator Rothschild	36
Ben	Willis	Major assigned to Luke Air Force Base	47

www.ingramcontent.com/pod-product-compliance
Lightning Source LLC
Chambersburg PA
CBHW020603310726
48979CB00008B/1323/J

* 9 7 8 1 7 3 2 8 1 8 2 0 0 *